FAR FOREST SCROLLS

Na Cearcaill

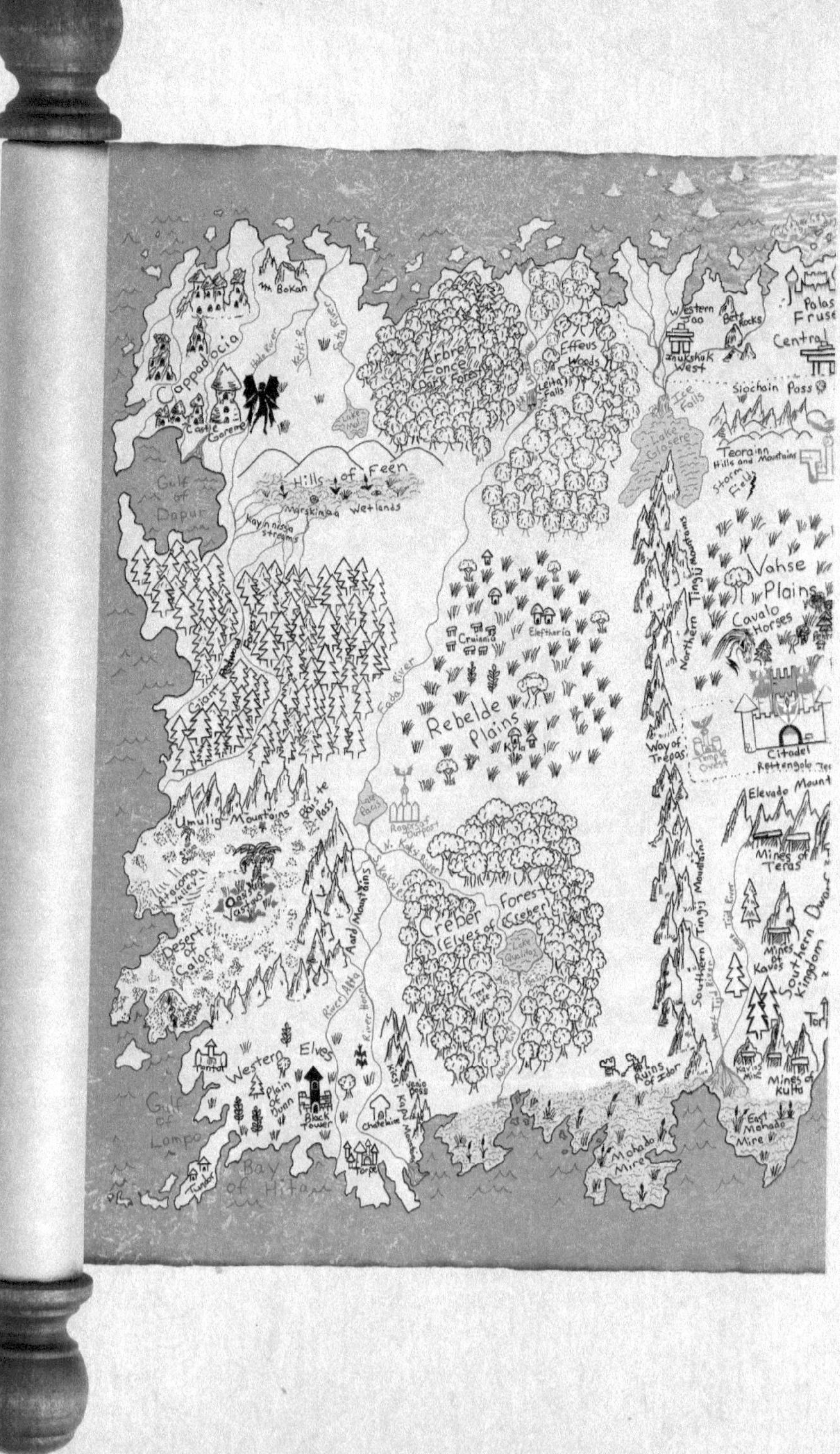

Cappadocia
mt. Bokan
Castle Goreme
Gulf of Dapur
Hale River
Keshi R.
Sota River
Arbre Fonce Dark Forest
Lake Ho
Effeus Woods
Leitha Falls
Hills of Feen
Marskinjaa Wetlands
Kay'n nissa streams
Western Jao
Inukshuk West
Betz Rocks
Palas Fruse
Central
Siochain Pass
Ice Falls
Lake Glosere
Teorainn Hills and Mountains
Storm Field
Vahse Plains
Cavalo Horses
Northern Tingji Mountains
Rebelde Plains
Cruinnia
Eleftheria
Kyla
Way of Trepas
Temple Ovest
Citadel Rettengole Ter
Elevado Mount
Mines of Teras
Southern Tingji Mountains
Tind River
Mines of Kavos
Southern Dwarf Kingdom
Tort
Creber Forest (Elves of Creber)
Lake Qualda
Ragostos Outpost
Kaky River
W. Kaky River
Giant Redwoods
Umulig Mountains
Bos te Pass
Lake Facil
Desert of Calor
Anacona Valley
Oasis Vastus
Aard Mountains
Western Elves
Plain of Quan
Black Tower
River Alta
River Hewa
Gulf of Lampo
Bay of Hita
Tunlot
Forge
Chalehian
Ruins of Izor
Mohado Mire
East Mohado Mire
Mines of Kulta
Kavlos Mine

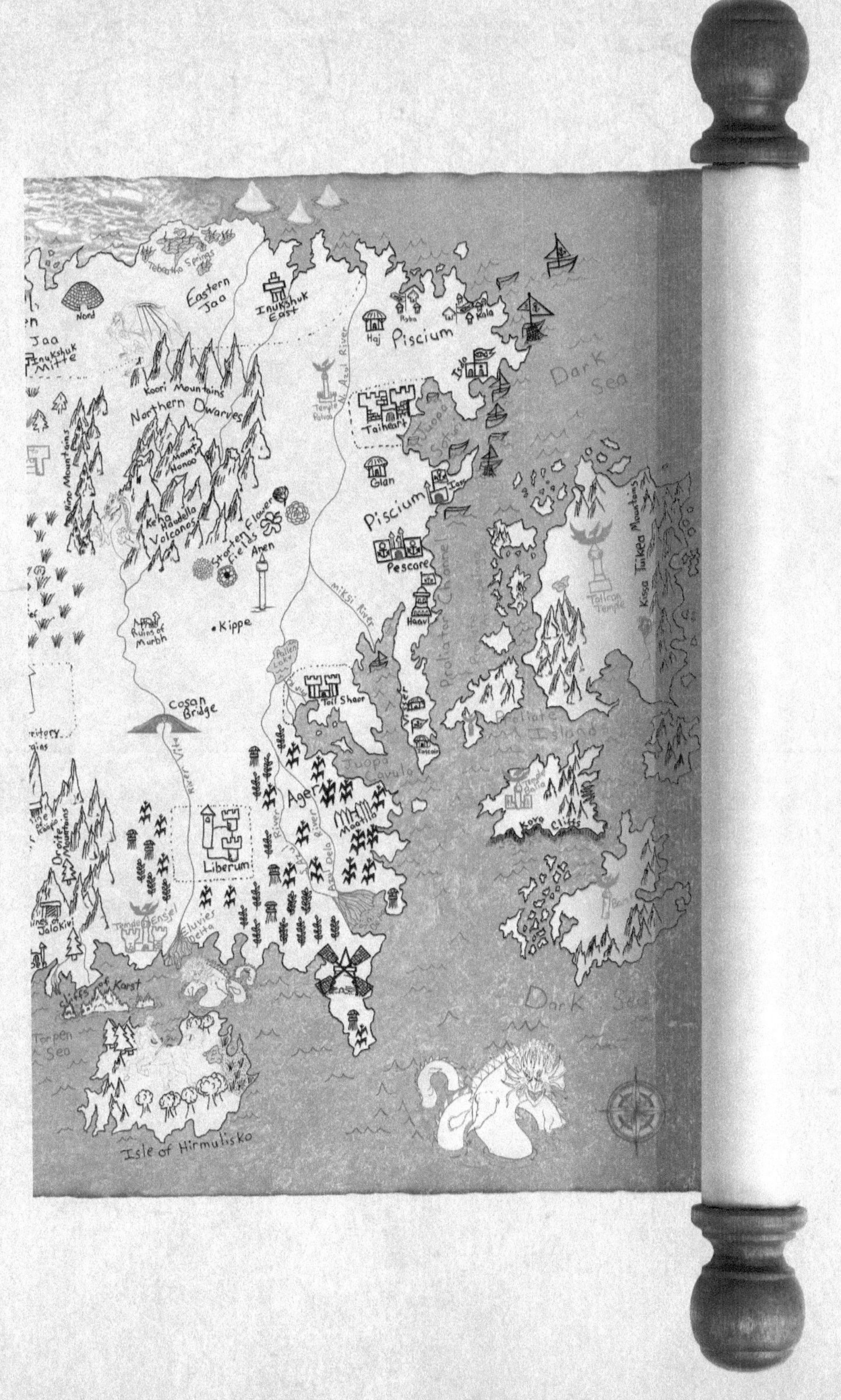

Tebattlo Springs
Eastern Jaa
Inukshuk East
Nord
Jaa
Inukshuk Mitte
Koori Mountains
Northern Dwarves
Mount Hanoo
Keha Haudella Volcanos
Starten Flower Fields
Anen
Ruins of Murbh
Kippe
Cosan Bridge
Temple Paloa
Taiheart
W. Azul River
Haj
Piscium
Ryba
Kala
Isle
Dark Sea
Tuopa Satun
Glan
Iasy
Piscium
Pescore
Prolator Channe
Haav
Miksi River
Tallron Temple
Kissa Tuikea Mountains
Pellan Lake
Tail Shaer
River Della
Ager
Maailla
Tuopa
Peliate Island
Kovo Cliffs
Liberum
Temple Ensel
Eluvies Delta
River Vista
Azul River
Oroite Mountains
Ruins of Jalokivi
Cliffs of Karst
Torpen Sea
Dark Sea
Isle of Hirmulisko

For more information and to view the illustrations for Book One online please visit:
www.FarForestScrolls.com

FAR FOREST SCROLLS

Na Cearcaill

BOOK ONE

ISBN (Hardcover, color edition) 978-1-7321499-0-8
ISBN (Paperback , color edition) 978-1-7321499-2-2
ISBN (Paperback , black & white edition) 978-1-7321499-3-9
ISBN (e-book) 978-1-7321499-1-5
Library of Congress Control Number: 2019914896

Symbolizing Book One, the rune Jera represents the insensate passage of time. Whether acknowledged or spurned, it is always a season of change.

A man's perspective
is limited by the brevity of his existence.

Even living deliberately, how far up can we reach?

Standing on our miniscule patch of time, how far into the future can we see? How much of the past can one truly understand?

Yet, only a recreant spends their precious drops of sand before dropping back into the abyss lounging in indulgence, not striving for understanding, knowledge, answers that those of us scourged/ consecrated with consciousness should seek with unconquerable passion.

Welcome to the world of the Far Forest Scrolls. Enter to increase your Wisdom of how to Live.

The significance of each change of season
is easily buried in the smallest of life's
mundanities and trivialities.

Yet, the true consequence of time's passage is
there, blaring within the subtle disguise of a
whisper for all who would listen.

A change of seasons is upon you ... and upon
those whom you are about to meet ...

TABLE OF CONTENTS

Figure 1: **Grand Master Elf Patuljak,** *originally from the Forest of Creber, his thick bark-like skin sags under the compulsion of time.*

Figure 2: Massive Elven warrior from the Forest of Creber, **Kempe.**

Chosen One

Scroll 1: Everything Is Different

*Three adults bound by friendship
lead three children fettered by grief.*

"Sometimes the start of a journey is unmistakable and obvious. Other times the start is a grey fog, lulling you away from the significance of the voyage you are walking on," Patuljak, the Grand Master Elf, mumbled.

"What?" asked the strapping young Elf of Creber, Kempe.

"Sometimes a journey can be the surprise and the destination familiar, and sometimes the journey is featureless and the destination shrouded in mystery."

"I have no idea what you're talking about."

"Your grandfather spoke of an unending cycle, Na Cearcaill, a chain of destruction alternating between light and dark blanketing Verngaurd for eternity."

"Seriously, I've no clue what you're talking about, Dad!"

"This journey, with these three children, is more profound than you know. We are at *the* crossroads that those in the League of Truth have dreaded. It is up to us to stand against this storm, this darkness. Whether we win, and free ourselves from this cycle, or lose on this journey, one way or another, innocence will be vanquished from Verngaurd."

"Are we even still talking about these kids?" Kempe asked.

"Sometimes we pick the journey, sometimes the journey picks us, but either way we will come out the other side either better or worse, never the same," Patuljak said, smiling at his son's annoyance.

"Lovely! You know how I *love* your cryptic nonsense!"

Patuljak laughed. "Remember, don't mention the Chosen One or Na Cearcaill to Friar. As far as Friar Pallium knows, these are simply three children needing a home."

The Grand Master Elf served as a bridge of peace between the two divergent Elf nations, the sylvan Elves of Creber and the urbanized Western Elves. The Western Elves broke off from the traditional forest life of the Elves of Creber countless generations ago with the intent of becoming more modern, soon becoming obsessed with separating from the symbiotic existence the Elves of Creber enjoyed with the trees of their forest.

"Why would I mention the Chosen One?" Kempe asked. "You haven't even told me which one of these three is *supposedly* the Chosen One."

"Soon enough the world will know. Before long, the prophecy that the League of Truth has been protecting for countless centuries will finally be fulfilled," Patuljak said.

"There have been hundreds of rumors over thousands of years about the coming of the 'Chosen One,'" Kempe scoffed. "What's different about this one?"

"Everything."

"If one of these three kids is the Chosen One, do you think they'll be safe training to be squires with the Knights?" Kempe asked. Like all Elves of Creber, his dark brown skin was thick, rutted, and streaked with green bands that resembled moss. It was the perfect camouflage for the forest dweller.

Only a few of the thirteen moons of Verngaurd were out in the cloudy night sky, making his bark-like skin blend into the darkness. The small group had crossed the Cosan Bridge several nights ago, and was walking towards Castle Liberum, the new capital of the Independent Knights.

"They will be safer behind the walls of Liberum. There have been too many attempts on my life for me to watch over them," Patuljak explained. "Resorting to assassins is a new low, even for the Evil One. It's too dangerous with me and no one will think to look for the Chosen One amongst simple squires."

He adjusted the plain cloak hanging over his aged skin. "Anyway, I shall see the Chosen One again, shortly."

"Shortly?"

"Yes, shortly."

"How shortly . . . I mean, how soon?"

"Soon, from an old Elf's perspective."

"What does that even mean?" Kempe asked, his voice leaking annoyance.

"It means the child needs to get older before beginning the quest described in the prophecy," the Grand Master Elf declared. "I just hope the world can wait that long."

"Patuljak, sometimes I think you are trying to drive me crazy!"

"Call me Dad."

"Well, *Patuljak*, obviously, the child should be older! Can you give me any details?"

"No."

"No?"

"No."

"No! Can you at least tell me how much older they have to be? Do they have to become an adult?"

"No."

"No, the child mustn't grow to adulthood, or no, you can't tell me?" Kempe demanded.

"Yes," Patuljak answered with a laugh.

"You know, Dad, I am starting to regret joining this League of 'Hide the Truth from those who are sworn to protect it!'" Kempe complained.

"No one can *join* our League of Truth. You are born into it. For countless generations our ancestors have protected the prophecy, waiting for the Chosen One who can break the Cearcaill."

Kempe huffed in frustration. "If you aren't going to tell me, just say so."

"I'm not going to tell you," Patuljak said, bursting into a fresh round of laughter.

Kempe shook his head and the two walked in silence that seemed deeper under the squeezing gloom of the night. The rolling plains of Eastern Verngaurd were pleasant enough to walk through, but the Elf preferred his woodland home. Here, only an occasional tree reared off the grassy plain. By day or night, the solitary trees seemed naked as they swayed awkwardly, uncomfortably alone. Kempe missed the thick Forest of Creber, but most of all he longed for his arbor breith, or birth tree. Like all Elves, he had lived most of his life under its protective roots in harmony with nature.

A muffled sob from one of the three children behind them made Patuljak turn. He instantly regretted laughing when they were in so much pain. Their mother had given birth to her third child but then died. "We shouldn't laugh in the face of their suffering."

Kempe thought of his own young son, Kainen, and nodded. He shuddered at the thought of not being able to see him grow up. He knew his son's life, and the constant training he was undertaking, was intricately linked to whichever of these children was the Chosen One. *My son doesn't have a choice about being in the League of Truth, but I guess they didn't get a say in their lives either.*

Even in the darkness, he could see the sadness draping over the older siblings. Gaining a new baby sister could hardly make up for losing your parents. Kempe wasn't sure how or why their father had died. The rumor was he had killed himself in grief over the loss of his wife. The one thing Kempe did know was that his friend, Aquila, had seen everything but would say nothing. Ever since the children's parents had died the large and beautiful creature had been keeping to himself. He hung back now, with the three newly orphaned children.

"I can't believe the Knights gave up their former capital Cumhacht without a fight!" Kempe finally stated. "Traveling all the way to Liberum is a major pain."

"The Proliate warriors have become incredibly strong since their victories in the Dark War decades ago. Their alliance with the Magicians has made them almost unbeatable," Patuljak commented. "I am not sure the Knights had much choice in the matter. Anyway, I like this new Friar, Pallium. He . . ."

"He's still the son of Isa!" Kempe interrupted scornfully. "Are the Knights returning to hereditary rule, like the days when they were ruled by kings?"

"No. With their ranks thinned, there were few choices."

"I am not prone to superstition, but that Friar Isa was plain and simply cursed. Whatever he touched turned to dust—including the Knights."

The Grand Master Elf stared at his warrior Elf son, wondering how to respond as he secretly agreed Isa had seemed cursed. "I concede Friar Isa had a string of horrendous luck and the Knights were reduced to a whisper of their former strength. However, give his son, Pallium, a chance. He is a driven man, expecting perfection from everyone, most of all himself. Even though the Knights are down to just three castles, Friar Pallium has doubled their mental and physical training over the last five years. They are a compact but deadly force. Who knows they may yet regain their former glory."

The two Elves settled back into a comfortable silence born of their close relationship as father and son. The stillness of the night was cracked only by muffled whimpers and periodic sniffles. The two distraught young children and their newborn sister were following about ten feet behind the two Elves and having a hard time thinking about anything but their dead parents. The uncertainty of moving to a castle to become squires heightened their fear and grief over the loss of their parents.

Shepherding the older two children and cradling the baby was Aquila, his features completely shrouded in a large, black cloak. His normally majestic head was crumpled down on his muscular chest and his shoulders were slouched. His keen eyes were fixed on the baby. The darkness and his tears worked in concert to obscure her tiny features.

Leaning in close, the hulking figure whispered into the newborn's ear the plea that had been playing repeatedly in his head, "Forgive me, child."

"What's wrong with Aquila?" Kempe asked. "He hasn't put that baby down since we left his home in the giant redwood forest. He didn't know the children's parents *that* well."

Patuljak sighed. "I cannot go into the details. I can only tell you that he was asked to perform a horrible act . . ."

"Aquila?" Kempe interrupted in total dismay. "Impossible! I don't believe it, not for one second! He is the most intimidating guy I know and happens to be the most principled. No one, I mean no one, in all of Verngaurd could make him do anything unethical or against his will!"

"Sometimes decisions don't come down to an uncomplicated right and wrong. We are occasionally challenged with two painful alternatives. Our friend Aquila was faced with a choice that was completely obscured in a hideous fog of wickedness. Whatever he chose, something evil would come from it."

Kempe stared at the elder Elf in confusion. "You make it sound heinous."

"It was . . . it is. However, he did what he believed was the right thing as a member of the League of Truth . . . a horrific act that just may save this troubled world. Still, the deed will haunt his dreams and weigh on his soul for all eternity."

"Bloody blight, Father! Tell me what happened!" Kempe demanded.

The elder Elf stared straight ahead in silence.

"Are you going to tell me?"

"Can't, my son," Patuljak answered.

"Can't or won't?"

"In this case, both are true."

"You are my father and the Grand Master Elf, and I know I ought to show you respect at all times, but right now you're really getting on my nerves!"

"I can live with that. Hey, I can make out torches . . . yep, there it is, Castle Liberum!" Patuljak announced, effectively putting an end to Kempe's rant.

Scroll 2: Nice Catch

Castle Liberum, the largest of the three remaining Independent Knight castles, nestled itself between excellent farmland and the River Vita. Its immense outer walls are flanked by large towers and surrounded by a moat.

"Rhyfeler? That man's as crazy as a woodpecker looking for bugs in a metal spear," Kempe declared as the eclectic group neared the castle.

Patuljak chuckled. "He takes his job as castle constable very seriously. There is nothing wrong with that. In fact, it makes me feel better leaving the children there."

"He is a keystone short of a complete arch. That's all I'm saying," Kempe added.

"Halt! Declare yourself!" a loud voice cried out of the darkness.

"Patuljak, Grand Master Elf, and friends. Friar Pallium is expecting us."

"Ah, Elves. We do need some firewood for our gatehouse! Raise the portcullis and open the gates!" a blaring voice announced, followed by fits of sporadic laughter.

"What did that fool say?" Kempe asked, his temperature rising.

"Be nice. We are their guests," Patuljak advised.

"Be nice? The guy just called us firewood! Proper etiquette has obviously been thrown into the moat!"

"Remember why we're here. Remember your duty."

Kempe's eyes blazed with anger but he needed no reminder of his obligations.

As the portcullis groaned upwards, the gates swung open to reveal a man in a flowing yellow surcoat over his armor.

"Rhyfeler," Kempe whittled under his breath.

"I hope my little joke didn't offend," Rhyfeler remarked.

"Why would being compared to firewood offend us?" Kempe scoffed.

"Of course not, old friend," Patuljak interjected loudly.

"It's merely that I have been waiting for the last six hours and had

Figure 3: Constable Rhyfeler of Castle Liberum is in charge of gatehouse defense.

nothing to do but come up with Elf jokes. That's too much time to *leaf* me alone! All that time on my hands to *pine* around was really the *root* of the problem!" Rhyfeler could hardly finish his words before bursting out laughing.

"Get it, leaves, roots, and pine trees . . . your skin is rough . . . like bark?" the castle constable spurted. Several Knights gathered around, their torches illuminating Rhyfeler's flowing blond hair and beard. The flickering light bounced off his fair complexion unkindly, giving him a haunted look.

"Oh, that's hysterical!" Kempe seethed. "No one has ever compared us to a tree before. How origi . . ."

"No harm done," Patuljak interjected. "Our dear Rhyfeler here has been waiting up for us and is behind on sleep."

"And common sense," Kempe snarled.

Ignoring his son's comment, Patuljak quickly changed the conversation. "Is Friar Pallium available?"

"He'll be here shortly, but he did have some chaperones ready for our recruits," Rhyfeler answered, keeping a keen eye on the hulking Elf warrior.

"Scelto! Come out here, boy!" the constable yelled.

After an awkward pause, he hollered the boy's name again.

"He's only six and a half, but a born warrior," Rhyfeler explained.

Finally, a boy shuffled out of the gate. He was obviously very tall for his age and broad shoulders stretched his cloak. Toddling behind him was a much smaller and gangly little boy with hair so glaringly yellow it was obvious even in the darkness.

"So, where are the recruits who need a home?" the constable queried.

"Come forward, children," Patuljak declared. "We have Jumeaux and his twin sister Gimelli. They are seven. Bellae, the newborn, is just behind with my good friend, Aquila."

"Welcome, children," Rhyfeler greeted. "This strapping young man bounding towards us is Scelto. He will show you to your quarters. You will be assigned to the Pantteri squad of Knights. You will join them as stablemates, but if you work hard, you can quickly achieve the rank squire. Oh, and the little guy behind Scelto is the famous Lontas."

A series of chuckles ran through the Knights.

"Famous?" Patuljak wondered.

"He's not yet three, but can *read* as well as any *teacher*! He has got to be the smartest tike to *ever* walk the grounds of Verngaurd!" Rhyfeler remarked.

"Is that so?" Patuljak said, amazed.

"Hey," Scelto said, standing in front of Gimelli. She was too sad to notice his stare.

"Ouch!" Jumeaux yelled as young Lontas plowed into his leg. The others turned to see Jumeaux standing over the trembling Lontas.

"Hey, watch it, new guy!" Scelto berated while gracefully moving in front of Lontas.

Jumeaux scowled, but turned away in silence. *I just lost my parents and now I get stuck here!*

"Easy, Scelto, Lontas just fell into Jumeaux. I forgot to mention the boy genius Lontas can read but not walk!" Rhyfeler blurted as a fresh round of laughter rippled through the Knights. "The boy was born with two left feet and ten big toes. He is simply the clumsiest critter to scurry over the face of the earth."

"Where's the third child, the baby?" Rhyfeler asked after the laughter died down.

"Jumeaux, get your sister, please."

Wordlessly the boy trudged back to where Aquila was concealed by cloak and darkness to take his baby sister, trembling at the sight of the mysterious Aquila and his massive arms. Silently the creature handed the baby to the boy and hopped away.

"What was that thing holding the baby?" Rhyfeler asked, squinting into the gloom.

"A friend and guardian," Patuljak answered cryptically.

"That's not what I meant," Rhyfeler replied.

Patuljak didn't have time to answer as Jumeaux began screaming. "Bloody wet! Great, just great!"

Disgusted by the urine dripping over him, Jumeaux stumbled. Gimelli screamed as Kempe dove through the air.

With outstretched arms he caught the falling newborn, Bellae. "I got her," he said, breathlessly.

"Unbelievable," Rhyfeler muttered. "Well done, Elf! Well done!"

"You threw your baby sister, Jumeaux!" Scelto shouted. "What's wrong with you?"

Jumeaux's eyes widened in irritation, "The freak peed on me! What did you expect me to do?"

"It's what babies do! They eat, sleep, poop, and pee! It's natural."

"Natural? If I peed on you, would that be natural?" Jumeaux challenged.

"You're not a baby! It only works for newborns. Anyway, pee or no pee, you *don't* throw a baby, especially your sister!"

"That's enough, Scelto," a new, aged voice commanded.

"Friar Pallium. This guy . . ."

"I know, Scelto. However, Jumeaux recently lost his parents and

Figure 4: Aged leader of the Independent Knights,
Friar Pallium.

then walked a very long distance for many nights to a place he does not know. He is tired and in mourning. Perhaps we should give him the benefit of the doubt," Friar Pallium, the leader of the Knights, suggested. He brushed aside his mostly grey hair and pushed down on his tired, blue eyes. "Rhyfeler, see the baby to the nursery. Scelto and Lontas, take the twins to your stablemate barracks."

"Yes, sir," Scelto obeyed. "Come on, Jumeaux, Gimelli, follow me."

"Are you going to show us how to be squires?" Gimelli asked as the four of them crossed the moat into the gatehouse.

"You have to pay your dues first. I'll show you how to be stablemates. We help the squires and prepare the stables. The Knights are divided into squads. Ours is the Pantteri, or Panther squad. If you prove yourself as a stablemate, you become a squire."

"Do you have dry clothes for me?" Jumeaux asked.

"Yeah, we'll get there, Whizzer," Scelto laughed.

"Not funny!" Jumeaux whined.

"What's up with the big guy in the cloak? The one who held your sister?"

"He kept constant watch over Bellae, but didn't talk to us," Gimelli answered. "His arms are human, but I don't think his face or legs were, and his back was hunched."

"You never saw him?"

"Not clearly. He kept under his cloak as we traveled by night, and we slept during the day."

The four walked in silence through the outer courtyard or bailey. As they neared the stablemate barracks, Scelto broke the quiet. For reasons he could not explain, he whispered only to Gimelli, "Hey, sorry about your parents."

The young girl smiled. "Thank you."

Jumeaux scowled, angry at being excluded.

"Friar Pallium," Patuljak said after the two wandered away for privacy. "I apologize for not coming to see you sooner. I was sorry to hear of your father's passing."

I doubt it. My father was a disaster for the Knights and all of Verngaurd.

"Thank you for saying so," Friar replied out loud.

After an uncomfortable moment, Friar continued, "I have to ask, my old friend, what in the world is the Grand Master Elf doing bringing me three children in the middle of the night?"

"Well, I was in the neighborhood, and thought I'd stop by," Patuljak replied, laughing.

"We can sure use the recruits, but that's a load of rubbish! Things have been pretty bleak around here lately." After a brief pause he continued, "Those attempts on your life have us all worried."

"Being Grand Master Elf used to mean trying to reconcile the differences between the Elves of Creber and Western Elves. Now it's about trying to prevent them from killing each other while staying alive!"

"Your son looks great, how's he doing?"

"Kempe's well. I'm very proud of him," Patuljak answered. The elder Elf kicked his feet nervously against the grass. "Friar, I need you, as a personal favor, to promise you will take special care of these youngsters without asking questions."

Friar chuckled. "You wouldn't have left your forest and escorted these children all the way out here in such secrecy if wasn't of the utmost importance! Did I see someone else with you?"

"Yes, but he's dealing with some personal issues. Don't think him rude," Patuljak commented.

"Understood. I'll watch over the children, you have my word."

"Well, I best be getting my son back to the Forest of Creber before his wife kills me."

"Safe journey . . . and thank you."

"Hey, Friar?" Patuljak's eyes clouded and his cheerful smile faded.
"Yes?"

"I will be lying low for the foreseeable future . . . given the attempts on my life."

"Seems wise, my old friend. Do you want a Knight escort?"

"I've taken enough of your time and we travel only at night. I'll be back someday to tell you the whole story about these kids. Until then, it is *vital* you keep them safe."

Scroll 3: The Deal

"You're joking!" Bellae said, giggling.

Years had passed and the newborn brought to Castle Liberum in the middle of the night with her twin siblings was now a freshly minted six year old.

"I'm serious!" the Knight Finn responded in counterfeit distress. He is one of a handful of Knights from the Forest of Creber. "I can't believe you would suggest such slander! It was just your birthday, and this is my present to you!" His green and brown eyes widened, and wrinkles of mock surprise creased through the bark-like furrows running the length of his brown Elvish skin. He was lean and muscular, moving with confident grace.

"A monster really lives in River Vita?"

"Yes, and today I will prove it to you," Finn declared.

"How?" the precocious six-year-old asked. Her large, brown eyes shone with an inner strength and understanding beyond her age. As her sandy-brown hair bobbed in the wind, the subtle, natural curls bounced merrily in the bright sunlight.

"I am going to catch the monster of Vita just for you!" Finn replied, laughing. "When I do, I want a full apology and let's see . . . what else should I demand?"

"I already have all the gross jobs as a stablemate, so I think an apology will be enough," Bellae said, chuckling.

"Okay, deal."

"What do I get if you don't catch it?"

"No need to worry about that. I *will* capture it," Finn said assuredly. "Are your brother and sister joining us, or are they too good for us now that they are squires?"

"Jumeaux and Gimelli will be here."

The stablemate and Knight had most of the long walk to the River Vita behind them. Despite the fact that the river snaked through the back end of Castle Liberum, the section of water that ran

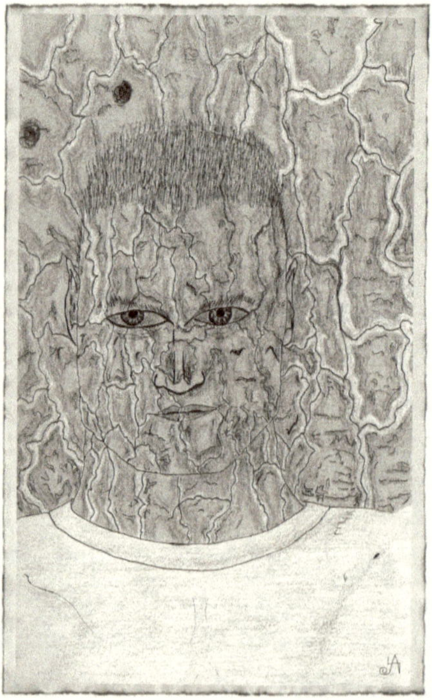

Figure 5: Originally from the Forest of Creber, **Knight Finn** *is known for the development and mastery of unique weapons.*

within the castle walls was set down in a deep gorge. That meant a long hike around the outside of the castle was necessary to reach the river's edge. The castle's water supply came from the plethora of underground aquifers.

Spring had finally come, punctuated by scattered wild flowers and a vernal coat of prairie grass waving energetically around them. Powered by the river breeze and encouraged by the warm suns overhead, the dance of the youthful spring growth added to the thrill rising within Bellae.

Could there really be a monster?

Bellae let her hand glide across the smooth but deadly weapon on Finn's belt.

"Tell me about your weapon!"

"Again?"

"Again."

"The kama has a wooden handle with the deadly curved beak of a tuima bird. The tuima are native to my Forest of Creber, and its beak is as hard as steel."

"Oh no! Do you kill them?"

"Again, *no!*" Finn laughed. "As I have said, we only use beaks of birds after they die naturally."

"That's not your usual fishing pole," she said, pointing to a massive rod in his hand.

"It's the largest one ever built, perfect for catching monsters!"

Bellae laughed. "What's in the bucket?"

"A surprise," Finn answered.

"Your surprise seems angry," Bellae commented as something in the bucket thrashed forcefully.

"Probably."

"Is it alive?" Bellae asked, already feeling the answer.

"Yes, obviously!" Finn chuckled.

"Oh, poor thing! What is it?"

"Do we need to review what the word 'surprise' means?"

"No!" Bellae chuckled. "It's just . . . I need to know. So, is it a bird?"

"No, and stop asking. You'll find out soon enough."

Bellae looked up at the tall Knight, her respect for him battling her intense curiosity.

Scrunching up her nose, she gave in to the craving to find out what was squirming in the bucket. "Uhm, a squirrel?"

"No."

"Cat?"

"I'm not answering."

"Dog?"

"Stop guessing."

"A puppy?"

"It's a *surprise,* girl! Let me walk in peace!"

"A raccoon?"

"Quit!" Finn jokingly implored.

Bellae was enjoying the game and her giggles grew louder. "Is it a tekorava?"

"Oh, that's it! I managed to snatch a vicious tekorava with fierce claws and a spiked tail and thrust it into a bucket. No!" Finn laughed.

"A horse?" Bellae snickered. "A dragon? Pegasus?" She was laughing so hard she had to stop, doubling over, her legs weakening under the energy drain of the deep merriment.

"Okay, okay!" Finn conceded. "Go ahead and look. I hope you don't feel too bad about ruining the surprise."

As soon as Finn slid the lid off the wooden bucket, water sloshed violently.

Bellae screamed. Stumbling backwards, she landed stiffly on her backside and started laughing even harder.

"A giant fish is your surprise? Why are we going fishing when you already *have* a large fish?"

"This, my young stablemate, is the bait that is going to catch a monster!"

"The river isn't deep enough for a monster!"

"Once every few years when the thirteen moons of Verngaurd line up just right, the waters flowing down to the Eluvies Delta move in reverse, causing the water to rise enough for the monster to travel across!"

Bellae scrunched her nose, not sure what to believe.

"You'll see."

Bellae couldn't stop laughing once they finally reached the river's edge. The fish's large tail repeatedly slapped the Elf in the face as he struggled to get it baited on a barb hanging below an immense three-pronged hook.

"Got it!" he finally proclaimed. "Time to catch a monster!

Scroll 4: A Bit of Bubbly

Bellae's eyes widened at the thick fishing line and massive fish struggling under the colossal hook as bait. *Could there really be a monster in there?*

Finn's laugh startled her. "Starting to believe, are we?"

"No!" Bellae answered emphatically. "Well . . ."

Finn cast out the enormous hook into the deep-blue water and they sat on the bank of the substantial river. Several large boulders stood like stone sentries around the edge of the river, and were the only diversion from the abundantly tall grass of the plains.

"You know Crann loves you?" Finn asked.

"He's an amazing horse and I love him, too."

"Good! My squire is going to test for Knighthood soon, maybe even next year. Would you think about being my squire?"

"Of course!" Bellae scooted close, resting her head on the Knight's shoulder. His bark-like skin felt cool compared to the heat of the three suns overhead, and the two cuddled into the relaxed patience required for any type of fishing, even for a monster.

"Is Lontas coming?" Finn wondered after an hour with no bites.

"He might come, or he might stay at the castle and read."

Suddenly, Finn bolted up from the ground, pulling hard on the thick fishing pole as the line tensed. "Whoa! We got something here!"

Bellae stood and started backing away. She could feel something, a strange surge of emotions. She could hear Finn talking, then yelling, but she couldn't make out the words. The intense feelings were blocking out his conversation. Closing her eyes and concentrating, she began to sense a blend of emotions bubbling up from under the water: hunger, panic, rage, and terror.

It's the monster! Finn's caught it. I can feel him! she thought.

"Bellae!"

The sound of her sister's scream shocked her back to the present.

Bellae opened her eyes and let out a nervous yelp. Finn's muscles were bulging as he leaned backwards, desperately trying to control whatever was on the other end of the line. Gimelli and Jumeaux rushed to Bellae. The features of Jumeaux's long and thin face were tense with fear. The thick black hair on his head shook in the wind as if it, too, was frightened. Gimelli managed to retain her staggering smile despite the dread in her deep-yellow eyes. Lontas clumsily struggled to catch up.

"Believing me now?" Finn asked with a strained laugh.

Suddenly Finn fell backwards and the massive fishing line went slack. He began chuckling. "The monster broke my line!"

Figure 6: The **River Monster of Vita.**

"Good!" Gimelli chimed. "With all due respect, Finn, what were you . . ."

Her words were cut off as a colossal creature rose out of the water, its massive jaws chomping, and rows of sharp teeth just missing Finn. The top of the creature's head had several horns offset with a crown of wing-like appendages. Its prominent snout was lined with a series of large tentacle-like feelers. Dozens of powerful flippers fluttered the width of its long scaled body.

Gimelli and Bellae screamed while Jumeaux stumbled backwards.

"Everyone back!" Finn ordered as the monster slurped beneath the surface into the tumultuous water.

They waited and stared. Slowly, the undulating water and their pounding hearts began to ebb.

"Is it gone?" wondered Gimelli.

"I don't know," Finn said. "To be safe, let's go."

Mesmerized by the lure of the extraordinary creature and the rhythmic lapping of the river's waves, Jumeaux's gangly body advanced towards the edge of the riverbank for a closer look.

"Hey, back up!" Finn ordered.

"Get away from the edge!" Gimelli yelled.

Jumeaux shook his head and stopped, finally realizing what he was doing.

"J-J-Ju-ma-ma-eaux," Lontas stuttered, arriving at last. He pointed frantically at something rising out of the water.

Jumeaux followed Lontas' finger out to the river. He screamed just as a massive tentacle shot out of the water. It swung around, lashing the backs of Jumeaux's legs. The girls screamed as his lean body awkwardly convulsed backwards. Seconds after his body slammed to the ground, several more tentacles whipped out and grabbed him, flipping him in a high arc towards the water.

The monster's hungry eyes rose further out of the water and instantly fixed on the squire flailing through the air. With blistering speed, the giant creature arched over and swallowed the boy whole before quickly diving back under the water.

Figure 7: **River Surprise:** *The surprised Knight and squires caught more than they anticipated.*

While the others stood in opened-mouth horror, Bellae instantly dove in after her brother. Stricken with panic, Finn pulled out his kama weapon and moved to the river's edge.

The bubbling water swirled savagely. Despite the foaming water and fierce thrashing, a shrill sound could be heard under the water. Incredibly, it sounded like Bellae screaming wildly.

The monster's head slowly rose out of the water, Jumeaux could be heard wailing within its mouth. Bellae popped out of the water, screaming in a singsong tone at the beast.

The creature seemed to almost nod before spitting out Jumeaux. The wet and terrified boy slammed into Finn. The force spun the Knight around, forcing him to drop his kama weapon into the water. Bellae snatched the sinking kama and swung wildly as the beast shot out its tentacles towards her. The beast let out a chattering howl as the sharp beak of the weapon easily sliced off an appendage.

"Finn!" Gimelli screamed as other tentacles slipped through Bellae's defenses.

The Knight shook his head, dazed from being plowed over by the flying Jumeaux. Bellae shrieked while being pulled under the water, the monster quickly joined her beneath the surface. The already churning water bubbled with fresh vigor.

A sickening black-red color bled into the white foam of the agitated river. Panic flooded Finn's body and he dove headlong into the water.

Jumeaux coughed and expelled a mix of water and ooze. Still traumatized by being swallowed and released, he began scraping off the viscous slime coating his body, wincing at the pain as his hands hit the innumerable cuts and gashes under his shredded pants.

"Save my sister!" Gimelli yelled even though Finn was already underwater.

Seconds sludged forward like hours. Bellae's screaming stopped, initially replaced by a deafening silence, but quickly succeeded by Finn's shouting. Gushes of blood exploded to the surface. The now crimson waves began thrashing more vigorously as the stormy water churned more violently.

"She's dead!" Jumeaux sputtered. The words surprised everyone, including himself. He was too young to comprehend the roots of his anger. He did understand that no one had screamed for him. He was, after all, the one who had been swallowed and vomited by the monster.

"Jumeaux!" Gimelli shrieked. "That's horrible! She has to be fine!"

Before her twin could reply a gasping Bellae and Finn emerged from the bloody water, his kama weapon coated in blood and gelatinous monster goo.

"Bellae!" Lontas screamed. The young stablemate shot in front of Gimelli and hugged his soggy friend as she hungrily savored the fresh air in deep gasps.

Gimelli's anxious tears turned to those of joy, and her spacious smile spread widely as she moved to embrace her sister.

"Away from the water's edge right now!" Finn demanded. "Move! Move! Move!"

Jumeaux stared resentfully at the affection being heaped upon his sister. Coughing up more of the nasty slime, he spat angrily. *Gimelli didn't come to my side,* he thought, turning his ire towards Bellae and Lontas.

"Nice job, Lontas, are you trying to get me killed, you clumsy, stuttering oaf? If you hadn't distracted me, it wouldn't have grabbed me. Oh, and let's not forget my precious baby sister, the freak! You were singing some sort of enchantment at that monster!"

"How can you say that? Lontas was trying to warn you, and Bellae is the one who jumped in to save you!" Gimelli said.

"She was talking to the monster, trying to get it to let you go," Lontas said.

"Not this nonsense again!" Jumeaux spat. "I'm already sick of you claiming she can 'talk' with animals and now you want me to believe she can communicate with a monster? Ridiculous!"

"I told it to let you go and take me instead," Bellae said. "Then I surprised it with Finn's weapon."

"Bellae saved your life," Gimelli said.

"No way that's what happened!" Jumeaux scowled.

"Stop bickering!" Finn said firmly. "Let's be thankful everyone's fine! Bellae, next time I get an idea like this, please slap me."

"Definitely!" Bellae said emphatically.

"I'll do more than slap you Finn!" Gimelli added.

"I deserve that," Finn chuckled.

"Has everyone gone mad?" Jumeaux pressed. "Bellae wasn't 'talking' to the monster, she's some sort of witch!"

"Jumeaux!" Gimelli scolded.

"Let it go," Finn warned, leaning down to look at the innumerable rips in Jumeaux's now blood soaked clothing. "You need to see a healer immediately!"

Jumeaux didn't hear the advice, instead glaring at his sister.

A smile slowly replaced Finn's panicked expression, "On the plus side Jumeaux, for the rest of your life you can tell a tale with the most interesting twist on the whole 'the one that got away' fish story. You can say, 'I got away from a monster this big!'" He held his arms out as wide as possible.

While the others laughed, Jumeaux scowled, stood, and hobbled towards Liberum.

"It's just a joke. Sorry!" Finn cried after him.

"Where did that thing come from?" Gimelli asked.

"Legend is that it swims up from the Isle of Hirmulisko when the water levels rise to look for new food sources."

"Hirmulisko? The island of creatures?"

"Yes."

"So, is it dead?"

"No, but it's wounded and long gone," Finn answered.

"What happened down there?"

"Bellae was . . . talking with it and holding my weapon out in front when I got down there. I took my kama and slashed at the monster until it left to find an easier meal."

The others stared, each one silently wondering what in the world had happened between Bellae and the monster. She blushed, feeling uncomfortable under their weighty gaze.

"Are you really okay?" Finn asked.

Bellae paused, a shimmering, ghostly figure flashed up on the hill. She couldn't make out any details before it disappeared completely.

What is that thing? she wondered. It had been showing up for several weeks, never staying long, but seemingly always watching her. Initially it only appeared during the night, now it had started appearing during the day. Unbeknownst to her, she wasn't the only one the spirit had visited.

Finn repeated his question.

"No," she said solemnly, trying to push the image of the ghost from her mind. "I'm not okay."

"What's wrong?"

"I'm imagining how many times I am going to have to hear, 'I told you so.'"

"What?"

"You were right, Finn. There's a monster in the river."

Scroll 5: Those Three?

"I know he's your son, Kempe, but Kainen's still a boy and you may be overestimating his abilities," Ailante, the elder Elf of Creber, proclaimed. "You expect me to believe those three . . . anemic individuals are the League of Truth's best offering to save the world?" The aged Elf's bark-like skin looked particularly droopy enveloped within his baggy robes. The grey streaks within his green eyes shimmered in the scattering light of dusk as he stood with two other Elves in their hallowed Forest of Creber. Immersed in shadows, several feet away, were the three subjects of the conversation.

The powerful Elf Kempe bristled at the notion his son might not be up to the task, but stayed silent. His thick, brown skin with black ruts allowed him to blend in perfectly with the surrounding trees.

"Kainen is a lifetime member of the League of Truth and has been training since he could stand," Patuljak answered. "He has overcome the connection with his birth tree to prepare all over Verngaurd."

Ailante scoffed. "Being the boy's father and grandfather does not exactly make you impartial! Also, this secretive 'League of Truth' notion means little to me. That's your family's obsession."

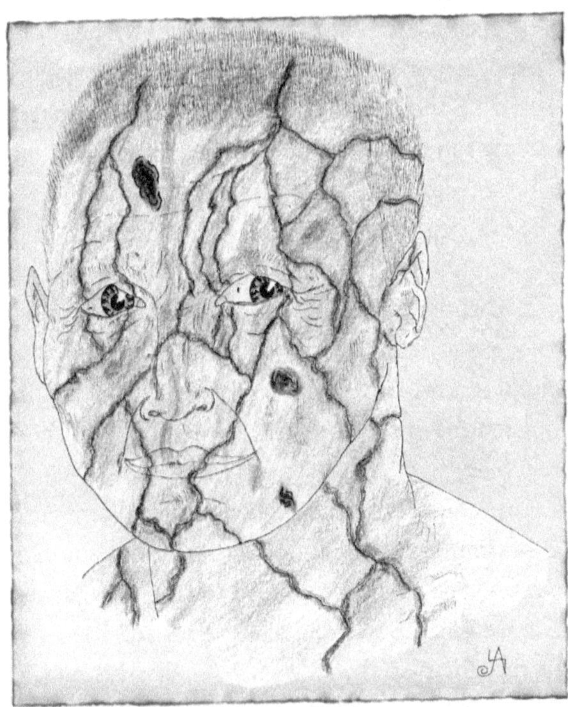

Figure 8: Ailante is an elder Elf of Creber and a member of the ruling class called Archerians.

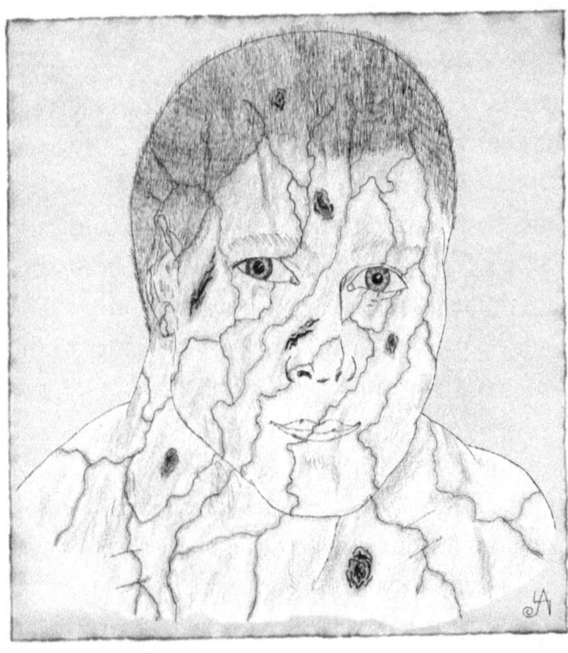

Figure 9: The young Elf of Creber Kainen is son to Kempe, grandson to Grand Master Elf Patuljak, and a lifelong member of the League of Truth.

"Obligation! Not obsession. Our family's responsibility has been passed down by my ancestors for millennia. Through countless generations we have prepared and waited for the time of the prophecy. Unfortunately, it falls to my son and grandson to contend with the ultimate purpose of the League, to ensure a successful resolution to the prophecy by guiding the Chosen One and avoiding the great chaos of the Cearcaill."

"The prophecy? The Cearcaill?" Ailante scoffed. "My family has been helping govern the Creber Forest for just as long as yours has been dabbling in the League of Truth. Each generation hears whispers it's finally time for the prophecy, the great chaos and the end of days. Those rumors have *always* been false."

"It's different this time. Dark forces are pouring across Verngaurd. The Dark Warriors are infiltrating our ranks to create divisions amongst the peace-loving nations. Do you think the winged warriors of the west would be mobilizing if it weren't time?" Patuljak questioned.

"Our 'friends' from the Giant Redwoods sat in their trees and let Verngaurd burn decades ago when the Dark Warriors invaded and the Knights failed us. I'll believe they are helping when I see more than the one youngling you bring before me. Our forest, a sanctuary and a fortress, will protect us, as we protect it."

"The sacred Forest of Creber is protective and nurturing but, for all the good it does, limits your view of the rest of the world. I have seen what is going on in the other countries. The Dark Warriors are back, the Magicians are expanding their ranks and training griffins for battle, and someone is raiding the Isle of Hirmulisko. They are stealing beasts that should be left alone, and training them for war," Patuljak said.

"Even if the time of the prophecy has arrived, your answer to this 'world-ending threat' is really the three puerile creatures I see over there?" Ailante asked.

"Yes. Kainen, Arend, and Sankari are sworn members of the League of Truth. Despite their age and size, they are knowledgeable and strong. Plus, it is imperative we have individuals who can make a deep connection with the youthful Chosen One, and they are perfect."

"A juvenile Elf, a youngling from the Redwoods, and a Fairy?" commented Ailante. "They are too young, too small."

"Did you just call me small?" a diminutive voice called out.

The young Elf Kainen grabbed the fuming Fairy, "No, Sankari!"

Her brown and tan spotted frame blended in with the dark forest, but her eyes glowed with anger. Her bifid wings beat frantically as she struggled to get free and confront her critic.

"She's spunky, I'll give her that," said Ailante.

"I apologize for her response," Patuljak said. "All three have been training nonstop. They are tired, yet anxious to begin their exercises in our forest. Soon it will be time for the youngling from the Redwoods to switch to direct guardian mode."

"Their experience and training should count for more than their age and size," Kempe added. "They will continue dedicating their lives to preparing for the prophecy."

Figure 10: Fairy Sankari is originally from Cappadocia and a member of the League of Truth.

"Assuming you are right, which I do not believe, when will this 'prophecy' come about?" Ailante wondered.

"Soon. Within a few years," Patuljak answered.

"We have many intrepid warriors, why not send them?" asked Ailante.

"Only the Chosen One can fulfill the prophecy. Plus, I don't think you fully grasp what's coming. The great chaos, Na Cearcaill, will drag the entire world into war, including our sacred forest. Our warriors will be needed on the battlefield trying to stop the world from burning. Fulfilling the prophecy is a job for the Chosen One and a small group mobile enough to weave their way through the coming turmoil to complete the tasks required," Patuljak answered.

"Tell me more about this prophecy," Ailante requested.

"That knowledge is only for the League of Truth. You know we are sworn to secrecy. We only mentioned the presence of these members within our forest out of respect for you."

"The League is welcome to prepare here. Will they be ready in time?"

"I'm not sure any of us can really be prepared for what's coming."

Chapter One

Of Day and Knights, Now Is the Time

Scroll 1: Hold a Star, in a Stable

The seven-year-old squire Bellae opened her eyes to a seemingly endless stream of particles stirred up by life in the stables. She watched them dance in the rays of the morning sunshine. Some moved leisurely, while others hustled with blustery motivation. Yawning contentedly, she enjoyed her soak in the foggy sunlight bath.

Her sandy-brown hair shimmered as she stretched on the mushy hay before snuggling in closer to Star. As the oldest stable cat of the castle, Star felt entitled to just about anything her heart desired. Most described her as obnoxiously lazy, except the devotee rats she ignored while growing fat on handouts.

The stable was a holding area for the castle's Pantteri Squad of the Independent Knights in Castle Liberum. Each of the five Knights had one section of the stable cordoned off for their horse and supplies. Bellae was squire to Elf Finn and his horse Crann.

"Bellae, I love nuzzling, but I would so enjoy a nice, plump fish fritter," Star purred.

"You want a fish fritter?" Bellae asked the cat in what sounded like

Figure 11: **Bellae** *is the youngest squire in the history of the Knights. Finn is her Knight.*

melodic chanting. Her first conversations as a toddler had been with animals, not people, and the tuneful singing she used to communicate with them came easier than words.

"*Of course,*" Star replied innocently. "*It's wonderful to have a human who understands me. What was it Friar Pallium said you are?*"

"*I have the gift of the Ainmhi Caint who used to live in Verngaurd. Everyone thought they disappeared.*"

"*Interesting,*" the cat draped in long, white hair purred. "*You're trying to distract me.*"

"*Never!*" the cat protested. "*Do you like being . . . whatever it is, so you can talk with us higher beings?*"

"*You know I love it, but you can't trick me!*" Bellae concentrated and could feel the cat's gorged stomach struggling to digest its bloated contents. "*You definitely don't need fritters, or anything else for that matter.*"

"*I hate it when you do that weird, 'feel what I'm feeling' thing. Everyone else must be jealous of your gift!*"

Bellae laughed. *"Not exactly. Mostly people ignore me . . . other than an occasional mocking whisper."*

"And they call us animals?"

Bellae chuckled as her stomach rumbled in protest, reminding her she hadn't eaten. Ignoring the hunger pangs, she laid back. For the moment, all was right with the world.

"Bellae!" a thin voice wailed.

She froze, a chill running through her. *I know that voice.* "Leave me alone!"

"Bellae!" the voice said again. "Follow me."

"Never!"

The normally lazy Star arched her back and hissed ferociously. *"Hide your eyes Bellae!"*

Bellae covered her eyes as the cat shrieked a warning. Eventually a wispy white form shimmered in front of the cat. Reaching out, the form put its ghostly hand through the cat. Overwhelmed with a cavernous chill, the cat fell like a block of ice to the ground.

"Star!" Bellae yelled, opening her eyes and coming face to face with a semi-transparent specter.

Its grey eyes sat back within deep, black circles and drops of what looked like dark blood dripping down the pale face.

Crann, the horse of her Knight, snorted threateningly and lashed out his hooves at the apparition as the other horses in the stable kicked and neighed loudly.

"What are you and why do you keep coming to me?"

"You should follow me when I call! All your worries will evaporate, and the coming agony you must endure can be avoided!"

"I'll never follow you!" Bellae said, drawing the cat to her and rubbing the frosty fur on Star's head.

"Too bad you animal-talking misfit! Eventually . . ."

The stable door opened and the ghostly figure disappeared in a flood of fresh sunlight.

"That ghost-thingy is sooooo annoying!" Star chattered, starting to thaw out.

"Are you okay?"

"Feeling warmer, and you're welcome for scaring it away."

"What does it want?"

"Maybe for you to get me some food after my delicate disposition was upset!"

"Star!"

"It seems to be popping up more frequently."

"I know! I even see it outside now."

"Good morning, Bellae," Virone greeted. "You realize you're a squire now, right? Let us stablemates get things ready for *you!*"

"Morning, Vir," she replied, trying to settle the fear rattling within her. "I enjoy being up to greet the gentle morning sun, Mardin. The other two suns seem hot and angry."

"Don't let the stablemates and squires from other squads get you down."

"What?"

"They're only jealous because you became the youngest squire in the history of the Knights. That's why you come in early, isn't it? To avoid their bullying?"

"I like being alone with my animals," Bellae replied. *But not ghosts!* "I guess I like it even more now that . . . everyone seems so angry at me. No one asked if I wanted to be the youngest squire!" she said, not understanding jealousy has a way of clouding logic.

Crann neighed loudly, demanding to know if she was okay and what was going on. After Bellae informed him she was fine and translated Virone's question about her being the youngest squire, he brayed loudly, *"Finn had to choose you!"*

"Thanks. I love you, too!"

"You need to tell Finn about that . . . thing."

"Not yet. I'm not sure what it is or what it wants from me."

"If that thing hurts you, it will be too late!" Crann brayed.

"Soon, I promise."

Crann nudged her for attention. Bellae obliged the patchy red Cavalo horse from the Vahse Plains. Crann, like most Cavalo horses, was taller and faster than other horse breeds. Bellae stroked his dark-brown mane, which rose eight inches off of his head, and wondered if it was time to brush his tail which consisted of thick, cord-like strands twice the length of other horses and deadly as a weapon.

"Is it okay if I wait and brush your tail tomorrow?" Bellae asked, still shaken up.

"Sure. I know it takes forever to groom, sorry!"

Bellae had no family other than her siblings and animals. In fact, she had no memory of her parents. She sometimes caught her twin siblings, Gimelli and Jumeaux, talking about them in hushed voices when they thought she was out of earshot. She hated that neither of them ever spoke of how her parents died.

Now the three siblings were all squires in Liberum, the last great castle of the Independent Knights. For thousands of years, the Knights had dominated and protected Verngaurd until their power was shattered by repeatedly suffering massive losses during the Dark War.

Figure 12: Knight Finn's horse, Crann, is a fierce Cavalo stallion from the Vahse Plains.

"Hello, Bellae," another Pantteri Squad squire, Scelto, called. "You're early."

Scelto's laugh made her look up. Gauging the amount of sunlight streaming through the stables, and the absence of stablemates, she realized it must be near six o'clock.

"Losing track of time again?" he asked, his large muscles flexing as he hoisted a substantial bale of hay into Crann's stall. Scelto's brown eyes sparkled, beneath his short black hair and surrounded by his rugged features.

"Chef Cookie told me she hadn't seen you this morning," he said, handing her a few oatmeal cookies.

"Thanks," she said, pocketing one for Grym and Borb, her mice friends living in the barracks.

At thirteen and a half, Scelto was as large as many Knights, but kind and humble. Scelto was squire for Ritari, the squad leader and the captain of all Knights.

"Good morning, you two," beamed Gimelli, Bellae's older sister. "It's going to be a great day!" Long, brown hair framed her fine features and yellow eyes.

"Hey," Scelto answered with an infatuated smile. He moved awkwardly towards her, but then nervously spun back to his duties.

"Hey, Lumi," Bellae replied.

"Why do you call her that?" Scelto asked.

"It's short for the second sun, Luminos, because she has such a sunny disposition!"

"She does indeed," Scelto whispered, blushing. "Yesterday Lontas was droning on about the third sun, Pheobus, and the first, Mardin, making up some sort of binary or twin star system that orbits the massive central sun, Luminos."

"Lontas loves to read everything, but he's particularly crazy about astronomy." Gimelli said. Frowning, she added, "Jumeaux better wake poor Lontas up!"

Figure 13: Large for his age, **Scelto** *is squire to Knight Ritari.*

Figure 14: **Gimelli** *is twin sister of Jumeaux and older sibling of Bellae. She is squire to Sorea.*

Figure 15: **Jumeaux** *is twin brother of Gimelli and older sibling of Bellae. He is squire to Luchar.*

"What's the forecast for your evil twin's mood?" Scelto asked.

"Jumeaux's not evil, but the outlook for his temper today is a robust grey," Gimelli replied, laughing.

"Ah! A relatively good day for the grouser, then? How do you stay so cheerful towards your grumpy twin?"

"If I can keep chipping away at whatever is making him so angry, maybe he can be happy. It could happen . . . if I keep smiling!"

"It smells horrid in here," Jumeaux complained, slamming through the stable doors.

"Good morning!" Gimelli said cheerfully.

"What a stench!" Jumeaux continued. His words leached their weeding-roots into the happy thoughts Gimelli had planted, quickly choking them out. Jumeaux was lean and gaunt, which made him look taller than he really was. His black hair was thick and comically unruly. His nose was long and thin and matched his feeble physique.

"Are these stablemates from the pigsty? We need to remind them to *remove* the shite, not spread it around," Jumeaux grumbled.

"You do realize this is a stable? You know, full of horses and what they eat, both before and *after* digestion?" Scelto retorted.

"Ha! Very funny! Is this the jester tent?" Jumeaux grouched.

"Do you want to change your forecast to black?" Scelto said, rolling his eyes.

Jumeaux ignored the comment and set to work with a purpose, motivated by fear of his always angry Knight, Luchar.

"J, did you make sure Lontas was up?" Gimelli inquired, beaming a warm smile.

"Hhhmpf!"

"Jumeaux, is Lontas up or not?"

"He was sitting."

"Were his eyes open or closed?"

"I'm not his keeper."

"Listen, Jumeaux," Scelto said. "If his eyes are open and he's moving around, he's up. If his eyes are closed and he's not in motion, likely snoring, he's asleep. Is that concept too hard for you?"

"You know, Scelto, I think it might be," Jumeaux said, feigning sadness at not having been able to complete the task.

"Jumeaux, don't be like this," Gimelli said telepathically to her brother. If they concentrated, the twins could converse, even at great distances. Bellae could usually tell when Gimelli was talking to him telepathically by her intense expression of frustration.

"I'll get him," Bellae said. "I'm ready."

"Show off," Jumeaux complained.

Ignoring him she winked at Crann and Star, *"Back in a minute."* Hopping off a stool, she headed out the door as Crann neighed and Star meowed for food.

Lontas was the fifth and last squire of their squad. At nine he had been the youngest squire until Bellae made her appearance. Their Pantteri Squad had five Knights and five squires.

Entering their squire barracks, Bellae found him asleep on his cot with an open codex, or book, lying on his chest. Lontas' blanching fingers were clutching it tenaciously as if it were a long-lost friend about to leave.

"Oh, Lontas, I know books are your refuge, but reading every night in the dark? Wake up," she implored, shaking his shoulder. His blond hairs shuddered back and forth as if they were awake and anxious to help arouse the rest of his body.

"I see you wore your clothes and shoes to bed to be on time . . . it didn't work!"

Lontas let out a groan and Bellae took a few steps back. Slowly, he sat up.

"Good job, Lontas!"

Bellae's optimism faded when he let loose a deep, contented snore.

"Wake up!" Bellae screamed.

"No, of course I didn't stay up reading," Lontas mumbled. His disheveled hair made it seem as if he'd slept well, but the bags under his closed eyes suggested otherwise.

"Lontas, always being late won't help your reputation as the worst squire in the castle. Please wake up!"

He was thin, gangly, and clumsy to a fault. Though steady in his work, he constantly dreamt of a place where he could read all night and sleep the day away.

"Lontas you're late!" Bellae yelled. Becoming increasingly anxious she nudged his shoulder, squealing as he fell backwards onto his bunk.

"Please, don't make me do it *again*," Bellae pleaded as he started to snore louder. Bracing his forearm with one hand, she tugged hard on the book until finally managing to yank it out of his hand. His fingers chomped hungrily after the absent book, sniffing like a mouse hunting for cheese. Eventually, he snorted in frustration and his hand stopped as she reluctantly made her way to the washbasin to collect some water.

Holding a bucket over his head, she sighed, "*Forgive me.*"

Figure 16: Known more for his clumsiness than his skill as a squire, Lontas *prefers books to brawls.*

Scroll 2: To Get Back Up

"Ahhhhhhh!" Lontas howled as the icy water washed over his face. His body shivered and jiggled as the frigid stream flowed down his chest.

"Sorry."

"My book! I can forgive getting wet, but my books? No way!"

"It's safe!" Bellae quickly reassured, pointing to show it had escaped the dousing.

He sighed with deep relief.

"We have to get going, like now!"

"Tell me I'm not late, again!" Lontas beseeched.

"I *could* tell you that, buuut . . . it wouldn't be true."

He stumbled out of bed and the two squires made a dash for the stables.

"Don't worry, we'll help you."

"Thanks, I . . ."

Thud!

Lontas tripped and fell face first into the apathetic dirt.

"Lontas!" Bellae shrieked, rushing back to help him up. "The ground here is really uneven."

"Nice try, but I know it isn't," he replied feebly, spitting dirt from his mouth. "I guess that's one for the LTC."

"I can't believe my brother Jumeaux started that silly Lontas Trip Counter game. Don't let him get you down. Just ignore him, you're better than that."

The sound of scornful clapping made them look up. They sighed heavily—Tiron and Stratto were approaching. The much older squires belonged to the rival Tilkeri Squad. Both boys had reached their adult height and their shirts bulged over youthful muscles. Their eyes shone with the zeal of hunters locked on easy prey, and their mouths watered at the inevitable feast awaiting them as they picked apart the spirit of the weak member of the squire herd.

Lontas' vulnerable nerves tingled in anticipation of the inescapable onslaught of insults as he plunged into the familiar role of quarry.

"Wow! Very nice, Lont-a-loser," Tiron said.

"Oh, I totally agree, well done!" Stratto added. "When was the last time you saw someone kiss dirt so successfully, so passionately?"

"Well, there was that blind and demented ex-Knight from the Infirmary who fell last week," Tiron taunted as they laughed haughtily.

Stratto nodded, "Good point. That guy really managed to look graceful as he face-planted his demented head. However, I give the nod to Lont-l-l-loser."

Bellae could see Lontas' already raw and battered self-confidence evaporating under their abrasive fire. "Grow up you two!"

"Nice comeback, Lontas. I love the ventriloquism. It really sounded as if your voice came out of this girl," Tiron said sarcastically. "Oh, wait. That wasn't you. Your pet girl talks for you!"

"Tiron, I have to correct you," Stratto stated with mock seriousness. "It's the girl-freak who 'talks' to animals who has taken Lontas as her pet. Not the other way around."

"Don't we put animals out of their misery when they are lame?" Tiron asked.

"You know, I think you're right. Maybe we should put the hobbling pet Lontas out of his misery?"

Without another word, Bellae quickly pulled Lontas towards their squad's stable.

"Look there, Stratto, he can walk!"

"Miracle of miracles! Thanks for sharing that with us." Stratto scowled scornfully. Tiring of such an easy target, the vulturous Tilkeri walked away laughing.

With his head down, Lontas trudged next to Bellae.

"We still have time to get your work done," Bellae said, trying to sound cheerful while leading him to the well outside their stable. "Forget about them. Let's get you cleaned up."

"Wait," Lontas cautioned, removing a small book from his shirt. "Yes! It's not damaged!"

"Oh, Lontas," Bellae giggled at her hopeless friend. "Bestilla from the library will kill you if you hurt one of her books."

"I know I shouldn't have. I just thought there might be time for me to look at it today." Lontas glanced in the direction of the retreating Tilkeri. "Why do I have to be stuck in this clumsy body?"

"It would be hard for anybody to hold up that one-of-a-kind amazing brain of yours!"

Lontas smiled at her tenderness, grateful the water Bellae was using to wash away the dirt concealed his tears born from equal parts shame and appreciation.

"Ready?" Bellae asked, finishing fixing his hair.

"Not really." His mind yearned for the day to be over before it could begin.

"Well, ready or not, we're going through those doors together!"

"I can't handle Jumeaux today."

"We can do it side by side. Maybe I'll ask Friar if we can ship him to the Tilkeri!"

Lontas smiled.

"Focus on getting your Knight Lovag ready for his day and I bet he'll take you to the library tonight."

Lontas' eyes brightened, realizing that a glimmer of hope, even a small one lingering tantalizingly far in the future, can help you face the trials in between.

"We've got this!"

"Hold it," Lontas said, clearing his throat awkwardly and glancing everywhere but Bellae's eyes. "Uhm, I want to thank you for helping me."

"Don't worry about it. They're bullies."

His cheeks heated with a crimson blush. "Not only for today. I mean thanks for all the times you fought to keep the bad parts of the world away."

"That's what friends are for! We're two misfit peas in our squire pod."

Scroll 3: A Day of Knights

The stable doors squeaked open and Scelto's eyes locked on Lontas' dejected expression and grimy, wet dog appearance. His eyebrows arched questioningly and Bellae mouthed, "Tilkeri."

Scelto squinted. *This is the last time they do this to Lontas without payback!*

"Everyone, please welcome our wonderful guest, sleeping beauty Lontasia. Please give her a hand," Jumeaux scowled with mocking grandeur as Lontas stumbled through the door bearing the scarlet scourge of embarrassment.

"Shut it, J! It was your turn to make sure he was up anyway," Scelto scolded.

Jumeaux ignored him. "I love the wet pig look!"

"*Not helpful, J,*" Gimelli told him telepathically. "It's okay, Lontas," Gimelli said. "Scelto and I have already started getting your Knight Lovag ready."

Grabbing a towel, she began drying him off.

"Listen, this squad will get our work done!" Scelto said, smiling at Lontas.

As the morning progressed, Lontas began to feel better as the refreshing pleasure of gratitude and friendship slowly overcame the hot embrace of humiliation.

"Uhm," Lontas began, attempting to distract from Jumeaux's angst. "I was at the library when Friar came through with fifteen Elves from Creber. They looked like Finn, with thick, dark skin and streaks of color."

"Listen, Lontasia, we are all happy to hear this fascinating story about your boyfriends, but what does this have to do with anything? Wait. Don't tell me. NOTHING!" Jumeaux hectored.

"I saw them, too. Ailante, an Elven leader, was with them," Scelto added. "Remember when we saw the Northern Dwarves a couple of months ago? Jumeaux, I'll tell you what Elves and Dwarves being here has to do with us. Something big is about to happen."

"Oh, really? What exactly is this 'BIG' thing?"

"I'm not sure. All I know is something *is* coming."

"Oh, that totally clears it up," Jumeaux blurted sarcastically. "I'll tell you what I know, Scelto. Right now, it's getting pretty thick in here with a lot of horse cra . . ."

"Jumeaux!" Gimelli interrupted.

Just as Scelto moved menacingly towards Jumeaux, the morning horn blew from the central tower of Liberum.

"Saved by the horn, Jumeaux," Scelto said, pointing. "Saved by the horn."

Jumeaux rolled his eyes, but was not bold enough to say anything.

On cue, the five Pantteri Squad squires stood at the ready awaiting their Knights.

"Finn!" the squires greeted as the first Knight entered. His graceful Elfin form moved effortlessly through the central walkway towards Bellae and Crann.

"Happy First Sun," Finn replied.

Like all the Elves of Creber, Finn had coarse brown skin that was thick and grooved to mimic the tree bark of his native forest. In contrast to his rough skin, Finn's facial features were fine and thin, and so perfect in shape as to appear important.

"Captain Ritari!" the squires greeted.

"Good Mardin," he replied.

"Crann and the other horses seem jittery today," Finn said.

"He's fine, they're fine," Bellae replied, turning a little red, upset at the ghost appearance and contrite at not telling her Knight.

Crann neighed loudly.

"I will tell Finn about the ghost later, once I know more," Bellae promised.

"How did I get so lucky to have a squire who can talk to my horse?"

Bellae smiled while strapping vambraces to his forearms and greaves to his lower legs. He wore no helmet to maximize his vision for his beloved archery.

"What weapons do you want?"

"For independent training time I will practice with my saighead . . ."

Figure 17: **Ritari,** *head of the Pantteri Squad and* **captain** *of the Knights of Liberum.*

"The perfect choice for shooting three enemies at once!" Bellae giggled.

"Hey, a triple shot bow can be very handy. I will also use my telescoping dagger and . . . those two." He pointed to his hailstorm weapon that shot spring-loaded flying stars, and a long rope with grappling hook on one end and a razor-sharp star on the other.

"Fighting an army today?"

"Once metal hits metal and battle begins, no one wishes they had practiced less," Finn replied as Bellae laughed.

Scelto helped his Knight, Ritari, into his black armor. His chest plate and shield were decorated with a panther in relief. His shoulder pauldrons and the part of his helmet protecting his mouth and chin were in the shape of panther claws. A central plume of short panther fur and a larger tuft of horsehair dyed red ran down the center of his helmet.

"Hurry up, Jumeaux!" Knight Luchar bellowed.

"The morning ritual of Luchar yelling at his squire has begun," Finn whispered.

"Even Jumeaux doesn't deserve that."

"Luchar holds to the old school belief that misery builds character. Plus, he's always grumpy before he has a chance to hit something or someone!"

"Will you be using your battle-axe and war hammer today?" Jumeaux asked, struggling to get Luchar's heavy armor over his padded aketon.

Figure 18: Knight Luchar, known for his short temper and monumental wrath.

Figure 19: Erudite Knight Lovag, known for his equestrian and archery skills.

"You know, I'm glad you asked. I was thinking that today . . ." Luchar said, putting his hand up to his chin in mock contemplation. " . . . I might train with a handkerchief and a doily." His face suddenly flushed with anger. "What the blazes else would I use Jumeaux, but my *WEAPONS?*" the short, stout, and incredibly strong Knight replied.

"Ready for the day?" Lovag asked, startling his squire, Lontas.

"You always enter so quietly!"

"Silent and overlooked can be great on the battlefield!" Lovag replied. This humble Knight was famous for his horsemanship, archery, and love of reading.

"I'm assuming you will ride Behalen out for practice today, and want both your long and recurve bow?" Lontas asked.

"Yes," Lovag replied, petting his all-black steed.

Lontas smiled at his easygoing Knight. He felt lucky to have one who loved books as much as he did and who had light armor that was easy to put on.

Lovag's glistening blue eyes were clearly visible in his black helmet which was cut back to improve his vision. A tall, black horsehair crest ran down the center. He wielded a curved scimitar sword for slashing from horseback.

Lontas sighed deeply. *Please, no falling today. Classes are after this,* he thought, looking forward to his comfort zone.

"Morning Sorea!" Gimelli greeted as her Knight arrived. She was one of thirty female Knights at Liberum. "Your crossbow is cleaned and the strings are waxed."

Figure 20: **Knight Sorea** *is known for her archery skills and expertise in siege engines.*

"Nice job!" Sorea said, inspecting her crossbow with an eagle head at the front, and the arms carved to look like wings. She wore light leather armor, relying on speed and mobility to avoid injury.

"Love the ponytail!" Gimelli admired. "However, it would look much, much better *under* a helmet protecting your head!"

Sorea tossed her long, dark hair playfully. "And ruin this?"

Gimelli shook her head, "For independent training, are we working on your new trebuchet?"

"Absolutely!" Sorea declared, salivating. As one of the most skilled mechanicians, she was constantly redesigning the castle's war machines, mostly catapults and trebuchets, to go farther and be more destructive.

"Do you want to start out wearing your talons today?"

Sorea nodded. The talons were two incredibly sharp blades with a slight curve to them as they arced along the length of her forearms, held in place via a series of leather straps. They allowed her to use her superior speed, balance, and trunk strength against larger opponents.

"What's on your mind?" Finn asked Bellae, seeing her gloomy expression.

Bellae recounted what happened to Lontas.

"Don't let what happens to you in life become so heavy that it prevents you from living. Learn something from the experience, then let the bad memories fall aside."

"But that's really hard to do!"

"Let your mind do what your body does . . . walk away. If you hold on to bad experiences, you give them power to disrupt your mind and weigh down your life."

Bellae smiled, "That's pretty good."

"I'm delighted you approve."

When the second horn rang, Finn rode out on Crann, and Lovag on Behalen while the rest of the Knights and their squires were on foot. Before moving to their designated practice area, they lined up with the other squads of Knights in the spacious grass-filled bailey that served as the practice grounds within the walls of Castle Liberum.

Centuries of Knights had trained and fought at this castle complex. However, it only became the main castle of the Independent Knights

Figure 21: The Pantteri Squad of Knights and Squires.

after a series of devastating defeats during the Dark War forced them to retreat from their former capital of Cumhacht.

The troubled leader of the Knights paused within his office despite knowing his Knights were waiting for him to appear. He unfurled a scroll from Supreme Master Magician Veneficus and reread the invitation to meet privately with him.

"A small bit of light in a dark world," Friar Pallium declared to the impassive and empty room. "If anyone can help guide the Knights and all of Verngaurd through these troubling times, it is my father's old advisor, Veneficus."

Friar nodded, excited to meet with the Supreme Master Magician at the upcoming Tournament. Sighing, he moved out onto the topmost balcony of the castle's keep. Before he could speak he paused again, letting his gaze linger on the storm clouds brooding on the distant horizon. His tired, blue eyes were flanked by deep wrinkles and sat within dark circles of sleep deprivation. He wore a simple black robe that made his greying hair even more noticeable.

"How many nights in a row must I suffer these nightmares, these visions?" he whispered to himself. "Are they some sort of warning? If so, from whom? From what?"

Do these nightly trials and those faraway dark clouds portent our future? Flashes from his recent string of nightmares raced before him: *howls of anger, bloody battles, shrieks of pain, despair, Castle Liberum being overrun by hordes of enemies.*

"Focus on today," he reminded himself. Shaking away his shadowy fears, he slowly raised his right arm until it covered his heart. The entire compound erupted in the oath extolling the four Knightly virtues taken from the old world.

> *"My life I dedicate to the search of wisdom,*
> *My heart I steel to courage.*
> *I shall live each day with temperance.*
> *For all citizens of Verngaurd, I defend justice.*
> *Never give up.*
> *Never give up.*
> *Never give up, Knights!"*

Each Knight thumped their chest twice before raising their right hand in the air, the palm facing backwards and all but the fourth, or heart finger, extended—forming an upright letter *K*. Silently they declared, *I give my whole self.* Next, they brought their hand in a fist to their left shoulder, making a quick slicing motion across their neck to finish the salute—affirming their willingness to give their life in battle.

Controlled chaos erupted, with each squad heading off to train.

Ritari's face grew animated as he barked out assignments. Finn and Lovag dismounted. The Knights and other squires ran to their assigned places as Bellae took Crann and Behalen to the horse holding area.

"I'll be right back," she whispered, kissing Crann on the nose before joining Finn at the footwork machine. Vir was running in a giant flywheel connected to a conveyor. As it turned, a different pattern of wooden rods rotated around, forcing Finn to move laterally and jump to avoid them.

"Bellae! Switch!" Vir panted after running feverishly in the wheel for several minutes.

Bellae moved next to him.

"Now!" he yelled, diving out onto the ground.

Bellae jumped in and kept pace with the wheel as best she could.

"Hey, Bellae!" Jumeaux yelled, his unruly black hair waving on top of his lanky body. "Don't stumble in there like Lontas, and become a human tossed salad!"

Jumeaux's laughter quickly morphed into a grimace as Luchar thwacked the back of his head. Lontas ignored the jab and continued timing Lovag using a device that looked like an abacus as the Knight ran a series of sprints.

Luchar lifted, then let a massive bag of rocks crash to the ground. Jumeaux cheered and Luchar raised both arms in jubilation. Using a complex series of pulleys to lift various amounts of rock, he could strengthen every muscle group.

A man dressed in a black shirt embroidered with a yellow *S*, a castle, and key approached Sorea. Everything about him spoke of efficiency and tidiness. Even his face was well organized to avoid unnecessary effort. His short, dark hair stood unwaveringly at attention above small and observant eyes. A straight and proper nose perched above a modest and narrow mouth.

"Hello, Baiulus!" Gimelli greeted. "What's the castle steward doing at practice?"

Without changing his solemn expression, he nodded over his shoulder to a dozen men hauling a tall wooden structure. As castle steward, or manager, he made sure every aspect of the castle ran smoothly.

"Sorea, as requested, your new inverted sit-up machine." He pointed to a wooden board that could rotate within a wooden A-frame.

"Excellent!"

Gimelli helped secure Sorea on the rotating board as the other four Pantteri Knights and their squires moved to observe the new training device.

"Rip it up, Sorea!" Ritari called.

"So, since Sorea is inverted, when we apply the phrase, 'Turn that frown upside down and smile,' does that mean you 'Turn that smile upside down and frown?'" Jumeaux joked.

Instead of laughter, he was greeted with stern looks.

"What? That's funny! Gimelli . . . come on!"

Gimelli rolled her eyes.

"I thought it was very clever," Bellae whispered.

"Like I care what you think, freak!"

She let out a gasp as Jumeaux answered her kindness with an elbow.

Not wanting him to get into more trouble, Bellae gingerly moved over to her sister, Gimelli. Jumeaux exhaled, grateful no one had seen his brotherly retribution.

"Luchar, are you next on this new contraption?" Finn questioned, looking at the Knight's portly belly as a round of laughter broke out.

"He's as familiar with sit-ups as he is with personal hygiene!" Ritari chided to a fresh helping of chuckles.

"Enough of this buffoonery! Strength of muscle and deadly weapons knock out your enemy, not sit-ups! Let's go, Jumeaux!" Luchar seethed before storming off.

"These are the targets you requested, Sorea," Baiulus said. "Hopefully, they will hold up. Your squire turns this crank to get them moving."

Gimelli began turning the crank and a series of targets began streaking around the top of the machine. Sorea used her intense abdominal muscles to sit upright. Reaching the top, she thrust her talons forward, easily piercing the targets with each blow.

Baiulus winced as the formerly pristine targets were quickly shredded.

Slowly the others went back to work as the targets continued to retch out silent screams of stuffing under the violence of her blows. Squire Scelto was manipulating a machine called the Rotator for his Knight, Ritari. It consisted of several circular towers with various weapons attached. Each tower could spin three hundred and sixty degrees, sending alternating weapons at his Knight.

After two and a half hours of work, they were ready for independent training. Bellae smiled, grateful to spend a little time with Crann before classes.

Suddenly Finn froze, "Something vile approaches."

Scroll 4: Red, Silver, and Blue

"What do you see Finn?" Bellae asked.

"Get Crann."

While leading Crann, she could see a scurry of activity at the gatehouse and outer wall, including Constable Rhyfeler's long blond hair and yellow surcoat. The wind was whipping the blue flags of the Independent Knights and intermittently showing their symbol, a white dove flying over two crossed swords and a castle tower.

Finn mounted his horse in a single leap, "Someone approaches."

"But what do you actually *see*?" Bellae questioned, curious about his unique sight.

"All Elves have the ability to see and feel emotion, health, and intention through nature. Right now, the ground is blood-red and seems to slither towards the gate, telling me something with foul intentions is approaching."

As Finn rode off, Bellae stooped until her nose nearly touched the earth, trying to sense the vibration and color like Finn, but saw merely dirt, and sensed only the awkward stares at her peculiar pose.

A series of communication flags were whipping in wide arcs at the top of the watchtowers. Bellae strained to follow them, whispering the words corresponding to their motion.

"What is it?" Lontas asked.

"Someone's coming."

"It can't be a large army or the Bells of Kadotus would be ringing."

"That's good, I guess," Bellae said.

Icy notes from the curled Horns of Infula rang from outside the castle walls, stopping every Knight in their tracks. It was the call of the Proliate and Magicians, first used during the Dark War when the Proliate army burst onto the scene of Verngaurd as a force to be reckoned with.

Friar Pallium abruptly appeared in their midst, and Rhyfeler gestured wildly to him from the top of the castle walls.

Friar nodded and Rhyfeler gave thumbs up to the castle porter. The heavy wooden gates wailed with a complaining groan until they crashed open against the castle walls. As the reverberation of the gates died down, riders entered Castle Liberum. Luchar immediately took off his helmet, poised to yell.

"Hold your tongue," Friar whispered. The expression on the Knight's broad face was more of a pained scowl than a smile, but he seemed to be trying.

Finn, Lovag, and other Knights on horseback moved in behind the visitors as they rode towards Friar.

The first sun, Mardin, was now well on its way to setting in the northeastern sky, and the second sun, Luminos, was directly overhead, painting everything with a yellow glow. As the gallop of the horses' hooves increased, the outlines of their riders grew crisper. The red capes of the Proliator warriors billowing out behind their horses were unmistakable.

"Red cloaks and armor . . ." Ritari groaned, " . . . they are the crazy Sanctus Division that guard the Proliate Temples."

"Temples? They're bloody fortresses!" Luchar growled.

"They are fierce, not crazy," Friar declared.

"You know they're called red death or Rutilus Obitus? Because they are *insane*!"

"Their other branch, the Ultor who wear silver, are not much better."

"When you get to that level of deranged, a slightly less batty is something to celebrate!" Ritari said with a tight smile.

The rays of the two suns reflected off the hyper-polished Proliator helmets, sending flashes of sunlight into the eyes of the Knights in perfect sync with the jostling of their horses. Two large phoenix wings flanked each of the Proliators' red helmets. A single burst of red plumage shot down its center. Their armor was red except for a thin, silver outline of a phoenix on their shields and chest plates.

"Oh, great, there's a Master Magician with them," Luchar groaned, spotting the telltale blue robes with yellow stars embroidered on it.

Long, greying brown hair flowed from underneath his headband into a long ponytail that bounced in stride with his mount. The center of his headband had a gold star underneath a red phoenix, designating him as a cleric of a Tallcon Temple. Steely grey eyes scanned the Knights and the castle hungrily, as if hoping for a fight.

The unwelcome warriors came to a choreographed stop before banging their spears and shields together and shouting, "All praise Tallcon, everlasting phoenix god!"

Friar Pallium spoke quickly, cutting off the cleric whom he instantly recognized. "Ah, welcome, Cleric Prast! By the light of the first sun, you look well."

Several Knights laughed at the derisive compliment since the first sun is the weakest of the three.

Friar continued innocently, "My Knights do not need a break, but perhaps I could entreat you to tea?"

"Knights?" snorted Prast. "Where are these Knights you speak of? Oh, dear me, I wonder if I am mistaken and these few anemic forms in front of me *are* your Knights? I'm embarrassed to admit I thought these ragtag and undernourished forms were squires."

Luchar's face flushed with anger, but he held his tongue, sliding his heavy helmet back on in order to mutter insults with some privacy.

Friar ignored the Magician's jibe and smiled, "Tea?"

Figure 22: A Proliate warrior. Their army has two main branches. The Sanctus Division wear red armor and are responsible for defense of their temples.

Figure 23: **Magician Prast** *is also a cleric for the Proliate, officiating their religious services.*

"That would most definitely be a no," Prast replied with a scornful smirk. "I have come to deliver a message from the Supreme Master Magician Veneficus."

Prast held out his crosier and began to chant. The crystal at the top of his wooden staff glowed blue, and a scroll from his saddlebag magically rose and unfurled itself. The scroll hovered leisurely in front of the Magician, its gentle vacillation presenting a stark contrast to the tension within the castle.

"Let all who hear this know, Supreme Master Magician Veneficus hereby proclaims the Independent Knights shall no longer address the leader of their three castles as 'Friar.' This term is misleading, as they do not serve Tallcon. They will choose another name so long as it is free from religious connotations. Failure to comply, especially at the upcoming Tournament of Flags, formerly called the Festival of Flags, will result in death at our hands and judgment thereafter as Tallcon sees fit."

Luchar rolled his eyes in disgust and grumbled more invectives within the seclusion of his helmet. Friar Pallium raised his hand to stay the Knights' quivering hostility.

"Veneficus wants this?"

"It was approved," Prast drawled, dodging the question.

"Do you Magicians have so little to do that you need to pick on an old man's title?"

"This is *no* trivial matter. In many native tongues, the words for 'friar' and 'cleric' are indistinguishable. We want the people of Verngaurd to have no trouble identifying their *true* protectors and spiritual guides."

Ritari began to draw his sword and the metal grated loudly in the strained silence. He stopped as Friar Pallium raised his hand for control.

"Prast," Friar said quietly, "I want to thank you for this valuable opportunity for us to grow. We shall journey into a new discovery and rethink the importance of having a title for me at all. If we decide one is needed, we shall select it."

While maintaining his unblinking gaze, Prast raised his head and turned it away slightly, probing to gauge Friar's sincerity.

"Yes, I should say," the Magician said tentatively. "I offer this list of titles which you may NOT use on your so-called 'journey.'"

The Magician chanted again. The scroll he had read from rolled itself up and plopped back in his saddlebag. On the way down, it passed a new and rather large scroll, which floated to Friar.

"I see, Pallium, that you are still letting your women fight for you?" the cleric said, smirking at Sorea. "You're no better than the primitive people of the North, Jaa. No wonder Verngaurd is so keen to have Proliators and Magicians defend them."

"Out here, in her armor, Sorea is a Knight. We are only men and women in our spare time."

As the Knights chuckled, Friar continued, "The Knights' sole mission for thousands of years has been to protect Verngaurd. We welcome any willing to help us in this endeavor. We appreciate the role the Proliator armies played in freeing Verngaurd from the Dark Warriors, but countless centuries have taught us that this 'help' comes and goes while we Knights stay steady and committed."

Prast chortled. "Referring to the Proliators as mere 'help' is an insult. Perhaps, you are too close to the situation to recognize how far the Knights have fallen. The Proliators need help with nothing! The day of the Knights is *over*!

"Who is patrolling the countryside hunting the Dark Warriors who have returned? It is the Proliate armies, working with the Magicians! We will stop them now as we did during the Dark War when your armies were obliterated!"

Before Friar Pallium could respond, Prast declared, "I tire of this conversation. Mark my words carefully, old man, you have nowhere to go but down. You've been spiraling for so long I expect you'll be able to handle this last bit of your fall into oblivion."

With great precision, the Proliators surrounded the Magician and paraded towards the gates, maintaining perfect lines as the wall of Knights parted to let them pass. The gates were closed as soon as they exited.

"How dare they insult you . . . us, in our own castle! I don't care what they say, they can't pry your title out of my lungs! Do they think they can change centuries of history with that foolish nonsense about Tallcon?" Luchar roared.

"Have you learned nothing about what is important?" Friar Pallium replied. "No amount of insult can change the height or grandeur of the world's tallest mountain, nor the length of time required to climb it. The mountain is unmoved even by the longest and harshest of criticisms. It simply does as it is supposed to. I, too, will function as I always have, no matter my title or the slurs hurled by that misguided traveler."

"Their fanatical religion spreads like pond scum!" Sorea added. "Proliators rely on their strength and the cheap tricks of Magicians to entertain the masses in their temples. We respect your wisdom, Friar, but it is the principle of the insult that boils our blood."

"If you cross the Desert of Calor at midday and call the sand cool, it will still burn your feet. To my thinking, the one who should feel foolish is the one who called the sand cool, not the sizzling sand itself. The sand should keep doing what it ought to be doing. Ah, perhaps there is a clue. All of you get back to training!"

Friar handed the scroll to Lovag. "I trust our book lover can come up with a solution that will calm our Knights and appease those who care so much about what does not concern them, or even matter. Now, back to training!"

Friar watched his Knights scurry back to work, but haunting visions of his recurring nightmares flooded back. He remembered standing on the castle wall as the Proliator's massive diezmar siege engines pounded at their walls.

In his mind's eye, he watched in horror as several large boulders exploded into the castle wall beneath him, blasting his body backwards. It seemed so real that a few beads of sweat formed on his brow.

His palpable fear, pounding heart, and dripping sweat overruled his mind's feeble attempt to convince himself, *There is time to change the future these visions portend.*

"Friar!" a voice shouted, wrestling the catastrophic images from his mind.

"Yes," he replied, wiping the sweat from his brow.

Several recently Knighted warriors surrounded Friar, watching him curiously.

"You were deep in thought."

"I suppose I was," he replied, smiling broadly enough to calm their fears.

"Please, settle an argument for us. Where is the best place to look when in combat? The hands, the weapon, the stomach, or the head?"

"An excellent question . . . for a squire!" he said. A round of nervous laughter went through the Knights.

"You must practice until you see *everything*. Analyze the fight's location, your opponent's mind, body, and spirit. Your foe's weapons and armor are strong, but these are the least important aspects of the fight. The most vulnerable part of any enemy is the flesh and blood wearing and wielding the cold, hard steel. Of his body, the easiest to attack is the brain. Defeat their mind and you conquer their will to fight and you win.

"Strive to understand the adversary's emotional state. Are they angry? Scared? Do they want to be there, or were they forced? Anyone with their back against the wall defending family or country will fight hardest.

"You must grasp that information in the context of the terrain. What movements would be impossible or unlikely if it is muddy or rocky? Is the ground sloping? Are there obstacles that change angles of attack? Generally speaking, uphill and with the brightest of the three suns to your back is desirable."

He chuckled at their dazed expressions. "Simple answers come from naive people blind to the true meaning of the question. Don't worry, complex answers become sharper with training. Keep these ideas in the back of your mind as you practice, practice, and then practice some more. One day it will make sense."

By this time, a large group of Knights and squires had gathered to hear his words. Tempaus, a Tilkeri Squad member almost of age to test for Knighthood, purposefully swung his elbow out and hit the side of Lontas' head while raising his hand.

"Oww!" Lontas wailed.

"Excuse me, Friar," Tempaus said, ignoring Lontas' cry of pain. "You always teach attack. So, isn't charging in the best strategy?"

Friar sighed in disappointment. "I do *not* always teach *attack*. I teach to take the *initiative*. The 'right' approach depends on the situation. There is a natural rhythm to every fight and fighter. Depending on the circumstances, you should change your tactics so you dictate the battle's pace. You may need to pull back to lure your opponent into attacking—forcing them to become off-balance or frustrated. Sometimes, you need to be still and observe. Other times, you may indeed need to attack rapidly.

"The sacrifice of victory occurs years before the war begins. Once the battle starts it's too late. The bells of defeat strike the unprepared. Observe, understand, and then formulate a plan. The more you train, the clearer this will become. Once the clash begins, you must constantly observe and rethink your strategy."

Despite the multitude of onlookers salivating for more, Friar began walking away. "Enough from this old man, for today."

Scroll 5: Squires & HK

Magician Prast's demeaning visit had lifted the masquerade of permanence and replaced it with a cloak of dejection, sending them spiraling into a nostalgic fog of how far the Knights had fallen after their devastating losses of the Dark War.

Doubt leached its tentacles into every crevice of their day. Suddenly each crack in the wall seemed larger, every weakness more profound, and the notion that the Knights could not only be defeated, but destroyed, hung around their necks like a millstone.

"That's it. Squires, head back to the stables," Ritari said as the long day finally withered. He removed his helmet and wiped the sweat from his forehead. "I'll stay until Luchar is done. The captain should be the last one from the field."

"Lovag's already at the library," Lontas declared.

"That guy loves reading books like Luchar likes hitting people," Scelto said, laughing.

"Doesn't Luchar ever want to sleep?" Gimelli asked, giggling.

"An eternity of sleep after I'm dead will be enough," Luchar growled after appearing amongst them. "Come on, Ritari. I promise *not* to take it easy on you tonight!"

"All stablemates, out!" Jumeaux demanded, shooing them from the stable.

"But . . ." Vir started.

"Don't care! Come back earlier tomorrow, stable rats!"

"Where's Bellae?" Gimelli asked.

"Talking with Finn," Scelto replied.

Jumeaux scoffed, "The key to stopping her blabbing is to distract her with an animal. She's insane about any four-legged creature!"

"That only works for you, Jumeaux, because if we compare their intelligence and looks to yours, ANIMALS will ALWAYS win!"

"Be nice, Scelto," Gimelli requested.

Jumeaux turned red, struggling for a comeback. "Scelto, you should transfer to Jester school. Wait! They don't take funny *looks* into consideration!"

Jumeaux and Scelto continued exchanging barbs until Gimelli managed to break it up.

Jumeaux looked to the rest of the squires, "I don't know about you, but I had no idea how far the Knights have fallen. I mean, we've all heard how few Knights there are now compared to the days before the Dark War, but I never expected this insult from the Magicians and Proliate. We blatantly got our pride handed to us."

"Jumeaux, put a bridle on it!" Scelto growled. "That Magician's a fool!"

"Things aren't that bad," Gimelli said. "The Knights we serve are no less than any that came before us, no matter what that birdbrain Magician said."

"Buuu," Lontas' voice cracked. Blushing, he cleared his throat and continued, "But the Knights used to have thirty-five castles, and now o-o-own-only three."

"See, even speech impediment fool Lontas agrees with me!" Jumeaux proclaimed.

Seeing the displeasure in Gimelli's eyes, Lontas added, "But I agree with Gimelli, our Knights are quite . . . uhm . . . quite good."

"Don't be a suck-up!" Jumeaux chided.

"Whether we like it or not, the fact is we are a fraction of what the Knights used to be," Scelto added.

"I heard a squad used to be twelve Knights, and now it's five. Liberum can muster five thousand Knights. This place could hold three times that," Jumeaux commented. "Isn't that right, Lontas? Scelto?"

Lontas, not thrilled about being singled out, backed against the stable wall, looking as if he would rather merge into the wood than answer. "Uhm . . . those numbers sound right. Technically we have a few hundred more in outposts. Either way, our numbers are way down. The highest number of Knights was seventy thousand in thirty-five castles right before the horrendous losses during the Dark War. After that, many castles were abandoned or taken over by the Proliate and Magicians."

"During the Dark War, the individual nations of Verngaurd started rearming their *own* armies with forced conscription instead of honoring their pact to send recruits to the Knights," Scelto added.

"Prast confirmed the rumor, the Dark Warriors are back," Jumeaux said. "They handed it to us last time and now we have waaaay fewer Knights. Plus, the Proliate and the Magicians hate us as much as the Dark Warriors do."

Gimelli smiled through her frustration, "We've had peace and tranquility for decades. No matter how you complain, times are good."

Both Jumeaux and Scelto looked as if they were planning a retort, but Jumeaux raised his voice, "The Knights are weak! If they wanted to, the Proliators *or* the Dark Warriors could come in here and kick our . . ."

He froze as Bellae and Finn walked into the stables.

"Finn," the squires uttered anxiously.

"Hello."

He and Bellae led Crann to their spot in the stable.

"Did Finn hear me?" Jumeaux asked Gimelli telepathically.

"I think so. You don't have to be so negative to make a point."

"By all means, Jumeaux, please finish your bold statement," Finn said.

Jumeaux's shoulders fell, and his thin face seemed even more gaunt than usual as his eyes darted frantically. Nervously, he swept his hand through his unruly black hair.

"I . . . *we,* were just talking," Jumeaux added, looking for affirmation from the other squires. When none came, his eyes dropped to the ground, restlessly watching the dust kicked up by his scuffling boots.

"Talking big in dark corners seldom achieves anything other than getting you into trouble. As it happens, Salus asked me to find someone to help in the Infirmary. Given your ample energy and bold attitude, I think you would make an excellent volunteer."

Jumeaux groaned loudly.

"So," Finn continued, "we are supposed to call Friar Pallium 'HK' for Head Knight."

"HK?" Scelto asked incredulously. "This is horse shhhii . . . I mean, this is absurd!"

Everyone laughed but Jumeaux. *Scelto blows off steam and it's funny? I do it and get sent to work at the loony bin Infirmary?*

"Finn, it was incredible when you saw the Proliate coming before anyone else! That's an amazing gift," Gimelli commented.

"There are advantages to seeing as we Elves do. It's a mixture of colors and emotions."

"That sounds wonderful!" Lontas said.

Finn paused. "Sometimes it is, but there are times I wish I had *your* gift of seeing things like a blue sky or flowers in their true colors."

"I hadn't thought about it that way. I imagined you saw what we do with something added," Gimelli commented.

"It's easy to overlook our own gifts while coveting others, often without knowing the full effort required to bear them," Finn answered.

"It's been an eventful day. Finish your work and get some rest. Jumeaux, head to the Infirmary when you're done."

"Okay," Jumeaux mumbled, gnashing his teeth at the perceived injustice. *No one sticks up for me, but everyone does for that freak Lontas.*

"Try to enjoy meeting the ailing and frail. Remember, soon enough we will be old and in the Infirmary with some young squire running over to wipe the drool off our mouths!"

The Knight leaned towards Bellae and whispered, "Don't forget your meeting tomorrow morning." She smiled and nodded despite feeling stressed about the private appointment as he headed towards the door.

"Everyone, sleep well because tomorrow is your next Squire Battle! Remember, you didn't hear this from me," Finn said in a mock whisper.

"Good night," they muttered over a collective groan.

Only the thud of a bucket being hung up or the jingling of bridle and saddle being put away broke the quiet for the longest time while the squires saw to their work, tacitly dreading the Squire Battle.

It was Bellae's laughter, standing on a stool stroking Crann's forehead that shattered the hefty silence.

"What's so funny?"

"Crann thinks the Proliator horses have their hooves shod too tight!"

Jumeaux rolled his eyes, "Not this again!"

"J, after everything you have seen how can you doubt her?" Gimelli asked.

"She's good with animals, yes, that I believe. But talking to them? No, not believing that! She hums, which they find soothing."

Ever since Bellae had saved him from the River Vita Monster, he had believed she could communicate with animals. However, he was in the mood to annoy. They needed payback for hanging him out to dry with Finn. His anger flared further as he rubbed his largest scar, one of the many cicatrices coursing through his skin after being swallowed. Each lesion served less as a reminder of the trauma endured than as an emotional symbol of the perceived spurn sustained from Finn and the other squires.

"You're just sore about what happened to you in the last Squire Battle," laughed Scelto. "Real fine piece of work that day." Everyone but Bellae and Jumeaux joined in the laughing. "Remember when . . ."

"It's okay everyone, we can stop talking about last year," Bellae interrupted.

She hummed quietly while grooming Crann. The sense of peace and natural ease that exuded from his younger sister only served to fire up Jumeaux's anger despite her coming to his aid. *Miss goody, goody!*

"I'm done and heading to the blasted Infirmary!" Jumeaux said in a gruff tone. *Thanks for leaving me hanging and not offering to help*! He wanted to share how angry he was to the oblivious squires, but faltered and lashed out instead.

"Anyway, Lontas, I think you should be proud. Your LTC and LCC are at record highs today. Good tripping, good making a fool of yourself, good clumsying!"

"'Clumsying' is not a real word, actually," Lontas corrected.

Jumeaux shot him a dirty look. "It's called sarcasm! Don't worry about me not sleeping. It's not like I need sleep to show up the likes of you incompetent ninnies tomorrow!" A thrown brush whizzed through the air and struck the door just as Jumeaux slammed it shut.

"I swear, Gimelli and Bellae," exclaimed Scelto, "how you three can be related I will never know!"

"He does have a good side," Gimelli commented.

"Oh, I agree completely," Scelto remarked. "Unfortunately, it's very small, and can only be seen if you squint really hard in perfect lighting."

They all giggled and Gimelli changed the subject, "What did you and Finn talk about, Bellae?"

"Finn told me about the old days when our capital was Cumhacht and the Knights ran the Festival of Flags. The Magicians and Proliate run it as the Citadel and are bringing the Festival back and calling it the Tournament of the Flags."

"Wow! Changing *Festival* to *Tournament* . . . what a huge change!"

"Long ago when the Knights were at full strength, the Festival of Flags was held every four years to test the different squads of the thirty-five Knight castles and determine the Knight Champion," Bellae continued. "It gave Knights a chance to see friends and family since they were gone for most of the year."

"Lovag told me that the donation taxes each country pays for us to protect them are drying up," Lontas added. "Instead of giving money to us to protect Verngaurd, they are spending it on their own armies or giving it to the Proliators. Think about the last time we had a new recruit for stablemate. A lot of people are sending their kids into their own country's army or to the Proliators."

"To get the protection of the Proliators, you have to let them build a temple to Tallcon and take their religion of the eternal phoenix!" Gimelli said grimly.

"The Knights have protected them for thousands of years! How can the nations of Verngaurd turn their backs on us?" Lontas asked.

"Are you kidding?" Scelto said. "We just talked about getting served in the Dark War. We lost credibility. The Proliate and the Magicians are the ones who beat the Dark Warriors and have the power, prestige, and money." He paused. "Boy, I would *love* to cut off Prast's ponytail."

"Some Magicians are good, Prast, not so much. Friar loves Veneficus who always looks out for the Knights," Gimelli replied. "Anyway, if the Dark Warriors are back in Verngaurd, it's better if we all work together to defeat them."

Gimelli playfully slapped Lontas on the back. "Dark Warriors aren't a cheerful thought to end the day, but you know what? It's time for bed. Finn is great. He didn't have to tell us about the Squire Battle tomorrow."

Scroll 6: The Lifeless are Calling

Jumeaux stood indignantly outside the door to the Infirmary while the other four squires drifted to their barracks buoyed by the promise of sleep. The white stone building had the word "Vetus" chiseled above the arched entrance and small windows lining the second floor, instantly conjuring the concept that "Infirmary" was a misnomer for prison.

"Jumeaux!" a strange voice muttered. Seeing a ghostly white form out of the corner of his eye he bolted through the door as he heard his name called a second time. *What the bloody latrine is that?* Jumeaux thought, having seen that spirit a couple of times before. *I so hate this castle! I soooo hate this castle, and everything in it!*

Once inside he instantly inhaled the loathsome stench that builds up when many dependent people are forced into a fixed area. His ears were assaulted with the erratic comings and goings of workers and patients who seemed to be bouncing around randomly. His eyes caromed back and forth fruitlessly trying to ascertain some pattern or purpose to the chaotic movements.

There were two bustling hallways stretching out to either side. The one to the left had a massive staircase leading up. Yellowing tapestries hung on white stonewalls but failed to dull the racket or add cheer.

"You the squire sent to help?" a large, muscular man asked before Jumeaux could bolt. He was wearing a white cloak and a red belt. His shaggy hair nearly covered his dull eyes. His massive hands were supporting a small, elderly patient who hung limply, like a heedless doll in the grasp of the immense man. "Little scrawny, aren't you?"

"I'll take it from here," a calm voice interrupted. "Please get that patient to his room. Hello, squire."

"I'm Jumeaux, from the Pantteri Squad. Finn sent me."

"I am Salus, I run the Infirmary. As you can see, you have come at our busiest time. We are getting everyone to their rooms for the night. Thank you for coming."

It's not like I had a choice.

"As you know, we take care of the sick of body and those with disordered minds. It is a gift to assist those who cannot take care of themselves."

Oh, yes, a "gift." That's why there are so many people beating down the door to help! Jumeaux thought.

"Come, let's get you to work," Salus continued. His voice remained as placid as his peaceful expression as if oblivious to the chaos of movement breaking around him like a wave.

Jumeaux was not so lucky, faltering behind him through the busy hallway towards the stairs. The urgency of the healers and orderlies

Figure 24: **Salus** *is head healer and surgeon at the Vetus Infirmary of Castle Liberum.*

stood in stark contrast to the listless despondency of the patients either motionless, except for dangling drool, or ambling in a hopeless haze, barely outpacing death, which ceaselessly hovered in the shadows brandishing its undefeated weapons, eternal optimism and unwavering patience.

Salus was a tall, spare man who wore a flowing white robe with a red sash over his right shoulder—designating him as a healer. His delicate, scarless, and callous-free appearance stood in stark contrast to the hardened appearance of the Knights. His spectacles reflected the flickering lantern lights, barely masquerading his emerald-green eyes. Petite ears were tucked neatly under his grey hair while standing sentry above a surprisingly broad jaw.

"We had an accident and desperately need help cleaning up."

Why can't you clean it up? Jumeaux thought. *You could use some manual labor.*

"I'm too busy running this place. We lose people all the time but no one steps up to take their place," Salus said, as if he had heard Jumeaux's thoughts.

Rattled, Jumeaux said nothing, Salus' response and the strange white figure from outside unnerving his mind.

"To make things worse, we have a few orderlies out sick. When it rains it pours," Salus said, pointing up the staircase. "Top of the stairs, first room on your right, a mop, buckets, and water are waiting to clean up days of soup rations, totally wasted!"

The squire glanced around nervously. "Uhm, up there?"

"Yes, Jumeaux. Go up and clean where the mess meets the floor, and the mop leans precariously propped but shamefully inactive. I assure you the mop is anxiously awaiting your arrival." As he spoke he used two of his fingers to mockingly climb imaginary, miniature stairs.

A chuckle from an orderly spurred Jumeaux up the stairs, flushed with self-consciousness. At the top, he was relieved to find less chaos with only a few orderlies helping patients into rooms down a long hallway. On his right, lying motionless on the floor, a puddle of disagreeable greenish fluid stared scornfully up at him.

That's food? Jumeaux thought with a shudder of revulsion.

The spill arched out from the doorway like an emerald tongue, mockingly sticking itself out and daring him to take a peek at the volume of slop hiding on the other side.

A solitary mop stood nonchalantly against the wall. Taking a deep breath, Jumeaux grabbed it and pushed one of a dozen large buckets of water closer to the spill. *You have to look,* Jumeaux told himself, leaning around the corner. Several large vats had overturned, hemorrhaging a massive spill of green goop.

Bloody, wretched . . . ah!

His thin arms tensed as he thrust the mop forward with all his might, each stroke stoking the fire of his ire. His untamed hair bobbed and weaved angrily in tune with his aggressive swabbing.

Finn, Friar, and the other squires are cozy in bed while I have to battle this sludge!

The mop moved furiously. *Dunk, splash.*

"Always me!" he yelled at the slime. "Everyone gang up on Jumeaux!"

Squish, splat, shove.

He ignored the ache in his slender arms and continued scrubbing. Each twinge of soreness in his muscles fueled the seed of fury growing in his heart.

"You missed a spot. Ha-ha. Funny joke, never gets old!" a male voice rang out, startling the squire.

Jumeaux cringed in disgust at a slovenly young man, perhaps a few years older than him, approaching. A fleshy mass of stomach had exiled the young man's stretched and despairing shirt up around his chest, leaving a breaking wave of fat smooshing out below. His disheveled black hair sprouted like greasy porcupine quills above impassive eyes, a bulbous nose, and inanely large ears.

He is obviously more than a few fritters short of a dozen.

A dribble of spittle dangling precariously at the corner of his mouth completed his slovenly ensemble. His pants stretched desperately above generous calves. His large toes, complete with yellowing nails, protruded from tattered work boots.

This guy works here? They really must be desperate.

Looking around, Jumeaux noted with relief that he was over halfway done. The ache of his muscles came hammering into his shoulder, back, and arms, causing him to momentarily forget the strange figure in front of him. Jumeaux dropped the mop and gently stretched his quaking muscles threatening to cramp.

"I'm sure glad they stuck you with this job. Who hates you? Ha-ha! Usually I do these jobs because I am such a hard worker," the bloated-belly-boy said.

Oh, yeah. Obviously!

"My name's Crassus. I work here," he said, proudly pointing to the perspiring red belt, its stretched fibers languishing under and around his profuse fat rolls. "Do you have food? They never feed me. It's always work, work, work. I always clean up messes. Do you have any food?" Crassus pleaded, picking at his belly button.

"What's your name?" he asked as his belly button mining expedition hit pay dirt. He smiled, extracting a large, tangled mass of hair and lint. Jumeaux squished up his face in revulsion.

"J-Jumeaux," he reluctantly answered, staring at the massive, hair laden ball of lint in Crassus' hand.

"How come you don't have a red belt like us workers?"

"Uhm, I'm a squire helping out."

"A squire!" Crassus said excitedly. "I could be a Knight, carry a swordsey . . . and ride a horsey."

Swordsey? Horsey? This guy's insane! "Didn't you have to be a squire before becoming an orderly?"

Crassus looked left and right nervously as if expecting someone to come and answer the question for him. A different finger nervously slurped up his nostril.

"Hey, man, what's wrong with you?" Jumeaux asked, feeling as if he were going to vomit. Crassus looked longingly as he squished his double mined treasure together.

"It tastes better if you get a little from both places!" Crassus announced excitedly.

"Don't do it, man, I beg you!" Jumeaux pleaded. Despite his request, the revolting morsel of belly button lint mixed with hot snot went plopping into his mouth.

"MMMMMhhh!" Crassus said as he swished the disgusting delicacy around in his mouth. Jumeaux retched but did not vomit.

"Crassus!" someone yelled from down the hall.

Ignoring the voice, Crassus moved towards Jumeaux. "Hey, Jay-OH-moh, I help you mop? Shall I?"

He crudely picked up the mop and ineffectively began to slosh the green slime around the floor.

"Hey, man, you're messing up my work!"

"I work here. I clean messes," Crassus mumbled as Jumeaux wrenched the mop out of his hands.

Crassus let loose a deafening bawl. "WAHHHHHHHHHH-HH-HA-HA."

"Uh," Jumeaux stammered, dumbfounded by the bizarre reaction.

"Hey, kid, what did you do to Crassus?"

"Me?"

The large orderly Jumeaux had seen downstairs pushed an elderly man in a rotasessius, or wheeled chair, up to them before gently patting Crassus, "It's okay."

"He not let me moppy! WAAAAAAHHHHHHH!" Crassus pushed the orderly aside and dove into the green slime, kicking and spinning his feet. The goop sloshed all over his tightly stretched white uniform while showering the area Jumeaux had already cleaned.

"Hey, I worked hard on that!"

The large orderly turned an angry eye on Jumeaux. "Haven't you done enough?"

"Me?"

"Me, me, me! Is that all you think about?" the orderly accused, picking up Crassus. "Let's get you to bed. How did you steal another uniform?"

"My uniform!" Crassus bawled. "Mine, mine, mine!"

"Okay, you're right. We'll get it washed so it's ready for you tomorrow," the large orderly soothed in a surprisingly gentle voice. Crassus cooed gently and rested his oversized head on the orderly's shoulder.

A bloody patient! Jumeaux thought. *Look at the mess that lunatic made!*

After they walked down the corridor a bit, the immense orderly turned. "Hey, squire, out in the hallway, now!"

Jumeaux obliged.

"While I get Crassus cleaned up and into bed, watch Necare," the orderly said, nodding to the elderly man in the wheeled chair.

"But, I have to . . ."

"You HAVE to watch Necare!"

"This my uniform. Right? Right? I cleaned well, didn't I?" Crassus whimpered. "If that nasty squire hadn't been there, I would have finished."

"It's your uniform and you did great," the orderly reassured. Both turned to glare hatefully at Jumeaux before disappearing into a room halfway down the hallway.

Jumeaux glanced longingly over his shoulder at the floor that was once again smeared with green slime. *If I leave this old guy to clean, something bad will happen and I'll get blamed.*

He looked more closely at the ancient Necare. The desiccated and gnarled old man appeared to have lost a desperately lopsided battle against the full brunt of time's vindictive abuse. His fissured skin sagged like friable drapery over wasted muscles. His head was thrown forward by a crumbling neck, warped by the years into an eternal bow. Sunken orbits held eyes drained of hope and turned an almost opaque grey by age. Tremors made his knotted hands contort an unconscious, dissonant dance. The ancient eyes suddenly flickered up at Jumeaux.

"A-bch-b-ch?" his dusty voice cracked and wavered through rusty vocal cords.

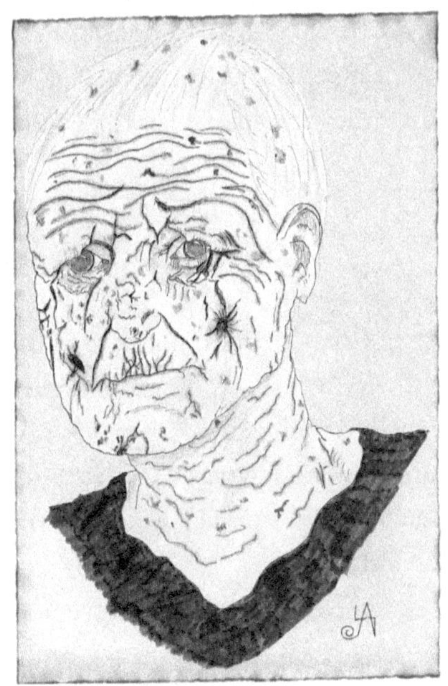

Figure 25: **Ancient former Knight Necare.** *One of the last Knights alive to have fought in the Dark War.*

A few decaying memories shook loose from decrepit mental rafters. Threadbare memories started and stopped like a carriage over large rocks, as he searched for youthful images of himself.

"Whhas Iahh boy?"

Fear, agony, and a cold sadness radiated from the ancient man, causing Jumeaux to shudder. The squire wallowed in the aged man's tangible despair, gripped by a nauseating mix of emotions.

"Was I a young boy?" Necare demanded.

"What?"

Necare sighed and repeated his question. A look of deep sincerity shone from behind the frail, clouded eyes. "Did I kill all those Dark Warriors?"

Jumeaux glanced around anxiously, willing the orderly to return. "I don't know, old man. I have a better question, is everybody in this place crazy?"

The elderly man shook his head in frustration and closed his eyes, seeming to instantly fall asleep.

A few moments later his eyes abruptly shot open, "It's gone!"

Scroll 7: The Dead Are Falling

"What's gone?" Jumeaux asked, startled by his sudden stir.

"My youth." A flicker of hope in the old man's eyes quickly departed, replaced with jaded fatigue.

"My village was between Pescare and the Koori Mountains. It has fields of wild flowers," he added, his voice quickened with a burst of lucidity.

"Have you seen the Storten Flower Fields? I ran through so many flowers it felt as if I were swimming in them. Oh, the smells, the sights. My muscles were strong and tireless. My whole life was in front of me. Now, look! I can't even stand and I get the pleasure of peeing myself daily!"

Jumeaux looked around in horror. Sweat began to bubble up on his forehead. He wiped it away, wondering if this night would ever end.

"How I wish I would just die."

"Oh, please, don't," the squire begged weakly.

With surprising quickness, he grabbed Jumeaux's wrist. "Just a whisper ago I was young like you. You're a blink of an eye away from sitting trapped like me in this seat of horrors, always tired, but perpetually bored, always in pain, and somehow always hungry but eternally full at the same time. Don't waste a single second of the time you have from now until you're sitting where I am!"

Panicking, Jumeaux began backing away towards the green slop and the stairs. The former Knight's gaze suddenly widened with intensity. Necare's grip tightened, causing Jumeaux to yelp as he dragged the wheeled chair forward. Necare sighed deeply, an endless fog settling behind his eyes. Without warning, his shoulders slumped, and his head collapsed while his entire body crumpled into the chair.

Jumeaux's mind impassively glanced at the old man's previous advice, but blinded by the youthful cloak of invincibility, he deflected them, sending the words spiraling into the green slime where they sat patiently waiting to be mopped up and discarded.

Seeing no one around, Jumeaux felt the man's neck with his free hand. *Please, be asleep.* "No pulse!" *Dead? You have got to be kidding me!*

Sweat poured off his forehead as he realized the man's hand was still clasped to his wrist. The leathery toughness of the skin surprised him as he frantically tried to remove it. Putting his foot on the front of the rotasessius, he pushed hard.

Nothing.

Leaning backwards in desperation, Jumeaux pulled harder.

Wham!

Instead of loosening the dead man's grip, Jumeaux managed to yank the dead man forward out of his chair. The lifeless body toppled onto him, and both were thrust backwards, sliding on the green goop. Necare's foot was caught in the wheeled chair, pulling it forward until it slammed against the wall, eventually toppling over, precariously resting on the top step.

Oh no! Oh no! Jumeaux lamented from his back. The old man's rigid body curled on top of him, his boney right shoulder pinching Jumeaux's neck.

Jumeaux managed to wriggle closer to the stairs, desperately reaching for the teetering wheeled chair. His fingers flailed wildly, barely touching the chair's side. Stars began flashing in front of his eyes from the lack of oxygen.

Have to grab . . . got it!

The creaking and wobbling of the rotasessius interrupted his thoughts as it hung precariously for a moment.

Don't got it.

The rotasessius fell, crashing and slamming down the stairs, quickly gaining speed.

"BOY! What are you doing? Don't you know Knight Necare fought in the Dark War?" the large orderly yelled.

Jumeaux whimpered.

"What the . . . ?" the orderly said, entering the hallway where the skeletal figure of Necare had Jumeaux pinned. Enraged, he flew down the hall.

"He's dead," Jumeaux said, feeling increasingly lightheaded under the dead weight lying across his neck.

"You killed him!"

"No!" Jumeaux gurgled, struggling to stay conscious.

A naked Crassus bolted towards them, excitedly flapping his soiled uniform like a corpulent bird desperate for flight. His lavish, fleshy belly rolls undulated in lumbering tune with each stomping flutter of his makeshift wings. Seeing the two of them lying on the floor, he dropped his clothes and began to jump up and down, clapping with unabashed enthusiasm. "The squire killed Necare! The squire killed Necare!"

Like a fire bell, Crassus' inappropriately joyous call had the residents of the Infirmary rushing into the hallway. Shouts of, "Murderer!" and "He really killed him!" flooded the hall and added to Jumeaux's terror.

Panicking at the orderly's anger and the chorus of patients, Jumeaux rocked back and forth to joggle Necare off him. He succeeded, gratefully sucking in a deep breath. His momentary reprieve was short-lived as brisk tug jerked his wrist, followed by a harsh sliding motion.

Jumeaux shouted, "Oh, NOOOOOO!" as the old man rattled down the stairs, pulling the squire after him down the bumpy course.

Thud-thud-thud-thud!

Finally clunking to a stop. Jumeaux looked up to see Salus standing above his throbbing and bruised body.

"This kid tormented Crassus and killed Necare!" the orderly shrieked.

Jumeaux looked pleadingly. Gently, but firmly, Salus broke the death grip of Necare before holding up his hand for silence.

"But . . ." the orderly protested.

"Enough!" Salus said with surprising force. "Carry Necare up to his room and prepare him for the death ritual."

"Sir, I didn't kill him," Jumeaux appealed. "Honest, I didn't. I was cleaning up the green slop when Crassus came pretending to be an orderly and eating nasty stuff he pulled out of all sorts of sick bodily places! Then, this mostly-dead guy starts freaking out about being a boy and peeing himself and . . ."

"It is okay, Jumeaux. I know it was not some action from you. The blanket of mortality has been nipping at his heels for years, and finally succeeded in settling its quietus upon him."

The orderly gently lifted the body of the old Knight, shooting Jumeaux a parting glare before disappearing up the stairs.

"I am sorry he's dead," Jumeaux said, averting his eyes from the healer.

"No, I'm the one who should be sorry. There's too much chaos here for a single squire to help. They should have sent ten of you. Do you want me to look at your injuries?"

"No, I'm okay," Jumeaux said, slowly standing. His whole body ached from the frantic mopping and painful fall.

"Do you need help getting to your barracks?"

Jumeaux grimaced, looking back up the stairs. "You don't need me to finish?"

"I'll have that hulk of an orderly take care of it," Salus said, winking.

"Thanks."

"I'll let you know when the funeral is," Salus called after him.

Oh, yeah, wouldn't miss it, Jumeaux thought wryly. A chorus of penetrating eyes greeted him as he made his way through the disapproving crowd and pushed through the door. The cool and crisp night air refreshed his lungs, but could not eradicate the brisk and icy memories of Crassus and Necare. Without remembering how he got there, Jumeaux made it to the barracks and changed out of his slimy clothes.

Everyone's sleeping! Lucky backstabbing weasels.

A chill went through him, *What was that white thing outside the Infirmary? If I tell anyone they'll only criticize me more than usual.*

As he scanned the room he noticed an empty cot.

Where's Scelto? Jumeaux's tired mind wondered apathetically. Gingerly he slid into his bed. Immediately, his exhausted mind raced into the sanctuary of sleep where he dreamed of wrestling patients in a frothy and turbulent sea of green slop.

Figure 26: Supreme Master Magician **Veneficus.**

Figure 27: **Valo** *are magical floating lights of foul temper, earning the nickname of floating crab apples. These round balls of light have human faces and a gift for sarcasm.*

Chapter Two

Battle Within, Battle Without

Scroll 1: Ancient Betrayal, Present-Day Pain

In the Citadel, Supreme Master Magician Veneficus rummaged through a mountain of disorganized scrolls in his secret vault. Sapphire eyes, accented by his like-colored robes, sat between his greying hair and goatee.

How could I have been so careless? I thought I would have more time!

He had been toiling to find the Prophecy Scroll for longer than he cared to admit. *Where have the last few hundred years gone?*

"Those cursed Ainmhi Caint!"

"What's that, Big Venney?" a glowing ball of light, one foot in diameter, with a distinctive face in the center asked. The magical orb floated six feet off the ground and, along with his nine counterparts, was responsible for lighting the room. His broad nose hung above full lips, and flourished beneath expressive eyes.

"Nico, you glowing cretin, address me as Master Veneficus!" the Magician thundered. "You know I hate being called Venney. I was lamenting those Ainmhi Caint animal talkers who were too smart for their own good! I offered them the world, and how did they repay me? Betrayal! They stole the Macht Power Crystals that our magic depends on."

"They don't sound too nice, *Master*," the glaring Nico declared.

Veneficus sighed. The relentless march of time since their treachery had not dimmed the potency of the duplicity. *I gave those animal talkers a chance to alter destiny, to save themselves. But they chose to steal and hide the crystals to "protect" the world from some imagined evil. I protect the world from evil! Now, with the world in chaos and the time of Na Cearcaill closing in, we are running short on our magic crystals.*

"Yet, there is hope. A simple squire in Castle Liberum has once again rekindled the gift of the Ainmhi Caint," Veneficus announced. "The reemergence of the gift of speaking with animals is the signal that the time of the Prophecy has finally arrived."

"Did you need something, *Master*?" the floating ball of light asked snidely.

"My greatest mistake in magic, and I have made many, was conjuring you ten magical Valo lights. What was I thinking? You're floating nuisances with faces!" Veneficus chided the creature levitating behind his shoulder.

"Hovering around you shedding light wherever and whenever you want is so gratifying that your harsh words pierce my nonexistent heart! Sorry, my nonexistent heart, *Master*." The face within the ball of light crinkled contemptuously.

"I should have made you mute! You do understand, you hot ball of sarcastic gas, that I can obliterate you with a sneeze?"

"Stopped by snot? What a noble death!" the Valo light proclaimed.

"Quit joking you glorified torch! The fate of the world is at stake, and I can't find the blasted Prophecy Scroll concocted by the animal talkers!"

The rising anger in Veneficus' words warned the mocking light to hold off on the sarcastic comment bubbling within.

"The White Wizard and his Dark Warriors are coming back in much greater numbers than during the Dark War. Our lesser crystals, the mindre, are running dangerously low."

"The mindre crystals are the ones on your crosier that you use for magic, right? So, how will you Magicians cast spells if those crystals all run out of magic?" the light asked.

"We won't be able to, you incandescent simpleton! That is why I *must find* the Prophecy Scroll that tells us how to find the true source of magic, the Macht Crystals. Once those crystals are discovered, we can recharge the lesser mindre crystals and properly fight the oncoming war. I had the Prophecy for hundreds of years before it was stolen from me by the wretched friends of the animal talkers."

"You mean the ones who stole the Macht Crystals also stole the Prophecy?"

"Sort of. The animal talkers stole the Crystals and then wrote the Prophecy to protect them from some fabricated 'evil.' I managed to find the Prophecy, but their collaborators stole it back from me."

"Those guys sure like to steal. If they have the Prophecy, why are you looking here?"

Veneficus shook his head in disgust. "I *was* able to get the Prophecy back from them, but misplaced it. You were with me for all of this, don't you remember?"

"I guess if I read my journal from eons ago it would contain all these sordid details that you expect me to remember. Oh, wait! You didn't see fit to give me arms or legs, *master!* I guess that precludes any literary aspirations."

"A warning my luminescent globule! Sarcasm wears out its welcome quickly."

"Really? I think of sarcasm as a socially acceptable way to mock with contempt," the Valo whispered.

Veneficus continued, "Anyway, just when it is time to fulfill the Prophecy, the scroll seems to be missing again."

"So, Boss, I guess the obvious question is why didn't you just do the Prophecy thingy when you had it a few hundred years ago? You know, before you were running low on magic?"

"Because, only an animal talker . . . or maybe it's her brother . . . I can't recall, can be the Chosen One. The blasted Ainmhi Caint put a safeguard on the Prophecy so that only the Chosen One can complete the tasks that will reveal the location of the Power Crystals."

"Did those animal talkers have magic or something?"

"They were an exceptional people with a special kind of magic."

"If they stopped you, they must have been awesome!" Nico said scornfully.

Reeling at the torment of their betrayal, Veneficus disregarded the comment. "The animal talkers completely disappeared from Verngaurd after making the Prophecy, and I feared their kind was lost forever until this squire showed up!"

"If they disappeared, who stole back the Prophecy Scroll from you?"

"I told you, their collaborators, some vile insurgent group calling themselves the League of Truth!" Veneficus smacked away the closest pile of scrolls in a fit of rage. Some of the ancient ones splintered, sending small pieces of shredded paper drifting down like brittle fall leaves.

"That'll teach those scrolls! Good hit there, *Master*!" the Valo spouted, before whispering, "Picking on defenseless paper, real tough guy!"

"To make matters worse I will have to work full time with the Proliate in the looming battle for Verngaurd."

"You don't like those Proliate boys?" the Valo asked.

"Not compared to the Knights. I greatly miss having the erudite Knights here in the Citadel. These over-religious Proliate are one-dimensional zealots and quickly become boring," Veneficus answered. "Teaching expands the mind, but over-preaching quickly becomes deafening to the ears and deadening to the unencumbered soul and inquisitive mind."

"That's quite profound Master!" the Valo fawned. "You have a great memory considering you've lived for eons."

"Time is an odd and cruel conqueror. The long days of our youth all too quickly blend into short years, eventually disintegrating into even shorter decades."

"If you say so boss," Nico scowled. "I definitely agree with you about the Knights. They should never have given up Cumhacht. I hardly ever get out of here and those Proliate even annoy me. It's like they have a spear shoved up their aa . . ."

"Enough Nico! I need to think," Veneficus said, closing his eyes. *I can't even remember if the Chosen One is the girl who can speak with animals or her brother? I want what's best for Verngaurd. Only I can protect it from the dark future looming.*

Scroll 2: Friar's Office—Say What?

Jumeaux grimaced as images of the green slop he had been dreaming about vanished thanks to rustling in the barracks. His tired eyes fluttered long enough to see his sister. *Bellae!* A surge of anger rushed through his aching body.

She's always getting up early to feed her idiotic critters!

He longed for the blissful ignorance of sleep to shelter his worry. *Everyone in the castle is going to find out what happened last night and make fun of me, including that misfit Lontas! Friar, Finn, and the other squires did this to me!*

Through sleep-weary eyes he turned to see Scelto's brawny form deep in slumber. *Where was he last night? If I try to get him in trouble for leaving barracks, no one will believe me over the golden boy.*

Fatigue overcame ire, and soon he was sinking back into unpleasant dreams.

Having arrived at the central tower of the castle, Bellae made her way through the grey stone maze towards Friar Pallium's office. Only a few of the torches were lit at this hour, though they did little to brighten her way or attitude. Her dainty fingers traced the rough walls as she ascended the stairs.

Arriving at his office, she found the heavy, wooden door to his office closed. Puffing out her lower lip, she blew her sandy-blonde hair out of her eyes. As time slowly passed she restlessly wandered around the waiting chamber. The lanterns hanging on the wall struggled to spread light against the oppressive darkness of the stone walls. Almost every inch of one wall held banners and shields commemorating centuries of Knight victories. Bellae shuddered as she ran her fingers across an immense dent in one of the shields. *What caused such a crater and what happened to the Knight holding it?*

The opposite wall was covered in rows of shelves holding hundreds of trophies from the old days when the Festival of Flags was a tournament for the legion of Knights. Her small hand wound its way around the old, and sometimes battered, forged metal trophies towards one in the back that seemed to shine despite its dusty veil. It was too heavy to slide forward, but she recognized one etched word, "Pallium."

"Funny to think Friar won that so long ago, huh?"

Bellae yelped, "You scared me, Ritari!"

"Sorry." The cloak he wore rippled over his muscular physique as he moved towards her.

"Friar was the youngest Knight to become Grand Champion of the Festival," Ritari said with a reflective smile on his face.

"Long ago, as a fledgling Knight, I stood right here and complimented Friar on his many trophies. To my amazement, he seemed disappointed, saying, 'Most people do not contemplate the motivation of their actions, or understand the importance of doing them well for the *right* reason. Move through life as if every one of your actions will echo forever. Actions inspired by hopes of glory or fortune result in false prizes that quickly decompose. When both the trophy and the combatant have faded to dust, and their memory has wilted from the world's consciousness, still the motivation of the deed will remain as an reverberation rippling through eternity.'"

The early wrinkles marring Ritari's chiseled face seemed deeper, making him appear old to the young squire. "Victory over self and virtuous inspiration are pure and never fade. Anyway, Friar's ready for you," he said, tousling her hair before heading down the stairs.

"Thank you for coming," Friar Pallium said from the open doorway.

"You're welcome," Bellae replied, following him into his office.

"I never thought Ritari would memorize those remarks." He chuckled, "I barely remember saying them! Yet, it is a reminder to choose our words carefully. You never know the size or length of the impact they will have."

"There are *a lot* of trophies."

"True, but . . ." Friar paused and slowly shook his head side to side, " . . . time continually strides forward, turning all that glitters to old."

Friar's office glimmered in the predawn glow shining through several windows and a walkout balcony. Both his desk and a tall chairless table had massive piles of books, papers, and scrolls draping precariously over the edges, stretching towards the ground like branches of a scholarly willow tree. A path in the middle of a red rug was worn threadbare and pallid from hours of pacing.

An ornate wooden settle had its cushions tattered and frayed by the many long and thoughtful conversations that had transpired within their embrace. Books and scrolls lined half the walls while the remaining space was crammed with paintings of past Friars.

Friar Pallium watched her scan the artwork. "These are only a few of our former leaders. When we held the fortress of Cumhacht, there was a great marble hall where all the past Friars and Kings of the Knights were laid out in order. It was awe-inspiring."

"Does losing all of that make you sad?" she asked, feeling melancholy herself.

To her surprise, he started laughing. "All things change. To think otherwise will only lead to disappointment. Accept and embrace change. If you think happiness is to be found in anything of this world, you are bound to be disappointed and distraught at its impermanence." Smiling he gestured towards the settle for them to sit.

"You have handled the burden of being the youngest squire in our long history with grace and dignity. It was your exceedingly rare gift of communicating with animals, and Finn's insistence, that persuaded me to allow such a responsibility to be placed upon your shoulders at the tender age of seven.

"Given the approaching turmoil, it's time for you to learn the truth. You have another hardship to bear. The world demands substantial sacrifice, often unfairly, from those upon whom it has bestowed the greatest ability."

Bellae stared blankly at Friar, dazed at the thought of an "approaching turmoil" and a "substantial sacrifice."

"You may have noticed all the unfamiliar visitors to the castle? One was a very important Elf, Patuljak. In fact, he was the one who brought you, Gimelli, and Jumeaux to us for protection over seven years ago. Eons in the past, a group of kindhearted and magical humans known as the Ainmhi Caint had your special gift, and had created a peaceful home on the islands now controlled by the Proliators."

A burst of excitement fluttered wildly in Bellae's heart. *Please tell me something about my parents!*

"Their selflessness drew the attention of Supreme Master Magician Veneficus. That should tell you how long he has been around! He loved them and came to favor them as his most trusted advisors. They eventually had a falling out, and without his protection the Ainmhi Caint were hunted into extinction, or so we thought. Veneficus grieved deeply at their apparent demise. Some believe the Proliators came down from the mountains and killed them. Others think the Dark Warriors slaughtered or captured them for the evil White Wizard of the East.

"Patuljak said that before the Ainmhi Caint disappeared, they somehow discovered that a horrific darkness would descend on, and destroy, all of Verngaurd far in the future. They also learned that it had happened before, perhaps *many* times before. He called it Nack . . . no . . ." Friar paused and searched the air above him for the answer.

"He called it Na Cearcaill. The Ainmhi Caint were being hunted, and realized they would not be around to stop the cycle of destruction from continuing, so they made a powerful Prophecy outlining the path the 'Chosen One' would take to find the powerful magic Macht Crystals and rid Verngaurd of this coming evil. They formed a secret band, the League of Truth, to protect the scrolls of the ancient Prophecy when they were gone. If the prize at the end of the quest falls to anyone but the Chosen One, it would be disastrous for the world."

Bellae shook her head in confusion. "Sorry, Friar, you totally lost me." Although his story was partly interesting and completely terrifying, she only wanted to hear about her absent mother and father.

"There's no easy way to say this. Many in the League of Truth think the time of great evil foretold in the Prophecy, the Cearcaill, is upon us, and that *you* are the Chosen One.

"Wait! What?" Bellae yelled. "You know I'm seven, right?"

"You have to realize this Prophecy is unimaginably old. No one knows for sure." Friar paused, *Should I tell her Patuljak said it is less likely, but that there's a small chance Jumeaux could be the Chosen One? No, I think not.* "That's the problem with secrets, the longer they are kept the more opaque they become," he said quietly.

"What exactly am I supposed to do?" Bellae asked, her head spinning.

"Right now—nothing. Patuljak only recently gave me this information, and despite his protests, I insisted on telling you. No one mentioned anything about the Chosen One or this Na Cearcaill when you and your siblings arrived."

Bellae was paralyzed with fear, struggling to comprehend the meaning of his words. *Evil? Prophecy? Chosen One?*

"I'm just as confused about this as you are. However, if the League of Truth is correct, you and your gift shall be put through a great test in the near future. I wish I knew more. I *can* confidently tell you I have complete faith in you! You never use your small size or young age as an excuse. Instead, you overcome and adapt."

Bellae's wide-eyed expression matched the confusion and uncertainty she felt.

Seeing her apprehension, he spoke, "I cannot predict the future, but I believe that you and the other Pantteri squires have some role to play in the coming war. I want you to watch out for yourself and the others who are going ..."

"War? What war and where am I going?" Bellae interrupted, springing to her feet.

"My apologies, I've done a horrible job explaining this. Please, sit."

She reluctantly did so.

"When profound evil rears its head, it responds only to the violence of war. Darkness is coming and that means we fight for our way of life, or die. The 'going' I was talking about is the upcoming Tournament of Flags. I want the entire Pantteri Squad to go. As for the Prophecy, nothing changes until we get more information. For now, simply keep being Finn's squire."

Bellae shook her head, her eyes fluttering with uncertainty.

"I sincerely apologize for overwhelming you with all this information, but must ask you a favor. For now, keep this between us."

Bellae nodded and Pallium continued, "The Proliate have not only brought back the Tournament of Flags, but also some of the ancient competitions, unfortunately including the formerly banned dragon fighting. I have nominated the Pantteri to represent our castle in the dragon battle. Generations ago, back when it was the Festival of Flags and under the Knights' control, we prudently dissolved that archaic tradition."

"Hold on . . ." Bellae murmured. Her stomach felt as if it had collapsed into the pit of her abdomen and was now flipping around violently. She had absolutely no desire to be the Chosen One, leave Liberum, or face a dragon. " . . . I'm going to the tournament, and the Pantteri Squad has to fight a dragon?"

"Yes, and probably. It's against my better judgment, but the Proliate are insistent we bring back the dragon battles one last time to honor the past as they revive the Tournament. One team of Knights will compete, and the Pantteri Squad will have a chance to be that squad.

"Bellae, would you be willing to have some private tutor sessions with me? I will do my best to prepare you for the uncertainty of the future that . . ."

A sudden, booming knock at the door startled Bellae and she jumped.

Scroll 3: Friar's Office—Who's That?

"Give us a minute!" Friar yelled.

He crossed to the tall table and somehow managed to slide an ornate wooden box out from under a large pile with only a few things falling to the ground.

"Here we go. I want you to have this," he said, taking out a sparkling gold-handled dagger with a silver blade.

"The Southern Dwarves forged it in the mine of Teras, so the blade will not fail you. My father, Isa, gave this to me, and now I bequeath it to you," he said, putting the dagger into her shaky hands.

"I can't take this."

"My dear, you already have!"

Raised voices could be heard outside the door.

"I fear time has caught us before we could talk through everything I had planned." Friar sighed, striding towards the door.

Drawings on the table caught Bellae's attention. Some sketches looked like giant metal birds. The shape was familiar, and she tried to remember where she had seen it before. Below the drawings were two sets of opposing battle lines. One side was labeled "Allies: Knights, Elves of Creber, Northern Dwarves, and Rebelde Plains."

Opposing them were the "Confederates: Proliators, Piscium, and Ager." Several names were written in the middle with question marks by them: "Jaa? Western Elves of Dunn? Southern Dwarves?"

Bellae thought of what Friar had said, "If darkness is coming, it means we must fight for our way of life, or die." *This is the coming war!*

Next to the drawings a book titled, *Sanctus Kirja Flamma: Book of Holy Fire* lay open. The shape of a bird stood next to the caption, "Tallcon, Phoenix of Life."

Of course! Bellae thought. *Those metal bird symbols are Tallcon, the phoenix god, worshiped by the Proliators.*

The inside cover held a handwritten message scrawled on the upper part of the page, "This might be useful. Your friend, Veneficus."

Bellae flipped through the book, stopping on a page where several passages were underlined multiple times:

Chapter 21, Rune 13: "For nothing is impossible with Tallcon. Harden not your heart against his will, you that are wise. He has the blessed path to salvation well marked. You need only drop what tethers you and heed His call. Let His fire cleanse doubt and weakness. Surrendering to Him leads to strength against all enemies."

Chapter 21, Rune 14: "In your hour of need, if you believe, His benefit shall be heaped upon you. He shall divide His infinite body and send down from the sky a terrible fire of retribution, a blazing sword, against your enemies. Behind the sword shall emerge innumerable images of the one true Tallcon, and your enemy will burn!"

A commotion by the door brought her back to the present as a wave of embarrassment for snooping washed over her.

"Listen, Pumilus, this fine Knight was only doing his job," Friar Pallium said.

"You send me an urgent message, yet after riding all night you now keep me waiting?" a voice Bellae did not recognize moaned. "You know I have a high metabolism and yet first sun is up and I have neither food nor drink after a frantic ride through dangerous territory. At one point, in the black of night, I felt the hot breath of a massive growling beast on my neck. Only my expert horsemanship allowed me . . ."

Friar laughed, "My fine Dwarf Pumilus, it's getting a little thick in here and the flies shall soon be upon this tall tale floating about the chamber."

"Tall tale? What a horrendous accu . . ." Out of the corner of his eye the Dwarf caught sight of Bellae. The young squire shifted her weight self-consciously.

The anxious Dwarf was the thinnest Bellae had ever seen. By Dwarf standards, his wispy reddish hair and delicate beard were a laughable turnout. His eyes darted about nervously, and he kept rocking forward on his toes and then back to his heels while rubbing his sparsely whiskered chin.

"Bellae is squire to Finn, and this is Pumilus, distinguished Dwarf of the Rebelde Plains and a friend to the Knights."

"How do you do?" Pumilus squeaked.

"It's nice to meet you."

"Sorry, Bellae, but we have *urgent* news to discuss," Friar winked.

Despite the two pairs of eyes boring down upon her, Bellae sidled next to Friar and tugged on his sleeve. He knelt, affording her easy

*Figure 28: A nervous Dwarf originally from the Southern Dwarf Kingdom, **Pumilus** was exiled and now lives in the Rebelde Plains.*

access to his ear. Pumilus made an aggravated huffing sound, mumbling under his breath.

"You mentioned the Ainmhi Caint. Did my parents speak with animals, too? Can you tell me about them?"

Friar Pallium looked up with sympathetic eyes. "I'm afraid there's not much I can say. Plus . . ." He glanced towards Pumilus whose toes were tapping with displeasure.

"Our other discussions will also have to wait." He smiled and gently nodded towards the door.

Bellae hurried out. Fear, excitement, disappointment, and her newly slung dagger all vied for her attention. She paused outside the door, not intending to eavesdrop, but listening anyway.

"I can't get my hands on a Saatana dragon!" Pumilus yelled. "The Northern Dwarves control them and hate Southern Dwarves, even ones from the Rebelde Plains!"

"I have a better use for your talents than stealing real dragons!" Friar reassured.

Movement by the back wall of the waiting chamber startled Bellae. Several Dwarves wearing white robes were twirling two white sticks that ended in blue orbs. *Are those weapons?*

Without waiting to find out, she hurried down the stairs. Pausing halfway she glanced nervously in the direction she had just come. No one was following her.

Bellae clutched her heart where she felt a void meant to be filled with loving memories of her parents. *Why won't anyone tell me about them?*

She tried to mentally swat away the jumbled images of prophecies, the Chosen One, Tallcon, the battle map, fighting dragons, and the Tournament of Flags.

"Bellae?" a voice whispered.

"Who's there?" Bellae asked, frantically looking up and down the stairs.

"Bell-aaaaaaa! Follow my voice and find peace!"

Bellae closed her eyes, "I will *not* follow you!"

After several minutes she opened her eyes to see a wispy form floating inches from her face. At first the ghost-like figure looked like Lontas, then Gimelli before turning into a gaunt woman with rotten teeth and dirty, scraggly hair.

"Your troubles and coming pain can be over before they begin, if next time you heed my call!"

"Never!"

The spirit's face contorted in rage, "There's no escaping your destiny you nasty orphan! Trust me, your fate is a future bathed in pure pain! See you tonight you dirty urchin!"

The apparition disappeared and Bellae ran, darting to the safest place she could think of.

Scroll 4: Nice Hat

"Good morning, darling, surprised I ain't seen you earlier," Chef Cookie said as Bellae entered the kitchen.

Bellae took a deep breath trying to calm herself, *I'm safe in here.*

Despite the enormous size of the main kitchen, it appeared undersized thanks to the chaotically jam-packed pots, pans, and other cooking utensils hanging from the ceiling and plunked on overpopulated surfaces in various stages of the baking process. There were several massive stone baking ovens at one end and assorted freestanding stove tops in between long counters. One entire wall was a giant doorless pantry overflowing with all manner of provisions and foodstuffs. Barrels lined the other walls and walkways, and half-empty canisters and sacks took up the remaining floor space.

"I had to see Friar . . ."

"Oh, my!" Cookie interrupted, stomping her feet excitedly, sending little clouds of flour and various other surprises puffing up. "Aren't you a fancy one, meeting with Friar at such a young age? I suppose I'll have to cook you something more elaborate now!"

"Oh, you know better," Bellae giggled, moving to pet the pretentious kitchen cat, Ri. The black cat had a distinctive white patch of fur in the shape of an inverted triangle on her forehead and a long, black tail save for a white tip.

"Scratch behind my ears and clean off the mess Cookie keeps spreading."

"You should be grateful for the attention," Bellae remarked. Ri's only reply was a meow of protest as she turned her head away demurely.

Cookie was as wide as she was tall due to her insistence on tasting and re-tasting everything she made during all the stages of food preparation. Despite her size, she moved with surprising deftness around her beloved kitchen.

"You're wearing your special hat!" Bellae said, pointing to the mushroom-shaped chef's hat embroidered with baking-themed battle scenes. Cleavers and knives endured culinary combat versus various kitchen utensils and foodstuffs.

"Oh, you noticed! Well, it's my prized possession, other than this," she said, fluffing her bright-red hair frosted in various edibles that had been flung or whisked into the air. "Cooking is a battle against hunger! The Knights have their wars, and I have mine! You know my credo, 'Life is food and food is life!'"

"Did you hear what those rascal Tilkeri Squad had done to 'em this very morn?"

"No. What?"

"Someone rigged their door to dump horse manure on the first one coming out!" Cookie blurted, laughing hysterically.

Figure 29: Head Cook of Castle Liberum's main kitchen, no one takes their job more seriously than **Chef Cookie.**

Smiling, Bellae immediately thought of Scelto.

"Serves those bullies right!" Cookie began excitedly, swinging her laden spoon around, depositing drizzles and splashing spritzes of dark-brown cookie batter everywhere, including on Bellae's face.

"Here, have a taste of this gingerbread for the feast tonight."

I've already had a small bath, Bellae thought, as Cookie waved a spoonful of gingerbread batter ominously close to her face. "I would try it myself but you know, must watch the old figure." Cookie patted her round belly. Her apron answered back by releasing a mist of "seasoning."

"I should eat breakfast fir ..."

Bellae's words were stifled as Cookie launched a surprise attack with well-practiced marksmanship, slipping the dough-filled spoon into Bellae's unsuspecting mouth.

"Uhmmfie hiffs ood!" Bellae managed in a muted mutter thanks to the gooey dough.

"I knew it, I knew it!" Cookie said. Being fluent in the culinary language of mouth-is-fullish, she understood Bellae had said, "Oh,

Cookie, this is good."

Cookie once again floured the freshly-cleaned top of Ri's head before returning triumphantly back to work. "I hate to come off as full of pride, but I am good!"

"Ghastly! Clean me off again!"

Bellae set about re-cleaning the cat's gingerbread encumbered head.

"She should know how it tastes," Ri snorted. *"The gobbler has been tasting that gunk all morning without washing the spoon. Disgusting humans, no better than dogs!"*

"Oh, be nice, Ri. Chef Cookie loves you," Bellae whispered, still trying to coerce the sticky dough from the fur.

"That cat can't have any gingerbread. I just knows it's a asking ya."

"You know her well!" Bellae agreed, rolling her eyes.

"You're one of my favorite people in the castle! That young stomach of yours can try all the food I throw at it!"

With breakneck speed Cookie had an omelet and milk sitting in front of the squire.

"Delicious. Thank you," Bellae commented, her mouth still full of the first hot bite.

"I'm glad you think so, my sweet one! Sweet? Every time I hear *sweet* it makes me ravenous for cookies."

The plump chef plopped two cookies in her mouth, creating two massive chipmunk cheeks.

"It's an unsolvable mystery why they call her Cookie," Ri mocked.

"I hate to leave, but today is a big day for squires," Bellae said, placing her empty plate and goblet near the washing barrel.

"Don't even think about leaving without your daily haul," Cookie warned, spraying a few crumbs out of her mouth.

"Excuse me for spitting some scattering scraps! Chalk up my bad manners to how good my cookies are! So, I have somethin' sweet for the Pantteri. Ah! I said *sweet* again, I get another cookie! There's fresh pynade and . . ." Cookie leaned forward, " . . . marchpane!"

Bellae gasped. Cookie rarely made marchpane because of the need for sugar instead of honey.

"Don't let those boys push you around. You and Gimelli give 'em what for, and show what us girls can do!" Cookie advocated, rising on her toes and cranking her arms to show her muscles.

"Thanks, Cookie, I'll try. Bye and thanks."

"Be good," Bellae whispered to Ri, who responded with a condescending purr.

Bellae stepped cautiously out into the fresh air, anxiously turning left and right for any sign of the strange spirit haunting her.

Scroll 5: Squire Battle: Fall Alone, Stands Together

Like so many things, the anticipation could be the worst part of the Squire Battles. Or so they hoped. Although pride and bragging rights were on the line, the Squire Battles were vital for older squires who would be ranked for consideration of Knighthood. The basic skills evaluated were always similar, but the actual tests constantly changed.

"Lontas, you okay?" Gimelli asked. "You look like you've seen a ghost!"

The eyes of Lontas and Jumeaux shot open in shock as they remembered the apparitions that had appeared to each of them individually several times. Both mistook the other's look of horror for mockery and quickly recovered, hiding their terror.

"Almost worse," Lontas said, trying to sound tougher than he felt, but appearing as if his breakfast were about to feel fresh air again.

"What's worse than a ghost, featherhead?" Jumeaux growled.

"Are you admitting you're afraid of ghosts then, Jumeaux?" Scelto asked.

Jumeaux's fear turned to anger, "Bugger off!" he said defensively. *If I tell them what I've been seeing, they will tease me even more!*

"Do you need a healer or something, Lontas?" Gimelli asked.

"No. It's just, Lovag and Behalen are here to watch."

"You're nervous about your Knight and his *horse* watching you? Trust me, feather duster, the horse couldn't care less about you," Jumeaux snickered.

"They're here to encourage you," Gimelli said, flashing her brother the evil eye.

Bellae entered the large castle bailey and sauntered over. The courtyard inside the walls of Liberum had been divided into sections for the different events of the competition. She tucked the treats behind her back when she saw the greenish nausea flickering across Lontas' face.

"You'll do great today, Lontas," Bellae said, trying to brighten his outlook. Before he could reply she shrieked, "Finn and Crann!"

She ran to Crann, hugging and nuzzling up against his sturdy head.

"After the meeting I had this morning with Friar, I needed to see you, my friend! You would not believe who . . . or what, I saw yet again!"

"That spirit thing? Tell Finn about that ghost right now! Right now!"

"I will, but not today."

The horse gently pulled away.

"I promise I will . . . at some point!"

"Okay, remember to focus on the battle and win!"

"I'll do my best. I'm not worried about winning."

Crann neighed his disapproval and stomped his hooves.

"Okay! I believe I have a chance to win!" she replied. "Finn, thanks for coming! These are treats from Cookie, Lontas' stomach can't handle them."

"We wouldn't miss it. Thanks for the goodies. Do your best and . . ." Finn leaned in close. With a serious look he added, " . . . have fun." After a final hug for Crann and friendly squeeze of Finn's hand, Bellae returned to the squires.

"Jumeaux!" Finn called. "Salus told me you worked hard last night despite a difficult task. Thank you for representing us well. I shouldn't have sent you by yourself, I apologize."

Jumeaux couldn't help grinning despite the terror of the night before. It felt good to have his labors acknowledged, especially since it had been a dreadful fiasco.

The horrible memories from the infirmary had created deep, raw scars. Unlike bodily ones, scars burrowed within our thoughts are living, changing injuries feeding on anger and starving on forgiveness. Until fully pardoned the unrest exists, swimming below the surface and coloring one's outlook. Jumeaux's smile disappeared under the other squires' inquisitive looks. *They're mocking me! Somehow, they know I was made a fool of last night!*

Bellae looked at Scelto suspiciously, then winked in thanks for paying back the Tilkeri Squad. Smiling, he shrugged his shoulders in feigned innocence.

"We're here for you, Lontas," she said, squeezing his hand.

"I wouldn't have made it without you, Bellae."

"Squad captains!" Tutor Ajatella shouted. Tutors are former Knights who teach everything from battle skills to history, military strategy, science, math, reading, writing, and music. Their grey robes have two crossed swords over an open book emblazoned on their chest.

After a few moments Scelto came back with a piece of red cloth tied around his arm designating him a captain. "Listen up, Pantteri. Squad captains go first, followed by oldest to youngest. That means I'm up first, then: Gimelli, Jumeaux, Lontas, and finally, Bellae. This year they are enforcing a time limit, so move fast or we lose.

"The next person goes when the person in front of you completes the task *or* their time is up. At the end of the competition, the top two squads compete to determine the overall squad champion. We win or lose *together*. Work hard and support one another," he finished, glaring at Jumeaux.

"Pantteri!" they shouted.

Jumeaux scowled, *Why single me out?*

"Our first event is dog commands."

Bellae squealed happily.

"How can you love the greyhound and spaniel hunting dogs but hate the hunt?" Jumeaux snarled.

"I feel pain when the prey gets hurt."

Jumeaux scoffed.

"Look! It's her majesty the dog lover," one of the dog trainers snarled at Bellae as the other handlers snickered.

Bellae ignored the comment and continued smiling.

"Are the trainers *still* mad at you for telling Cookie they were withholding food from the war hounds?" Lontas questioned.

"Definitely. They tried to defend starving them by saying a hungry wolfhound is a 'better war dog.' Seriously?"

"How did Cookie get them to start feeding the dogs better?"

"She threatened to limit the trainers' own meals to make them 'better trainers.'"

Bellae and Lontas laughed.

"Focus!" Scelto reminded.

The two suppressed their giggles while lining up with the other Pantteri squires behind a barrier. The stands were filled with spectators: teachers, Knights, stablemates, as well as squires waiting to compete.

"First up is Scelto, captain of the Pantteri," a tutor bellowed through the enchanted Huuto, one of the ancient shells given to the Knights by the Magicians centuries ago that, when held up in front of the vocal cords, amplifies the user's voice.

Scelto moved forward as a packhorse towed in a large crate with several openings. Standing between Scelto and the box were a series of obstacles.

"You will each be randomly assigned one of three tasks to complete in less than three minutes. If a spaniel is released, you must command the dog to come to you, and then fetch a replica bird placed at the opposite end of the arena. It is the same for the greyhound except that it's a replica rabbit. If a war hound comes out, you must command it to stay while you cross the arena towards the dog. Then order the dog to run through all five obstacles. The squad with the most successful commands in the shortest amount of time wins."

Scelto nodded and the tutor shouted, "Start the time and release!" The front of the box fell forward, and a giant war dog covered with spiked armor bolted out. The crowd cheered wildly for the black wolfhound.

Scelto yelled, "DESINO!" The dog cocked his head, confused by the crowd noise and a mere squire giving commands. However, it stopped. Scelto continued to intermittently yell "Desino!" He then led the dog through four of the five obstacles before time ran out.

Gimelli drew a spaniel that completed the course in less than two minutes.

"Come on, Jumeaux. You can do it little brother," she encouraged.

Little brother? We're twins, she was born like a minute before me. Why does she have to embarrass me? Jumeaux wondered. He also drew a spaniel, and was successful in two and a half minutes.

Lontas was sweating profusely by his turn. "Go get 'em, Lontas," Gimelli cheered.

Shaking, Lontas made his way into the arena.

"Stand strong, Lontas, you can do this!"

Lontas wanted to say thank you, but was afraid of vomiting.

"Time and release!" the tutor yelled. Lontas whipped around, his heart thumping faster and faster until he felt it was about to rupture. The box swung open.

"Oh no, a war dog!" Gimelli breathed.

The dog had a short, grey coat covering its heftily muscled body encased in intimidating red armor with spikes. It immediately bolted towards Lontas.

"Come on!" Bellae yelled, watching in horror and resisting the temptation to run out and give the command herself.

The wolfhound galloped closer.

Lontas could hear the muffled cries of his friends, but could not make out their meaning. His feet felt as heavy as lead, and hands bulky and numb. He futilely smacked his cracked lips. Arching his head forward, his suddenly parched throat bobbed ineffectually as he tried, and failed, to swallow.

With each stride, *thump-thump, thump-thump,* the dog bounded ever closer to the inert Lontas.

"Move!" Scelto shouted, desperate to wake him out of his stupor. The dog was halfway to the petrified squire. Sensing Lontas' fear, the dog uttered a guttural growl.

Thump-thump, thump-thump, "GRRRRRRRRRRRRRRRRRRRR!"

Lontas watched with horror as the dog seemed to move in slow motion. He could see its red eyes clearly set off by the red armor.

Even Jumeaux, who normally loved to see Lontas suffer, felt anxious.

A sharp, savage bark burgeoned from the murky entrails of the war dog. Lontas jumped and another wave of fear rattled through him.

Vaguely a word began forming in the back of his brain. His thirsty tongue bumpily grated over his parched lips without adding moisture.

Thump-thump, thump-thump. The beast was three-fourths of the way.

"Lontas, Lontas, Lontas!" Bellae yelled, hysterically.

Ten feet. *Thump-thump, thump-thump.*

Even the dog's trainer stood in a panic, "Don't kill the boy!"

Five feet. *Thump-thump, thump-thump.*

"Lontas!" Bellae screeched. Her shout finally woke him. Slowly, he stuck out his right hand.

Three feet.

Thump-thump, thump-thump.

He let out a hoarse cry, "DEEEE—"

The intimidating dog jumped, and for a split second could be seen completely stretched out in midair.

The armored beast slammed into Lontas and his voice trailed off into a full force scream, "AHHHHHHHHHHH!"

The squire slammed to the ground under the weight of the hound. The dog's face contorted into a terrifying snarl, baring its massive teeth. The dog pressed his armor so close the spikes were inches away from Lontas.

A tutor held Bellae from moving to help her friend.

Lontas whimpered as the dog let loose a sharp, penetrating bark that rang through the cowering squire and shook body and confidence to the core. A steady spray of spittle rained down on his face. Time finally ended and the trainers mercifully led the jumping and clawing wolfhound away.

"Come on, Canities!" a trainer yelled, straining against the lunging dog. "You've beaten up enough of that boy's confidence and spirit!"

Rising feebly, Lontas used his sleeve to wipe off the saliva coating his face. Making his way back to the squires, he passed Bellae stepping forward to take her turn.

"It's okay, Lontas," she said, smiling. "That was a tough dog." Lontas groaned pitiably and stared blankly, burdened by embarrassment more than the grass, dirt, and saliva coating his face, body, and tousled hair.

Figure 30: Red armored war hound, Canities, introduces himself to squire Lontas.

Gimelli put her arm around him, "I got you." Lontas looked up pathetically as she cleaned him off.

A few members of the Tilkeri Squad moved closer.

"You're supposed to bathe in water, not dog drool!" A round of nervous laughter rippled through the crowd.

"I didn't know you had a girlfriend, Lontas! She looks absolutely fantastic in red!"

A collective gasp on the other side of the arena caused the crowd to lose interest in Lontas and the tormenting Tilkeri. The tutors exchanged nervous glances between the upcoming box and Bellae.

A sneering trainer mouthed, "Good luck, your highness."

"Something's obviously wrong with that dog," Scelto breathed nervously.

"It can't be worse than Lontas' war dog, can it?"

The tutor shouted, "Time and release!"

The gate swung open and an enormous sandy red wolfhound wearing black armor bounded out of the box, letting out an ear-splitting howl as gasps rang through the spectators. Bellae calmly marched towards the charging beast.

"Fochmhar, that's enough," Bellae said, holding out both arms in front. The dog howled, then skidded to a stop as he recognized the small figure before him.

"Is she singing to that dog?" a spectator asked as others mumbled.

After a moment of conversation, Bellae replied, *"Easily fixed."*

She gently loosened the straps on the dog's armor and confirmed they were secure. *"Does that feel better?"*

"Now I need a favor, my friend. Would you please run through these obstacles? If you do, I promise some steak."

The massive dog quickly ran through all five obstacles stunning the audience into silence.

"Every time that girl chants, the dog adjusts his course. Maybe the rumors are true," someone said.

After the dog finished, Bellae playfully scratched him under his armor. An edgy chuckle went through the crowd at the peculiar sight.

After listening to him a bit more, Bellae stood up to scan the crowd until spotting the trainers, *"Which one?"*

The war hound pointed his muzzle.

"You there! Boman!" she said, pointing to the dazed trainer. "This dog has not had any water. Secondly, his armor was strapped so tightly it cut into his skin."

"Uh?" Boman managed.

Friar Pallium appeared, "Perhaps you should see how she did it."

Boman's shock at Bellae's handling of the wolfhound disappeared after observing the grooves in the dog's fur and around its legs, and his anger boiled over. "Now hold on, little girl . . ." On seeing Friar Pallium's expression, he wisely stopped.

"Perhaps she should visit the dogs more often, to help?" Friar offered.

"As you wish," Boman replied with a resentful bow. "She already comes around too much," he mumbled.

"Bye, my dear Fochmhar, and thank you. I'll see you tonight," Bellae said. Fochmhar licked her hand playfully as Friar winked approvingly.

The Pantteri handled the next two events easily. Given all of their experience with Lontas injuring himself, and Luchar indiscriminately lashing out at others, they could have won the wound management contest with their eyes closed. While all Pantteri squires did well at the subsequent event, food preparation, Lontas was particularly adept.

"Good job, everyone," Scelto said. "We're in third place and if two of us do well in the last challenge, we're guaranteed a spot in the final!"

"Any idea what it will be?" Gimelli asked.

"Not yet."

"Probably archery or projectiles," Jumeaux stated.

"I think it will be writing," Lontas added optimistically.

"Writing? What, are you defective or something?" Jumeaux asked. "Don't be dense. They won't have a bloody writing contest!"

"Enough!" Scelto commanded. "We're close to the finals."

Scroll 6: Squire Battle: A Blow of Innovation

"It's weapons repair," Scelto said despondently as the others groaned.

"There will be a mock battle between two Knights. One will have a faulty weapon rigged to break. The Knight will then call on us to repair it."

"We've hardly practiced that," Lontas said.

"Cearta will be there to help."

"That guy's disturbing," said Jumeaux.

"Show some respect. As head armorer someday he'll make a weapon that could save your life," Scelto said.

"I'm only saying the top of his head is flat, like an anvil."

"Jumeaux!" Gimelli said. *"Quiet, he's coming."*

Cearta's lumbering frame came stomping towards them, indeed topped with a broad face ending rather horizontally. A beaklike nose plunged over a downturned chin, both appearing to have melted under the heat of decades in front of a forge. His pocked jaw had been singed so frequently that no beard could grow. He wore a leather apron and belt that held various tools and a medium-sized sword. His forearms were bare except for scars and gnarled patches of thickened skin, a visual history of past forging injuries.

"Good luck, squires," Cearta's deep voice resonated. "You'll need it."

Scelto managed to repair a battle-axe by replacing its wooden shaft in just under the five minutes allowed. Gimelli, Jumeaux, and Lontas failed to repair a shield, crossbow, and mace respectively.

"There isn't enough time for these repairs!" Jumeaux griped.

"I agree with you," Gimelli answered, puffing the hair out of her yellow eyes.

"Does the tutor have to say, 'Congratulations, young squire, your Knight just died?' I mean, we feel bad enough as it is!" Lontas said dejectedly.

"The Tilkeri Squad didn't seem to get the message that Scel . . . I mean 'someone' sent them this morning. They heckled Lontas mercilessly," Gimelli said.

Scelto blushed but said nothing.

"Send in the last competitor," the tutor stated as a Knight with a broadsword began fighting an attacker with a heavy battle-axe. Soon after they started, the Knight with the axe smashed the other's defective sword with a loud *CRACK.*

"That wasn't supposed to happen," the Knight whispered, before quickly recovering. Switching to a mace, the Knight yelled for a squire. Bellae ran forward and began picking up the three large sword pieces off the ground. "I need my sword!" the Knight shouted while still battling the counterfeit attacker. Several boys from other squads laughed or chanted for her to quit.

Spheres of sweat advanced on Bellae's forehead. *What am I going to do?*

Using the bottom of her cloak she struggled to get the heavy sword pieces back to Cearta. "Ow!" she howled, nicking her left arm.

Despite the tension and disappointment amongst the Pantteri squad, Jumeaux chuckled, "I wonder if that sword maker got the *point* of that sword, or if he left it for others, like Bellae, to find! Ha-ha!"

The other squires gave him disapproving glances. His eyes darted hastily from face to face, "What? It's a joke."

"So not funny. Your sister just got cut!" Gimelli scolded.

"What do you expect me to do with that wreckage that used to be sword?" Cearta prompted, smiling down at the minuscule Bellae and the shattered sword at her feet. "Even back at my forge it would take days to fix, and never be perfect."

Bellae thought a moment. An idea percolated in the back of her head. *Could it work?* Something Friar Pallium said echoed in her ear, *"Enormous problems break only with a blow of innovation."*

Mustering her widest smile, she went for it. "I'll take yours."

"What?" he mumbled, his singed eyebrows arching questioningly.

Holding out her hand, she repeated, "I'll take *your* sword!"

"Well, that's-that's . . . out of the question," Cearta stammered.

"If our Knight falls, the enemy will come after you."

"You little terror," Cearta stammered. "It can't be fixed!"

"I know. So, I humbly ask you, hand me your sword."

"Humbly?" Cearta repeated incredulously. "You need to take another look at that definition. Your brazen request to relinquish my sword is against the rules!"

Without flinching Bellae looked him straight in the eyes, "No, it's not, and you know it." Actually, she had no idea, but she had nothing to lose.

Cearta scowled. Placing her hands on her hips, she returned an unblinking stare. *Either he gives me the sword or time runs out*, she told herself, willing her knees not to buckle.

Bellae saw a faint smile wash across the armorer's tough face as he reluctantly took out his sword. Smiling, she grasped the handle and said genuinely, "Thank you, master armorer."

The crowd gasped as she took his sword and began walking back to the fight. "Knight, at your moment, a sword is ready at your right, back three feet." The mock fight stopped as laughter swept through the crowd.

"I believe that's a victory, dear Tutor," Friar Pallium said encouragingly.

"She cheated!" One of the other squad leaders shouted. Several Knights were close behind, all yelling protests.

"There's nothing in the rules against it. Our code demands we fight with honor, but that doesn't mean we can't be resourceful!"

As a mix of cheers and whistles erupted around her, Friar stooped down, "Very nice. There's always a way to win, even when the odds seem impossible. Don't be afraid to think about a problem from a different angle."

Bellae turned to the cheering crowd and raised her arms up high overhead. They responded, roaring even louder. Bellae smiled at the unbridled thrill as the sensation of victory and the cheer of the crowd tingled down her spine.

"Excellent, Scelto! You led from the front!" Friar stated. "The Pantteri Squad is in second place and headed for the finals. Gimelli and Jumeaux, nice job. Go join your prodigious sister."

Prodigious sister? Jumeaux thought scornfully. *More like pain-in-the-ous sister.*

Finally, Friar came to Lontas, disheveled and shaken, "Let's walk."

Lontas blinked as if he were dreaming, half expecting Friar to disappear. Instead, Friar reached down and grabbed his hand.

Scroll 7: Something Aflutter

"Facing off for the squire championship will be the Tilkeri and Pantteri Squads!" the tutor with the Huuto shell announced as the crowd cheered.

Friar and Lontas walked against the horde thronging towards the top two squads. Many onlookers stared at the odd couple marching away from the field of victory, but no one questioned Friar.

"Let's talk about perception versus potential," Friar began when they separated themselves. Lontas was confused, but interested.

"Overconfidence sets one on a brisk path to the merciless jaws of defeat. The reverse shortcoming, living in fear, swallows you in the same failure. Don't let the greatness that lies untouched in your heart be squandered. Abandon the feeble perception of yourself you espouse, and wake up your true self lying neglected deep within."

Lontas stared at Friar in complete bewilderment. Sensing a slight downward slope underfoot, he realized they were heading far away from the competition fields to the commorancy, where the tutors lived. "Won't I miss the competition?"

"That's the golden question that only you can answer."

Lontas felt flushed and hot under his intense gaze. "Uhm, whether we make it back in time probably depends on how far we're walking in the opposite direction."

Friar laughed, "I had something else in mind."

The buildings of the tutors' commorancy were stone with wood-framed windows and thatched roofs. Many shutters were open, giving Lontas brief glimpses of the inhabitants. In one a woman drifted quickly into view rocking a fussing child, another displayed a man pacing and reading.

"Are we meeting someone?" Lontas questioned nervously.

"Yes and no," Friar answered. "We're going to the cemetery."

Cemetery? Knowing the destination definitely did not make him feel better.

Unlike the gridded layout of the rest of Liberum, the tutor houses were set about haphazardly, making a maze of winding paths. After walking a little longer, the small houses gave way to a horizon filled with a deep gorge and a massive burial ground. Nestled in isolation on the other side of the canyon sat neat rows of tombstones, representing the legions of fallen Knights.

The ancient cemetery sat silent and somber beneath the massive shadows of the large walls protecting three of its sides. The deep river valley protected the fourth edge. The only link to the main castle grounds was a frail-looking suspension bridge dancing apathetically in the wind.

As they drew closer Lontas flushed with dread. *That bridge has seen better days.*

Out of the corner of his eye, Lontas saw something moving between two of the tombstones and stopped. Squinting, he could just make out a large, black shape peering back at him. *What is that?*

"Keep up, Lontas."

"But . . ." Lontas began. Two large, wing-like shapes shot out from behind the dark figure and beat vigorously as it flew over several tombs before disappearing.

"Friar! Wh-wh-what's that?"

"Hmm?"

"I saw something . . . huge flying over there," he said, pointing to the now empty sky.

"When the suns catch the tombstones exactly right, the ripple of light and shadows can play tricks on your eyes."

"Yes, sir," Lontas replied, unconvinced. A small chill ran down his spine as a similar fluttering shadow caught his eye in a deeper part of the cemetery.

Friar gracefully strode down the decline and Lontas followed, struggling to keep his balance. Finally, they came to the cable and wood suspension bridge.

Lontas' head was spinning at the mere thought of the height while Friar marched confidently onto the bridge. Respect for Friar eventually outweighed his aversion to heights, and Lontas stepped tentatively onto the swaying walkway, seizing the ropes so tightly the rough strands jabbed his skin.

Don't look down. Focus on Friar's back, he thought, forcing his feet to move.

I think this bridge is getting longer, he imagined, shuffling along the wooden planks. Despite the burning in his hands from rigidly sliding them along the rope, dread forbade him from loosening his grip.

After what seemed like hours, he stepped gratefully onto solid ground, and was greeted by a black sandstone arch curving over the entrance to the cemetery. Deep-green strands of ivy clawed their way up its sides, barb-like roots cutting deeply into the sandstone's skeleton for traction on a quest for sun. The skin of ivy growth was unchecked except for a rectangular section on top of the archway which bore the inscription:

> *"Enter to increase your Wisdom,*
> *Not of Death, but of how to Live."*

Lontas stepped through the archway, stretching before them was a dizzying array of grey stone arches, each with seemingly endless rows of tombstones lined up behind them.

"Each arch and the graves beyond represent a different era in the long history of the Knights," Friar proclaimed. "Each section represents a combination of years, historical events, and leaders. That archway reading 'King Leon–Friar Eerste' marks our transition from King to Friar."

Without another word, Friar walked towards their right and strode through one of the grey arches. Beyond it, the path branched into five separate rows, each one lined with a seemingly infinite number of head-stones.

As Friar gazed down the seemingly endless rows, Lontas glanced at one of the older tombstones with an obscured name. Etched below was an ancient writing, *"Non fui, non sum, non curo."*

"What does this mean?" Lontas asked, frustrated he could not read it. Simply for fun he had taught himself many extinct languages.

"It's an ancient tongue. Remember, even when we held what is today the Citadel, this has always been the Knight Burial ground." Friar smiled. "However, a professor once told me it means, 'I didn't exist, then I existed. I don't exist now and don't give a damn!' It was a popular epitaph many centuries ago.

"If you work hard and make it to Knighthood, you spend your last night as a squire in a sleepless vigil amongst these tombstones reading inscriptions in order to come up with a draft of how yours will read one day."

Lontas shivered as they began walking again. "Seems morbid."

"Does it? Understanding how fragile the human experience is and grasping your inevitable demise, if you allow it, will guide your life decisions and inspire you to a greater existence."

Eventually Friar stopped in front of a newer, ten-foot tall grave marker that was a white sandstone obelisk, "Read this one."

Lontas enjoyed the tranquil silence cradling his ears and the cool, crisp gust swirling up from the gorge. The Squire Battle seemed a million miles away and suddenly, much less important.

A sniffling noise brought Lontas back to the present. Looking to his right he saw Friar holding back tears and quickly read the headstone.

Friar Isa

Born: 36 B.D.W.   Knighted: 18 B.D.W.
Friar: 1 B.D.W.   Died: 36 A.D.W.

For me, it's too late,
Don't suffer my fate.
I once walked the earth
Inert to life's worth.
Routine, my shield,
I loathed foreign field.
Too late did I wake up

Far Forest Scrolls

To drink from life's cup.
Be bold in life,
Do not shun strife.
Soon you will be here
And lost all you hold dear.

"You know BDW and ADW mean Before and After the Dark War?"

Lontas nodded. Despite their sadness, Friar's eyes shone with intimidating intensity.

He wants me to say something. Unfortunately, Lontas' mind went blank.

"This is my father's grave," Friar said mournfully, breaking the increasingly awkward silence.

"Till his dying day, he lamented being nominated Friar right before the devastating Dark War. Even after the main army of Dark Warriors was driven out by the Proliate in five ADW, a scourge of them remained fighting a guerilla war. They weakened our outposts, killed innocents and, most importantly, caused the countries of Verngaurd to lose even more faith in us.

"After the blistering defeats of the Dark War, my father became so entangled in the flawed belief we could hide from our troubles that he forgot about living and winning. He stayed close to our old capitol, Cumhacht, and made deal after deal with the Proliators."

Lontas could see the regret and pain in Friar's eyes.

"It was a vicious cycle. The more we physically gave up, the less confidence other nations had in us. On his last lucid day, he said, 'Live life as if it were a grand adventure. Don't let fear paralyze you. Feel the splendor of each day. Have no regrets, my son. Glide on air . . . on air . . .'

"His true final words went unspoken, forever silenced in his last moments of breathless desperation. The message for you, Lontas? Attack and enjoy life with no regrets. Do your talking while your heart is powerful and your muscles have the strength to chase your dreams."

While struggling to think of what to say, a black shadow moved with lightning quickness behind Friar. Lontas peered around him as a faint fluttering sound echoed through the stone sentries of the grave-yard.

"Each precious here and now moment is your life, Lontas. What you do every day in the present—that is the story and substance of your life. It doesn't start at some magical point in the future."

Lontas' head was spinning under the weighty words and frightening figure.

"Friar, I'm honored to be here, but I'm only a squire, and not a good one. I'll never qualify for Knighthood or go on any grand adventures," Lontas said in a grateful tone.

Thinking of Bellae, the Prophecy, and the coming war, Friar Pallium sighed. *As the Chosen One's best friend, he must step up and be her companion during the coming trials.* Suddenly, his words seemed woefully inadequate. *Is Patuljak right? Can a seven-year-old and her friends, no matter how amazing, be responsible for our fate?*

"I cannot see the future, but I can tell you that opportunities, both good and bad, rarely ask permission before opening the door and hauling us through. Each of us stares at four simple words: 'living,' 'dreams,' 'your,' and 'in.' But how we mold them transforms everything."

"I'm not sure I understand."

"*Living in your dreams* at night changes nothing, but *living your dreams in* daylight reshapes your soul and the world. Start living your dreams out in the day and let sleep be a time of rest for living rather than an escape from life."

Lontas blushed as he felt the words settle on his shoulders with a weighty importance too heavy for his small back.

"Shall we return to the question you so astutely asked earlier? Will you miss the competition?" Friar smiled as if he could see the gears of understanding shaking off their rust and moving together in Lontas' head.

"You were wondering whether I will I actually show up and compete, or fold under fear as I have in the past?"

"You've got it! Come on, let's head back and find out. Most people take advice like a rock in their boot, an annoyance to be discarded as quickly as possible. I hope you take it to heart."

Lontas was reluctant to leave this peaceful place for the crowded pressure of the Squire Battle. "Any chance we missed the final?"

"Oh, don't you worry, you'll get a chance to show me how much you heard."

Great, I was so hoping for more pressure.

Friar kept walking across the bridge while Lontas stopped at the black sandstone arch positioned before the cavernous ravine. The vines were just as thick on the arch's back except for another small, rectangular clearing:

"Leave to Genuinely Live.
Savor each instant for what it Truly Is.

"Lontas," a voice whispered.

The squire swiveled back and forth searching for the source. His eyes swelled at the sight of a ghostly white figure staring back at him from the tombstones.

"Loooontas!" the spirit howled.

I'm sick of seeing this strange specter, Lontas thought, shivering. It had last come to him in the library, but disappeared when the librarian walked by. "What do you want?" he asked, but a forceful fluttering sound caught his attention. A black shape with enormous wings scampered in the shadows behind the ghostly apparition. Even hidden in murkiness, Lontas could tell it stood upright, but something appeared wrong with its legs.

Abruptly the winged figure burst from the shade, punching wildly at the spirit. The spirit's mouth opened into a howl before shutting under the creature's pummeling.

Lontas froze, entranced by the creature's enormous, bright-yellow eyes. Something sharp and yellow flashed out of its mouth. It's muscular arms lashed out at the figure of light until it disappeared.

Scream! he thought, but his voice did not respond. The yellow-eyed figure moved farther into the light and a human hand reached out, desperately gesturing for him to return to the cemetery.

Wracked with fear, Lontas turned and ran. His toes struck the edge of the first board of the undulating bridge, pitching him forward onto his right shoulder. Pain ripped through his right arm and back as he slid on the rickety bridge. Wincing, he looked back to see a pair of enormous wings shoot out from the creature's back. Terror prevailed over pain, and in seconds he was on his feet scampering across the bridge.

Whoosh! Whoosh! Whoosh! The creature's towering wing beats grew louder.

Halfway across the bridge he risked a quick glance back. His gaze locked with the beast's large, yellow eyes and it stopped to angrily shake its human hands, as if irritated with Lontas for not following him back into the tombstones.

Its fiery eyes turned towards Friar, who was facing away towards the castle grounds. It briefly raised one index finger before flying back and disappearing amongst the headstones.

"Friii . . ." Lontas wheezed through paralyzed vocal cords.

Did that gesture mean he wanted me to wait . . . or is he warning he'll come after me?

Once on the other side he scanned the silent headstones standing in eternal, tedious attention, draped in stultified indifference. There was no sign of the creature or the light. *Why did it stop? It could have easily caught me, and what the bloody herring is that ghost thing?*

Suddenly, a hand clamped down on his arm.

"Aaaaahhhhhhhh!" Lontas screamed.

"It's only me," Friar responded. "Let's keep moving."

Embarrassed, Lontas followed. After walking for a few minutes, he stopped to look over his shoulder. His fear and nausea were subsiding, but there was no denying that a flying creature was living in the graveyard and had scared him half to death.

Should I tell Friar? But tell him what? A ghost called my name twice, and then a giant flying creature appeared and fought with the ghost to see who could attack me, but all this happened so quietly, you saw nothing? Yeah, that won't end well.

As they neared the practice bailey, Friar took a deep breath. *Will my efforts be enough to help this boy stand by the Chosen One during the evils ahead?*

"Lontas, free yourself from the bonds of doubt and allow your strength to come out and you can sleep well tonight, secure in the knowledge that you fought your fight in the sun's light with all that you had. Live your dreams during the day."

Scroll 8: Squire Battle: Big Endings

"Those are the obstacle courses for the finals," Friar said as they approached the scene of the Squire Battle finals.

"Looks long," Lontas said of the two extensive wooden structures snaking across the giant castle courtyard.

"The course is difficult, but survivable."

Survivable? Lontas' stomach lurched, *Horrible choice of words!* He knew it was not unheard of for squires to die in the competition, especially the finals.

The Pantteri squires were anxiously talking in front of one of the structures. Except for Scelto, they appeared minuscule compared to the much older competition.

The Tilkeri Squad snickered with easy self-confidence. They had won every Squire Battle for the last three years. Two, Tempaus and Saccade, were weeks away from their eighteenth breithlá when they would be eligible for the Knight exams and trials. The other three: Tiron, Stratto, and Atla were only a year away.

"Hey, Lontas, did ya' soil your garments and have to change?" Tempaus bellowed. "Or maybe ya' snuck off to kiss your hairy girlfriend wearing red?"

Lontas turned scarlet under their malicious laughter.

"Tempaus, can you think of nothing more original?" Friar Pallium asked. "I would think someone like you, with such a rich history of disparaging comments would be more inventive."

The older squires' smile vanished as those around laughed, but the apology he released was nothing more than an apathetic, "Sorry."

"You know Tempaus, bullying is a cowardly form of evil that targets those less imposing than the persecutor, and serves only to show the world how small your ego and ingenuity really are."

The Tilkeri squire bristled under he insult but only looked down.

The weight of more and more faces piling on Lontas caused his conviction and legs to wobble. Friar reached out to brace him, "The difference between you and the other squires is not lack of talent, but lack of faith."

"Come on, Lontas!" Scelto yelled urgently. "It's time!"

Lontas took a few deep breaths and his legs steadied as Friar nodded and left for the stands.

"For the finals, the squire with the lowest score goes first," Scelto paused sympathetically. "For us, that's you."

"I go first?" Lontas cried.

Scelto was talking, but the words bounced off Lontas' panic. Then, the young squire surprised himself, thinking of Friar a chill ran up his spine, *Today I fight.*

Scelto grabbed Lontas' face. "Hey, are you listening? Strap on this sword!"

"I'm ready," Lontas said with a steadiness that astounded Scelto.

Lontas could hear Friar's voice, *"Live your dreams out during the day."*

"Not at night," Lontas said.

Scelto cocked his head curiously. "You're right, the final isn't tonight, it's right now! Just . . . do your best."

"Squires, ready!" a tutor shouted. "First squad to finish wins! Ready? Go!"

The doors to the two obstacle courses swung open.

"Where did Friar take Lontas?" Gimelli asked.

"Didn't say. But, he seems different . . . determined," Scelto replied.

"Our Lontas?"

Scelto shrugged his shoulders.

Lontas scuffed his way up a lengthy flight of stairs before jumping across a sizable gap to a doorway. He entered a small room devoid of windows, and jumped as the door slammed shut behind him, drawing complete darkness across the space other than a sliver of light that came and went on the opposite wall with a faint squeak, announcing there was a handleless door swaying on hinges.

The entire room suddenly pitched upward violently, sending him airborne, but gravity quickly, and jealously, regained dominance, planting him face first onto the floor. His sword barely missed hitting his already sore shoulder. While struggling to stand, the room jerked forward so far, he slammed into the wall with the hinged door, which now served as the gravitational floor.

Reaching down he attempted to open it, but with the lack of a handle and gravity teaming up, it was impossible. The room began to pitch and roll back and forth, side to side. Lontas held his sword out, desperately trying not to cut himself.

When the far wall was facing the sky, light burst into the room as the hinged door swung open. All other upheavals led to complete darkness as it slammed shut. The gesticulating room mercifully slowed, he quickly sheathed his sword and waited for the room to make another revolution. When the door swung open, he jumped off the "floor," which had been the wall when he entered a few minutes ago, grabbing the frame of the door he hung on for dear life as the room continued its spasmodic movements.

When the room lurched forward, he managed to raise his legs up and block the door from closing. Half-scooting, half-lunging, Lontas dove out and rolled down a net onto a floor that was firm but not solid.

At least it's not moving, he thought, closing his eyes tightly until his mind caught up with the reality that he was no longer being thrashed about.

Opening his eyes, he discovered he was resting on a suspension bridge. Looking behind he saw dozens of Knights controlling long wooden levers that had been responsible for tossing him about. Several waved.

Lontas waved back contemptuously, *Thanks so much for almost killing me!*

Standing, he carefully moved along the undulating bridge until he came to another door and moved through.

Nice, Lontas thought, stamping his feet on the solid wood floor.

"AHHHHHHHHH!" a battle cry rang, shattering his joy.

Lontas looked up to see the form of a Knight hurtling towards him with a flail raised menacingly above his head. The flail consisted of two pieces of wood separated by a short chain. The Knight held onto the longer piece while the shorter one was covered in metal spikes.

Lontas quickly dove forward, rolling repeatedly until stopped by the wall. Pain from the hilt of his sword reminded him of his weapon. He unsheathed it as the Knight charged. Jumping to his feet, Lontas adjusted his sword to deflect the flail hurtling towards him. A horrific clang reverberated in his ears as a violent vibration cascaded down his arms. The force flung his sword towards the floor, embedding the tip deeply in the wood.

Momentum carried the spiked end of the flail down the edge of Lontas' blade, summoning a shower of sparks. The Knight untangled the flail, then swung it around as the squire quickly ducked behind the implanted sword, the weapon whooshing narrowly overhead. Lontas decided to leave his blade lodged in the floor and ran to the opposite wall. His eyes scoured the monochromatic wood, but there were no obvious crevices or breaks.

"No escape, boy!" the thickly muscled Knight growled, advancing on Lontas who began backpedaling.

The Knight cut him off and Lontas leapt to the center of the room right as the spiked flail slammed down in front of him. He was backpedaling again, fear coercing him to move faster until his back slammed into a wall.

"Lucky weasel!" the Knight admonished.

Lontas was confused until he heard a loud *click*, and tumbled through a trap door. He landed hard and a low-pitched wheeze escaped as the wind was knocked out of him.

The hidden door he had fallen through had barely closed as a thunderous strike from the Knight's flail splintered the wood with a loud *CRACK!* Shattered pieces exploded from the newly born jagged opening. The Knight's face appeared in the breach, "Come here, boy!"

"Rather not, actually," Lontas whimpered, hastily scrambling up while air sluggishly returned to his lungs. He scampered towards a solitary darkened doorway directly across from the trap door he had toppled through.

Another pitch-black room! How original.

After taking a few steps, his right foot sunk and he heard another *click* followed by a loud crashing sound as a wooden barrier dropped from the ceiling right behind him, encasing him in blackness. Suddenly sightless, his breathing seemed as loud as a thunderstorm and his nose awoke to perceive the mustiness of the air.

A resounding blow from the Knight's flail on the wall that had just fallen behind him sent splintered shards raining down on his back. The only bonus was a faint, but meaningful, light snaking its way tenuously through the dark.

This guy really hates wood! Lontas thought, groping forward.

After several hard falls he quickly discovered the floor was congested with obstacles. After a few minutes of blundering over stairs, ramps, and metal barriers, the weak light from the broken wall faded, soaking him in utter gloom once again.

A loud creaking sound made him stop. The blare of his thumping heart pounded in his ears. Frozen, Lontas was expecting, could almost feel, a hand reaching through the darkness to grab him. Slowly, he turned, but saw nothing other than a faint light from the splintered wall.

Did I blink or did somebody bounce in front of the light?

"Lontas?" a soft voiced creaked.

That's not the Knight! he trembled.

Shivering in the darkness, too afraid to speak, his eyes searched frantically.

"Loooontaaaaass!" the same voice hissed.

Petrified, he listened. The wind sweeping along the sides and roof rattled, and an occasional creaking board added to his rising panic. After several minutes, an eerie white face appeared in front of his eyes, its hair danced outwards away from its head as its deep-set eyes flashed hatred, "Next time, klutz-boy, follow my call or suffer a lifetime of agony the likes of which you cannot imagine!"

The ghostly face shot towards Lontas, traveling through his head. His brain instantly felt frozen and, moaning, he tried to pop his ears and move his face which felt numb and wind burnt.

Squueeeeeeak. Someone stepped on a loose floorboard right next to him. Spurred by terror, he floundered ahead, sticky blood running freely from scrapes and cuts serving as reminders of his failures in dealing with previous obstacles.

For several minutes he moved forward as a shadowy weight grew in his mind, increasingly sensing someone closing in. He could almost feel hands reaching and snatching the air behind him. Sweat poured liberally under the stale air and steamy heat, causing each of his cuts and scrapes to scream a painful roll call.

Stopping, he listened intently. Someone else's panting breath was drawing closer in the blackness.

"I told you to quit." The Knight's hot exhalation singed the back of Lontas' neck, and his gauntleted hand landed heavily on Lontas' shoulder. The grip of fear was stronger than the Knight's grasp and Lontas violently swiveled until he ended up facing the Knight.

The squire flung his body backwards to put some distance between himself and his attacker, and found himself on a downward sloping ramp. Gravity and momentum quickly accelerated him, his arms swinging wildly.

Losing his footing, he skidded a moment before being tossed into a series of backward rolls. Tucking his head, nausea rose in his stomach and vertigo whirled in his head.

The decline abruptly turned upwards, flinging him into the air. No longer in a tight sphere, his body tumbled frantically until slamming into a wooden wall. A fresh surge of pain ripped through him. The wall gave way and Lontas thrashed through the serendipitously discovered trap door, slowly rolling to a stop on soft grass. His lungs sucked deeply at the fresh air as his eyes squinted under sunlight's assault.

I'm outside! Am I done?

Remembering the Knight and the phantom, he quickly stood. Dizziness washed over him and he staggered backwards. A foreign growl hit his ears right as a red fog surrounded him. Lontas fell, skidding to a stop exhausted and battered. Craning his neck to look behind, he was greeted by an upside-down image of an angry-looking Dwarf.

Rolling onto his stomach he got a better look at the thin, red-haired

Dwarf rhythmically moving two white wooden sticks with glowing blue orbs and black tassels.

"Better lucky than good, clumsy squire!" Dwarf Pumilus spoke testily. "It's hard to be afraid of my dragon if you fall backwards and never see it."

Dragon? Lontas wondered, totally confused.

"Get up and find a healer. Either way, bloodied boy, you're finished."

A wry smile crossed Lontas' face at the word "finished."

His eyes quickly widened in terror as he finally realized what the red fog was. Scrambling to his feet he found his upper body sticking out of the tail of a very solid and real looking red dragon. His lower body was still "in" the "dragon." A fine mist of red vapor swirled around his abdomen, trying in vain to seal the hole.

"Magic!"

"I'm *not* a corrupt Magician! It's the virtuous art of prestidigitation, the illusionary side of magic!" Pumilus stated coldly, looking increasingly annoyed.

"Those are loitsia sticks that contain minuscule amounts of the same magic crystals the Magicians use in their crosiers! Beating them rhythmically allows you to conjure this 'false' dragon."

"Thanks for stating the obvious!" the Dwarf huffed. "I can create anything, not just dragons."

"The Southern Dwarves created prestidigitation—you must be from there?" Lontas asked, moving closer until exhaustion gave a tug, and he sat down.

"I *was* from there. Now, get lost!" Pumilus scolded. "This might look easy, but it takes a great deal of concentration."

The adrenaline that had flooded his body during the course rapidly departed and fatigue began to overwhelm his wailing aches and pains causing his eyes to flutter.

"Oh no you don't!" Pumilus cried, reaching out to kick the fading squire. "They've replaced the broken wood at the beginning of the course and the next squire is starting.

"Implore your uncoordinated limbs to stand and stumble your appallingly bloodstained carcass somewhere the bloody abyss else!"

Lontas was about to protest when Leigh, one of the healers or parantaa, helped him up. As they moved to the rear of the courtyard, Lontas could see carpenters quickly tending to the wooden portal he had crashed through.

"Lontas, it may hurt to move, but there are no restrictions on your duties," the healer said once the wounds were cleaned and dressed. "See a healer once a day until told otherwise. Head up to the observation deck."

Lontas could see a large crowd, including several Tilkeri who had already finished their course, pointing and smiling at him from the stands.

"Here's good," Lontas said, snuggling into the grass.

He watched in silence as the other Pantteri squires slowly made their way across the finish line. Just as Scelto sat to have his wounds dressed, a bell went off.

"The Tilkeri have won!"

Gimelli looked hopeful, "Does that mean Bellae doesn't have to compete?"

"Once she's through the first door, she finishes. Don't worry, she can handle herself," Scelto said, trying to erase the worry spread thickly on Gimelli's face.

The Pantteri Squad fell into anxious silence awaiting the youngest squire as the Tilkeri celebrated.

A murmur dribbled through the crowd as Bellae calmly marched through the last wood panel. Her outer cloak had a single small tear, but otherwise she looked none the worse for wear. Pumilus' red Saatana dragon shot sham fire into the air and howled. Bellae's tranquil expression did not change, except for a hint of contempt. Her gifts immediately let her know this was not a living creature. Without hesitating, she walked straight through the dragon to a beaming Friar.

"You never cease to amaze," he said. "You had the fastest time!"

"Bellae!" Gimelli shouted, rushing up to hug her sister.

Lontas rose stiffly and saw Bellae's two mice, Grym and Borb, duck into her pocket. *Those two would make excellent guides!*

Friar stepped in front of Lontas, "The greatest victory is not always

Figure 31: Bellae's friend and bunkmate, **mouse Grym,** *is known for his small size and gruff voice.* **Borb** *is known for his jagged ear and the black patch of fur around his right eye.*

marked with a trophy or adulation. Today, you took your first steps towards the most any of us can hope to achieve, victory over self."

Lontas looked down with timid embarrassment, "But Friar, I was terrified the whole time."

"That only makes it more impressive that you completed the course."

"More like I *fell* through it," Lontas whispered.

"Don't second-guess your achievements. True victory comes from acknowledging your fear, calming your emotions, and bringing mind, body, and spirit into a single and just purpose. You faced your fear today, that's heroism. That is victory."

Scroll 9: Trophy or Steak

"Wait up!" Finn yelled, running after his squire. "You did amazingly!"

"Thank you for coming," Bellae replied with a hug.

"What are you doing way out here away from the celebration?"

"I have a friend to repay."

Finn smiled at his eccentric young squire. Friar Pallium's voice could be heard in the distance presenting the Tilkeri with their trophies.

Bellae could tell there was something on Finn's mind, and had the sense to wait as he pursued the correct words. His eyes searched the air above as if the sky might be hiding the perfect script.

"Bellae, I chose you as my squire because we have a special bond. We make an excellent team on and off the training grounds. You've always reminded me of my sister back where I come from, Creber Forest. You two precocious girls have a wisdom and poise well beyond your years.

"Elven daughters are given an Inion medallion by their fathers. The Inion's never-ending weave is a reminder of the eternal love between father and daughter. It is forged with some of the father's blood to represent his willingness to die before letting harm come to her. A sliver of bark from his birth tree is added to remind us of our connection with nature.

"I offer this Inion medallion, and ask you to be my adopted daughter. It was forged by our armorers with my blood and a shard of my birth tree which the recently visiting Elves brought. I promise to do my best to guide and protect you forever."

Bellae was so caught off guard she could only stare at the intricate knot design spinning in front of her. As it pirouetted, she saw the word "Inion" flicker in and out of view. Gleaming orbs of tears had gathered in Finn's brown and green eyes.

"Finn," was all she could utter. She experienced, but could not vocalize, the joy she felt filling up a slice of the emptiness inside her created by the void of her parents' absence.

Slowly, she took the Inion and slipped it over her head. Pressing its cool metal against her skin, she could feel a warm glow surge in her heart. With her own tears flowing, she said, "I'll never take it off, or forget this."

The two embraced as surrogate father and daughter.

"The kindness in your heart and joy of your actions make each day special. You stand up to every challenge with a courage that few Knights could muster. Go repay your friend," Finn said with one last tearful embrace.

Lontas desperately searched for Bellae while caught in the middle of the celebrating throng. Finally, spotting her heading off the practice fields, he sighed with relief. She always seemed to know what to do and had a confidence that Lontas admired. The idea of running after her was quickly squashed by loud protests from his wounds and he settled into a determined hobble.

By the time he caught up to her, she was exiting Chef Cookie's kitchen and struggling with a plump sack.

"If any of them trainer fanatics give you any grief, you let ol' Cookie know and they'll eat horse rations for a week!"

"Thanks, Cookie!" Bellae laughed, giving Lontas a friendly wave.

"Bellae!" Lontas called when she started moving away. Despite the bag's weight on her small frame, she almost seemed to skip, moving as if she was none the worse for wear.

She stopped and offered a sympathetic smile as he limped, "How are you?"

"Not too bad. Having a picnic with an *army?*"

"No!" she laughed. "It's not *that* much food. I'm keeping a promise. You can come if you like."

"I'll take that for you."

"No, you look pretty sore."

"I'm fine," he said, taking the sack. Her eyes were red as though she had been crying, but she seemed content enough, so he said nothing. *Should I tell her about the ghost and winged creature?*

He hesitated and decided to ask, "How did you come through the Squire Battles with no injuries?"

"My mice friends helped me." Seeing his pained expression, she

Figure 32: The armored war hounds of Castle Liberum are fierce and well trained.

added, "They gave me an unfair advantage. You had it worst, going first."

"That's nice of you to say."

The sound of barking shook Lontas to the core. "The k-kennels?"

"Yes!"

With each step, the intensity of the barking grew, cultivating Bellae's mushrooming smile and Lontas' sprouting trepidation.

"Shut your traps!" a man's voice boomed.

Bellae's smile vanished. A man moved amongst the shadows, wildly shaking his fists in the air and occasionally kicking a cage. Bellae whispered something Lontas could not make out. She began walking faster and Lontas struggled to keep up, his wounds and the heavy sack causing him to fall behind.

"Boman!" Bellae shrieked with such strength that it even surprised her.

The trainer froze, flashing a look of trepidation quickly followed by anger. "Listen, gurl, the kennels are my world, not yours, not Friar's!"

The dogs let out a thunderous roar of warning to Boman that resonated around the courtyard. Feeling empowered by their protective growl, Bellae inched forward to position herself between the dogs and Boman.

"What do ya want?" Boman spat, this time with less anger. He seemed worn out by his previous outburst and the passion of the dogs who were continuing to bark and yip all around him.

"These dogs need to be paid back for being so good today!"

"Oh, now ya got one thing right. There will be payback! But, it's ya getting paid back for showing me up today. There ain't no Friar here, gurl!" Boman scowled to the background of barking dogs.

Just then, he noticed the immotile Lontas. Seeing his scared expression energized the dog trainer.

Suddenly, a high-pitched bark stung the air. Bellae had taken advantage of Boman's distraction to release four of the dogs. Their fierce eyes and bared teeth immediately deflated his bravado.

"Boman, I will be spending some time with the dogs. You may stay or go. I take responsibility for them not escaping."

He hesitated, weighing his options.

"By the way, I will report back to Cookie about how things go. I believe she mentioned something about horse rations for you?" Bellae stated innocently. Fochmhar, the massive hound from the squire competition, stepped closer to Boman to help him make up his mind.

"All right, gurl. Have your time. I have more important things to get done anyway. If anything happens to them dogs . . ." he paused for a phlegmy snort and to swipe at his nose, " . . . I'll have your head."

With Boman gone, the dogs turned their attention to Lontas. His body shivered in a frosty bath of panic as Bellae released the rest of the dogs.

No eating me, no eating me! Lontas closed his eyes and waited for teeth to tear into him. He could hear dozens of them panting and circling.

Then it happened, first one, then another.

Some of the dogs gently nudged, others licked his hands.

"Don't keep them waiting!"

"Oh, I forgot!"

He found two separate sacks in the larger bag. The first was full of juicy steaks. The dogs began to howl and Lontas quickly threw one to each dog. With military precision, they caught their allotment and settled down to feast.

"Good job!" Bellae smiled. "See, they like you."

Lontas had to admit he was starting to feel more comfortable.

A sharp growl broke through Lontas' happiness. Even without the red armor, Lontas instantly recognized the grey-furred dog that had humiliated him earlier. "Good d-d-doggy."

"*Canities, Lontas is your friend,*" she chanted, instantly calming the hound.

"Give him a steak."

Lontas obliged and wearily plunked down. Bellae opened the second sack and handed Lontas a honey crisp cookie and a covered pint of hunaja sauce. They took turns dipping their cookie in the thick, honey-based sauce. After eating their fill, they sat quietly enjoying the cool air and warm company. Every once in a while, a dog would nuzzle against her, and occasionally she would remind them not to wander off.

"If I tell you something, do you promise not to think I'm crazy or laugh?"

"Of course," Bellae smiled.

"No laughing . . . hey, you're already laughing!"

"You can't tell me *not* to laugh, Lontas! It makes me crack up!"

Do I start with the ghost or winged creature? He shook his head, *Both sound ridiculous!* Sighing heavily, Lontas recounted the story of the winged creature he had encountered at the cemetery, deciding to skip the story of the ghost, at least for the moment.

"Why are you squinting? I knew it, you think I'm crazy."

"It's some sort of . . . bird-thing," she finally said.

"Can't be. It stood upright, taller than me, and motioned with *human* arms!"

"I've glimpsed and felt something like a large bird on the practice field a couple of times in the last few months. The last time, I was out late with Finn, and it was circling very high above us. It was gone in a flash and Finn didn't notice."

Lontas sighed, grateful she believed him.

"We need to find out exactly what it is and . . ."

Lontas coughed and sputtered. "Are you insane?"

She didn't get a chance to answer as an exasperated cry rang out from the dog trainers' quarters. Bellae snickered.

"What?"

"The dogs ate the trainers' steaks. Chef Cookie made them gruel!"

Lontas and Bellae laughed. Between giggles Bellae added, "The best part is she made it with a bit of hay because they are horses aaa . . . well, the back part of the horse!"

The two laughed harder. The stress from earlier evaporated on the evening breeze. With the third sun slipping behind the horizon, Lontas smiled, "Friar was right, sometimes the days we think are the worst are the ones we'll remember forever."

Scroll 10: Sister's Sister

"Bellae!"

"What?" Bellae mumbled, struggling to wake up.

"Bellae! Come here, sister."

Sitting up, she searched for the source of her wakeup call. Gimelli stood by the barracks' door motioning for her.

"Okay, be right there."

Bellae groggily put on her boots becoming vaguely aware of her two mice friends squeaking furiously. Still bleary, she was having trouble figuring out what they were saying.

"Not in the mood you guys. The Squire Battle was rough!"

They scurried down the cot's leg and began running in frantic circles.

"What's wrong with you two?"

Screeching louder, they began to run back and forth from Bellae to one of the other cots. It took a moment for her to realize it was Gimelli's cot and that her sister was fast asleep.

Whirling around, Bellae was confronted with a ghostly white face with deep, black circles under corrupt eyes. The specter's hair floated around its head in tangled factions. The horrifying specter hovered off the floor glaring at her with profound rage.

"Your ignorant and shortsighted vermin think they saved you. But, trust me, they've only prolonged the pain about to engulf you!"

Frozen in fear, Bellae could only stare at the apparition in front of her.

"Appearing as your sister, your sister," it hissed in a spiteful, singsong voice. "As your sister, your sister, I almost, I almost haaaad youuuuu!"

Glaring maliciously, its gnarled hand rose to the squire's face. Her knobbly and neglected nails scraped across Bellae's face filling the squire with a bitter and sorrowful feeling. Shivering from the frosty fingers and a deep sadness Bellae sat on her cot.

The spirit put her twisted index finger between the squire's eyes and pushed. Bellae fell backwards, more from the hollow cold feeling than physical pressure.

"It's not too late to come with me," the specter wheezed moving to float completely horizontal over Bellae. Her ghostly face distorted into a simulated smile that made it even more terrifying.

"Come now, join us and you will avoid *so* much agony, *so* much suffering! Help master find what he needs and then we'll kill you quickly and reasonably, pseudo-sort-of painless. We have to have some fun, don't you know!"

Grym and Borb scampered onto Bellae's chest, and began chattering as ferociously as their small size would allow. Standing on their back legs, they tried in vain to swat at the apparition.

Bellae shook her head, "I'm never going with you!"

"Darling, you have no choice. Sooner or later you *will* do his bidding. So, it has been, so the cycle, Na Cearcaill, forever shall be. There is no escaping your fate or his never-ending wheel of predestination! Your destiny became sealed the moment your scum of a mother gave birth to you!"

The remark about her mother filled Bellae with rage. Scooping up her mice with one arm, she swatted at the apparition with the other. Her arm went completely through the phantom. Every hair stood on end, and her entire arm felt exceptionally cold and numb.

"Another reminder of why I detest mewling children. So be it. See you soon enough!" it said, vanishing.

"Thanks, guys," Bellae said cuddling her mice.

"It's like you were in a trance or something," Borb said.

"I know, sorry. I couldn't help it."

"Why would you follow that . . . thing?"

"Initially, it looked like my sister," Bellae said, quickly getting under the covers. The room seemed freezing.

"We won't be sleeping anymore tonight, guys."

"You think?" Grym squeaked.

"Ready for class, my Inion?" Finn asked.

Tell Finn about the ghost! Bellae's mind screamed the next morning. Thinking about what the spirit said about destiny, she instead asked, "Do you think there is such a thing as fate? As destiny?"

"That's a deep and existential topic! Why do you ask?"

"Just something I've been thinking about. Is our life already decided?"

"Definitely not! We are all born within a certain time, at a certain place, with the opportunities that era and our status bestow. Beyond that, fate is simply an excuse for failure and a justification for power."

Bellae cocked her head back and studied her Knight while contemplating his words. "I like it."

"Oh good! You know I live to impress."

"You're pretty smart, Finn."

"You're just figuring this out?" he laughed.

"Not as smart as Crann, but . . ." she giggled.

"Very funny. Now, get off to class and learn something!"

With a genuine hug she left, *Suck on that ghostly shrew and your stupid destiny!*

Chapter Three

Of Dwarves, Dragons, and Distant Stars

Scroll 1: Class of Stars

"I'm not sure I can handle Professor Lehtori today," Gimelli admitted.

The previous day's ordeal seemed a long time ago as the bruised Pantteri sat at their wooden desks in the dusky classroom. Scrolls, books, and astronomy gadgets adorned the stone walls while the dark wood ceiling was pocked with garishly rendered planetary and solar models.

"Lehtori? I've never heard old Star-Brain talk about anything but astronomy," Scelto said. "If she says the name of these lectures one more time . . ."

"You mean, 'The Practical Uses of Armillary Spheres: Getting to Know the Model of the Heavenly Bodies!'" Gimelli snickered.

Scelto groaned.

"La-Lontasia, what are you studying?" Jumeaux growled.

"Pantteri stick together! Knock it off, Jumeaux," Scelto commanded. "You okay, Lontas?"

"What? Yeah, I'm all right." Reading about the stars, suns, and planetary movements had almost been enchanting enough for him to forget about his injuries.

He quickly scanned the room, *No Tilkeri, yet.* Even the gravitational pull of the heavenly bodies couldn't overcome his dread of the Tilkeri Squad and their inevitable tormenting.

"The Tilkeri probably won't come since they won the Squire Battle. Maybe it'll just be us, the Karhuteri, and the Elandiri Squads for class," Bellae said.

"Even though they barely beat us, they're so obnoxious I'm sure we're in for it."

Just then, Stratto entered with hands cupped around his mouth like a mock trumpet, complete with chafing simulated music. Bellae closed her eyes in disappointment.

"Ignore them," Scelto whispered.

"Your attention, ladies and louse-covered dogs! Please rise and give a hand to your Squire Champions, the Tilkeri!" Stratto bellowed, temporarily halting his out-of-tune musical penance.

The Tilkeri smiled maliciously as the formerly sleeping Mykka from the Elandiri Squad stood up and began clapping loudly.

"That's the way, Mykka!" Stratto bawled as the rest of the Tilkeri bowed deeply before raising their hands in triumph.

Realizing he'd been duped, Mykka quickly hunched in shame.

"Thanks, everyone!" the Tilkeri said, as if the entire class had greeted them with applause.

"We want to give a special thanks to Lontas. If we had a sixth trophy, we would give it to you for all your help yesterday."

Bellae was happy to see that Lontas did not shrink quite as much as usual under the weight of their insults.

"Sit down and give it a rest," Scelto said.

"Hey, Lontas," Tempaus said, ignoring him in favor of the smell of blood coming from Lontas. "Where's your girlfriend in the spiky red dress? She's better looking than I expected and, I guess, not too bad if you don't mind the drool and fleas."

"Nice feet, jester-boy," Tiron snickered, kicking Lontas' feet as he passed.

In mock sympathy, Atla whispered, "Hey, cut it out. Lontas can't help it if his boots were on backwards. He thought he was running *towards* the dragon, poor guy didn't even know he was falling!"

"Leave him alone," Bellae stated, but the Tilkeri pretended not to hear.

"Better lucky, I mean clumsy, than good," Atla added before walking by Lontas, and bumping into his bandaged legs. Lontas grimaced as they laughed.

Scelto moved towards them menacingly, "Touch him again and you'll pay!"

"We know it was you who rigged our door, boy. You're already on our list!"

"All right, everyone, settle down and attend to details," Professor Lehtori said while walking in. "Astronomy is all about details. Life is also all about details. Hence, learning the details of astronomy is just like learning about life, and a life without astronomy is a detail not worth living. The more details you know of astronomy, and hence life, the better. Therefore, detailed details in living life can ..." Professor Lehtori looked up, lost in the maze of fluttering concepts orbiting her jumbled thoughts.

"As I was saying, anything you want to do well in life is always about the details and hence, by the product of reason, astronomy itself."

She set her things down and immediately gravitated to her armillary sphere as if it were a long-lost friend. Her hands moved around it caressingly without touching it. Her absurdly large necklace bumped rhythmically against it with a periodic *ting*. "All thirteen moons and three suns of Verngaurd are here! Isn't it deliciously gorgeous?"

"Would you like us to leave you two alone?" Tiron snickered as the Tilkeri laughed.

Professor Lehtori slowly stood up, draped in a hurt expression. "You there, Squire Tiron, rattle off to me what the ancients were referring to when they said, 'saphaea.'"

Tiron silently looked down.

"Tell me the difference between the ancient astrolabe and the later saphaea."

After another awkward silence, he said, "I'm not sure, Professor Lehtori."

"Ah, it seems to me that you have too much time to boast, bully, and throw around hurtful humor, but not enough to study. I will confide in you that I tried very hard to convince Friar to transform the Squire Battles into something truly magnificent and genuinely useful, the Astronomy Battles!"

A burst of laughter shot through the class. It was only after she flashed another anguished expression they realized she was not kidding.

"You're as bad as them! Do you not appreciate that life is astronomy and astronomy is life? You will be delighted to know I need a one-scroll summary of the differences between a saphaea, an astrolabe, and the current day armillary on my desk before Mardin rises tomorrow."

An audible groan united the room.

"I know, I know. It's exciting, isn't it? However, do try to hold in your enthusiasm, and there's no need to thank me."

Their abusive humor, and picking on Lontas suddenly did not seem so fruitful to the Tilkeri.

Despite Professor Lehtori's unbridled passion for the subject, her cadence turned dry and monotonous the longer she lectured, eventually settling on coma-inducing.

"Time for the fun," she eventually said. "We're working on the armillary spheres that create a working model of Verngaurd and its celestial bodies. We can predict the location of the heavenly bodies in relation to each other. The first piece we will add is the Mardin Armillary, or morning sun phase. Then we'll add Luminos and finally Pheobus to complete the solar trio, next class we'll add the moons.

"I know everyone is dying to hear the thirteen moons. Lontas, rattle them off!"

Lontas grimaced, knowing each correct answer would translate into some later punishment from the Tilkeri, "Kuu and Vegrandis." He closed his eyes, picturing each one, "Migrus Luna, Feinelaud, Mane,

Tungl, Mond, Celi, Himmel, Nefol, I Fyny, Oeri, and finally Stor-Ma-nen."

"Wonderful. Simply wonderful!" Professor Lehtori held her hand over her heart. "You Tilkeri should note this information is *required* for the trials into Knighthood. Being a Knight is more than simply beating someone's brains in."

As the professor rambled, Bellae wondered what Crann and Finn were doing. She pulled out her Inion pendant, a sense of happiness washed over her. She suddenly felt guilty about her intense longing to find out more about her parents. *I have all the family I need right here in Liberum.*

Professor Lehtori's distant voice continued to spout absurd directions. "... continue this easy assembly. Make sure equinoctial A has the three hundred and sixty degrees facing up. Next, attach the three ellipses of the suns starting with Mardin. It passes through both celestial meridians L-Z. Solstitial closure H and the quadrantal wire must be firmly tied ..."

Something's wrong with the creature Lontas saw that's been following me, otherwise, it would have simply flown away. Plus, should I tell him about the ghost thing that has been haunting me or would that be too much for him to handle? Too much for now I think.

A plan began to take shape in her mind as Professor Lehtori showed up next to Bellae's disheveled armillary where she had been randomly attaching pieces.

"What you have here resembles ... well, it looks like the universe threw up on your desk now, doesn't it?"

Bellae blushed and the Tilkeri chortled.

"If the world was designed as you have it, I'm afraid our planet would be destroyed. You attached several moons in the sun's orbit and over here ... well, I'm not sure what you were thinking."

The next ten minutes felt like twenty years to Bellae as the professor took over the construction. "You see, I told you this was easy."

"Excuse me, Professor. I thought we were only supposed to work through the suns?" Mykka asked.

"Whoopsie! My fault. Bellae and I got too excited, didn't we, dear?"

Bellae forced a halfhearted smile and nodded despite the fact she had been daydreaming.

"This class is about unleashing the heavens! So, how can we keep from getting excited?" Professor Lehtori screeched, gently patting Bellae.

"Need a hand, Tiron?"

"Professor, that's kind of you, but then I'd have three hands, which would be weird, and you would only have one, which would be bad."

"Looking at your work, I would say it wouldn't matter how many hands you have."

"Nice, Professor!" Scelto exclaimed. His smile vanished at her reproachful look.

"Let's see who else needs help. Lontas, do you . . . oh, of course, you don't. Excellent job! Perfect, as always. Looks as if you got carried away and did the whole thing as well!"

"Ahhm-suck-hhm-up-ahhhm," one of the Tilkeri coughed.

Scroll 2: Evolution-Dilution

With classes over, Bellae gently tugged on Lontas' shirt, pulling him away from the stream of dazed students heading towards their barracks. Most, but not all, were too drained to notice.

"Hey, suck-ups!" Tiron shouted as the Tilkeri quickly surrounded them.

"What did you call them?" Professor Lehtori asked.

"Nothing, Professor," he answered sweetly.

"Better be. Right now I want all you big shot Tilkeri to go *orbit* the exercise field until you burn off your negative energy!"

"Thank you," Bellae said. Professor Lehtori nodded and followed the Tilkeri to make sure they left.

Tiron pointed and mouthed, "Later."

"Ready for my plan?" Bellae asked.

"Hmm?" Lontas mumbled absently, still dreaming of spinning suns and moons.

"I have a great idea!"

"Oh no! No, no, no and no!" Lontas cried, his thoughts of the heavens crashed to the ground under the gravity of her scheming. "Your 'great ideas' get me in big trouble."

"What?" Bellae asked, trying to sound hurt and innocent.

"You can't fool me. You're plotting something that will end up with us in a mess."

"Plotting?" Bellae repeated, sounding offended. "Someone needs our help."

"Ohhhhhh nooohhh!"

"What? Come on, you haven't even heard my idea." Flashing her sad eyes, she continued, "You have to at least listen to the idea before you say no."

"Okay."

"I don't have *all* the details worked out yet, but we're going to find the creature in the cemetery!"

Lontas turned ashen while Bellae continued, "Cookie will give us food for the poor creature, and we'll sneak out tonight."

Feeling the pressure of Lontas' silent dread and deadpan stare, she quickly added, "I just *know* it needs us."

He continued staring straight ahead.

"Are you going to say something?"

"No!"

"No to the plan, ooorrrrr no to saying something?"

"Both."

"Finn's on guard duty tonight so even if we get caught, which we definitely won't, he can keep us out of trouble."

"This isn't some cute and cuddly stray you can hide under a floor board! There is no way we should look for it. If I thought anyone else would believe me, I would have already told them."

"Let's . . ."

"No, and no! I draw the line at searching for winged *demons!*"

"Would a demon try to help you?"

"That thing tried to bloody kill me!"

"Come on, Lontas. You said yourself it could have grabbed you and disappeared before anyone even knew what happened. It only wanted your attention."

"Did you hear yourself? You're exactly correct! It easily could have grabbed me and flown off! Yet you want to go to the cemetery to find *it*, at *night*?"

"You're being dramatic. If we don't look for it, the creature will find us."

"Nah," Lontas whined, envisioning stumbling along the dark, twisting path trying to find a terrifying creature.

His resolve melted as Bellae continued outlining the reasons her plan would work. Lontas' refusals slowly evolved from a loud prehistoric, "No!" progressing into a huddled, "Nah," before transforming into an upright and unassuming "Yeah."

Bellae squeezed his arm, "You'll be so happy you did this!"

I sincerely doubt it.

Scroll 3: Sounds of Alarm and Nesting Birds

A thunderous gong reverberated throughout the castle, startling the squires.

"The Bells of Kadotus? Is this for real?" Lontas whispered.

Their resonance sent a ripple of fear through the fortress. The giant, ancient bells had warned Knights of attack for centuries, including when they were housed at the previous capitol, Cumhacht.

The answer came swiftly as a Knight screamed, "Let's go squires! Get your lazy hides to your Knights!"

Bellae grabbed Lontas' hand and they sprinted to the Pantteri stable.

They entered to hear Luchar berating Jumeaux, "Get moving, ya dunce!"

"Dig your heels to the flanks, Pantteri! Go through your checklists. We can't fight with good intentions!" Ritari yelled as Scelto worked on his armor.

"Bellae, here!" Finn called.

"Let me help with your armor," Bellae said, hands shaking.

Finn looked around cautiously, "I think it's only a mock attack."

"You think?" she scoffed, fumbling badly with his armor.

"Pretty sure. Focus on getting Crann in full-dress battle gear," Finn said.

Bellae embraced Crann's neck as he warmly nuzzled her back and, as her Knight predicted, the interaction managed to calm her nerves. Finn smiled, knowing Bellae would never remember this tender moment, but it would live forever in his heart.

"Ask Finn if I can skip the caparisons," Crann requested. *"I look like I'm wearing a tapestry!"*

"Is it okay if Crann skips his coverings? He thinks he looks like a tapestry!"

Finn's laugh was interrupted by Luchar shouting. "Get it strapped or I will use it to hang you from the highest tree as food for the buzzards!"

Jumeaux winced, sweat pouring profusely as he worked with the heavy armor.

"Watch the signal flags and listen to the drums for instructions. Fall back if ordered," Finn reminded her.

"Thanks for worrying about me," Bellae said, giving him a quick hug.

"Hey, you're my Inion now and forever."

"If you two-legged creatures are done fawning over each other, I could sure use some food," Star purred. Bellae could feel his bloated stomach and shook her head before quickly getting back to work.

After preparations were finished, the Pantteri headed to the large training bailey chock-full of Knights in glistening armor.

Using the enchanted Huuto to amplify his voice, Friar spoke, "Too slow! We will practice this until you get it in half the time! An army is marching on these walls and will not wait for you!" An anxious murmur arose from the crowd.

"Move out and into formation one! Adaptability and innovation are the root of victory! Chaos and fear are the birth of defeat!"

"Bottleneck gates are great only if you don't have to move through them," Finn said as they struggled out the gates, across the moat, and onto the sloping Plains of Keto.

"Even without seeing them, the enemies' war cries and drum beats are scaring the crap out of me," Lontas said.

Bellae squeezed his hand as they began forming up lines on the high ground, just before the plains dipped down into a low-lying basin of grassland.

Most squires were wide-eyed and tense, while the Knights waited eagerly.

They had drawn up in their standard formation of repeating six-deep lines so the depth of the line could change to become deeper, twelve or even eighteen fighters if facing an army with heavy cavalry. The line could also easily be spread out to match a larger force in order to deter a flanking movement.

Keeping fresh troops is a key strategy for the Knights, and the secondary depth provides that flexibility. These formations are dependent on precise, well-timed maneuvers of large numbers of Knights and their squires, but are not without risk. In several instances, both Knights and squires suffered massive losses during the Dark War.

"They're here," Lontas wheezed as the enemy crested the opposite slope.

Bellae drew in her breath sharply at the sight of so many combatants lined out against them. With one voice the army shouted, "Victory!"

The force of their cry sent a shiver of fear through Bellae. The Liberum Knights and squires screamed back, "Knights!"

The beating of drums and snapping of signal flags pulled Bellae back to her current duty. She recognized the order, *Prepare for frontal charge.*

At this signal the squires looked imploringly to Ritari. "They're Knights from the castles of Taiheart and Toil Shaor, here to practice maneuvers."

"You could have told us that!"

"We needed to see how you handle fear and pressure."

For the next several hours, Knights and squires on both sides practiced large-scale maneuvers, each army making and countering moves without any actual fighting.

"Son of a dried mushroom! Let me hit someone!" Luchar yelled, becoming increasingly agitated at the maneuvers with no chance to vent his soaring rage.

"I think we need to practice *that* again," Jumeaux said sarcastically, smiling at the chuckles it drew.

The flags finally signaled, "Last maneuver." The Knights of Liberum had fallen back as part of a feigned retreat and reformed their lines as the signal for charge commenced.

"Finally!" Luchar screamed, rushing forward, anticipating the first blow with his axe. This time, horns blared in addition to the signal flags and drums. All three indicating an immediate stop. The two sides slowed to a halt a dozen yards from each other. Bellae could now make out details of the army across from them and each side sized up the other one Knight and squire at a time.

Bellae locked in on the soft-green eyes of an Elf from Taiheart Castle, Gleoi Dea. Her tannish-brown skin had gentle celadon hues running down it instead of the deep grooves of Finn's.

"Finn, it's Gleoi Dea!" Bellae exclaimed, but the two Elves were already staring at each other so intensely there appeared to be visible connection stretching between them.

"I didn't know tree bark could blush," Sorea joked.

Gleoi Dea rode a fearsome-looking kameli from the Desert of Calor. Massive twisting horns coiled out menacingly from its head while two large tusks pointed downward. All were striped with black and white swirls, making you feel dizzy with even the quickest glance. Its feral ears had overhanging tufts of hair to deflect sand. Its light-tan fur deflected heat and insulated from the cold. Kameli are extremely difficult to train, but if won over, are fiercely loyal.

After an awkward moment, Bellae followed Finn towards the object of his unblinking stare. *He can't take his eyes off her. What if he gets married and leaves?*

Crann snorted, *"That creature smells horrible!"*

"Calm down!" Finn yelled, struggling to stay on as Crann reared up, futilely flailing his front hooves against the odor drifting from the kameli. All the while Gleoi Dea and her beast stared with curious amusement.

Figure 33: A Knight from Taiheart, Gleoi Dea's grandparents came from the Forest of Creber. She is famous for riding a kameli instead of a horse.

*Figure 34: Fierce creatures from the Desert of Calor, **Kameli** sport massive horns and tusks.*

"Crann!" Bellae yelled forcefully. The horse immediately settled, the fear of harming her overwhelming his disgust of the fetor.

"Kameli are disgusting!"

"The other horses don't mind."

"They're anosmic."

"Anosmic? What does that even mean?" Bellae laughed as Finn dismounted. "I'll take Crann so you can talk to Gleoi Dea." She batted her eyelashes and flashed a knowing look at Finn.

He rolled his eyes.

After leading Crann away, Bellae gently stroked his neck while he ate some of the mostly trampled grass.

A loud blast of horns suddenly rang out, shattering the preceding tranquility.

"Bloody Helvetti! That's it? They call that a meet and greet?" Luchar bellowed, even though he had been sitting alone on the grass scowling indiscriminately. "I better get to hit or smash someone!" he said, eagerly cramming his helmet back on.

Finn came running and deftly jumped onto his horse.

Gimelli smiled deviously and raised her eyebrows.

"What?" Finn asked innocently.

Bellae, Sorea, and Gimelli laughed.

"What's so funny?" Jumeaux asked, mirroring Scelto's, Luchar's, and Lontas' guileless expressions.

The girls and Sorea rolled their eyes.

"What?" Jumeaux demanded.

"She's cute," Sorea said.

Lontas, Jumeaux, and Luchar exchanged puzzled looks.

"Bellae's cute?" Jumeaux asked.

Ritari walked up, "What's going on?"

"The ladies have a secret about Finn."

"Get used to it," Ritari said.

"Open your eyes, fellows, and shut your jaws before birds build nests in there," Sorea said, laughing.

"This day is getting more annoying by the second!" Luchar grumbled.

"Squads from Castle Taiheart, Gyronny and Chevron; from Toil Shaor, Squad Three; from Liberum I need the Pantteri!" Friar yelled.

"That's us, let's move!" Ritari said excitedly.

"Why are there two squads from the Taiheart?" Jumeaux asked.

"Because they need two in order to compete with us!" Luchar snarled.

The sharply arranged squads from Taiheart stood next to Friar. They stared threateningly as the Pantteri sauntered by. Luchar met their gaze, his own eyes blazing with antagonizing fire, daring them to make a move.

A line of tutors began forming a barrier behind the selected squads. "Those of you not chosen move elsewhere!" one of them yelled.

"This should be good!" Ritari exclaimed.

Scroll 4: Contrasting Veli

Friar Pallium stood conversing with the two polar opposite Veli, or heads of the other two remaining Knight Castles.

"Who's that guy with the dirty cloak?"

"That's Veli Pingius, leader of Castle Toil Shaor, known for his massive girth!" Lontas chuckled. "It's said he never turns down a second, or third, helping!"

A simple long-sleeved garment stretched around Veli Pingius' generously proportioned body. It was unadorned save for a splattering of smeared casualties from past meals scattered haphazardly in various colors and ages. His most celebrated feature was tucked cozily between his burgeoning cheeks, a mirthful and blithe smile.

"Why are the Veli wearing crowns?" Jumeaux asked.

"They're totally *not* crowns, they're wreathes," Gimelli giggled.

"Uhm, they are so totally crowns!"

*Figure 35: The ample **Veli** of Castle Toil Shaor, **Pingius**, is never lacking an appetite or a smile. **Veli Falciss** aggressively runs Castle Taiheart with unyielding precision.*

Gimelli laughed. "After the Knights stopped being ruled by kings, the lords of Knight Castles became known as Veli. They kept their crowns by changing the name to 'wreath.'"

"That other Veli looks intense!" Bellae said, a little intimidated.

"Or constipated!" Jumeaux remarked, huffing as no one laughed.

"That's Falciss from Castle Taiheart," Lontas said, watching the Veli's black eyes aggressively scan the environment. "He's fierce! Do you think his eyelids ever close for sleep?"

The features of Falciss' face glistened with greedy efficiency. He wore a lanky nose, notable for a snobbish downward hook. The muscles on his lean frame quivered slightly, as if seething with energy and annoyed at having to stand still.

The corpulent Veli Pingius moved towards his Squad Three with surprising grace, his well-aired teeth gleaming their jovial welcome. His undomesticated hair waved as if cheering each hefty stride in the breezy pastures around his head. His Knights wore frowzy armor with hints of rust. Their breastplates held the old kingdom numeral "III" as well as shells that paid homage to their seaside location around the gulf of Joupa Cavala.

The slouching squires of Squad Three wore a hodgepodge of old clothes, standing idly with an occasional yawn punctuating their apathetic demeanor.

Veli Falciss strode with brisk self-assurance towards his Castle's two entries, the Chevron and Gyronny. The Knights and squires of Taiheart took after their leader and stood motionless in precise military formation, their armor and weapons shone from excellent care.

"Knights, you have the honor of more challenges today," Friar informed.

Groans of complaint came from the squires and Knights of Toil Shaor. Veli Pingius smiled, ignoring the outburst of those under his charge. However, Veli Falciss' face contorted angrily as though he was contemplating attacking them.

Ignoring their protest, Friar continued, "One squad of Knights will compete in the Dragon Battle . . ."

A loud murmur went through the Knights.

" . . . at the upcoming Tournament of Flags. These challenges will determine which of you will represent the Knights. Squires are not needed. Please wait on the other side of the line of tutors."

The squires moved off, quickly swallowed by waves of flowing white robes worn by the tutors. Bellae lingered under the pretense of handling Crann's reins.

"Good luck!" she said encouragingly.

Suddenly a large red dragon appeared. It let out a roar and Crann startled. *"It's a pretend dragon,"* she reassured.

Scroll 5: First Try?

After what seemed liked hours, the great wall of tutors finally let down their intertwined arms with a collective sigh of relief.

"We've finished! Dinner in one hour!" Friar Pallium yelled.

"That's it? He's not going to tell us whether we have to fight *a dragon* at the Tournament?" Lontas puzzled.

"I guess not," Bellae said.

"That seems like an oh-so-important teensy-weensy little detail!"

Bellae laughed, then raised her eyebrows expectantly.

"Oh no. Not tonight!" Lontas pleaded with a tired edge. "You heard Friar. We have to get ready for dinner."

"You don't need an hour to prepare," Bellae said with her sweetest intonation. "Let's find somewhere to plan our quest to help the poor creature."

"You say poor creature, I say rabid demon."

"Not funny! With all the other Knights and squires, the castle will be crazy. Let's go this way."

While everyone else headed for Liberum, Bellae pulled the reluctant Lontas against the flow towards the simulated dragon. Like two fish struggling upstream, they paddled through the crowds, ignoring the occasional spray of mumbled insults. Finally breaking through, they saw Luchar berating a red-haired Dwarf.

"Hey, I met him, that's Pumilus," Bellae whispered to Lontas.

Luchar was waving a broken loitsia stick in front of the angry Dwarf, "Honestly, do you think I care about your little broken sticks or your flimsy command center? I will smash it the rest of the way . . ."

Pumilus discretely nodded to Lontas and Bellae then winked at two other Dwarves dressed in white robes. They quickly began whipping their loitsia sticks in geometric patterns in the air in front of them.

Bellowing, Luchar pulled back his battle-axe and took aim at the wooden structure that meant so much to the Dwarves. Suddenly, two figures appeared before him. With a howl of fear, Luchar held his massive swing. "You fool squires! I could have cut you both in half!"

Bellae and Lontas looked at each other to confirm the bizarre sight confronting them. Incredulously, they saw the spitting image of themselves, standing indifferently between a ranting Luchar and the wooden structure.

Drawn to the rhythmic movements of the white rods, Bellae walked in front of the Dwarves. Her eyes followed the swift path of the loitsia whizzing through the air. Like a fading memory, a surreal mist of white trailed behind the rods. Fascinated, Bellae thrust her hand through the hazy blur of light behind the fast-moving sticks. A gasp of awe went through the gathered Knights.

Bellae glanced up to see the image of herself in front of Luchar shimmering like a desert mirage before solidifying again. Tilting her head to the side, she repeated the process. Each time her hand broke through the trailing light the image briefly fragmented.

"Pumilus!" Luchar roared, finally understanding the illusion. "Of all the dirty tricks! Using a little girl? When I get my hands on you . . ."

"Enough!" Friar Pallium bellowed. The Dwarves wielding the loitsia stopped, and the apparitions of Bellae and Lontas evaporated.

"We should thank our Dwarf allies for their assistance," Friar encouraged to a lukewarm round of clapping. "Knights, go get ready for the feast."

Weighed down by fatigue and thirst, the Knights who had competed to participate in the Dragon Battle trudged towards Liberum, except Luchar. He stood ten feet away glaring at Pumilus and the other Dwarves.

Lontas tugged on Bellae's arm, "Let's leave."

She shook her head and smiled at one of the Dwarves, "May I hold those, please?"

Lontas quivered, self-conscious around new people. The Dwarf glanced at Pumilus. Surprisingly, he nodded. Perhaps the near-death experience with Luchar had jarred some kindness loose which landed on Bellae's request.

"They're called loitsia or control sticks," he said, handing them to her.

"These Dwarves are from the Rebelde Plains, but their ancestors hail from the Southern Dwarf Kingdom, and they are skilled in the art of prestidigitation—creating illusions," a smiling Friar Pallium said.

"It takes years of study to accomplish even the slightest apparition!" Pumilus said haughtily. "Just to be clear, Friar, I expect *lots* of *extra* compensation for your oaf of a Knight breaking my priceless loitsia!"

Bellae moved the sticks back and forth rhythmically. The sight and feel of them evoked a strong emotion of familiarity and comfort.

The crystal orbs on the tops of the two sticks began to glow. Bellae started to hear a humming sound. Looking around she saw the Dwarves talking with Friar. From their expressionless faces, it appeared they did not hear the growing noise. She turned to Lontas. He raised his eyebrows and feverishly gestured with his head to communicate that they should leave, but obviously he could not hear the droning noise.

Bellae closed her eyes and concentrated. Her head jerked back, and she found her mind streaming down a blindingly bright tunnel. She was about to open her eyes when visions appeared in the fast-moving passage of light, including a saber-toothed cat, a kameli, Castle Liberum, Friar Pallium, and Lontas. An orchestra of out-of-tune buzzing came from each image, creating a head-splitting screech within her mind.

Now here's something interesting. A sleek and majestic red bird came swooping towards her through the tunnel of light.

Locking in on the bird, everything else faded, including the humming. A beautiful trilling sound emanated from the bird. Concentrating on its music, she began to understand words within its song. When she thought of an action for the bird, its melody would tell her how to move the loitsia sticks. She imagined the great wings flapping gracefully, banking right and then left.

Suddenly, Pumilus ripped the sticks out of her hand and it all disappeared, replaced by a blinding flash of light then total darkness. Bellae's eyes fluttered until a blurry image of Friar began to take shape.

"Hello, Friar."

"Hello young squire," he chuckled.

Bellae realized that she was on the ground with the Dwarves staring at her suspiciously and Lontas eyeing her with wonder tinged alarm.

"Conjuring a prestidigitation phoenix, on your first try?" Friar admired.

"What were you saying, Dwarf?" Luchar bellowed. "Something about years of practice? Ha! This little girl . . ."

"Silence," Friar ordered, helping Bellae up.

Pumilus' cheeks glowed red with abashed anger.

"I expect everyone to keep quiet about what just happened. Now go prepare for dinner," Friar said, grinning broadly. *Yes, she's the one. Now is the time of the prophecy.*

Lontas and Bellae trudged slowly back to their barracks.

"Conjuring a phoenix was . . . amazing! It looked soooo real!"

Bellae smiled. He hadn't asked how she did it, merely accepted it. Without looking at him, she grabbed his hand and squeezed affectionately.

Scroll 6: Dinner Discord

"What are you Pantteri squires doing?" Friar asked.

"Helping prepare the feast," Scelto answered.

"Well, stop!"

"Sir?"

"No duties for the squires of the winning squad. Congratulations! The Pantteri will be representing the Knights in the Dragon Battle!"

"Yes!" Scelto said, pumping his fist in the air.

"Lovely!" Jumeaux said sarcastically. "You do know that dragon heartburn comes out as *FIRE*! Yeah, the chance to be roasted by a dragon sounds super, super great!"

"J, show this squad and Friar some respect. Although, you should know about indigestion because you give it to us every day."

"All right," Friar said. "Jumeaux, if you are cautioning us that only time will tell how this adventure will eventually turn out, you're right. Sometimes what we think is good news turns out to be bad, and the opposite can also occur. However, speaking with malice corrodes hearts, especially for the one talking.

"Come, let others serve you for a change." He led them to a table situated right behind where he, the Pantteri Knights, and the Veli, Falciss and Pingius, were sitting.

On the left were the austere Chevron and Gyronny Squads, and on the right sat the tousled Squad Three eating and drinking noisily.

The Pantteri squires strained to listen to Veli Falciss complaining of attacks in his territory. "We are losing the faith of the people we are sworn to protect. Our ranks are too thin to handle these Dark Warrior assaults. Entire towns are turning away from us and seeking aid from the Proliators."

Bellae and Lontas exchanged looks of horror.

"They multiply like rabbits, spreading across our lands like a red plague! How long must we swallow this bitter Proliator affliction bleeding the inhabitants of Verngaurd of their trust in the Knights?

"We must attack the Proliators and throw them into the sea! After that, we aggressively recruit new Knights and prepare them to battle the Dark Warriors. Ager, Jaa, Piscium, and even the Rebelde Plains need to have their armies siphoned into ours. With these troops, we can adequately protect our lands against the Dark Warriors!

"We should also take this opportunity to retool our training, tactics, and discipline." Looking at the fleshy Veli Pingius, Falciss whispered, "Or lack of discipline."

He continued in a loud voice, "We need uniformity, discipline, toughness, and austere conditions. Though I am loathe to say it, we would do well to mimic the Proliate's techniques."

"Our strength is in the individual Knight's ability to innovate as a battle changes," Friar answered. "It doesn't make sense to give up our identity and become an exact copy of the Proliate. Is that any different than being defeated and assimilated?"

Falciss snorted in disgust, and his sharpened eyes grew more enraged.

To diffuse the situation, Friar Pallium quickly continued, "Our goal is peace for the people of Verngaurd. Power is only respected if it is not used, otherwise it is simply intimidation and imposing fear. These lands are ... "

"These lands?" Veli Falciss interrupted. "We have fallen from thirty-five castles to three! Verngaurd has gone from an open, ordered, and learned society to a fractured one soaking in nationalism, riddled with fear, disarray, and fire-worshiping Proliate! What lands? Like father, like son! You sit and do nothing while *our lands* disappear!"

The air instantly became thickly tense with the biting words *"like father, like son"* hovering like a storm cloud. Awkward silence filled the tiny crevices squished in-between the insult still hanging insolently above them.

Friar Pallium sighed, "I would remind you we are not a kingdom, and I'm no king. If we become expansionistic warriors instead of protectors, we would become like the Proliators."

"What you call expansionistic, I say, is *defending* our way of life! We have just enough strength to defeat the fire-worshiping Proliators, but only if we surprise them!"

All the Liberum Knights seemed appalled, except Luchar, who nodded his head in agreement while voraciously eating his chicken. "Kill them all!" he exclaimed as food refugees fled his chomping jaws.

"Those fire worshipers, as you call them, are still our allies. The Proliate fought beside us against the Dark Warriors."

"That alliance is as reliable as the crumbling scroll the treaty was signed on," replied Veli Falciss. "Wake up! The Proliate aren't much better than the Dark Warriors. In another few years we will either be dead or wearing Proliator red. The Proliate are more interested in spreading their extremist phoenix faith than protecting an open and free Verngaurd. I shouldn't have to remind you that woven into the blood that mortars this institution *is* a history of kings looking out purely for greedy advancement."

Silent contemplation nestled onto the surrounding tables as the words of Veli Falciss braided themselves together with those of Friar Pallium.

Veli Pingius laughed into the uncomfortable quiet, "Now boys, let's not be too hasty in words *or* actions, unless that action is to reach for pudding! Ha-ha! Ah, pudding! Reach for it fast, eat it faster, as long as it can last, be the pudding master! So, they say." He stared longingly at the table willing pudding to appear.

"You realize no one says that, or has a clue what you're talking about!" Falciss huffed.

Pingius continued, "Except in relation to the aforementioned, and unfortunately absent, pudding, *caution* is better, Falciss. We cannot beat the Dark Warriors and the White Wizard without help from the Proliate. Besides, Friar has provided us with highly detailed plans in case of a war with the Prolia ..." For once, the genial expression faded from Pingius' face, replaced with panic as he realized the secret he had started to spill.

"Pingius!" Friar Pallium said crisply. "That private discussion is for later. Until we have solid evidence to the contrary, the Proliate will be considered allies. It's my job, however, to plan for all possibilities." Raising his mug, he said, "To the Pantteri, the Knights' dragon warriors!"

Everyone raised their tankard and shouted, "Pantteri!"

The conversation stayed genial for a short time before slithering back to the Proliators and Dark Warriors. As the tension escalated, the Pantteri squires excused themselves and headed to their barracks.

"The White Wizard and his Dark Warriors are back, and bringing a huge war, aren't they?" Lontas asked.

"I think so." Everything Friar had told her in his office came rushing back to Bellae, and she grimaced, "Actually, yes. It's definitely coming."

Scroll 7: Black Magic of the Night

Wearing her own, Bellae quietly crept towards the rack and grabbed Lontas' cloak. She tiptoed to his bunk, carefully avoiding squeaky floorboards. After making sure the other squires were sleeping, she placed the cloak over his mouth while shaking him vigorously.

Lontas' eyes snapped wide with panic. Feeling his mouth distorting into a yell under the deep folds of his cloak, Bellae felt justified in her tactics. Once the terror had completely drained from his face, Bellae removed the cloak and he took several deep, restorative breaths.

"Ready?" she whispered.

He shook his head, mouthing, "No."

Bellae took advantage of his grogginess to pull him up, carefully placing the book he had been reading on his bed before mothering him to the door and checking her bag. Satisfied, she carefully lifted the latch and pushed the door open just wide enough to let Lontas squeeze through. She grabbed a lantern and hooked it onto her bag before grabbing a phosphorous stick and a flint stone to light it.

Scelto groaned and flopped over. She stared hard, trying to force the darkness apart to see whether his eyes were open. After several moments with no other movement, she slipped out the door. Even before it was shut, Lontas' hand alighted on her shoulder.

"Something's wrong."

Bellae froze and concentrated. "What's that tinging?"

"Don't know, but there are *a lot* of unusual noises." They listened to the repetitive sounds echoing around the castle.

"Maybe it's the Knights from the other castles?"

"No. They're camping outside the walls and leave in the morning."

Everything from the ground to the air felt restless and galvanized. Doubt crept into Bellae's mind while staring into Lontas' pleading eyes.

"No," she said, shaking her head passionately enough to try and reassure them both. "Every part of me is screaming to help this creature."

She tugged his arm, pulling against the magnetic hold of fear and uncertainty rooting him to the ground. He whimpered but begrudgingly began walking. They tread softly around the different buildings that made up the wooden barracks.

"Friar's up," Lontas noted.

Bellae glanced up at the central tower. The flickering candlelight from Friar's windows bobbed from side to side and Bellae could imagine it symbolizing his head shaking in disapproval of their late-night antics. The shield of darkness guarding the chill night detained the humble light fighting to escape his office to a pale aura.

They were about to cut in front of the tower, when loud barking erupted from that direction. Lontas froze, squeezing Bellae's hand so tightly she gasped.

"Hand!"

"Sorry," he whispered, relaxing his grasp.

"I think we should head past the armory," Bellae suggested.

For the next several minutes, they made good progress with only a few sightings of dancing flames from the torches of the guards walking patrol. The orbs of light contrasted so sharply with the black sky that the fiery trail continued its pirouette even in the gloom behind their closed eyes.

A gust of wind chilled the air and rustled the trees. Lontas' head whipped in the direction of the motion.

Who's there? Please not the ghost!

The rustling grew louder, the leaves protesting with increasing fury under the wind's oppressive command. Beneath the veil of darkness, the movement seemed more intense. Swarming murkiness covered each tree, bush, and building so completely that their natural shapes transfigured into all manner of unfamiliar and frightening creatures.

"What's wrong, Lontas?"

"It's dark."

"Yeah, that's generally what happens at night!"

"'The Black Magic of the Night,'" Lontas whispered.

"What?"

"The old fable from Jaa about the spirit of the night that comes and transforms normal objects into monsters after dark."

Talking about class made Lontas relax, and he continued in a calmer voice, "The warrior maidens from Jaa have to sleep during the day and hunt in the dark for thirty-three straight nights. They are not given food or water, and must battle the monsters created by the magic of the night for survival. It's really a metaphor about facing fear, but could be viewed . . ."

He abruptly stopped as she shook her head. "Interesting, but not the time."

"Sorry, but it's so much easier to not be afraid in sunlight."

As Bellae scanned the horizon, Lontas suddenly jumped, smothering her in a taut embrace, "A growl!"

"Loosen!" Bellae gasped, her ribs constricted. Lontas relaxed his grip and they both took a deep breath. A sharp bark from a dog, and the movement of two torches in the distance, caught Bellae's attention.

"Those lights are moving towards us, and fast. Back to the barracks," Bellae declared. *It'll have to be another night.*

Not needing to hear it twice, Lontas immediately ran towards their barracks. As the dogs moved closer, their barking turned into exaggerated howls meant to intimidate. Bellae looked behind to see their shapes closing quickly.

"The guards are some ways off, but the dogs are going to catch us."

"What should we do?"

"I can talk . . . watch out . . ." Bellae exclaimed, but too late.

Lontas found himself slamming into a large hedge hidden in the shadows. The branches bent as they dug into his body. Once his momentum slowed, the boughs recoiled, springing him backwards.

He landed hard on his back. His old injuries screamed loudly at the fresh insult. Bellae had been holding his hand and was spun around, landing next to him on the ground.

The barking grew louder and Lontas arched his head backward to see the inverted image of the dogs closing in.

"Move!" she pleaded while trying to lift him up. Realizing the dogs were too close, she stopped, "Get under the bush!"

"Let's run for it."

"Too late!" She could feel the hostility radiating off the dogs. *If I can get them to slow down and talk, we have a chance.*

"I guess getting maimed under a bush is as good as out in the open," he whimpered.

Sliding back, Lontas felt the jabs and snares of the branches impeding his progress. Several of his scabs ripped off, and fresh blood oozed freely. From the twangs and breaking sounds, he knew Bellae was suffering a similar fate. From their spot below the undergrowth, they could only see about a foot above the soil.

The cold, hard ground began pushing its icy fingers up from below, weaving through the fabric of their clothes and delving deep into their bodies, making them even more uncomfortable as the savage barking grew louder.

"Stay still and no matter what happens, say *nothing*."

"Okay, but what's the plan?"

"You be quiet."

"Starting now?"

"Starting now."

"I thought you . . ." Lontas let his words trail off. Even in the dark he could feel Bellae's biting look.

"But . . ." he said, shivering under terrifying flashbacks from the Squire Battles.

"Quiet!"

"Sorry."

"Lontas!" Bellae said, as loudly as she dared.

The dogs were so close now the squires could see the dynamic pumping of their legs and occasional splashes of drool sparkling in the patchy torch light. In another moment they could see the war hounds' eyes hungrily reflecting the scant nocturnal light.

The branches of the bush exploded apart as four hounds burst into their hiding place with teeth bared.

Bellae's melodic chanting collided against their harsh growls while she flung several items from her rucksack. Lontas, feeling claustrophobic, was getting ready to scoot out the other end when the dogs calmed, tearing into the steaks she had brought for the creature.

"Lead the guards away, please. I'll see you tomorrow."

The night guards arrived outside the bush as Lontas' "friend" from the Squire Battles caught his scent. Three of the four dogs darted away, barking contentedly. Smelling the rising fear and tasting the vivid memories of his domination of Lontas at the Squire Battles, the dog in red armor remained locked on the trembling squire.

"Go, Canities, please!"

He nodded before tearing off after the other dogs.

"Close your eyes," Bellae breathed, trying to avoid the red reflex from their eyes giving them away.

The watchmen waved their torches, trying to pierce the darkness of the branches. After a tense moment, they started walking away.

"What was in there?"

"With Canities, who knows? That dog is a bridle and a couple of shanks short of a rein," the other watchmen laughed.

"You have to admit, he did a number on that goofy kid at the Squire Battle!"

Bellae winced in sympathy for her friend. They stayed still for several moments, letting the guards move away.

"Loooontas!" the eerie voice they had both heard before called out. Even in the dark Bellae could feel her friend constrict in terror.

"I-I-I've heard th-that voice before," he whispered, his voice trembling with fear.

"You have? Me too! I was afraid to tell . . ."

"Loooontas!" the voice called out a second time, seemingly right next to them.

The two squires bolted out from under the bush and started sprinting.

"What is that blasted thing?"

"No idea!"

"You should have told me!"

"*You* should have told *me!*"

"I didn't want to stress you out," Bellae explained.

"And I didn't want you to think I was crazy," Lontas added. "Have you seen it?"

"Yes, it's ugly and terrifying! Let's get further away from it!" Bellae said as they swept behind the great hall.

"Rest . . . here," Lontas puffed, leaning and panting against the rough, square stones that made up the sturdy building. Slowly their breathing calmed under the cool night breeze that caressed their faces.

"I've heard that voice many times before," Bellae whispered. "Actually, for years now."

"Me too! Not as long, but for a while. It always calls my name twice," Lontas replied as Bellae nodded. "There's something familiar about this ghost thing. I've heard or read about something similar before, yet I can't remember where."

"You should . . ."

"Bellae!" the disturbing voice called out.

A shiver of dread quivered through the squires.

A semitransparent form floated towards them. Its face was that of a beautiful woman. Although Bellae knew she had never seen it, the appearance seemed familiar.

"Bellae!" the voice rang out again, this time sounding almost tranquil.

The two bolted, weaving and dodging shrubs and buildings until finally rounding a corner near the kitchen, and halting near the now thunderous clanging noise.

"That thing is really starting to make me angry! Terrified, but irate! Also, what in the world's going on with all this annoying racket?"

"No idea," Bellae said, suddenly stopping to look frantically through her bag.

"What?"

"The lantern's gone. I must have lost it when we were hiding from the guards. First the dogs eat the steak, and now no lantern."

"We should go back," Lontas said nervously. "Although, I don't want to run into the ghost thing and there's no way I'm sleeping tonight!"

"I have a feeling the creature will know what that specter is and be waiting."

"Oh, the winged demon will be waiting with information on the ghost? Why didn't you say so?"

Scroll 8: What the Hephaestus?

The two squires moved with a mix of lusty terror and quiet frustration at how the night had gone so far. Eventually, they tucked themselves near the back corner of the craftsmen's living quarters.

"The armory should be shut down for the night, but just look."

Lontas peered through the branches. All the sounds they were hearing suddenly made sense. The yellow-orange glow of hot forges reflected brightly off the eyes of workers battling flame and steel. The forge was busier than Lontas had ever seen it. There was a flurry of movement, only loosely conducted by the head armorer, Cearta.

His eyes blazed like the fire he commanded. His muscular arms flexed taut as he gestured instructions. "Hephaestus!" he howled so loudly both squires jumped, huddling together behind their paper-thin defense, the shadows.

"Yes," Hephaestus, the chief designer and a master innovator, answered calmly. Known more for his humility than his size, his soft-blue eyes glowed with turbulent contemplation. His fine-featured face was forested with lush and unruly hair.

"Get this armor to the tunnels! Make sure your sluggards don't trip! The halfwits spilled everything last time, and *I* had to pick up their bloody mess!"

"Of course." Unruffled, Hephaestus turned and began giving orders of his own to get the armor to the storage tunnels.

"Let's follow them," whispered Bellae.

"Are you crazy?" Lontas asked a little too loudly.

Bellae pulled him to the ground.

Lontas' growing frustration and fatigue evaporated as Cearta thundered towards the crouching squires.

"Show yourself!" Cearta roared.

"What should we do?"

He was only ten feet away when Cookie's unmistakable voice cut through the night, "Cearta!"

"Cookie to the rescue," Bellae sighed with relief.

Cearta slowed as Cookie bellowed, "Get over to the kitchen and pick up the cheese wheels and cured pork hangings. I have to get started on the morning fare. No complaining when you have leftovers for breakfast!"

Cearta scowled at Hephaestus, who called some of his men to help.

"Aren't you going with them?" Cearta demanded.

"I'm going to the tunnels, as you ordered."

"Fine!" Cearta muttered, moving reluctantly towards Cookie. The blistering heat of the forge suddenly seemed more comfortable compared to Cookie's white-hot tongue.

"Now!" Bellae said. Jumping up, they sprinted in the direction Hephaestus had travelled. Dodging and hiding when necessary, they trailed the armor-laden procession.

The two squires stopped in the shadows and watched the bewildering array of supplies and armor being stockpiled in the storage tunnels.

"How much longer do we have to pull these ridiculous hours?" one of the men asked.

"We're ahead of schedule and almost done," Hephaestus answered. "We have supplies to last nine months, and enough armor and weaponry to supply all the Knights three times over. Now for the hard part."

"What does that mean?"

"Nothing for you. The foundry workers and I have a list of special requests from Friar. He ordered all sorts of metal sculptures, special weapons, and tons of hollowed-out stones. Plus, he wants it done before the Festival ends!"

"Hephaestus, that tunnel can't hold any more."

"Seal it and open another."

"I sure hope Friar knows what he's doing. I thought guard duty was bad, but this is horrible."

Hephaestus grunted, "Come on, the others can finish without us watching."

"This has to do with the Dark Warriors, huh?" the man asked.

Bellae and Lontas exchanged a frightened look.

"Yes. The Dark Warriors are tearing up the eastern seaboard and moving inland."

"Are there a lot of them?"

"No idea. I am so tired, a splat of bird shite could knock me over, and we still have a long night of work ahead of us," Hephaestus replied, walking off.

"You would only need that much reserve if you were expecting a drawn-out siege or battles requiring long marches away from the castle," Lontas said.

"Friar mentioned something about war to me, but why are they hiding this from the rest of the squires? We'll be right in the middle of the fight when the battles come."

"Does that ghost thing have anything to do with the Dark Warriors?"

Bellae thought of what Friar had told her about the coming war and her being the Chosen One. "I think it does," she said, looking up at the largest moon, Stor-Manen, which seemed to hang precariously in the black of the sky. Out of nowhere a band of swift traveling clouds swirled above them, blotting out almost all the reflected moonlight. *I don't believe in omens,* she tried to tell herself as the clouds draped them in near-total darkness.

"Let's cut through the tutors' quarters," Bellae suggested.

"What are the odds this creature's still there? It probably flew off."

Contradicting his words, a smooth but loud, flapping noise came from overhead. Crossing through breaks in the clouds, a dark shape was intermittently outlined flying above. A sharp, piercing cry punctured the air. Lontas and Bellae looked at each other with opposite expressions. Bellae smiled while Lontas froze in terror.

"Demon!"

"Creature in need," Bellae corrected. "Look!" she said excitedly. "It's heading for the cemetery!"

"A demon-monster, a cemetery full of dead people, a ghost calling out our names twice, and all in pitch-black darkness. What else could I ask for?"

Scroll 9: Flight Night, Mighty Fright Night

"There's a narrow path down the hill that sweeps through the gardens. We can hook back up with the main path to the cemetery down there."

Lontas' stomach churned at the thought of crossing the suspension bridge in near total darkness. His gut lurched and he vomited into a blackberry bush.

The next thing he knew, Bellae was cradling him and fanning his face.

"Did I pass out?"

"Only for a second."

Lontas sat up and swallowed, trying to get the acid taste out of his mouth and longing for water. He thought of Friar Pallium's words earlier that day.

I don't feel brave, but I am tired of being a weakling.

His shaky legs protested as he stood. He saw Bellae's concern for him intermingling with her desire to meet the creature. Worn out, Lontas only wanted to get back to the security of his bed. The two stared into the silent darkness, both wanting to travel in opposite directions, but neither wanting to let down the other.

"It's okay, tonight has been stressful already. Let's head back."

"I can make it," Lontas said, surprising himself as much as Bellae. *Is this opportunity knocking without permission?*

Bellae smiled with gratitude and relief, warming his heart. *I need to pay Bellae back for all the times she stood by me.* Arm in arm, the pair made their way to the bridge.

Bellae looked uncertainly at the ominously swaying structure. "Quite the bridge!"

"It's something," Lontas agreed, glad to have already emptied his stomach.

Lontas kicked a stone over the drop-off. Both squires peered cautiously over the edge, watching the spiraling stone until it was swallowed by the darkness of a canyon so cavernous they never heard it hit bottom.

"Do you think the river monster is down there?"

Bellae shook her head, "Not sure. That was a long time ago."

"Not long enough! Once we cross, where are we going?"

"Don't know. How about where you and Friar went?"

Images of tombstones and thoughts of the rotting corpses they stood sentry over flashed through his mind. The two stepped gingerly onto the wooden planks which creaked and moaned as if in protest, angry at being woken from their slumber on such a brisk night. An energetic wind commanded the fuming bridge to sway and lurch, adding to the squires' dread. They stopped and strained their eyes, trying to make sense of the shadowy shapes of graves rising and falling ominously like barren trees.

A songlike shrill whistled through the cemetery just as a frigid gust of wind rushed across their body.

"What's that?"

"It's only the breeze flowing past the tombstones."

"Sounds like ghosts singing. I'm so totally done with ghosts!"

"Come o . . ." Bellae stopped abruptly.

A tall, dark figure sprinted between two of the tombs. The speed and size of the creature struck Bellae with a wave of doubt as Lontas shivered, his thin veil of courage, woven from Friar's words, shredded under the deep darkness and his flourishing fear.

"You can wait here, I'll go ahead," Bellae said determinedly. After a few feet, she turned and flashed a thin smile before continuing across the bridge.

She's not going alone, Lontas thought guiltily. Feeling exposed and vulnerable, he hurried to catch up to his friend.

Bellae gasped.

Lontas looked up to see the outline of a crouching and well-muscled figure about ten feet in front of her blocking the opening of the bridge. Its features were covered in gloom, but they could see it gesturing for them to follow. In the blink of an eye, it turned and dashed into the forest of tombstones.

An icy wave of fear weakened Lontas' knees.

"The creature seems sad," Bellae said.

"You mean terrifying? If it needed us, it wouldn't keep disappearing. We saw it, and it left, which is exactly what we should do!"

"It was *beckoning*. The creature's smart and knows the cemetery isn't guarded."

Lontas thought the planks of wood bending beneath his weight looked relaxed, as if lounging with their hands behind their head on a gently swaying rope hammock. Their placid bearing stood in stark contrast to his utter dread as Bellae guided him across the tottering bridge.

The shadowy darkness surrounding the gravestones made them seem infinitely more terrifying. The wind shrieked a warning, furiously trilling at having to traverse an obstacle course memorializing the dead.

"The tombstones are bigger than I thought," Bellae said. "I wish we had our lantern."

"Yeah."

"Look at that tall one. It's lovely."

Lovely? "Not the words that come to mind as I stare at graves in the middle of the night," he said as Bellae grabbed his arm and pulled him forward.

Figure 36: Lontas and Bellae are drawn to the tallest gravestone in the ancient Cemetery of the Knights.

"Lontas, I can *feel* him as plain as day. He's close."

"So not comforting," Lontas said feebly. "Anyway, the top of that tombstone . . . I don't remember . . ."

"Let's take a closer look!" she interrupted, moving with magnetic allure towards the towering tombstone.

"Must be someone important to have the tallest one."

"He probably doesn't care so much now."

"Why is the gargoyle on top black?"

Lontas said nothing but stared up in frozen horror.

"It's very realistic and quite unique."

"That-that wasn't there before," Lontas whimpered, hyperventilating and pointing to the figure.

Bellae looked up in time to see the gargoyle-like creature tilt its head to one side. The shock of seeing what they had taken as a statue move made them stagger backwards. Spreading out its massive wings, it blocked out the light from the cloud-cloaked moons and stars. Fresh terror pulsated through them. Screaming, they half-stumbled, half-sprinted away.

Leaping onto the bridge caused it to bounce and dance wildly. After several strides on the oscillating boards, Lontas stumbled and fell. Unable to bring his hands up in time, he slid shoulder first along the wooden planks. His feet skidded under the ropes and flailed wildly outside the rickety confines of the bridge. His hands clawed desperately at the wood, his eyes wide with terror.

Scroll 10: Night Flight, Mighty Flight at Night

Lontas tried to call for help, but only managed a pathetic wheeze. It was enough for Bellae to stop and turn.

"Lontas! Hold on!"

The creature jumped from its perch on the tombstone uttering a shriek. With lightning speed it swooped towards Lontas, snatching at his legs flailing off the bridge. The massive talons that served as feet missed Lontas, but several of its claws raked roughly against the wood, creating an ear-splitting grating noise.

"It's trying to kill me!" Lontas yelled.

"I'm coming!" Bellae screamed.

The creature circled around for another pass as Bellae tried to feel its intentions. The sheer panic in Lontas' eyes made it too hard for her to concentrate. He was desperately clinging to a wooden plank while his legs dangled under the ropes and over the side of the bridge.

A booming screech of frustration startled her. She was thumped by a dynamic gust of air from the creature's powerful wings as it flew barely overhead. The violent blast, just as she was turning around, sent her petite body careening forward, right into Lontas. His eyes shot open even wider as his upper body joined his legs, sliding over the edge of the bridge. His tender fingers blanched with effort, struggling to keep his tenuous grip.

"NO!" Bellae yelled, desperately grasping his wrists. She heaved with all her might. *Too heavy*, she realized. His weight pulled her forward to the edge of the bridge as the little progress she made evaporated.

"Don't let go!" Lontas pleaded. His fingers slipped off, and his life was now totally at the mercy of her straining, fledgling muscles.

Putting her feet against the ropes of the bridge for leverage, she pulled again. He slowly started to move up.

"Help me!" Bellae pleaded.

"Help you? I'm the one dangling here!"

A loud squawk pierced the air as the beast swooped directly for them. Their screams were inaudible over the ear-splitting cry of the creature.

Taking a deep breath, Bellae pulled with all her might. Lontas started to ascend. Suddenly, her feet slipped below the ropes and out over the edge of the bridge. Her body slammed into the bristly ropes as the air was knocked from her lungs.

"Lontas!" she wheezed, his wrists sliding from her clutches. With her body pressed against the ropes, the urgent desperation of her floundering arms struggled as his hands slipped through her fingers until she futilely grasped empty air. She could do nothing but weep as he screamed.

"Bellaaaaaaaaaaaaaaaaaaaaaaaahhhhhhhhhhhh!"

Looking down in horror she watched helplessly as the darkness swallowed him. The creature abruptly zipped upwards in front of Bellae, the force of its wings blasting her once again. She could feel the power and sensed the creature's blind excitement.

Bellae closed her eyes, *I'm going to die,* expecting its talons to shred her flesh.

Nothing.

Instead, the creature did a one eighty and whooshed downward right in front of her face. She opened her eyes to see the claw-like feet of the creature hurtling after Lontas, its mighty wings tucked tightly against its body to assist its dive.

"Down there, in the cemetery!" came a shout from tutor hill.

"Get more torches, wake up the reserve guards!"

This is all my fault. The creature or fall will surely kill him. Lontas was right, we shouldn't have come.

She searched the dark canyon, but the ocean of blackness and veil of tears obscured everything. A wave of nausea hit her as dreadful images flashed in her mind: dusky tombstones, creaky bridge, Lontas falling, sharp talons.

Torches streamed together to form a lake of fire right outside the tutor cottages. She numbly staggered up and headed down the bridge, *maybe they can find his body.*

She tried to yell for help, but felt too weak, a wave of exhaustion and grief tugged ruthlessly on her energy.

Unexpectedly, a rhythmic beating noise squirmed its way into her grief-stricken and exhausted brain. She felt something tighten on her right arm and shoulder followed quickly by a gentle, but brisk lifting sensation.

Suddenly, someone was next to her. Slowly she realized it was Lontas. Relief flooded her body. The fragile solace of seeing him was washed away as she realized the creature had them in his talons.

"Lontas!" His limp body slumped in the grip of the powerful creature. *Is he dead?* "Lontas?"

"Please, stop yelling," a voice rang out above her.

Reaching over, she felt a strong pulse in Lontas' neck. Scanning his body, she didn't see any new injuries. The wind rushing past her started to move faster. Through tear-stained eyes, she watched the ground whir by. Unexpectedly a sense of calm washed over her.

There's kindness in the creature, Bellae thought. *He didn't need our help, it wants to help us!*

She looked up to see powerful wings beating smoothly against the night air. Examining her own shoulder, she noticed how gently the massive talon was holding her. Despite her aching body, she felt relaxed and free flying through the air.

"We made too much noise. I will distract the guards while you two get out of here. I'm sorry we cannot talk now, but the day we spend lots of time together approaches. I have been watching you for a long time, and shouldn't have let you see me, but decided to move closer because the strange spirits invading the castle have become more powerful and emboldened. I don't know what they are, but I'm worried the Evil One is making a move against you," the creature said in a human voice, like that of a boy.

The ground slowly came into focus. Arching back, the creature deftly laid Lontas on the ground and then set Bellae next to him. Bellae struggled to make out his face, but it was quickly lost amongst the wing beats and darkness as he bolted into the sky.

"Wait!" Bellae called out. "Who are you? What are you?"

"Don't seek me out again, my friend. We'll meet soon enough. I am your guardian and will continue watching over you from a distance."

"Can I do anything for you?"

The creature let out a screeching laugh, "You're too nice. Just make sure you and your family stay safe. Lontas is smart, have him figure out what those spirits are and how to deal with them."

What had been a quiet flight turned noisy. The creatures' wings beat loudly and it let out several shrieking cries. Bellae peeked up over the tall wild grass to see the torches of the tutors and guards streaming towards the bridge as shouts of "There it is!" and "Get it!" arose from the mob.

A groan from Lontas grabbed her attention. She brushed the matted hair away as he struggled to open his eyes.

"You fell and the creature saved you! You're safe now."

At the mention of the creature, Lontas sat bolt upright. Images of the beast, the dark, the bridge, and falling all slammed through his mind.

"It's okay, he said we would talk soon."

"Soon?" Lontas mouthed, unconvinced of the creature's good intentions.

"He said you need to figure out what those spirits are," Bellae said, looking down sheepishly. Tears once again streamed down her cheeks. "I'm sorry I fell into you and can't believe I dropped you!"

She hugged Lontas so tightly he gasped. Suddenly, he began laughing.

"What?" she said, taken aback at his reaction.

"Maybe we need to start a 'Bellae trip counter,'" he said, bursting into heartier laughter.

"So not funny!"

A loud screech from the creature woke them to the current reality.

"He's distracting the tutors and guards. We need to move."

"You mean *they* are scaring it away. It was probably taking us to its lair to eat us when their shouts scared it off!"

"Lontas, seriously? I *felt* kindness in him, and he was so gentle. He could have ripped us to shreds or had us miles from here in a flash, but instead he specifically told me to leave. Plus, he has been watching me for a long time, and the only reason I saw him is because he's worried about these spirits. As I mentioned, he wants you to research them."

"The winged beast wants me to learn about the spirits?" Lontas said, a tinge of pride biting through the spinning sea of fearful emotions being stirred by an aching tiredness.

"He said you're smart enough to find out what they are."

Lontas smiled, "Actually, I have an idea where to look."

Slowly the two stood up and started the sluggish climb up the trail. With each sore step, they were reminded that it is always easier to walk down than climb back up.

"The creature's really trying to help?" Lontas asked.

"Yes, and he spoke to me in plain language. Do you know what he is?"

"I'm not sure. I didn't really see it. My priority will be to find out about these spirits. Are you certain it can talk in the plain language? You do talk to animals."

The idea gave Bellae pause. "I'm pretty sure, but not a hundred percent. Even though I could feel him *like* other animals, there's something different."

The fall winds were blowing harder now, and the promise of an abrupt end to the growing season echoed within the ruffling air. Despite the wind, the rows of crops, embarrassed to be caught in the act of changing into their autumnal browns, seemed to stand tall and stiff at attention.

They limped along in silence for several minutes before Bellae stopped. "Something's wrong."

Lontas looked into the darkness, "I don't hear anything but the forges."

The hair on the back of Bellae's neck was standing up as she scanned for trouble.

"Going somewhere?" a voice from the darkness startled their frayed nerves.

When will this night end? Lontas wondered despairingly.

"Are you all right?" a different, friendly voice asked.

"Finn?" Bellae called.

"It's me. Are you hurt?"

"We're okay," she answered, relief washing over her.

"I'm glad you're okay," said the first voice. "However, I might have to kill you for putting us through so much worry!"

"Scelto?"

"Yeah. Sorry I scared you. It's payback for the worry you put me through. I woke up to find you missing, and panicked. Gimelli would have flipped out, so I found Finn."

Finn used the igniting stones to light a torch.

"Good gracious!" he exclaimed. "I wish I hadn't lit that! Matted hair, dirty clothes, ripped cloaks, and bloodstains? Have you been fighting a wolf-bear?"

"It's a long, long story," Bellae answered.

"Try us."

"Promise not to tell anyone else?"

"Promise."

"Lontas and I have both seen a huge bird creature. He thought it was a demon, but I thought he needed help. He scared us when we thought he was a statue, but now we know he's nice!"

Leaning into Lontas she whispered, "Should we tell them about the ghosts?"

"No. The demon-thing is enough for now," he whispered back.

"You met a creature with wings and thought it was a statue, but it's nice?" Finn wondered in disbelief.

"Yes, we're telling the truth!" Bellae said.

"Where did you meet this scary, but nice, breathing statue?" Scelto asked.

"The cemetery."

"When Lontas fell off the suspension bridge I thought he was dead, but the creature saved him before all the tutors came," Bellae stated as Finn and Scelto exchanged stunned looks.

"Wait, wait, wait! You fell off the cemetery bridge?" Finn asked.

Lontas nodded.

"Falling off bridges, meeting a winged cemetery creature . . . statue thing, and looking as if you've been through the meat grinder," Finn said, shaking his head in amazement. "I guess we should be grateful you're alive!"

"I suppose we're going to Friar Pallium's office?" Bellae winced.

Finn chuckled. "I cannot, in good conscience, get you into trouble if you weren't off having fun. If he asks, I will tell the truth. Then again, I am not sure I even believe what you told me."

"Thank you," Bellae said.

"You must vow to never pull a stunt like this again!"

"Never, ever, ever!" Lontas uttered with earnest conviction.

"Not ever again," Bellae agreed.

"Well then, let's get you cleaned up and into bed. Your chores will still come due in the morning," Finn said. He whispered to Bellae, "No more crazy adventures, my Inion!"

Not sure I'll have much choice!

Chapter Four

Distant Journey, In-Steps, and In-Sides

Scroll 1: Factual Future? Blooming Blush

A gaunt-looking boy wearing blue Magician robes let out a malicious laugh. He grew in size: doubling, then tripling, faster and faster until he towered over Friar Pallium who let his sword and jaw drop in dismay. He looked around helplessly at his Knights' and squires' bodies lying in bloody heaps around him. Ritari, Finn, Lontas, Bellae, Sorea, and Gimelli were closest. His mantra of "Never give up. There's always a way to win," seemed absurd.

How can I fight this? Friar thought.

Hearing his name being called Friar swiveled his head but only saw dead bodies and the demonic young Magician whose face contorted and shook before changing into Jumeaux's.

"Jumeaux?"

Another vindictive laugh bellowed from the enormous Magician.

Someone began calling out his name with increasing urgency.

"Friar. Friar!"

"Who's there? Where are you?"

"Friar! FRIAR!"

Bolting upright, Friar woke to see Baiulus, the castle steward, standing over him, his eyes wide with alarm.

"Another vision?"

"Yet another. What's worse is I feel as if I haven't slept at all. They are so real . . ."

"What was it this time? Bellae, or the Proliate attacking Liberum?"

"Neither. It was a Magician with the face of Jumeaux," Friar answered. "I know it's tough being Luchar's squire, but he hasn't adjusted well. I believe he, like his sister Bellae, has a part to play in the time ahead."

"It seems ridiculous that Jumeaux could be the Chosen One."

"I know. But that's what Patuljak told me. Unlikely, but possible. Either way, those young squires will play a role in our future," Friar whispered.

"Well," Baiulus said, "there's one thing about the future, it comes whether we are prepared for it or not, and it's time for you to rise for the day."

Shortly before the morning horn, Scelto leaned close to Bellae, "You forgot to mention you stirred up the *ENTIRE* tutor camp and guard reserve in your little caper to the cemetery."

"I'm so sorry. It was my idea to look for the winged creature."

Scelto regarded her questioningly. He still had doubts about what they saw, but succumbed to her trustworthy eyes, "A winged monster, huh?"

"He's *not* a monster. He's good."

"Really?" he asked, smiling.

"Thanks again for looking out for me and Lontas."

"Just don't make a habit of it."

"Lontas, what's your problem?" Jumeaux howled. "You've been moaning all morning! I'm going to throw your clumsy butt to the dragon at the Tournament."

Lontas grimaced, but ignored the comment. The bumps and bruises from the Squire Battle and the previous night were haunting his every movement.

Scelto deftly moved to stand between them. "Back to work, Jumeaux, the horn is about to sound. Plus, you better bring extra underwear for when we see the dragon at the Tournament of Flags. It's going to be soil city for you."

"Are you really okay?" Gimelli asked Lontas.

"Yeah, thanks."

Scelto stopped to gaze at Gimelli. The two stared at each other in awkward silence while Scelto tried to calm his racing heart.

"Hey," he finally said.

"Hello . . . again," she replied, giggling.

"Give it a rest, you two," Jumeaux retorted, and quickly changed the subject. "So Lontas, what happened to you and Bellae? You two are acting like you fell from the towers. Now, Lontas I believe. That klutz can fall anywhere, anytime."

Bellae looked up in alarm, but Scelto answered, "Let it go, Jumeaux."

"*Lontas takes enough abuse from the Tilkeri Squad,*" Gimelli told Jumeaux telepathically.

"*You just focus on your boyfriend, Scelto.*"

"*He is not!*" Gimelli replied, blushing.

Scroll 2: Future to Ponder, Pondering the Future

"Bellae, would you come with me, please?" Friar asked later that day. She smiled politely and nodded.

Scelto and Lontas exchanged anxious looks, fearing she was in trouble for last night. She held back a grimace at the aches and pains serving as a reminder of yesterday's misadventure, gently squeezing Lontas' shoulder for reassurance.

"You have your dagger?" Friar asked.

"Yes." She drew back her cloak to show the hilt.

"Great. I want to add some skill to go with your new armament," he said as they walked to a small courtyard off the main bailey.

The two sat on a bench under a small tree within the grassy courtyard.

She decided to ask the question foremost on her mind, "So, Friar, what's going on with the . . ." she hesitated under his intense gaze, " . . . Dark Warriors?"

To Bellae's surprise, Friar Pallium laughed. "Dark Warriors, eh? Well, I can tell you I would prefer not to see them again. What have you heard?"

"Rumors about their attacks."

"There's never a shortage of rumors. That much I can tell you. Unfortunately, they are back, and we don't have the number of Knights we once had," he said softly, as if it were a secret. "Despite that, I think we have a role to play in the coming struggle."

Bellae thought of all the cached supplies she had seen, "You mean war!"

Friar stood up and calmly pulled his short sword. Bellae's self-congratulatory expression quickly faded. "Friar?" she whimpered, fearing she had offended him.

"Draw your weapon."

When she hesitated, he raised his eyebrows expectantly. Slowly she pulled out her dagger. As Friar's sword whizzed through the air, she managed to lean away and slash her dagger at his blade. The metal edges slammed together in an unfriendly *clang*.

"Friar?" she asked urgently.

"Use your training, trust yourself. From the beginning of your life to its end, you are all you really have."

Friar made her block strikes from various angles and strengths. Although she knew he was taking it easy on her, she had to work furiously to keep up.

"Remember, you will always be the smaller combatant, so don't take the full brunt of their attacks. Elude and deflect your opponents' blows until they make a mistake."

After what seemed like hours, Friar stepped back, "Well done. Shall we sit?" he asked casually, as if they had been on a lovely stroll instead of battling.

Her arms felt like wet noodles as she shakily sheathed her dagger. She stood motionless for a moment, catching her breath, and slowly wiping the cascades of sweat billowing down her forehead before alighting next to him.

"You mentioned war and I wanted to give you a small flavor of it," Friar said with a sly smile.

Bellae raised her eyebrows, "I definitely won't ask about it again!"

Friar laughed. "Many who have never experienced it like to imagine it is glamorous. In truth, war is ghastly and bloody chaos."

"That little 'war' was harder than I expected."

"War always costs more than you anticipate. Hostility takes over every facet of your accustomed life. It worms and digs its way into each tiny crevice, spreading, ripping, and shredding everything familiar. Eventually, the fighting reforms itself into a living, breathing reality that consumes everything you know."

"That sounds ridiculously awful!"

"War is a fierce, self-serving, and unforgiving master. It demands the surrender of your freewill as it dictates the future to you. Then, as a tribute of sacrifice, it requires nothing less than your friendships, humanity, love . . . all that makes life worth living."

"Why lead the Knights if war is so horrible?"

"There is always evil roaming the world, seeking to exploit the weakness of the virtuous. This is one of the few constants of life. Sometimes, fighting against the vile forces is not a choice but an imperative."

The two sat in silence as white wisps of clouds swirled lazily in the sky, forming and reforming under the sculpting hands of a slow wind. The same breeze was blowing tunefully through the trees and grasses which swayed in gentle music. Bellae's head ached while trying to grasp the nebulous and terrifying future taking shape. She thought about everyone who made up her life, imagining them training, studying, sleeping, laughing, loving–all the routine sights and emotions that made up her life at Liberum.

I couldn't stand to lose them or my life here. Should I tell Friar about the winged creature or the spirit?

Before she could decide, he spoke, "You have an important role in what lies ahead. In the little time we have before the future descends upon us, I hope to impart some knowledge, some grain of benefit that might help you . . . help all of us I guess."

"I wish you would stop saying that. What role could I possibly play?"

"Merely keep being yourself, train hard, and stay open-minded. Learn as much as you can before the Tournament of Flags."

"It's only, when you unsheathed your sword I felt so . . . nervous. How can I ever be ready for what you are saying?"

Friar smiled, "That nervous feeling before battle is simply nature's energy boost."

Bellae scrunched her nose at the peculiar comment.

"It's nature's adrenaline energy boost juice coursing through your veins!"

"Boost juice?" Bellae began laughing so hard, she nearly fell off the bench.

"Ah, certainly not my finest oration!" Smiling, Friar stood. "Speaking of the future, you need to prepare for our journey. Ritari has a plan for the next few weeks so we are organized for the Tournament."

Bellae was having a hard time comprehending Friar's comments and what exactly would be expected of her. Sighing, she moved towards the barracks.

"Bellae!" Luchar's angry voice rang out, "Why aren't you with the other squires? Ritari is outlining our preparation for the Tournament."

"I was talking with Friar."

"Were you?" he said, calming. "Well, what did Friar tell our favorite little squire?"

"He was talking about how war destroys everything. How it is super complicated. How . . ."

Luchar interrupted her with hearty laughter.

"Complicated? War? Nothing's further from the truth, dearest girl. I love Friar, don't get me wrong, but all rulers make this mistake. They take something simple and pure and twist it into something complicated. It's part of their job description. If only life were as straightforward as war.

"Two or more warriors stand across from each other and fight. The best and smartest side wins, the other side loses. War is simplicity: straightforward and uncomplicated. No blasted chatter. No fool leader talking out the side of his mouth. There are enough complicated things in life. Don't waste your time making simple things difficult.

"Now, go see Ritari. And make sure your bonehead brother has his act together."

Luchar's answer had immediate appeal to Bellae, especially when contrasted to Friar's convoluted and terrifying version.

Scroll 3: Getting Absorbed in Her Job

"Bellae!" Lontas called out. "Here, now!"

Smiling she ran towards her friend as he stood outside the large stone library. The front was meant to look like a castle, and the entire building was made up of a series of repeating turrets.

As she moved closer, her smile shriveled. Lontas looked pale, waving frantically in front of a pair of doors intended to look like a drawbridge.

"What is it?"

"Nishi!" he yelled before darting back into the library.

"Nishi?" she questioned, but Lontas was gone and the doors closed.

Bellae entered and scanned the large building. Reading tables and benches stood at attention down neat rows, each with several candles or lanterns. Around the edge, each circular turret held seven levels of books accessible by repeating coils of spiral staircases.

Finally, she spotted Lontas feverishly beckoning to her from the back and took off.

"Walk! I say walk, squire Bellae!" Bestilla, the librarian, yelled. "And be quiet!"

Bellae slowed, nodded, and then walked towards her friend who was tapping an open page on a massive codex.

"Nishi," he whispered.

Bellae leaned over and read the brief passage.

"They are night-spirits from Ifrean. Ifrean? Where the White Wizard and Dark Warriors are from?" Bellae asked.

"Yes, and no one has *ever* seen them in Verngaurd before. They are most powerful at night but can rarely be seen in the day. They always call a person's name *two* times!"

"Exactly what's happening to us!"

"Watch your voices! Soft whispers only!" Bestilla shrieked, despite the fact they were the only ones there.

"Sorry," Lontas apologized before continuing in a hushed voice. "It also says something about them being able to hypnotize you if you respond and follow them immediately after those two calls of your name. It goes on to mention something about becoming a 'soulless shade' forever in their power."

"That's horrible! What else?" Bellae asked as Lontas' face contorted into disappointment.

"Sorry, is that bad to ask?"

"No, but that's all I've found. Because they aren't ... weren't in Verngaurd, even finding this took me days. Since no one can legally trade with Ifrean, and the White Wizard is known to be outrageously tyrannical, there is almost no information on those lands. I did find mention of a reference book that contains more information on Nishi."

"Great!"

"Not really, it's crazy old and locked away in the Athenaeum section—for professors only!"

Bellae smiled at her friend.

"No. No!"

"What else do you want to do? No one is going to believe us and we need to find out how to get rid of, or at least fight, them!"

"Lontas!" Bestilla called.

Lontas smiled and stood up.

"No wait. Something's off ..." Bellae gasped.

"It's only Bestilla she ..."

"Loooooontas!"

Bellae was staring into Lontas' eyes when a white film dropped over them. His muscles slumped and his gait turned into a shuffle. Bellae turned to see Bestilla floating a few inches off the ground. Her glowing eyes were sunken with dark circles underneath and her mouth stretched into a vile grin.

"Bestilla?" Bellae asked, but the librarian did not break eye contact with Lontas, who continued tottering ahead.

Bellae moved towards Lontas, but Bestilla let out a horrifying, inhuman wail. Raising her arms, the librarian's body was engulfed in light. She chanted something, and a brisk gale surged through the room, blowing out all lanterns and candles.

Bellae trembled in the dark, she could hear Lontas limping towards the possessed librarian, her glowing white eyes providing the only light.

"It's not night, you're supposed to come at night!"

An evil laugh from Bestilla made Bellae falter, "The Evil One endowed us with extra power! Now, I get to have fun in the daytime!"

"Evil One? The White Wizard!"

Bestilla laughed again, "The White Wizard? You're cute. Ignorant, but cute. That's it my ordure, come to me squire!"

"What do you want with Lontas?"

"Not just him, you and your family too!"

Enraged at the mention of her family, Bellae ran blindly forward. She rammed her thigh against a bench, spun around, and fell hard. Undeterred, she rose, focusing on the terrifying light coming from Bestilla's eyes she sprinted towards them.

"I am the spirit of the East! On souls I feast! Come to me and you fade, forced to live your life as a shade!"

Bellae slammed into Lontas tackling him harshly to the ground. His head struck the floor hard, bounced up and hit again, knocking him out.

Bestilla's whole body shook as a bright light flashed creating a thunderclap noise. Her eyes stopped glowing and her body fell hard to the floor. Bellae looked up to see an angry looking spirit floating towards her. Her eyes were black, pushed deep in her skull surrounded by gaunt cheeks. Shimmering robes flowed down her body.

Figure 37: Bellae and Lontas encounter a Nishi spirit while in the library.

"You think you've won? I have a little secret for you, dearie, even if you manage to 'win' this battle with us, you will lose absolutely everything and everyone you love in this ordeal!" the spirit said as Bestilla started to groan. "This is the coming of Na Cearcaill, the recurring darkness!"

The door to the library crashed open, spreading a steady stream of light into the dark library. The spirit disappeared as Bestilla sat up.

"What the . . ." Lovag uttered, holding the door open.

"What's happening?" Bestilla asked. "How did I end up down here, and why are the candles and lanterns out?"

"Is Lontas okay?" Lovag asked, propping the door open before moving towards his squire.

Lontas began moaning softly.

"A huge gust of wind came through the library and blew out the lights. Lontas and I panicked and ran towards the door. He fell and hit his head. Bestilla was coming to help us when she fell," Bellae said.

Despite the explanation's obvious deficiencies, the adults seemed satisfied, as no other logical explanation would account for the calamitous scene.

"Let's get Lontas to a healer," Lovag said.

"I'll take him!" Bellae briskly interjected. "You two can get the candles and lanterns going . . . you know, for safety."

Bellae carefully observed her friend as she walked him to the Infirmary, "Sorry about knocking you down."

"Better than being taken by that thing and . . . turned into a soulless shade."

"Looks like we have another nighttime expedition!"

Lontas hesitated, but Bellae, remembering what it said about her family, was not backing down. "No way does this . . . Nishi thing get to come and terrorize me and my family!"

"Family?"

"It said it was coming after me and my family. That includes you, by the way," Bellae said, gently squeezing his arm.

"Tonight then?"

"Tonight."

Scroll 4: Innocence

Bellae's eyes fluttered, she struggled to understand what was happening. Slowly the giant smile on Lontas' face and the darkened squire barracks came into focus.

"I got to wake you up!" he whispered, barely able to contain his excitement. "It feels soooo wonderful to be on the other side!"

Bellae smiled deeply and hugged her friend. The two squires quickly got ready and cautiously peered out the door into the inky night. After making sure the area was clear, they quickly headed out. Once they had traveled twenty feet, a floating Bestilla, complete with glowing eyes and fiendish smile, rounded the barracks corner behind them and followed.

"Do you think we're breaking our promise to Finn?" Bellae asked. "I still feel sick about making up that story to Lovag and Bestilla."

"I'm pretty sure going to the library is totally different than the cemetery!"

"How do we get in?"

"No worries. I know the library like the back of my hand!" Lontas swelled.

"How does that help?"

"What?"

"How well do you know the back of your hand, and how does that help?"

Lontas looked confused, "I'm not sure, I guess I never thought about it."

Bellae burst out laughing, "I'm only kidding with you, although it's pretty silly!"

Lontas peered back and forth between his friend and the back of his hand, "Actually it's idiotic. I rarely even look at the back of my hands."

"So, you know how we can get in?"

"The Athenaeum section was actually an addition, added to the library when Liberum became the lead castle for the Knights after leaving Cumhacht."

"So?"

"So, we could fight our way through the library gates, then struggle through the pitch-black reading room, before encountering several locked doors inside or . . . we could sneak in a back window."

"Are you saying you've done this before?"

Despite the dark, Bellae could feel him blushing. "Lontas, you rascal!"

"Well . . . I . . . I . . . was just . . ."

"I'm totally joking, but seriously tell me."

"A couple years ago there were a few historical records that I wanted to research in the Athenaeum area, and one of the professors let me see the room. I noticed the row of windows, and may have unlocked the shutters when he wasn't looking."

Bellae laughed, but Lontas froze, they were at the library. A few torches were lit outside the door, but the rows of turrets created a massive number of sinister shadows.

"It would look creepy even if we hadn't had a Nishi attack us and hypnotize you," Bellae uttered.

Surprisingly, Lontas' face filled with rage, "No! Not this place! This is *my* library, *my* refuge! They can't have it!"

Impressed, Bellae nodded and lit a lantern before grabbing her friend by the arm. They marched together around to the back of the library where Lontas, with well-practiced efficiency, moved a stashed barrel next to the back wall. Holding up the lantern Bellae noticed a small piece of metal sticking out below the thick shutters. Lontas slid a rope through a hole in the metal and easily opened the shutters.

"You see the rope and my effort force easily overcome the load force of the . . . oh, I see, not the right time for physics," Lontas said, seeing Bellae's deadpan expression.

Bellae handed the lantern to Lontas and duplicated his technique for sliding through the window. Once in the Athenaeum she shivered, the memories of earlier in the day were too vivid and the shadows cast by the lantern too eerie as they bounced across row after row of shelves filled with scrolls, codices, and artifacts. The fireplace had a large stone hearth and mantle that covered the opening on all sides to protect the valuable books from sparks.

"You've done this more than once," Bellae said as Lontas moved comfortably along the room.

"I don't always stay and read in the barracks. This is my home, one of them anyway."

"Do as I do," Lontas said. He went to the front of the room and washed and rinsed his hands four times in separate washing stations. "The oils on our hands are bad for the manuscripts."

He then carefully placed a series of book supports wrapped in felt into a V-shape. "These will support and protect the codex, once I find it."

Lontas then set about scouring the Athenaeum's classification system.

"Wake up, *again!*" Lontas said, enjoying himself a little too much. "Twice in one night I get to rouse you. Good news, I've found the reference number!"

Bellae watched groggily and tuned out Lontas' description of how he could then locate the book as he moved fluidly in his home away from home.

"Do *not* bend the pages!" Lontas said after carefully propping open the book using the felt supports. He then painstakingly turned each page using a felt-tipped set of tweezers, looking for something on the Nishi spirits.

"Can you read this? What language even is it?"

"Hmm? Of course, I read it, them actually. This book has passages added over the last thousand years and . . ." Lontas started chuckling. "Here it is! Okay, night spirits . . . can cause possession . . .'"

"Tell us something we don't know."

"I'll summarize the highlights. So, they can only call your name twice in spirit form . . . can mimic any voice . . . take on any likeness, temporarily . . . you become hypnotized and under their control if you follow after they call your name . . . if it lasts too long, it leads to a *permanent* soulless life as a sullen shade . . . for brief periods, a Nishi can carry out full possession!"

"Lontas, you are not allowed to be possessed . . . or leave me for any reason!"

"That would be my strong preference!" Lontas said without looking up. "Okay, okay here's the good part, 'Centuries before the age of Kings, legend says a half-starved ascetic washed up on the shores of Verngaurd rambling about the Evil One and the coming end of days. In his brief periods of lucidity, he spoke of the Nishi, evil spirits of the dark, similar to what is in the text above. I include his verse here. However, I cannot attest its validity in protecting yourself should you encounter these specters:

> *Stay hidden unless the call is one or three,*
> *For a Nishi it could be.*
> *Seek to protect your back:*
> *Obsidian black,*
> *Iron or kyanite blue*
> *Can also do.*
> *Finally, neverita duplicate,*
> *Can avoid a sealed-soulless fate!'"*

"What? That's it? Disappointing."

"Not at all! This passage tells us everything we need to protect ourselves! Obsidian is relatively easy to find since it is a glasslike volcanic rock, and there are plenty of volcanoes in the Northern Dwarves' land. Iron is easy, obviously, and the neverita duplicate is the fancy name for a shark-eyed shell found all over the East Coast of Verngaurd."

"Shark-eyed?"

"It's simply a grey moon shell with a blue swirl on the side resembling an eye!"

"Will these things kill or only fight off the Nishi?"

"I'm not—" a loud knock on the door startled the squires.

"What do we do?" Bellae mouthed.

Lontas shrugged his shoulders as the pounding on the door increased.

"Hello, sister," a voice called from the other side of the door.

"Jumeaux?"

"Yes. Yes, it is."

"What are you doing here?"

"Please unlock the door, Lontas or sister Bellae."

"How did you know we were here?" Bellae asked as Lontas carefully put the codex back.

"I am your caring brother."

"Uhm, not so much with the caring, but okay. What do you want?"

"Just to talk to you two, my sister and friend."

Lontas' eyes widened, "No way is that Jumeaux. He would never call me friend! Plus he hasn't insulted me once. He's never gone more than a minute without hurling abuse!"

A bright light suddenly shone through the door as the head of a specter appeared. "You squire swine think you are sooo smart?"

The skeletal-like head had waving hair floating around it, as if underwater. It bared its foul teeth and screeched, "Open *this* door!"

Lontas leaned against the table, his knees buckling in fear. Without warning the ghostly head disappeared back to the other side of the door. Bellae grabbed Lontas' hand and they stared, waiting.

Another harsh pounding on the door commenced.

"Hey there kids, open the door," another voice called out. "You can't be in the library at this hour, and you're never allowed in that room!"

"Bestilla?"

"Of course it is. Now, I can unlock the door, but it's better if you let me in. There are a lot of different keys on this chain."

"Is anyone else out there?"

"Nope."

Despite her denial the squires could hear a conversation going on outside the door. Lontas looked at Bellae horrified. As the voices continued they could hear the jingling of keys. After several minutes of fumbling and arguing about which key they should try, the first lock clicked open.

Another spirit head popped through the door, "Soon! To keep you halfwits updated, we're coming in, and soon!"

Lontas jumped, "I seriously wish they would stop doing that! Out the back window!"

The squires turned to see three spirits floating outside the back windows. Lontas mumbled, "Iron," and ran to the fireplace, grabbing a fireplace poker as the last lock clicked open.

Bestilla and Jumeaux, both with glowing white eyes, floated into the room.

"Once I possess someone it is super easy thereafter!" the Nishi within the librarian said. "Did you find what you were searching for? Don't you stupid squires know to avoid reading? Take it from me, knowledge is a menace!"

Lontas brandished the iron fireplace poker at Bestilla.

"Go ahead and hit her! See if I care," the Nishi inhabiting the woman cackled.

"Bellae!" one of the Nishi from the window called.

"Don't look at it!" Lontas advised.

"Go to her, Bellae! It's your mother!" the ghost said through Bestilla.

Bellae looked up in horror, one of the ghosts had taken the same, somehow familiar, face of the woman Bellae had seen during their late-night adventure to the cemetery.

"Belllllllllll-aaaae!" the beautiful spirit called again.

Is that what my mother looked like?

"Come with us to the Evil One now and your suffering will be quick and semi-quasi-painless!" Bestilla howled.

"Resist, and you shall know a hundred lifetimes of pain in the few miserable months you have left to live," the spirit said. Bellae shivered at hearing her brother's voice mixed with the Nishi's.

Lontas jabbed the iron poker towards Jumeaux, when it hit him the ghostly light behind his eyes flashed and the spirit within let out a roaring wail.

"Iron? Do that again and I put it through your head, boy! Last warning scum! Your innocence is forever deceased! It's only a matter of how *much* suffering you endure! Obviously, you found the book about us. No matter, other things, not in books, will come for you!"

Bestilla and Jumeaux floated towards the squires, their whited-out eyes stared viciously, unblinkingly forward as their mouths contorted into demented grins.

With a sudden burst of speed, Bestilla flew to Bellae, grabbing her by the neck and chest then zooming upwards until she slammed the squire to the ceiling. Bellae gagged, kicking and flailing with her back plastered to the ceiling. Lontas swiped at Bestilla with the poker, but missed. He didn't have time to try again as Jumeaux hurtled towards him.

Swinging wildly, Lontas smashed the poker into Jumeaux's head. The Nishi wailed in agony, and shot out of Jumeaux as the squire's body crumpled to the floor.

Lontas swung at the flying spirit. The poker seemed to cut it in two as the semi-transparent form disappeared with a loud swishing sound. The Nishi outside the window began to screech, their malevolent faces morphing into rage.

"Someone comes!" one howled before the Nishi beyond the windows disappeared.

The door to the Athenaeum slammed open. "Let her go!" Finn thundered.

The possessed Bestilla turned, her face contorting with anger, "Back away bark-boy!"

"You will not hurt my Bellae!" Finn yelled, his voice shaking with rage.

"Anything iron!" Lontas called out as Bellae's face began to turn blue and her eyes fluttered.

"Make a move and I will kill this squire-pup!" Bestilla said.

Finn nodded to the poker in Lontas' hand, then sprinted towards a table in the center of the room. He pointed to Lontas while jumping up on the table in a single leap.

Lontas threw the poker, it was off the mark, but Finn managed to kick it up with his foot, then contorted his body to grab it while vaulting towards the ceiling where Bestilla had Bellae pinned.

He slammed the poker on the librarian's back, tossed the poker towards Lontas, then grabbed Bellae as the spirit released her.

Finn fell to the table, but managed to somersault backwards to dissipate the force, rolling until eventually landing with Bellae safely on the floor. Bestilla dropped hard, a nauseating *crack* signaling she had broken at least one of her legs as the spirit howled in frustration.

"There is no escape from the pain you simpleton squires! You are all going to die! Trust me, you will hear from us again. You have *no* idea what is coming for you!"

"Suck on this!" Lontas yelled.

He tripped on his way to the Nishi, but managed to swing the poker Finn had thrown to him, and swatted the spirit away.

At that moment, Friar burst through the door. "Is Bellae okay?"

Finn looked taken aback by Friar's appearance and passionate concern. "She seems okay. She passed out but is breathing."

Jumeaux started groaning loudly, reaching for his sore head. Lontas drew back the poker and wacked him on the top of his head, knocking him out again.

"Lontas!"

"What? I'm just being cautious! The Nishi may have come back," Lontas said, sheepishly trying to hide his pleasure.

"Nishi?" Finn wondered.

"That's what those ghost things are," Lontas said.

"I thought they were a myth," Friar said, moving to examine the still unconscious Bestilla.

"They're not, but Bellae and I found out a few things to protect us from them."

Lontas explained what had happened, what the Nishi said, and what they had learned as Bellae and Jumeaux woke up.

"Did I mention I take this Inion business seriously?" Finn chuckled nervously, grateful that she seemed okay.

Bellae snuggled into his side, "Thanks, and I'm sorry for going out at night again."

"Why does my head hurt?" Jumeaux asked. "Why . . . where am I?"

"Finn, take Jumeaux, who was *sleepwalking* and fell, back to his barracks and send several healers urgently for Bestilla. I want to talk with Lontas and Bellae," Friar ordered. "Oh, and Finn, keep this information between us, for now."

Bellae began sobbing after Finn and Jumeaux left. "That spirit said, my 'innocence is forever deceased.' What's happening?"

Friar sighed, "I wish I could change this reality for you, or at least delay it, but the simple truth is the storm is here and getting stronger. The good news is that whether you come out of the other end stronger or splintered is up to you, and how you handle the journey."

Bellae stopped crying but buried her face in Friar's robe.

"Both of you need to rely on yourselves and each other. Keep fighting and this struggle will make you stronger."

Lontas moved and put his hand on Bellae's shoulder, he already knew there was something else going on with Bellae, all her extra training and meetings with Friar. Now he understood why Friar was interested in him, he was connected with whatever "this struggle" was as well.

"Let's get you to bed, I will post a guard outside your building. It was lucky Finn was on duty tonight." Friar paused. "I think I know someone who can help us make some custom protection pieces based on the information you discovered."

Scroll 5: Attending to Business

"I'm so happy we're finally close to leaving for the Tournament!" Gimelli said.

"I don't know," Lontas ventured. "We're going to miss classes."

"Oh no, 'we're going to miss classes!' Boohoo!" Jumeaux said spitefully. "You are *sooo* lame."

"How's that headache?" Lontas mumbled to himself, stifling a laugh.

"Jumeaux, do you have to be negative all the time?" Scelto asked. "Don't worry, Lontas. Friar made sure we won't be penalized for being gone."

Gimelli quickly changed the subject, "Jumeaux, don't forget to pack your nice clothes for the opening ceremony and your nightshirt."

"I have no *Knight* shirt," Jumeaux said, lackadaisically sitting on his bed.

"We both know you do."

"I can tell you with complete confidence that I don't own, nor have I ever owned, a *Knight* shirt."

Cocking her head to one side, Gimelli giggled playfully. "Jumeaux, don't act so strange, you wore it last night."

"Strange?" Jumeaux repeated in mock surprise. "It's strange to me that all of you think I'm a Knight. I am but a humble squire who has no shirt of a Knight."

The other squires groaned as Jumeaux laughed.

"Jumeaux, everyone's nervous about leaving," Gimelli said telepathically.

"It's called humor. Lighten up."

"Come on! That was funny!" Jumeaux said out loud.

"We don't have time for this," Scelto fumed.

"What about time for *that* or the *other thing*?" Though Jumeaux giggled at first, his expression quickly morphed into anger when the others did not share in his merriment. "Don't you get it? Scelto said 'No time for *this*.' Then I said, '*that* or the *other thing*.' This, that, and the other thing?"

"Jumeaux! Pack your nightshirt or don't, just get ready. We still need to help our Knights," Scelto said.

"Are they wearing their *Knight* shirts?" Jumeaux asked as the others groaned again.

Bellae knelt and gently pulled up a floorboard under her bunk.

"Borb, Grym?" Bellae called in Ainmhi Caint.

A few small squeaks echoed back followed by faint scratching.

"Hi, guys! Here are some cheese treats from Chef Cookie."

"Thanks, Bellae." Grym's small, black tail wagged ferociously side-to-side, reminding Bellae of a dog.

"I'm sorry, but I have to leave the castle for a few weeks."

Both mice looked up in horror.

"Don't worry, I'll stock you up with plenty of food," she said, trying to sound reassuring. *"Please stay out of sight and . . . do your business outside."*

"Our business? Do you mean the business of living? Eating?" Grym asked, playing naive while rolling a mound of cheese into a ball with his front paws.

"Your dirty business," Bellae replied. *"I don't want to see any of your feces, droppings, manure . . . whatever you want to call it, around the barracks!"*

"Oh, come now. A few strategically placed in Jumeaux's bed would serve things well. In fact, we can move our nest up there while you are gone!" Grym squeaked, starting in on the cheese.

Bellae smiled before thinking better of it. *"You'll do no such thing!"* she said, louder than she intended.

"Are you talking to those two poop monsters?" Jumeaux asked with a sickened grimace. "Disgusting mice!"

As Jumeaux approached, the two scurried under the floorboard. Bellae stomped it down just as Jumeaux's head peeked under her bed.

"Where are the buggers? My bed still stinks from the shite they left last month!" Jumeaux's face turned scarlet with anger and disgust.

"I'm going to . . ." Jumeaux's voice trailed off as Scelto emerged.

"Leave it alone," Scelto said menacingly.

Jumeaux stood his ground, sizing up his resolve. Satisfied that Scelto was serious, Jumeaux backed away.

"All right, everyone, fifteen minutes and we're heading over to finish the supply wagons. Tomorrow, we pick our horses," Scelto said.

Bellae squealed with delight. "Horses! Yay!"

Jumeaux rolled his eyes, but said nothing.

Scroll 6: What Is Sleep?

Later that night, Friar glanced out the window into the oppressive blackness that was conspiring with the autumn chill to mercilessly push through the windows. The fire was losing ground, and the candles' flames wobbled weakly, struggling to hold back the hostile darkness.

"Friar?" Baiulus said. "Are you still with me?"

"Yes and sorry. It has been a long night."

The castle steward ran his fingers though his short, black hair and sat down. As he did, he let the papers he was holding fall to the table. They joined legions of others spread haphazardly. Some layers indicated the hours of work already completed, while others showed how much still needed to be done.

"May I speak freely?" Baiulus asked, gesturing questioningly with his hands.

"Of course."

"These preparations are extravagant and costly, especially when we don't even know whether war will come. With our dwindling resources, are we acting irrationally?"

"War is always a question of who and when, not if," Friar replied.

"Okay, I get it, the Dark Warriors are back. However, most of the elaborate plans you have focus on the Proliate. At least on paper they are still our allies."

"My dreams are powerful, almost palpably authentic. I absolutely do not want to fight the Proliate or order these preparations. However, I feel compelled to follow my visions. I am certain that, sooner or later, we will have need for these arrangements," Friar said, ending in a shivering yawn born of fatigue and nightmares of what his father lost or gave away of the Knight's power and prestige.

"If I've offended . . ." Baiulus started.

"For the love of Verngaurd! We know each other too well for such formality! As the old saying goes, 'If you have a friend who only flings flatter, you will soon find out it's fecal matter.'" Both burst into a genuine laughter that comes only after toiling at a grueling task, when the tired brain cries out for distraction.

"That's the worst joke ever."

"Oh, I doubt it's the worst. As with all jokes, there is truth hidden within. I don't want empty praise. I need honest opinions."

The two men silently slumped in their chairs, exhaustion teaming up with gravity to accentuate their slouching frames.

"I have to admit that when the three suns rise and spread their warmth, logic grabs hold of my plans and shakes them so hard they fracture around me," Friar finally said. "However, as the suns set, my nightmare visions reconstruct their necessity."

Baiulus frowned. "Sometimes I think the glaring light of day hides the truths that can only be perceived in the shadows of the night. It is only in the darkness, away from the comfort and mirage of welfare that flourishes within the bounds of sunlight, that we awake to see the true reality of our circumstances."

"Look at you becoming philosophical."

"I can't comprehend your visions, but I do trust *you*. We were discussing the placement of the new outer walls. Hollowed stones will not be strong enough . . ."

"Ah, but that's the point. Their strength is in their ability to deceive, and Hephaestus will come through with a copy of the castle gate and second moat."

"I think I understand. Anyway, are you excited about returning to Cumhacht?"

Images born from childhood within the beautiful glistening white marble buildings raced through Friar's mind. Memories of the great libraries and gathering halls, his friends and his father all came hurtling back.

Friar shook his head and the images withered, "Cumhacht died and the Citadel was born the day we abandoned it to the Proliate and Magicians. I know nothing is permanent in this world, but that was a magnificent city. I hope I'm making the right decisions so the Knights don't get caught off guard and lose anything else. Which reminds me, you were telling me about our patrols and outposts before I interrupted you earlier."

"Much, much earlier," Baiulus said, chuckling out of exhaustion rather than humor.

"Unfortunately, there are still sporadic and unpredictable Dark Warrior attacks. We simply have too few Knights to adequately patrol our assigned areas. Your idea of concentrating our forces on various sections in a sweeping rotation was a good idea, but the Dark Warriors adapted to this tactic, and now attack right after we patrol an area.

"As you know, the individual countries are building greater and greater national armies to defend their own borders—giving less into our coffers."

"I could have done with good news."

"It gets worse. More communities are inviting the Proliate in. Of course, they have to build a temple and start worshiping Tallcon before they will help."

"You've got to be kidding me!"

"The villages are desperate." Baiulus responded, raising his hands up as if ridding himself of any responsibility before continuing.

"One new trend is a sharp decline in support from our Southern Dwarf 'allies.' Our friends in the Rebelde Plains have increased their exports, so the supply of iron ore and other raw materials have not decreased. However, their limited supplies make this a short-term fix."

"Ah!" Friar huffed in frustration. "The Southern Dwarves have always been unreliable in everything but greed."

"They are supplying the Proliate who pay more," Baiulus added.

"When was the last time we had a solid recruit from any of our main supporters: the Elves of Creber, the Rebelde Plains, or the Northern Dwarves?" Friar asked rhetorically, knowing it had been a long time.

"If our allies don't support us, how can we expect the more fickle countries to give their share of assistance? The Southern Dwarves, Western Elves, Piscians, and Agerians are sick of promises of the return of our strength."

"I can't blame them," Friar admitted. "With the Dark Warriors back, the safety of their people trumps loyalty to us, and the Proliate are strong."

"Oh, any other ghostly attacks on Bellae and Lontas?"

"No, the primitive defenses and extra guards seem to be working, the Northern Dwarf King is sending someone who apparently knows of these Nishi. He did caution that the man is . . . eccentric and sometimes exceedingly hard to deal with."

"Eccentric? Great, just what we need! The world is changing, becoming more terrifying!" Baiulus exclaimed.

"Even when they don't venture into our view, the vile creatures of the world are there, hiding and waiting."

The two embraced cordially and Baiulus left, eager to mine a little sleep out of the fleeting night. Once alone, Friar shivered with fear. A deep-seated uneasiness about the future had been growing ever stronger in his mind.

"Conquering what you are afraid of might be a reasonable definition of a true hero, but it doesn't make it any easier," Friar said to himself, feeling alone and uncertain.

Will the Knights be destroyed in the coming storm? History judges my father as the Friar who threw away the Knight's power. How will I be judged?

His eyes felt heavy when images of Supreme Master Magician Veneficus walking with his father down the glorious halls of Cumhacht came flooding back.

I shall seek Veneficus' consul as my father did so many times before, Friar thought before falling asleep where he sat.

Scroll 7: Awake to Prepare, Prepare to Awake

Clang-clang-clang! A sword pounding against a shield rang through the Pantteri barracks. Bellae startled awake, desperately reaching for her mice friends, Grym and Borb. Her hand finally stumbled onto their soft fur as Scelto continued banging.

Borb's raggedy ears flopped lazily about his head, "*What's that fool doing?*"

"*Get under the floorboards. I'll see what's going on.*" Bellae said, gently scooting them into their house.

"Up and at 'em Pantteri squires!" Scelto said. "We need to go!"

"What blasted time is it?" Jumeaux asked, lying in bed with his eyes closed.

"It's four in the morning, and time to get moving if we're going to finish our preparations for the Tournament of Flags and pick horses!" he said, mercifully stopping the racket.

"All right!" Gimelli said. "This is going to be great!"

"Can you give the one-girl-cheer-show a break today?" Jumeaux chided.

"I'm excited and there's no reason I can't show it."

"Is making me want to vomit a good enough reason?"

Bellae was quickly standing next to Scelto, holding on to his arm, and bobbing up and down with unbridled excitement. "Can I pick any horse?"

"Well . . ." Scelto started.

"No way!" Jumeaux interjected. "They're not giving you some destrier-war steed, if that's what you're thinking. A shrimp like you will get a pygmy horse!"

"Jumeaux!" Scelto roared. "Shape up, or you'll ride a donkey!"

"I was just trying to bug her," Jumeaux said, a little taken aback.

"I know, J, but take it easy today."

"Good morning, Scelto!" Gimelli said cheerfully.

"Hey!" Scelto said, his mouth wearing a wide grin.

"Can he ever greet you with anything other than, 'Hey'?" Jumeaux teased.

"Ready to get your horse?" Scelto finally asked Gimelli.

"Not as excited as Bellae, but close."

"Ha! See, Jumeaux. He said something else!"

"Congratulations, you have my permission to marry."

"Gimelli, will you and Bellae see Cookie about the food for our trip? She'll give you two the best rations," Scelto stated.

"No problem."

"Great. The rest of us will finish with the weapons and other supplies."

Ritari burst through the door, "Everyone ready?"

"Yes, sir," Scelto said.

"Great. We have a lot to do, so you need to pick your horses quickly!" Ritari clapped his large hands together, "All right, Pantteri, move out."

The squires followed him through the early morning darkness to the stables. The entire complex was illuminated with a substantial series of lanterns. Multiple barns were visible beyond the wooden fence encircling a large exercise yard.

"Is that Finn?" Lontas asked.

Bellae could hear her Knight arguing loudly next to a large crowd restraining a struggling horse inside the fence.

"Where are you going?" Ritari yelled as Bellae took off in a sprint. "Finn!"

"He can take care of himself!"

She began to make out what Finn was shouting, "Quengeln, give this horse to me!"

Bellae had been expecting Quengeln to be a hulking, boisterous man, as Finn rarely yelled. Instead, she saw a gruff-looking elderly man, his scraggly white hair escaping in quiet desperation from underneath the burgundy-riding hat of a groom. His face was cut deep with wrinkles and leathery brown from decades of exposure to Verngaurd's suns. He wore a black shirt and trousers overlaid with a burgundy short cloak that arched along a spine curved spitefully by age. His gnarled left hand trembled on a walking stick.

Suddenly, a deep, searing pain cut into Bellae's side. She winced and fell to her knees, desperately looking for the source. Someone had jabbed a pole into the side of the horse Finn was quarreling about.

The elderly groom continued in a firm, but slightly shaky voice. "Finn, this dumb brute of a filly sauntered up to our gates out of the blue two months ago, and has been nothing but trouble ever since. My best trainers haven't made an inch of headway. Plus, you are leaving for the Tournament and have no time to train this unbroken beast."

"Bellae!" Finn called out as she pushed past him in a full sprint.

The horse she had felt came into full view. A massive golden-brown mare was writhing under the taut ropes of a dozen struggling stable hands.

"This is the last time we have to put up with this garbage!" one howled.

"Horse burgers for breakfast, boys!" another proclaimed to a round of laughter.

The horse regarded Bellae carefully as she ran up. Its eyes, radiating sadness and fury, bore into Bellae's heart. Buoyed by her anger and the horse's desperation, Bellae thundered, "Stop, and release that horse!"

Everyone, including the mare, stared incredulously. A few snickers came from the grooms as they beheld the small squire.

"What sh' say?"

"Everything will be okay," Bellae said to the horse. A flicker of hope flashed behind the black eyes of the horse at the realization they could communicate.

"Is she singing to it?"

"Gurl, what do you think you're doing? This dangerous horse is about to be put out to the pasture in the sky, if you get my drift. Move along!"

Bellae looked at him with all the fierceness her young body could muster. "I'm not going anywhere! You release her!"

Finn smiled, *My amazing Inion.*

"Stay calm while I work this out," Bellae told the mare, observing a slight nod, the best response the taut ropes would allow.

"Hold on, hold on here," Quengeln called, hobbling over to Bellae.

"Stop this before you get injured. Aren't you here to get a horse for the Tournament? So, go and get one! Won't that be nice?"

"No, I don't think so. It'll be 'nice' when you let this horse go and back away!"

The mare rocked a little under the biting ropes.

"You're exciting the horse, gurl. Let us do our work!"

Without warning, a sharp stabbing pain racked Bellae's side as the horse shivered in pain. Bellae's knees buckled, but she did not fall. She looked up to see a groom poking a sharp stick into the horse's side.

"See, she's stirring up the horse! Somebody get this crazy girl out of here!"

"Bellae!" Gimelli called as the other squires caught up with her. Ritari motioned for her and the others to stand back and let Finn handle it.

"Stop exciting this horse! I'm losing my patience. Come now, and I'll get you a quality riding horse, a nice palfrey, eh? No hackney for you. What do you say?"

"I would say your men pulling the ropes tight enough to cut her skin and the twit jabbing a stick into her side are responsible for 'exciting' the horse!"

"You want to be ground into meat with this beast?" the elderly man asked, his patience evaporating.

"All I can tell you is one way or another, we are leaving together."

"Finn, get this crazy kid under control before I call the guards, if not Friar himself!"

Bellae saw the panic welling up in the mare's eyes, *"I swear on my life I will not leave without you!"*

"What's this sing-songy nonsense? This gurl is not right in the head," Quengeln uttered in disgust.

"She has a gift with animals," Finn said. "Release the horse."

"This is ludicrous!" Quengeln shrieked. "Four of our best grooms have already been hurt. This ends today! Your lunatic gurl thinks she can handle *this* horse? Absurd! You there, get the guards. The rest of you, take this horse to the slaughter house, now!"

The grooms tightened the ropes further, and began to drag the horse away.

"Noooo!" Bellae cried, wincing in pain as the horse fought.

"Wait, wait!" Finn said. "Please wait! Give Bellae one chance. If she can ride the horse, we will move her to the Pantteri stables, and she will be off your hands."

"Preposterous!" Quengeln spouted.

"What do you have to lose? Captain Ritari can be witness to our pact. The full responsibility of what happens will be on us. If I'm wrong, we'll leave you to your business."

Quengeln mulled the offer. "One try and you'll leave?"

"Yes."

A sly, self-satisfied smile carved its way through the old groom's parched wrinkles. "Ritari, you take responsibility if this gurl, or anyone else, gets hurt?"

"I do."

"You expect us to simply release her, then?" Quengeln asked.

Finn looked to Bellae questioningly.

"I can get them to release you, but I need two favors. First, you must stay calm. Second, if you are to come with us, you need to let me ride you. The horse nodded as best she could. "Release her!"

The dozen grooms laughed.

"This is insane! We've been looking forward to seeing this nightmare boiled!" one of them complained.

"Go on. Release her," the old stableman said to loud groans of disapproval.

Bellae could feel the horse's relief as she was freed from the ropes.

"Thank you," she said, finally able to speak once the ropes were removed. The horse's sweet and light voice seemed at odds with her huge size.

"You're welcome. What's your name?"

"Honey. I feel as if I have known you a long, long time already."

"We will become great friends!"

"Her name's Honey!" Bellae said excitedly.

"This horse's name is Brute," Quengeln said with more than a hint of disgust.

"Actually, it isn't."

"Are you hurt?"

"Not really. But I have to do one thing before you can have a ride."

Without looking, Honey kicked the stick out of the hand of the groom who had been poking her. The stick shattered under the powerful blow, and the man's arm was flung backwards.

"Scared the water out of ya'?" Ritari laughed.

Bellae peered around Honey to see the front of the man's trousers darken with moisture. He turned and ran as the other grooms laughed. Honey stamped triumphantly and neighed what sounded like a snicker.

"I'm ready," Honey said in a merry tone.

"Finn, help me up, please."

"I doubt the beast will let us put on a saddle before it throws you off and breaks every bone in your body, but we can try," Quengeln said derisively.

"Do you need one?" Finn asked.

"We'll be fine."

"I didn't realize how large she is. I've never seen a stallion this large, much less a mare."

Bellae was filled with an instant feeling of harmony as she slid onto

Honey's back. The grooms gasped as the vast mare bolted with the small girl effortlessly floating on her back. Bellae could feel and anticipate Honey's darting movements, easily shifting her weight to match. After a vigorous sprint around the yard, Honey trotted up to Quengeln and neighed loudly, spraying spittle all over his face and hat.

He wiped it off, muttering, "I didn't think . . . didn't know . . ."

Bellae and Honey marched over to Finn, "I've found my horse!"

"Looks that way," he said, chuckling. "I'm proud of you."

Bellae smiled brightly, kissing her Inion medal before putting it back under her cloak.

"Why don't you introduce Honey to Crann, and get her settled while we pick out some hackneys for the others," Finn said.

"All right," she replied. *Let's go, my friend. I have someone to introduce you to.*"

"*Bellae always has to show off and be the center of attention,*" Jumeaux complained to Gimelli.

"*You have got to be kidding me, Jumeaux. She genuinely cares about that horse and just saved its life. She wasn't showing off.*"

"*Looked like it to me.*"

"*J, you should be looking out for your sister, not criticizing her.*"

"*You mean like your boyfriend, Scelto, looks out for you?*"

"Jumeaux, give it a rest," Gimelli said out loud.

Scroll 8: Lesson and Learning

"I heard you made quite the impression at the stables today," Friar said later that afternoon.

Bellae smiled but, breathing heavily, said nothing.

"I'm glad you put those stable boys in their place. They need to treat those horses better. An apple can be better than a lash.

"Let's resume your training. Keep your vision centered on mine, but *see* my entire body and the field of battle. Be alert for another attacker from the side or back. Anticipate moves . . . look for openings and watch for any weakness in your opponent. If you see one, exploit it vigorously."

"Block!" he shouted as he thrust an overhead blow upon her.

Bellae raised her dagger and blocked. The vibration rattled down her arms and into her chest.

"Muscles move before the weapon. Look for any twitch to anticipate their strike. Remember to angle your blade and move so that part of the force is deflected."

Right when Bellae's arms were about to give out, he told her to stop.

"Now, close your eyes and take deep breaths. Feel. Listen. Learn to process each sound, recognizing in an instant if it is danger or something to ignore. This takes time and practice. Feel the rhythm of the world and its energy swirling around you."

Bellae listened to the wind on the trees and the grass rustling. Slowly, she began to envision waves of energy cascading across the world around her.

"Now," Friar said, startling Bellae from her trance. "Listen and *feel* how the blade slices the air, separating the energy flowing around you as a warning."

She squinted more strenuously and listened to his sword whistle around her.

"It has been a long day. Why don't you head back to the barracks?"

"Okay, Friar. Thanks."

"You're welcome."

On a hunch, she headed to the gatehouse. As she approached Rhyfeler, the constable of Liberum in charge of the gatehouse and defense of the castle, waved, "Looking for Lontas?"

"He's here then?"

"Of course! It's good you came. He has more books than usual in his hideout!" Rhyfeler said, laughing so hard his unruly, yellow hair bounced above his scruffy face. Leaning into the gatehouse, he yelled, "Bellae's coming up for Lontas!"

Bellae walked through the open wooden door that served as the back gate, running her fingers over the steel studs. A moat and drawbridge served as the first line of defense and were followed by a thick, heavily studded front gate. If an intruder made it past that, they entered a long, narrow hallway with two metal portcullises on either end. The ceiling above was lined with openings called murder holes used to fire projectiles, drop rocks, or pour boiling liquids on any attacker that made their way through the first portcullis. If they managed to get past all of that, they still had the back gate to deal with.

After reaching the second floor she entered a door to her right that led to the room above the hallway with all the murder holes. Several pits for boiling unpleasant liquids along with many weapons lined the room. Lontas was lying on his stomach reading with books and scrolls scattered about. The torches were lit and the arrow loops let in a little of the fading sunlight.

"Interesting book?"

"It is. I heard you coming but wanted to finish this page."

Bellae nestled close, laid her head on the small of his back, and a wave of fatigue closed around her. She shut her eyes, *I'll rest for a bit.*

"Bellae! Wake up!" Lontas declared urgently.

She slowly came around. "Did I fall asleep?"

"For quite a while."

"Hey, you two, I said get back to your barracks!" Rhyfeler yelled from the hallway below. "We're about to drop the portcullises for the night."

Bellae whipped her head around to see pitch-blackness glaring at her from the arrow loops. "Oh no!" she exclaimed. "I'll help you get your books back."

"Thanks."

The two squires quickly gathered up the books and scrolls.

"Release the front portcullis!" Rhyfeler yelled.

They could hear the Knights on the floor above releasing the brake on the winch. With loud groans and angry creaking, the portcullis dropped with a deafening thud. The two friends burst down the small stairway and ran through the cloud of dust thrown up from the front portcullis landing.

"Lontas and Bellae are through, release the back portcullis!" the constable cried as the two squires ran towards the library.

"You two!" Friar yelled.

The squires slowed.

"Once you return those to the library, Baiulus will lead you to my private foundry. We have some business to take care of."

"Okay, Friar!" Bellae said.

"Are we in trouble?" Lontas whispered.

"I guess we'll find out."

Scroll 9: That's Normal

"With all due respect Friar, I once again advise against letting that loon in here!" Rhyfeler exclaimed. "How do you know this Trelos character?"

"He has my permission to enter," Friar said simply.

"But, he is absolutely out of his mind . . ."

"Let him in and escort him to my foundry as discretely as possible."

Friar left the petulant Rhyfeler and joined Finn, Bellae, Lontas, and Baiulus in his private foundry with Hephaestus.

"In there!" Rhyfeler shouted, nudging a feeble-looking man through the door before shutting it. The diminutive man wore a disheveled brown robe and carried two large satchels, making it hard to tell if his hunched back was from deformity or the weight of the bags. His long, narrow face grew a pointed nose between black eyes protruding so far you could see white around the entire iris.

"Welcome! I am Friar Pallium, and you are?"

"I'm human! By the heavens are you *insane*?" the small man yelped.

"One of you is," Finn whispered.

"What have I gotten myself into," the protuberant-eyed man said, scanning the room nervously. Suddenly, he jumped more than walked forward, proceeding to invade their personal space, sniffing each of them in turn.

"Uhm . . . is this normal?" Hephaestus asked.

"Of course, it's normal!" the man said, still smelling Bellae. He was so diminutive and hunched that they were of similar height. "Sniffing is a well-established method of determining my safety! Unless, you don't care about my welfare?"

The man pointed at Lontas, "Are you peeing normally?"

Lontas paused, taken aback by the question, "Uh, sure . . . I guess."

"Why would you have to guess? Does someone urinate for you?"

"Uh?"

"You!" he said, switching to Bellae. "Are blackberries black?"

Bellae shook her head in speechless confusion.

"Or . . . is all visible light simply absorbed by objects appearing black? If that is so, what color are they really?"

"What's your name, friend?" Friar asked.

"Trelos! Now, you, old man!" he said to Friar. "Can walking in circles get you to a destination?"

"It depends on how big of a circle and where you are going, I would guess," Friar said. "Do these questions help you?"

"No of course not! What are you a brain trauma victim?" Trelos howled.

"Watch it little man!" Hephaestus grunted.

"Watch what?"

"Be respectful! Watch what you say," Finn said.

"I cannot imagine a circumstance where one could *see* what they are saying. Are you suggesting you *see* spoken words? Do you also *hear* voices no one else does?"

"Friar, seriously?" Hephaestus complained.

"Are you the armorer?" Trelos asked, but continued before Hephaestus could reply. "Does iron melt at a lower temperature if it is very, very, very, very hot outside? If so, how many 'verys' would it take? Wait!

Don't answer that, I wouldn't trust your answer anyway, you smell odd."

"Perhaps we should step back and introduce ourselves—" Friar started.

"How would knowing your names help me?"

"It is customary—"

"It's customary in Jaa for their warriors to jump into freezing water, that doesn't mean we all have to, does it? Do you expect me to swim in freezing water?"

"No, but I don't understand how your questions will help us—"

"Does everything I do have to help you? Is that all you think of me?" Trelos shouted, his already proptotic eyes bulging even more as he leaned in close.

As if forgetting why he was angry, Trelos suddenly looked down and spun around three times while clapping his hands in a series of complex, rhythmic movements. Opening his satchels, he said, "Show me what you have."

"So, you're the expert in the Nishi, Trelos?" Friar asked still taken aback.

"Yes, squared. I am an expert and that is my name."

"King Abernan of the Northern Dwarves recommended you to help us with our spirit problem. Have you done this before?"

"No, I'm really supreme ruler of all of Verngaurd taking a holiday to visit Liberum! Of course it's what I do! Shall we proceed or do you have more stupid questions? Show me what you have!"

Friar nodded and the squires showed the visitor their homemade protection devices: clunky belts studded with iron and obsidian. The man sneered, "Amateurish! Recount what happened."

Lontas and Bellae told the stories of their various encounters.

"If the Nishi perceive you've discovered how to protect yourselves, they won't attack again. Still, it would be wise to fit you with custom and superior protection that doesn't look like a toddler ate, and then retched and defecated it out!"

"We need something for two other squires, Jumeaux and Gimelli, Bellae's siblings. However, they don't know about the spirits, and we want to keep it that way."

"So, you want me to make them attractive?"

"That would be ideal."

Trelos threw his hands in the air and huffed loudly, "According to you I have to be supreme leader of Verngaurd and now a fashionista?"

"Actually, I didn't—"

"Don't care. You . . ." the man said, pointing to Lontas, " . . . what's your favorite animal?"

"Uhm?"

"What, you hate animals? Do you also hate dirt and the air? What—"

"Trelos, please," Friar interrupted. "We appreciate you being here—"

"Where else could I be but here? One is always here and other people there! My bloody goodness, how did you get to be Friar? Please stay on topic!"

"We would love to be on topic, it's only we are not sure what the topic is."

"Wow!" Trelos huffed. "This is not difficult! The topic is preventing Nishi possession and hypnotism! Seriously, is there anyone else to talk with?"

Finn stepped forward, "We have many preparations to make before the tournament, and the safety of these squires is our top priority. Please tell us only what we need to know!"

"Your skin, Elf, is exactly like bark!" Trelos mumbled moving close to touch it as Finn scowled.

"Enough distractions! You Knights need to learn to stay on task!" the odd man said. "For you squires we'll make a small forearm charm from iron with obsidian and some shark-eye shell pieces, that no one will ever see, yet will repel the Nishi. For your siblings: a necklace for the girl and a belt for the boy."

"Everyone but Trelos and Hephaestus can go," Friar declared after various measurements had been taken. "We can fabricate the protective gear while the rest of you attend to preparations."

"But!" Trelos whined. "I need to ask them about insects!"

"Perhaps another time," Friar said, hastily waving the others out.

Scroll 10: Awake to Leave, Leave to Awake

The walls of Liberum seemed to be alive, fluttering with flags representing the Independent Knights: a blue background with a large, white dove flying over crossed swords and a white castle tower. Knights not traveling to the Tournament stood glistening in their finest armor along the length of the castle walls. Rhyfeler was waving in front of the gatehouse in his archetypal yellow.

Figure 38: **Castle Liberum,** *one of the last three Knight Castles.*

"Bestilla and I will save your spots, boy!" he yelled to Lontas.

Knowing his voice would not make it back, Lontas waved enthusiastically to him and Bestilla in her wheeled chair, both of her legs splinted heavily. He patted the neck of his hackney. He had always been afraid of horses, but the short, gangly, and skittish Klaufi was a perfect fit.

"Tell me again what the groom said!" Jumeaux asked, laughing.

Lontas sighed, "It was the oldest horse he had ever seen."

"Then what?"

"No one alive had ever seen a horse turn completely grey before. I don't care, I love Klaufi."

The grey horse swayed nervously, its aged eyes darting furtively for any sign of trouble. The supply wagons were loaded, and the packhorses cropped idly at the grass, waiting to leave for the Tournament. Lontas spotted Cookie gesticulating wildly to the pale driver of the first wagon who anxiously thumbed the reins, willing it to be time to move out.

Lontas adjusted his forearm armlet, grateful to have had no further encounters with the Nishi. He smiled at Jumeaux's belt, it was somehow gratifying to keep a secret from him. The extra, and completely unnecessary, whack on his head in the library also brightened his outlook.

"I hate dismantling siege engines for transport!" Sorea lamented.

"Why do they have wheels if we can't pull them?" Gimelli wondered.

"Siege engine are too heavy to be rolled for any length. The wheels absorb the recoil generated when the siege engines are fired. Without them, the frame would fall apart when a projectile is launched."

"Luchar! Stop picking a fight with Arquero," Sanar, a healer, said.

Only the Pantteri would be traveling as an intact unit to compete in the Tournament, but several individual Knights from other squads would be participating, including the archer, Arquero.

Lontas started hunting for his friend as Sanar tried to calm Luchar's ire.

"Bellae!" Lontas called, smiling broadly at her minuscule stature compared to the massive frame of her new horse, Honey. The two had been nearly inseparable since she rescued it from death.

Bellae didn't notice him—she was silently sauntering towards a small group including Finn, Friar, Hephaestus, and Baiulus.

"*Try to be super quiet, Honey,*" Bellae entreated. The giant horse looked comical almost tiptoeing forward.

"The tutors won't be happy digging a new moat," Hephaestus said.

"It doesn't have to be deep," Friar reminded him.

"They still won't like it."

"Friar wouldn't ask unless it was important," Baiulus stated.

"Do you feel comfortable with the drawings of the new defensive weaponry that needs building?"

"Yes!" Hephaestus said, becoming animated. "I have some ideas that can add devastation and power to the weapons Finn designed—"

"Of course, the new gate gets done first?" Friar interrupted, raising his eyebrows expectedly.

"Yes. But . . ."

"Gate first. Without it nothing else matters."

Hephaestus angled towards the gatehouse, and caught sight of Bellae. His strange expression made Friar look as well.

"Bellae, nice to see you."

"Come with me, my Inion, this isn't a conversation for you," Finn said, leading Bellae away.

Bellae perked her ears to hear Hephaestus say, "Replicating the gatehouse will be hard, and take longer than you think."

"Remember, just like the stones for the new 'wall,' we only need to create the perception the gate is real . . ." Friar's voice faded as they moved away.

A new "fake" gate and moat? she wondered.

"Are you going to make some lame excuse to conceal your spying?" Finn asked, interrupting her musings.

"Lame excuse? Me?" Bellae smiled, purposefully averting her sheepish grin.

"Did you hear anything interesting while eavesdropping?"

Bellae turned towards him and they burst out laughing. Both were still smiling when they joined the other Pantteri.

"Yes, Luchar. The weapons were triple-checked, including by Scelto and Jumeaux," Ritari explained.

"Excuse me if I'm not overwhelmed with confidence at hearing that!" Luchar said, swaying to release some of the pent-up energy boiling beneath the surface.

"Given your wrath is still at its boiling point, I'm guessing Arquero didn't take the bait and fight?" Ritari said, chuckling.

"Ah, that string jockey isn't worth my time," Luchar said. "No offense, Lovag."

"Line up!" Friar Pallium ordered.

A cheer rose from those gathered on the wall as the individuals leaving for the Tournament moved into position. Friar headed to the front on a reddish-brown horse. Ritari was next to him on his black steed, Musta-Yo. Finn and Bellae were next, followed by the rest of the Pantteri Knights and their squires lined up two by two.

"The beginning of the journey is always the most invigorating, the middle and end . . . well, the unknown is part of the excitement." Friar said, raising his right hand high in the air.

The Knights lining the castle walls shouted, "Search for wisdom, steel on your courage, proceed with temperance, and defend justice!"

Those leaving shouted, "Never give up! Knights!"

"Are the scouts prepared?"

"Yes, Friar. Three squads of experienced Knights familiar with the trip to the Citadel will make up our rear and advance guard."

"Excellent," Friar said faintly before shouting, "Scouts, to the Cosan Bridge!"

Bellae felt a surge of exhilaration flow through her as Honey burst forward, almost overtaking Ritari and his horse, Musta-Yo, who neighed loudly in protest.

"Easy, Honey!"

"Sorry, Bellae. I feel like running!"

"Me too, but we need to stay in line!"

Slowly, stride after stride, the initial excitement began to wither, replaced by the aching drudgery of the saddle on a long journey.

It's even smaller! Bellae thought desperately as Castle Liberum dwindled on the distant horizon behind them. The wider world seemed to be growing infinitely larger as her castle shrunk.

Watching the only home she had ever known, and the most prominent landmark in her life, shrink made Bellae feel off-balance. The thin blanket of the familiar was evaporating, leaving her feeling exposed and lost without Liberum's looming walls and strict, but comfortable and predictable schedule.

Enthusiasm plummeted further with opportunistic fear and doubt slithering up to take its place. Although it was autumn, the air was becoming hot as the second sun, Luminos, rose to join Mardin. The river Vita to their left reflected large, burly clouds rolling excitedly across the sky like heralds, warning the suns their season to rule would soon end, replaced by winter.

"Nervous, my Inion?" Finn asked, reaching over to squeeze Bellae's hand.

She nodded, forcing a smile in a vain attempt to hold back the tears welling up in her eyes.

Finn smiled sympathetically, "The familiar is comforting, there is no doubt. However, it can also be a cover, which, while shielding us from fear, obscures the opportunity for adventure."

Bellae chuckled and wiped away her tears. "That's pretty good."

Finn leaned towards her and whispered, "Remember, whatever comes, whenever it comes, we go, and fight, together, forever."

Bellae smiled, but said nothing. Sometimes the softest whisper of encouragement can blow with the strength of rolling thunder, well past the initial lightning strike of the kind words spoken out of love.

"Finn, track down the advance guard," Friar said several hours later. "I had hoped for an update by now. We will meet our counterpart Knights from Taiheart and Toil Shaor on this side of the River Vita and cross the Cosan Bridge together in two days."

"Yes, Friar," Finn answered, gently squeezing Bellae's hand.

"Don't leave!"

"I won't be gone long. Hey, silly, let go!" Finn said, playfully looking at her hand clutching his.

She bowed her head, ashamed of how anxious she felt.

"Hey, Inion! You're still holding on!"

"Sorry," she muttered, finally letting go.

"Remember, I'm always in your heart and medallion." Crann reared up and snorted at Honey before galloping away, happy to be out on the open plain.

"It's okay, Bellae. He can take care of himself," a telltale squeak whispered.

"Borb? What in the world are you doing here?"

"You didn't honestly think we would stay without you?" the gruff voice of Grym added, both of their heads poking out from her saddlebag.

"Stowaways?" she laughed, letting tears of joy replace those born of fear. She put the two mice inside her cloak pocket.

"You might as well ride in your usual spot. Your timing is perfect. I so needed to see you. But, be careful no one else does, okay?"

"Of course."

Grym squirmed in her cloak. Bellae laughed at the tickling as Friar rode by with a questioning glance. Preoccupied, he said nothing. He was haunted by his recurring dreams of Jumeaux rising above him in Magician robes. Struggling to find meaning in his visions, and disturbed that Patuljak had mentioned there was a chance Jumeaux—not Bellae—was the Chosen One, he decided to talk with the troubled squire.

"Jumeaux, ride with me away from the others."

"How are you feeling, son?" he asked once the two were riding together.

Jumeaux glared at him. *Why are you singling me out?* Seeing the questioning stares coming from the other squires, he felt a flame of anger and embarrassment.

"Are you excited to see the Citadel?" Friar asked.

"Yes."

"Do you know the way?"

"I've never been there!" Jumeaux balked.

"Ah! That's true. Life is a lot like that as well."

Jumeaux looked at him, puzzled.

"Every morning sets us on a voyage to a place cloaked in fog that we have never seen, our unknown future. There's the problem. We have to make good decisions without seeing what is in front of us. Each day is a step towards an uncertain fate, creating our destiny one stride at a time. Make a conscious decision on where you want to go, and how agreeably you will walk your life's journey. Understand?"

"Uhm," Jumeaux said.

"Don't wait too long to start living and enjoying the present. Life is the right here, right now. Grasp the moment in front of you and breathe it in, treasure it for what it is, the most important time of your existence. Each second we live, and each decision we make, creates our lives, our legacies."

"Friar, do you have to . . ." Jumeaux started angrily before turning away.

"Don't let anger or frustration rule your days. Like a wall can break your hand when you punch it, the anger you lash out towards others splatters back on your *own* heart."

Jumeaux felt like galloping away, but nodded his head in agreement, hoping his feigned interest would be enough to make Friar stop talking.

"Your experience drives your perception, and your perception drives your experience."

Jumeaux glanced at him in baffled irritation.

"In Jaa, if I grab your forearm it's impolite. In the rest of Verngaurd, if you refused, that would be rude. Where you are from, and what you have experienced, determines how you perceive the same action."

"I guess that makes sense."

"The other side is perception driving experience. Take your trip to the Infirmary."

Jumeaux grimaced as flashes of green goop and Necare's bulging eyes assailed his mind.

"You went there with the perception that it would be a bad experience. A negative emotion or preconception about an activity tends to become a self-fulfilling prophecy."

A wave of nausea bubbled up at the thought of Necare's dead body clinging to him. *Why would he blame me for what happened at the Infirmary? Is he trying to torment me?* Jumeaux wondered. Friar could see the swarming mental shield, more formidable than the thickest metal armor, Jumeaux had erected around himself.

"We are family. For better or worse, we stand together."

"Yes, sir," Jumeaux said, longing for the conversation to end.

"If you ever want to talk, let me know."

"I will. Can I please go now?"

"Go ahead."

Jumeaux hastily steered his horse back in line under the uncomfortable stares of the others as Friar sighed. *It is a scary thought that I am more comfortable with his petite seven-year-old sister being the Chosen One than him.*

"In trouble again, Jumeaux?" Luchar howled gruffly. "Boy, you better behave once we get to the Citadel!"

It's always the same, Jumeaux thought angrily. *I'm always the bad guy.*

Scroll II: Tree of Birth, Mire of Rebirth

"The advance guard is scouting the area around our encampment, but so far there's no sign of the Knights from Toil Shaor or Taiheart," Ritari said two days later.

"We are camped in the right spot, northeast of Cosan Bridge. I'm sure they're simply late and will show up tomorrow."

As Ritari left, Bellae stared at the sunset. The third sun, Pheobus, was saying goodbye with a rose-colored wink, arching over the horizon.

Finn saw the anxiety floating behind her misty stare. "What's wrong?"

"You know about the Nishi, of course, but . . ."

Tears were teetering precariously on her lower eyelids. At first, she spoke evenly and calmly. The tempo of her words intensified in tune with the increasing flow of tears. She recounted the conversation with Friar mentioning her special role in the future, the extra training, the stockpiled supplies, her fear of war, and her unease at leaving Liberum. Finn listened intently, keen enough to not interrupt what she needed to divulge.

After the cathartic release, she felt tranquil, as if a weight had been lifted, and the tears subsided. "Something big is happening, and I'm trapped into being some sort of hero?"

"I'm glad you told me. I'm sorry you're feeling trapped and under so much pressure."

"What am I supposed to do?"

"I know what lies ahead seems overwhelming, but in reality, it's no different than any other day. We may not understand, or want, the future to be uncertain, but it *always* is whether we recognize that or not. All you can do is give your best effort, follow your heart, and make the best decisions you can."

Bellae scrunched up her nose.

"Disappointed in that answer? Ah, but life is rarely simple. Remember, I will be by your side every step of the way."

Bellae sighed.

"Want a story?"

"Is it funny?"

"Well, it's very embarrassing for me!"

She nodded, "What's embarrassing for you is super funny to me!"

"When I was about your age I, like you, felt nervous and ensnared by *my* future."

"Really?"

"Yes. Cages come in all shapes and sizes, and do not always have a key. Whether it be from custom, tradition, worry of being different, or fear, our own minds can create powerful prisons binding us to what is familiar and comfortable."

Bellae squealed as Borb pawed to get out of her cloak. His ragged ears and white face peeked over the top of her pocket.

"You brought a rat?" Finn asked in disgust.

"He thinks you're a rat!" she managed between laughs.

"Tell tree-boy we are handsome mice," Borb squeaked, showing off his face by turning it side to side.

"Wow, that's a talkative little guy."

"They don't appreciate being compared to rats," she giggled, deciding to leave out the tree-boy comment. "Honestly, they snuck into my saddlebag."

"They? How many are there?"

"Two."

"Don't let Friar see them, or a farm cat along the way is going to be very happy."

"Thanks for not telling on me," Bellae said. "Grym is the crabby black one. The feisty white one with the black patch around his jagged ear is Borb."

The mice's heads disappeared and Finn smiled, looking at the fading sunlight as it began its slow surrender to the encroaching darkness.

"Where the true Elves live, the Forest of Creber, each of us has a special birth tree, our arbor breith. There is a deep spiritual connection to that tree, and most Elves never stray far from it. It begins to take on a physical, sinewy partnership. I remember growing to fear that attachment.

"My family and friends felt they were gaining something, but I felt I was losing myself."

"What was it like?"

"I could feel and see as my tree did: the air breezing through the leaves, the deep-blue of the sky, the intense orange glow from the life-giving suns, the nutrients coming up from the earth, and the cold blackness of night."

"Being close to nature doesn't sound bad."

"It created a cycle that was starting to consume me. The more time I spent with my arbor breith, the stronger the pull became. I found myself exploring the forest less and less. Like you, I felt trapped, but my family and friends thought I was crazy."

Bellae tried to imagine being so close to a tree. She felt close to animals, but she had their friendship, not some possessive connection.

"I had to leave or risk becoming imprisoned. I didn't want to drift, letting the current of circumstance decide my path. I wanted to take a paddle and control my destiny."

"Was it hard leaving?" Bellae asked, longing for her parents and family.

"I still miss my family, friends, even my arbor breith. However, I never regret my decision. The first night away from my arbor breith,

Figure 39: Stag Moose: *these massive creatures live in the dense vegetation of the mires of Southern Verngaurd. Their fearsome horns and immense size make them immune from attack from all but the most powerful warriors.*

I went through withdrawal, vomiting and suffering hot flashes and chills. The next morning, I felt better and kept going.

"For the first time in my life, I burst through the edge of the Forest of Creber. It felt like breaking through the surface of the sea, breathing air, and seeing the horizon for the first time. The sight was nourishing to my soul, but not my stomach!"

Bellae smiled and grabbed his forearm.

"Yielding to my hunger, I marched south, trudging into the beautiful Mohado Mire. Even growing up in the Forest of Creber didn't prepare me for the unfathomable array of plants and trees aggressively sprouting there. There is a thick, green growth floating on the surface of the marsh that makes the water seem alive, trying to shimmy up your legs and assimilate you into the mire!

"Every surface is a platform for green vegetation to grope, cling, and grow. There is a tall toboz tree with two sets of branches: a thin one with needlelike leaves, and a thick one with red fruit called piros. I took a fruit out of desperation, and it was delicious! I was feeling proud of myself when I felt a hot, snorting breath on my shoulder. Slowly turning, I saw a giant stag moose!"

Bellae let out a little laugh as Finn's eyes grew wide.

"It was enormous and covered in short, brown fur except around its neck where it had a shaggy, black mane. Its antlers were wider than it was tall and had wide, smooth sections with occasional sharp, dagger-like points. Its large, dark eyes seemed at once disinterested, yet fierce enough to serve as a warning."

"I looked up at the beast and proceeded to bravely . . ." Finn paused to lean in close, glancing around to confirm they were alone, " . . . pee myself."

Bellae moved back slightly before they both burst into laughter. "You did not!"

"I did! Thankfully, the water I was standing in covered my accident. There I stood, looking up at the stag moose in absolute awe as he lazily chewed on needles of the toboz tree. He could probably smell the odor of my fear, which was now intermingled with the mire water!

"Suddenly, *twang, thud!* A fine mist of blood showered over me as several spear tips slammed through the moose's neck. The creature had a brief wide-eyed expression before collapsing into the mire, sending a shock wave of green water splashing over me."

"I did *not* see that coming," Bellae gasped.

"If I hadn't already wet myself, I would have then!"

"What happened next?"

"I heard a terrifying voice yell, 'What are you doing, crazy Creber?' A giant hulking man came limping through the emerald water. He had smooth, very unbark-like, monochromatic skin. Is 'unbark-like' even a word?"

"I don't think so, but I know what you mean," Bellae giggled.

"Anyway, he was covered in a mixture of furs and carrying a large axe. He ensured that the stag moose was dead. Satisfied, he asked, 'You lost or insane?' I'm pretty sure I answered with something profound like, 'Yes.'

"He said, 'Since that was not a yes or no question, I'm guessing you're just plain crazy.' I suppose he was right," Finn said, and they both laughed.

"He was an ex-Independent Knight called Kappi. A few former Knights continued to live and train at the famous Castle of Idor on the eastern edge of the Mire even after it was officially closed during the Dark War.

"After he cut off the antlers, some other ex-Knights pulled the stag moose out of the mire with horses. While they prepared it, Kappi told me stories of battles and faraway adventures, and I was hooked. He offered to let me be a squire, but only after I returned home and told my parents. I didn't want to, but he said, 'You will never regret doing the right thing, but will frequently mourn avoiding it.'"

The last finger of reddish light slipped off the horizon, swirling darkness restlessly filled the void as silence just as eagerly took the place of Finn's fleeing words. The campfires behind them were now the only light.

"Do all Elves get sick if they leave the forest?"

"No. My arbor breith knew I was abandoning it. We can leave without symptoms if we intend to come back, for instance, during a war. Also, if a religious leader, or Prete, performs a ceremony to release us, we don't get sick. That is what used to happen when the Elves would send their young to train to become Knights.

"You and I, together, will handle *whatever* your future brings . . . hopefully without urinating on ourselves!"

He leaned in and hugged her tight, "Are you feeling better?"

"Much. Thanks."

The two embraced warmly. "Anytime, anywhere."

*Figure 40: Previously thought to be mythological lore, **minotaurs** are massive humanoid-bull creatures from across the Dark Sea in Ifrean. Up to nine feet tall, they have two massive horns and hooves on their feet and in place of one hand.*

Chapter Five

Plea for Help

Scroll 1: Early Bird

Bellae swatted at something tickling her nose. A stiff, aching pain shot up her back and legs, making her long for sleep to return and take away the soreness that comes from lying on the frigid, rigid earth.

"Bellae? Bellae!"

Her eyes fluttered open to the ghostly white form of Borb, *"Your whiskers tickle! It's pre-Mardin. What's going on?"*

"Something's wrong. Finn left to check it out."

"We can take whatever comes," Grym said confidently. *"But, we better get some food first!"*

"Wait, is this a ploy for food?"

"No way!" Borb said defiantly. *"However, a snack would be appreciated."*

"Finn went that way," Grym squeaked, pointing his nose over his right shoulder.

Bellae glanced through the darkness to where the Knights were sleeping. Luchar grunted restlessly, sounding angry even while dozing. An empty spot on the other side of the dying fire made it clear that Finn had indeed gone. Seeing her siblings, Gimelli and Jumeaux, and the other squires, Lontas and Scelto, sleeping made her feel better.

"All right, let's go," she said, scooping up the mice.

Once through camp she started up a gently sloping hill. The sleek outline of Finn's Elfin form stood at the top scanning the horizon.

"What is it?"

"Oh, hey, Bellae. Something unpleasant is far, *far* to the north, I only sense a faint whiff of it. I sent the sentries to scout it out. I'm having trouble figuring out what I'm seeing. It's almost as if there are two different things. Neither one is good, but the larger one is . . . just really unpleasant and something I have never felt before. What are you doing up?"

"My two stowaways were hungry," Bellae giggled. The first hint of the Mardin Sun was cresting the eastern horizon, and a blanket of red began spreading over the skyline. The cool fall wind was kind and peaceful as it gently massaged her skin. Looking at the sunrise, and listening to the morning birds chirping, it was hard for Bellae to feel afraid of whatever Finn was sensing.

Shouting erupted from behind them, shattering the dawning tranquility.

"Trouble with the horses!" Bellae said, breaking into a run.

When she arrived, Crann and Honey were rearing up and exchanging blows with their hooves. Ritari and Luchar were circling in a vain attempt to calm them.

"What a way to wake up, crazy horses!" Luchar shouted.

"I will kill you before I let you hurt her!" Crann said. Despite the fierceness of his eyes, Crann looked small compared to the towering Honey.

"Stop, now!" Bellae thundered. The horses looked at her guiltily before halting.

"You better get these bloody horses under control!" Luchar huffed.

"Crann, I'm disappointed. Honey is new and you haven't exactly welcomed her," Bellae admonished.

Honey neighed arrogantly.

"Honey, I'm disappointed in your behavior as well."

Crann neighed defiantly, *"Honey is plotting agai—"*

"That's it!" Honey retorted, rearing up and lunging towards Crann. Crann deftly moved sideways to avoid the flailing hooves before

crouching and springing forward, smashing his shoulder into Honey.

The sheer surprise of Crann's attack made Honey stagger backwards despite their size difference.

"Enough!" Bellae screamed, stepping in front of the horses.

"Finn, get Crann!" she said, nodding. *"Honey, with me."*

Jumeaux wandered over. "Why is everyone up so early?"

"The early bird gets the worm," Sorea answered, patting his shoulder.

"How exactly is that an incentive?" Jumeaux asked. "I mean, how would eating a slimy, wriggling, pee-laden worm encourage me to get up early? If early birds get delicious pancakes and sausages . . . now that's motivation."

Sorea stared at him. "It's a metaphor teaching you to get up early and work hard in order to achieve your goals."

"I still think 'the early person gets a great breakfast and no chores,' is way better."

"Learn to keep your mouth shut, squire," Luchar growled, stomping away.

"What?" Jumeaux queried, left alone with his scowl. "None of you have a sense of humor."

"What do you think is up ahead?" Lontas whispered.

"Not sure," Bellae said, trying to remain calm as the Knights marched northeast towards the danger Finn saw.

"Aren't we going *away* from the Tournament?"

"Yes, but we have to find out what's going on first. It could be that the Knights from the other castles are in trouble, and that's why they haven't showed up yet," Bellae explained.

"We're halfway to the watchtower of Anen. This is much further off course than I had anticipated travelling. Any idea how much farther to the danger you are seeing?" Friar asked.

"Sorry, no. I've never sensed anything this . . . abnormal or this far away before. All I can say is, we are heading in the correct direction. It is definitely getting stronger," Finn replied.

"Well, it's getting dark and we pushed the horses, we camp for the night."

Scroll 2: Inauspicious Beginning

"A few of the advance guard are finally returning!"

"Let's hope they have some news," Friar stated the next morning.

Bellae urged Honey towards Friar, Arquero, and the Pantteri Knights. Honey's long strides made the distance vanish instantly, and she arrived before the returning advance guard.

"Friar, we found an unarmed villager bearing the Affiso," one said, huffing with excitement.

The Knights filled with pride and sat up a little straighter at the name.

"What are they talking about?" Honey asked.

"Someone has an Affiso, a special seal given to villages under our protection. The villagers promise food and supplies, and we promise to protect them. They simply need to show it to any Knight for help."

"Ritari and Arquero, organize the rearguard and squires to prepare the supply wagons to move out. Catch up to us as soon as possible. The rest of you with me! Bellae and Lontas, since you're here you may ride with us," Friar directed. There was a sense of vitality and excitement in him that the others had not seen before.

"Lontas," Bellae whispered. "I didn't see you ride up."

"Couldn't let you leave without me."

Bellae held Honey back as her long, graceful strides could have easily outpaced the other horses. A pale-looking Lontas bounced uncomfortably on the floundering Klaufi. The grey horse quickly fell behind lathered in sweat.

"We're close," the advance guard stated.

Rounding some trees, they saw the rest of the advance guard surrounding a hollow-cheeked villager, thin from starvation and pale from fear. His eyes were set back and highlighted by dark circles. His tattered cloak was covered in filth. An emaciated donkey swayed woozily behind him.

The pit of Bellae's stomach lurched in sympathy.

The villager smiled meekly and waved the circular bronze Affiso nervously as Friar and the other Knights approached. The outer circumference of the six-inch medal was engraved with four words, "Wisdom-Courage-Temperance-Justice." A picture of the former Knight capital of Cumhacht was in the center.

"I am Friar Pallium of Liberum. What is your name and problem?"

The man's eyes darted anxiously between the Knights as he stammered, "Bar . . . I-I-I Bar-Bar-Bar-Bar . . ."

"That's all he does! We can't get anything else out of him!" one of the advance guard said angrily.

The villager winced at the ire in the Knight's words.

"One of the colors I saw was this man's distress," Finn whispered to Friar. "The other is clearly danger and, unfortunately, death somewhere in the distance."

Friar nodded.

"Finn, I want you and the advance guard scouting our perimeter. Make sure we are not walking into a trap, and then rejoin us," Friar said calmly.

Finn and Crann burst into motion with the advance guard following.

"Sa-sa-sorry," the villager uttered.

"It's fine," Friar said, dismounting and handing the man his water skin.

The man drank greedily as Friar continued in a relaxed tone, "There, now. What did you say your name was?"

"Bardus."

"Well, Bardus, what village do you come from?"

"K-K-Kippe."

"Wonderful. What seems to be the problem in Kippe?"

The brief calm that had come over Bardus vanished. "Min-min-a-min . . ."

"Take a deep breath, you're safe now."

"It was a m-m-m-m and the . . . d-d-d . . ." he sputtered, his sunken eyes widening in panic. He paused and took a deep, gasping breath before continuing. "Dar-Dar Warr . . . attack."

"Dark Warriors!" Luchar howled, swaying with excitement.

"How many?" Friar asked.

"Th-th-thirty!"

"Did you send for help from one of our outposts?"

"We t-t-t-t-tried repeated-d-dly. Th-th-they never came. A-a-a cup-cup-couple of us escaped to look for help."

In an instant, Friar was back on his horse and pointing at Bellae.

"Wait, th . . . th-there's a m-m-m-m-min . . ." the villager started.

"Bardus, leave your donkey and ride behind this squire. You lead!"

"Honey, please let this man ride."

Honey reluctantly nodded.

"Okay, sir, come on up," Bellae smiled. The man moved like he talked, slowly and awkwardly. Luchar huffed, dismounted, and roughly hoisted him up behind her. A foul smell choked its way through Bellae's mouth and nose. It was pungent, with an acrid quality of body odor and grime. She smiled through it.

"Tell her which way to go! There are Dark Warriors that need to die!" Luchar bellowed, heaving himself into his saddle.

Bardus pointed a shaky finger towards the northeast.

"The smell! I can't!" Honey said, refusing to move.

Bellae leaned forward, *"The sooner we get there, the sooner he gets off."*

"All right. I would hold on now . . . if I were you."

As Honey bolted into a sprint, Bardus clamped his arms tightly around the small squire. Despite his suffocating grip, he struggled to stay on. Friar and the Knights fought to keep up with Honey's speed. Bellae could hear their urgent appeals to slow down, but Bardus' presence threw off her rhythm.

"I m-m-must men-men-mention . . . min-min-mina-min!" Bardus stuttered.

"What?"

Bardus repeated himself, but Bellae could not understand. Her sides ached from his desperate grip, and she wasn't sure she could stand his clasp or foul odor much longer.

"J-j-j-just ov-ov-over th-th-that r-rise," Bardus finally said.

She could see smoke billowing angrily over the crest of the next hill.

"Bellae, hold!" Friar shouted fearfully. He signaled for Finn and the advance guard, who were far to the west, to return.

"Honey, we have to let the others catch up!"

"If I have to slow down, he gets off."

"Sir, we're going to stop. You'll need to get off . . . for your own safety," Bellae added quickly, her nostrils burning from the stench.

"Okay to stop . . . " Honey halted so quickly, Bellae and Bardus were nearly thrown off. The jostled villager happily dismounted the wild horse.

Friar and the Knights were closing in quickly. Finn and the advance guard were off to Bellae's left. Straight back, she saw Ritari and Arquero passing Lontas and his huffing horse. The rearguard and the supply wagons were even farther away, but still visible.

"Arm!" Friar Pallium shouted. The grind of metal on metal screeched their zeal for battle. "Bardus, linger here until the battle is over."

"Wa-wa-w-wait!" Bardus said desperately. "A min-min-min . . ." Turning green, his contracted and distressed stomach disgorged the water he had drunk. "S-s-s-savage horse r-r-rattled my bell-bell-belly."

"What's he trying to say?" Luchar growled.

"Not sure. He mumbled something on the ride about a mine or men?" Bellae said.

A courage-shattering howl startled the air.

Bardus curled into a fetal position. "I t-t-t-tried t-t-to warn u-u-you."

Scroll 3: Beginning of Inauspiciousness

"Luchar, join me in the center! Sorea, to the right! Lovag, to the left! Bellae, to the rearguard!" Friar commanded. "Bardus, move back!"

The villager curled into a more compact whimpering ball. Bellae's trembling hands pulled hard on the reins, but Honey refused to budge. She could feel the mare's resolve to fight whatever made that howl.

"I'll protect you. Let me stay and fight!"

"What was that?" Lovag asked, quickly nocking an arrow.

Two twisted horns crested the hill. The face of an angry-looking bull quickly joined the massive horns framing it. His thickly furred neck was massive and descended into a human torso. His right arm terminated in a hoof, but his left hand was human and wielding a massive war hammer with a long spear tip on top. A shendyt covered his hooved legs.

"A minotaur . . . in Verngaurd?" Friar wheezed.

"Thanks for yelling to let me know of your approach, appreciate that. Now, turn around and crawl back to your crumbling castle, Knights!" the nine-foot tall beast growled. "Wait in your hovel like the cowardly dogs you are, for the sure death that is coming from the Evil One as the time of Na Cearcaill has arrived!"

"We are sworn to protect . . ."

"Talky-talk-talk blah, blah, AHHHHHHHHHHH!" the minotaur's words evolved into a raging scream as he rushed towards Friar and the three Knights.

"Bring it down, now!" Friar yelled.

The bolt from Sorea's crossbow sunk into the minotaur's massive chest while Lovag's arrow pierced his right shoulder. It howled in pain before dropping into a three-point stance. Using his right hand as a third leg, the creature exploded forward.

"Die!" Luchar snarled, commanding his horse into a sprint towards the beast.

"Stay in line!" Friar ordered, but too late.

"Taste my war hammer, you savage!" Luchar screamed.

When they were a few feet away, the minotaur lowered his right shoulder before blasting up into the chest of Luchar's horse. The horse was thrown backwards with a sickening crunch as its sternum, humeri, and scapulae were obliterated. Before the horse could crumple to the ground, the minotaur's war hammer battered its head.

The entire jawbone and most the skull were instantly pulverized, turning its face into a bloody bag of mush and bone shards. The horse was dead before it hit the ground. Luchar dove off and swung his own war hammer towards the beasts' right arm. With surprising speed, the minotaur brandished his own weapon to block.

The two war hammers slammed together. The mismatch in strength was obvious, resulting in Luchar flipping into the air. His flailing body somersaulted several times before thudding to the ground. Lovag and Sorea quickly put two more projectiles into the minotaur's chest. His absurdly thick muscles and tough skin protected his vital organs and he charged towards Friar.

At the last second, Friar skillfully moved to the side of the charging beast. Swinging his sword in a half circle, he deflected the power of the massive war hammer before urging his horse forward and slashing his sword on the minotaur's back. The blade struck the thick mane of hair and did little except infuriate the beast.

"Bellae! Get out of there!" Finn yelled as he and the advance guard rushed towards the fight.

Honey agreed to move back, but refused to leave.

The minotaur twisted around, swinging his hammer upward, barely missing Friar's horse as two more projectiles pierced the beast's abdomen. The creature ignored the arrows and bolts, taking off after Friar who was desperately leading his horse away.

Luchar recovered enough to crouch in waiting. As the minotaur sprinted by, he swung his battle-axe and sliced into the beast's left quadriceps muscle. The beast howled in pain and reflexively elbowed Luchar in the chest, knocking the air out of him, and sending him flailing backwards. Blood gushed in rhythmic spurts from the minotaur's deep gash as both toppled to the ground.

Finn rode up with the advance guard and signaled to Lovag.

Grinding his teeth, the beast dove for Luchar. Before the minotaur landed, Finn put an arrow into his right eye and Lovag shot one into his left. A guttural cry of misery roared from the beast as he tore at the arrows. Finn's smaller gauge arrow slurped out, bringing the majority of the eye trailing behind, while leaving a bloody vault filled with dangling eye muscles, bone fragments, and aqueous humor.

Lovag's thicker arrow penetrated so deeply into the orbital bones that it would not come out. Luchar caught his breath enough to get up and swing again at the kneeling minotaur. The blade of his axe bit

Figure 41: The Knights battle a minotaur.

deeply into the creature's left side, obliterating ribs and gashing into the spleen. A massive geyser of blood burst through the wound, soaking the ground three feet out. Two more arrows and a crossbow bolt bit into the minotaur's chest as the advance guard dismounted. Surrounding the minotaur, they began raining down blows.

The beast blindly thrust its hammer forward. The spear-like tip caught one of the advance guard in the abdomen. The minotaur pulled the flailing Knight towards him, and leapt on top of his bleeding body. In a sightless rage he repeatedly brought his war hammer down on the Knight's head.

The helmet dented on the first blow, the second and third blows completely collapsed the metal with sickening cracks ringing out as the skull splintered. Scraps of bloody hair, bits of scalp, pulverized skull fragments, and blood exploded through the cracks in the crumpled helmet. The other advance guard increased the intensity of slashing and stabbing.

The dying minotaur ignored them and continued to bring his war hammer down on the puddle of brains, flesh, and flattened metal. The minotaur's body was so covered in cuts and oozing blood that it looked as if he had been skinned by the countless blows.

Finally succumbing to his wounds, the minotaur dropped his hammer. "You will all die soon enough," he said, teetering weakly.

In a final burst of energy, the minotaur leapt forward, goring a second Knight in the chest and abdomen with his horns. The Knight fell and the beast landed on top. The minotaur repeatedly slashed his horns downward, ripping and tearing the chest and abdomen of the fallen Knight until it was a soupy blend of blood, organs, bone, and intestines.

"Move!" Luchar bellowed, pushing the advance guard out of the way.

The first blow with his massive battle-axe cracked through the minotaur's cervical spine and severed his spinal cord. The minotaur instantly dropped, his horns piercing the fileted goo that had once been the Knight's torso one last time.

Luchar kept swinging his axe in rage-fueled strikes. When the head, still with Lovag's broken arrow embedded, rolled away from the minotaur's body, Luchar switched to its already bloody back.

"Enough!" Friar yelled.

Luchar managed to get in two more colossal chops before stopping and spitting at the beast.

Ritari and Arquero finally arrived. A member of the rearguard was fifty yards behind with an extra horse for Luchar.

"A minotaur?" Ritari asked.

"I didn't think they existed," Lovag added.

"I have to admit, I wasn't sure they were real until now," Friar said. "They were rumored to live in Ifrean, but have never been seen in Verngaurd."

"Friar, there's a lot of smoke coming from over that hill," Ritari stated. "There may be more."

"Bardus said thirty Dark Warriors are waiting for us as well. Form up a line and move out!" Friar yelled. "We will avenge the death of our two Knights!"

Luchar jumped on his new horse with a low guttural growl, his eyes sharpened by the rage of anticipation. "My axe is still hungry!" he yelled, brandishing his fur- and blood-coated weapon.

They topped the crest of the hill with the second sun hanging low in the sky, lazily floating upwards with a red banner of mist relaxing around it. Enviously not wanting to be outdone, the late morning clouds reflected its light in purples and reds. Drab smoke from the burning village below rose up in jealous swirls to block the elegant hues. The horses strode ferociously, feeling the anxious exhilaration of their riders.

One by one they flew down the hill expecting a fierce battle. However, drawing closer, they came to a stunned stop. Their jaws dropped and their weapons lowered as they surveyed a village ravaged and ablaze. With burning huts as a backdrop, the villagers huddled together in small, isolated groups.

"What are they doing?"

Looking closer, the truth became nauseatingly clear. They were not huddling, but trapped in roughly made wooden cages. Their slouching body postures belied their vanquished spirit. Each one was as dirty and poorly dressed as Bardus, but those in the cages had the added fashion accessory of layers of soot heaped on top. Occasionally, red blood snaked its way across the grimy landscape of their skin to add the only hint of color in the otherwise monotonously macabre scene.

Seeing a White Wizard hat and staff painted upon a large plank of wood, Friar muttered, "The Dark Warriors and the White Wizard they serve."

Scroll 4: Friendships and Stomachs Fall, Foes and Tension Rise

Bellae dismounted, drawn to an enclosure holding a girl about her age huddling in the corner with a filthy cloak pulled up over her eyes. Dark-brown hair clung to her grungy forehead in odd branching patterns. A seemingly endless array of blood, stains, shed tears, and ripped tears ran the length of her tattered garment.

Sensing Bellae, the girl lowered her cloak to reveal two inky brown eyes propped wide by the sheer weight of the horrors witnessed. Their haunting look was amplified by gaunt hunger drawing her face tight around her skull.

The girl stared at Bellae's clean, unblemished cloak, and a wave of embarrassing guilt, from being so filthy and helpless, washed over her. Bellae suffered guilty embarrassment for being so fortunate and clean.

A creaking noise made Bellae look over the cage. Rocking gently in the breeze were rotting corpses of village animals hanging from wooden beams or impaled on stakes. Entrails and unpleasant visceral fluids spilled out from deep gashes lining their defiled bodies. Several bore massive bite marks on their uncooked flesh.

The minotaur, Bellae thought.

The horrors her eyes sustained had previously shielded the stench from her olfactory system, but now the odor of the decaying flesh assaulted her nose.

Bellae returned to the hollow stare of the girl. The experiences she lived through had done more than cage her body, forever deadening part of her spirit. She rubbed her soiled forehead. Bellae gasped at the sight of her bloody fingers and mangled fingernails, torn apart with broken shards pointing in all manner of unnatural directions, some with whole sections missing. Inside the cage, Bellae noticed deep scratches of anguish slicing the wood in arcs of desperation painted in blood.

Blinded by tears and anger, Bellae took her dagger and let her emotions transform into fury, hammering the lock until the entire door fell off.

A wave of exhaustion swept over her, and she dropped to the ground. Focusing back on the girl, Bellae saw her cowering in the corner. The girl was afraid, but not surprised. She had witnessed plenty of heedless rage.

Bellae heard Finn approaching and collapsed into his arms as the world went black.

"She all right?" the girl in the cage asked.

"Should be. You?"

The girl averted her eyes. Sometimes, when there is too much to say, there is nowhere to begin, no way to convey the evil experiences endured.

The silence was shattered by the shouts of several irate villagers standing just outside their cages verbally assaulting Friar. Convinced the Dark Warriors were gone, Bardus crept slowly over the hill to join them.

"Is this protection?" an emaciated man in a hooded cloak yelled, his body quaking with anger and hypoglycemia. His drawn-out nose stood at attention below large, dark eyes and perched above a prolific mouth.

"Our crops burned, our livestock plundered, we are tortured and put into cages! The Dark Warriors came right after your Knights passed by on one of their futile patrols. Even a bloody minotaur showed up!" He lunged ineptly at Friar who deftly stepped aside. The man stumbled forward, caught by Ritari.

"Dalvo, enough," an older man with a tight, grey beard said. "My name is Bilek." His face was ringed with cavernous wrinkles paying homage to the trampling power of the years he had endured and terrors survived.

"Bardus, welcome back," the old man said. Bardus handed him the Affiso.

"People of Kippe, pity these Knights as much as ourselves. Look at how far they have fallen. We begged for help from your outposts and the watchtower of Anen. At first, we thought you abandoned us. Then we saw they were destroyed and sent messengers farther away."

Friar and Ritari exchanged a quick look of panic.

"So, you didn't know? Pathetic."

"We had no knowledge of these attacks, or that our garrison at the Watchtower of Anen had been destroyed," Ritari pleaded.

Bilek ignored him and continued, "The Dark Warriors are back and it's obvious you can no longer protect us, but the Proliate can."

"Let us help start the cleanup process. We ..." Friar started.

"NO!" the elderly man screamed. "There's no need to start what you cannot finish. The warriors of Tallcon will come. Dalvo had escaped, found them, and accepted their terms before being recaptured by the Dark Warriors.

"It was incredibly lucky I found one of their lost patrols!" Dalvo said.

Bilek nodded before tossing the Affiso seal to Friar, "We have no need of this!"

"You're saying Dalvo ..." *The man who can hardly stand up!* "... escaped the Dark Warriors and managed to happen upon a Proliate patrol? All before being recaptured?" Friar asked incredulously.

"Yes, several of our brave villagers, including Bardus, the one who found you, escaped."

Friar paused, processing the improbable information before adding, "Let me send word to Liberum ..."

The old man scoffed. "Before word reaches your castle, the Proliators will be here and stay *permanently.*"

Bellae stirred in Finn's arms. His warm smile could not break the dark visions racing remorselessly in her head. The girl's sunken eyes, her mangled fingernails, and tortured animals flashed before her. She shifted her gaze towards one of the freed women crawling towards Friar.

At one time, the village woman's shirt had been white, but it now radiated a sickly grey-brown tone under hordes of stains. Her grimy face was burdened with such sadness it seemed frozen in a desperate grimace.

"AHHHHH," the women gargled. She clawed Friar's thigh, and he gently helped her stand.

"My boys," she said, hoarsely.

She cleared her throat and let out a dry cough. Gimelli had just arrived with Lontas and brought the woman some water. She drank hungrily before continuing in a cracked voice, "Hengeton and Kuollut were twelve and fifteen years old. Both as big and strong as ten horses!" she said, looking through Friar rather than at him.

"Sukea, let's get you cleaned up," a villager advised.

Sukea ignored the request and grabbed on tightly to Friar's shoulders.

"When the Dark Warriors came, my boys fought them off by the dozens, they did. They were so brave. They cut down the villains, but there were just too many. They were murdered!" her voice rose to a wail, and for the first time her eyes locked on Friar's. "They died doing your job! Where were you?"

She stared with wide-eyed fury at Friar who was stunned into silence.

"Do you have any idea what great things they would have done? Hengeton possessed a silver tongue, and would have made a wonderful Magician ... or king! Kuollut was as strong as any three of your Knights. Can you imagine, only fifteen and as strong as any four or five of your Knights? Kuollut the Invincible ..."

She slumped to the ground in spasms of tears that shook her whole body. Her reddened eyes once again retreated to an embellished and flawless image of her boys on the day they died: young, strong, and burdened with the limitless potential that only a mother can conjure and believe. Doubts about their heroic strength or brilliant future were not allowed in her mind. She never considered they might stumble on any of life's innumerable obstacles. Within the cozy confines of her consciousness she could dream and boast about them with the self-assured confidence that no one could contradict a future that could never materialize.

"Come on, dear," a village woman stated. Sukea followed her only in body, unable to bear gazing in the present for too long. Her absent mind and spirit were nailed down in memories and concoctions. Silence lingered, frosting the air until the emotional leftovers of Sukea's pain fully evaporated.

"The Knights . . ." Friar started.

Bilek held up his hand. "Your words are an anachronism. Your glorious deeds are locked in history, and past triumphs provide no protection today!

"Your banners no longer invoke respect. The Dark Warriors taunted us mercilessly, 'Oh listen, I think I hear the Knights coming,' then they laughed as we cried!"

"We never asked much of you. Can you say the same of the Proliate?"

Bilek shook his head slowly. "Do you think swearing an oath to Tallcon and letting them build a temple is too high of a price to pay for safety?" he said with a wave of his hand before walking away.

"Let's go, Friar," Ritari finally implored.

"We'll wait until the Proliators arrive, in case the Dark Warriors return," Friar pleaded.

Bilek slowed, turning his head disdainfully to look over his shoulder, "With the only patience I have left, I ask you one last time to leave."

Wordlessly, the demoralized Knights and squires returned to their horses and rode off. Bellae looked back at the little girl released from the cage. A few strands of her dirty hair had managed to escape the grunge gluing them to her head, their feeble wave in the wind made up their only farewell.

Once at the top of the hill, Friar pulled Ritari aside. "Why did the Dark Warriors and minotaur spare the villagers?"

Ritari was taken aback. "I don't know, but shouldn't we be grateful?"

"Of course I'm glad, but the Dark Warriors did not pardon them out of decency and were known for *never* sparing *anyone*, civilian or soldier. I think they did it to weaken our reputation and push Kippe, and others, towards the Proliate."

"I don't know. Why would the Dark Warriors do that? Making the

Proliate stronger doesn't exactly help them. The Proliate pushed them back during the Dark War half a century ago."

Friar nodded. "You may be correct, but perhaps they want to get rid of us. When we are destroyed, they can turn on the Proliate."

"Divide and conquer?" Ritari stated. "Now that I think about it, the fact that several villagers 'escaped' seems odd."

"Exactly! Bardus and Dalvo could barely stand, much less plan and execute an escape from the Dark Warriors! They were let go on purpose, leading us to this exact humiliating moment."

"It feels like we are always ten steps behind!" Ritari huffed.

"Agreed. It is absolutely vital we discover something at the Tournament and shore up our relationships with our allies. The White Wizard is up to something. His agenda, wiping us out, we know, but the storyline I do not yet fully understand."

"Does this have something to do with your visions?"

Friar shook his head, "I honestly don't know. I think . . ."

Shouting below the hill shook the Knights from their despondency.

"The rearguard is under attack!"

Scroll 5: Watch and Burn

Filled with adrenaline, they sprinted their horses towards the rearguard and supply wagons.

"Something's burning!" Luchar shouted.

To the left of the flames the rearguard, remaining squires, and supply wagons stood opposite several haunting figures.

"What the . . . ?" Ritari wondered as they moved closer.

To the right of the flames stood three revolting humanoid creatures with wings.

"This detour can't get any more bizarre," Lovag hissed.

"Are those the creatures you saw in the cemetery?" Finn asked Bellae.

Her face twisted in agony, "No! They radiate evil and make me feel numb."

Surprisingly, it was Scelto standing in front of the Knights, his face red with anger. "We bury our dead *in* Liberum!"

The three creatures chuckled. The one standing directly across from Scelto wore a collared robe that left most of his chest and all of his arms bare. Deep fissures cracked through his skin like chasms through a land devoid of rain. His ice-blue eyes were pocked with white streaks under a hairless head. Four wings sprouted from his massive back muscles. The two other winged beings stood back, their faces cloaked under hoods.

Figure 42: **A Watcher:** *The Knights encounter mysterious four-winged creatures from Ifrean. Eventually they discover the creatures are underlings of the White Wizard. Their ice-blue eyes, massive wings, and dry-fissured skin create a horrifying appearance.*

"Welcome, Friar, Knights, and younglings," the creature in front said without turning. "I apologize for not leaving before your arrival. Since we see almost everything, that's quite the embarrassing oversight."

"Form lines!" Friar yelled.

The Pantteri and advance guard moved forward, the rearguard was next, and finally the squires.

"No need for hostility . . . yet. The time of your demise still lingers tenuously in the future. How did you like the Nishi?" The creature smiled, distorting the fault lines cutting through his face and misting a fine dust into the air.

"Shut your foul mouth!" Friar said, glancing nervously at the others.

"Oh, I see," the creature laughed. "Only the Chosen One and those close to them know! You think you can hide the rising evil? You presume you can avoid your painful demise? Your baseless optimism is absolutely delightful, charming even! As if you could wish away or hide from the coming darkness! The fire of purification requiring the execution of innocence, is here, once again, as Na Cearcaill looms."

"Scelto, get back!" Ritari ordered as the squire moved forward.

"But they're burning our Knights!" Scelto screamed, refusing to back down.

"This one has spunk, it's almost unfortunate you all have to die."

It was only then Friar and the newcomers realized the flames in front of them were engulfing the charred remains of the minotaur and the two dead Knights.

"How dare you defile their bodies!" Friar shouted.

"Funny. Friar's funny. Desecration . . . it's kind of our thing."

"Arquero, Finn, Lovag, Sorea!" Friar rumbled ominously.

Seconds later three arrows and a bolt whirred through the air. With an annoyed expression, the creature held out his hand. The projectiles froze in midair, hovered briefly, then fell harmlessly to the ground.

"That's irksome. Refrain from future aggression."

"You'll pay for destroying innocent villages and burning our Knights!" Luchar howled.

"There really is no limit to your ignorance! Watchers observe and guide. Killing the hapless is not our mission . . . yet."

"You didn't destroy Kippe?"

"So I have said. We observe and guide the Dark Warriors, Nishi, minotaurs, and those you have not met thus far. They do the dirty work. You . . ."

"Then you're no better than them!"

"Before I was rudely interrupted, I was going to say you are blind to the script playing out in front of you, as it has so many times before over countless eons, Na Cearcaill. Your destiny, while yet to be suffered, is already sealed. These wretched, burning Knights should be the least of your concerns. All of Verngaurd is about to go up in flames. A world purified by fire will rise, cleansed by rebirth. Soon is the time when we will join the fight and lustily kill you all!"

Luchar charged forward. "Suck on this, demon!"

With a flick of the winged creature's wrist, Luchar was tossed backwards, flipping into several unwieldy rolls before skidding to a stop. "What did he hit me with?"

"Magic," Ritari huffed.

"If you keep annoying us, we will make an exception and kill you now."

"The Evil One won't be happy if you do," one of the hooded creatures stated. "He still needs them."

"He won't be pleased they killed one of his precious minotaurs either," the one in front countered. His smile quickly turned into a grimace as a blinding beam of hot light coming from far behind the Knights slammed into him. He screamed as his fissured skin splintered under the streaking glare, sending flakes and powdered bits of flesh into the air. The three creatures instantly took to the sky. Once they were thirty feet away, the light stopped.

"You will pay for this Tacet-Vand!" the hoodless creature yelled. "Knights, remember, you're all going to die!"

"Friar! Two men approaching from the south! One is . . . floating and looks like a . . . Magician?"

Light shot out from behind the Knights once again. After wailing in pain, the three creatures flew out of sight and the beam of light ceased.

"Advance guard, watch the north to make sure the creatures don't return. Pantteri and rearguard, form up to the south!"

"I stand corrected," Lovag said. "A bearded guy floating towards us who can fire demon-scattering light makes this diversion even more bizarre."

A balding man in a grey robe came floating towards them holding out a decorated crosier. His bushy eyebrows, kind brown eyes, and long curly beard made him seem friendly despite the obvious power brewing below the surface. Several mysterious-looking vials hung from an ornate belt.

Running effortlessly next to him was a sleek-looking warrior in silver armor and a red cape. The soldier had flowing blond hair with several long braids on either side of his face. His powerful cheeks guarded concave dimples and a square, military jaw. His soft, yellow eyes were wide and observant. He carried a large wooden bow with fearsome blades on either end.

Figure 43: A fierce warrior who fights with a bladed-bow, IleZuri is attendant to, and voice for, the mysterious wizard.

"Friar?" Ritari questioned.

"No idea," he sighed, sincerely wishing they hadn't been drawn into this misadventure. "Prepare for battle . . . just in case."

Weapons were drawn and bows nocked as the two strangers neared.

"No need for your weapons, boys," the armored warrior said.

"Forgive us, after the day we've had, we can't take anything for granted."

Figure 44: **Tacet-Vand** *is the mysterious wizard who drove off the Watchers. He has taken a vow of silence and travels with IleZuri.*

"I'm IleZuri, and this is Tacet-Vand. He drove off the Watchers."

"I am Friar Pallium. Tacet-Vand must be a powerful Magician."

"No! He's a wizard, not reliant on magical crystals for spells," he explained, pointing to the all-wooden crosier as the wizened man alighted onto the ground.

"Weapons down," Friar ordered, moving to grasp the forearm of the wizard.

The warrior quickly stepped forward. "No one may touch or talk to Tacet-Vand!"

"I only wanted to thank him," Friar stated, a little taken aback.

The old man nodded kindly.

"He is under an oath of silence until the day he confronts the Evil One once again."

"We can certainly use all the help we can get," Friar said.

"We remain autonomous. It is another provision of his oath. We travel Verngaurd assisting those in need."

"Do you know Venefi—"

"Cease!" IleZuri interrupted. "Tacet-Vand and the Magician you speak of had a falling out. We seek truth and an end to the Evil One."

"Do you know the Dark Warrior's endgame?" Friar asked.

"I can only tell you what you already know: they want to destroy Verngaurd."

"Are they trying to turn everyone against us?"

"Would that be helpful for them if they wanted Verngaurd razed to the ground?"

"Yes," Friar answered simply.

IleZuri raised his eyebrows, encouraging Friar to make his own conclusions.

"What were those winged creatures?" Lovag asked.

"They are Watchers from Ifrean working for the Evil One," IleZuri said. "They have magic that comes through him."

"Are they with the Proliate? They mentioned rebirth from flames. Isn't that Tallcon imagery?" Lovag asked.

"I can't answer that."

"When you say, 'the Evil One,' you mean the White Wizard?" Friar asked. "Okay, okay," he added with a sigh. "I get it—you can't answer."

"I'm sorry about your Knights. To be honest, bringing down a minotaur usually results in many more casualties. A guardian watching over you informed us of your predicament," IleZuri said, nodding to Bellae.

She glanced to Lontas and mouthed, "The winged creature from the cemetery!"

"What guardian?" Friar asked.

"You'll know soon enough."

Tacet-Vand began to levitate and nodded to the warrior.

"We will follow the Watchers to make sure they don't return to harass you. Our paths will cross again. Until then, stay safe," IleZuri said.

"Wait!" Friar yelled, but the two were already off, heading east.

"What happened over the hill?" Jumeaux asked as Friar and Ritari talked privately.

"It was horrible!" Gimelli told him telepathically.

"Did someone die?"

"Not just someone—something. We lost the village of Kippe to the Proliate. The Dark Warriors had been torturing them, and we did nothing."

"We didn't know. How is that our fault?"

"If you had seen them, seen what they had been through, you would understand why it doesn't really matter who's at fault."

Scroll 6: Should We Wave?

"You fell asleep! Time to get up," Bellae said, gently shaking her friend.

"Time for chores?" Lontas asked, his mind clinging to the promise of sleep.

Bellae smiled, "We're not in Liberum, silly."

Lontas quickly sat up. Seeing the Knights and squires in formation on the plains of Eastern Verngaurd made him remember where he was. "With all the weird stuff we've seen, it's obvious we're not in Liberum anymore! Why is my horse tied up?"

"You'll ride on a supply wagon to rest poor Klaufi."

"Okay."

Once Lontas was seated, the dejected Knights wordlessly headed out. After twenty minutes of silent riding, one of the advance guards came darting towards the main column of Knights.

After speaking with him, Friar shouted, "Dress your ranks!"

The marching columns quickly straightened and tightened. Ritari went back to one of the equipment wagons and handed out dress banners bearing the white emblem of the Knights against a blue background. The flags reminded everyone of their joyous send-off from Liberum, the rampant optimism at the beginning of the journey now a distant and hollow dream.

"What's going on?" Honey asked.

"Isn't it obvious?" Grym said. *"We're preparing for something."*

"Oh, very profound! Of course, we're preparing for something, Captain Obvious!" Borb chastised.

"Quiet. Whatever's coming, we should be ready," Bellae pleaded as the advance guard rode hard towards them.

They lined up next to the squires, making a three-deep column. The Knight next to Bellae was wide-eyed and had beads of sweat dripping down her furrowed face. She had just lost two of her friends, and they would not even get a proper burial. Their ashes had burned so thoroughly under the Watcher's magical flame, that they had fused with those of the minotaur, all of which were buried in an impromptu grave.

Bellae looked at Finn questioningly.

"The Proliator troops are coming."

"Do you see anything?" Bellae asked.

"I sense they are seeking to do good." Finn let his voice fade away.

"But?" Bellae prompted.

"I recognize a shadow of corruption. I do not believe this comes from the Proliators. But, I'm not sure."

"Wow!" Honey neighed upon seeing the Proliate mounts.

Six Proliate Red Guards riding horses appeared in front of the Knights. The familiar blood-red figure of a phoenix fluttered on a white standard.

Bellae gasped at the four-legged creatures behind the horses.

"What are they?" Bellae asked in horror.

"Spraks from the Proliate Islands," Finn whispered.

"Steady!" Ritari yelled as Knight horses reared or neighed anxiously. Only the rope tying Lontas' Klaufi to the back of the supply wagon kept him from falling over.

The Proliator Warriors riding the spraks made constant and strenuous adjustments to the thick chains serving as reins. The six lizard-like creatures were greyish black, like the rocks of the Proliate Islands. They were twenty feet long and four feet tall at the shoulders. Large, yellow eyes scoured the horizon as their bodies jerked in awkward, halting movements owing to their sprawling hips.

Their jaws were long and thin with forked tongues repeatedly flickering in and out over their sharp and backward slanting teeth. The

*Figure 45: Sprawling lizards from the rocky Proliate Islands, the **Sprak** are not so much controlled as unleashed on enemies. The twenty-foot long creatures have four sail-like appendages and razor-sharp teeth. Sprak trainers suffer a high mortality rate.*

*Figure 46: **Tilkeri:** fearsome creatures from the Proliate Islands famous for their dagger-like front teeth. They are not fully domesticated, but trained enough to attack their enemies when released.*

Proliators gave a cry in unison and the spraks spread out four sail-like appendages. Two smaller ones came from their heads and two larger ones from their backs. The spine-like projections had rough scales over them colored red and black, with a yellow center resembling an ominous-looking eye.

"Pansies!" Honey snorted as they passed the drooling and profanely howling spraks.

The closest sprak hissed and flicked its pronged tongue in response, its wing-like sails billowing out intimidatingly.

"I like your spirit, Honey, but we can't fight them," Bellae said, feeling a surge of defiant pride.

Behind the spraks followed several squads of Proliators and mule-drawn cages holding large tilkeri or saber-toothed cats, also from the Proliate Islands. Next were a series of supply wagons heaped with wood, food, and clothing.

One of the tilkeri roared ferociously. Bellae's mice shivered violently. *"I always knew I hated cats,"* Borb said, looking at the intimidating teeth of the caged animal.

"Those are a little bigger than stable cats," Bellae said.

Luchar stared with wide-eyed fury, quietly mumbling an insult at each passing Proliator. None responded, living up to their reputation for discipline. Once the two forces had passed each other, Friar Pallium called a halt.

Scroll 7: A Field of Flowers, Flowering Feelings

The tall plains grass waved restlessly in the wind, too busy with their frenetic dance to be concerned with the morose Knights.

Friar and Ritari continued their discussion at a confidential distance. "Captain, I need your honest opinion. Should we go home or continue to the Tournament despite these somber omens?"

Ritari stared at his commander, struck by how delicate and irresolute he appeared. The weight of Friar's doubts seemed to be pushing down his spirit.

"I'd hoped you would know."

Friar sighed deeply. "I don't. Even in my position of authority the idea of control in most situations is a laughable illusion. My gut says to turn back, but there is much we need to learn at this Tournament. Plus, with Veneficus' help, perhaps, we can diffuse the situation with the Proliators and unite Verngaurd against the return of the Dark Warriors and their propaganda campaign to drive us apart."

"If they aren't working together that is."

Friar thought a moment before continuing, "How are the Dark Warriors being supplied? Burning Kippe's food supplies and slaughtering their animals must mean they have more than enough. Are they being supplied from the sea?"

"With the number of troops involved, supply from the sea seems unsustainable."

"Perhaps they are receiving support from the air? Maybe magic from the White Wizard?" Friar rubbed his eyes, frustrated to be left with even more questions and zero answers.

"What do you think of continuing north to see the Flower Fields near the Northern Dwarves before cutting across the river up there?"

Ritari scrunched his nose. "I think fresh scenery would be good for us, and there are few better sights than the Flower Fields. By the way, what are Nishi?"

Friar explained them to Ritari before yelling to the other Knights, "Gather around!"

He first explained the Nishi to all of them, describing what Bellae and Lontas had been through, and since Lontas had discovered the keys to neutralizing the threat, Friar had decided not to scare the rest of the castle.

Of course, precious little Bellae and the bumbling Lontas get lots of praise. Jumeaux thought. *I had to endure those ghosts too! I hate Bellae and Lontas as much as those stupid spirits!*

" . . . so, the rearguard will head back to Liberum," Friar was saying. "Tell our Knights the tragic news about our fallen brothers, and have

Baiulus send troops to the Watchtower of Anen. If you see the Knights from Toil Shaor and Taiheart, tell them to go on to the Tournament without us."

"Yes, Friar," they responded before riding off.

"The rest of us will make our way north to the Storten Flower Fields and then cut under the Keha Haudella Volcanoes."

"There's no path across the river that far north," Sorea said, puzzled.

"Just because it's not on a map doesn't mean it's not there," Friar answered. "Advance guard, head out!"

"Squires, to me!" Friar commanded after they had been riding north for several hours.

"I wish I could tell you the horrible things you saw today won't happen again, but you are smart enough to realize that would be a lie. Acknowledge what happened. You may not be able to make sense of it, but you should try and come to terms with it. When we attempt to suppress negative thoughts, our minds have the nasty habit of thrusting them back at us in a larger and more dangerous version."

With a gust of wind, a vibrant fragrance rushed into their nostrils from the still unseen Flower Fields.

"Lovely!" Gimelli cried out.

Tall prairie grass, and occasional bursts of trees tentacled up from the landscape before them while, in the background, large mountains sat in quiet contemplation, a halo of murky clouds circling their tops.

"Beauty can restore faith," Finn whispered. "Isn't it funny how a winsome smell or sight can quiet unrest churning inside you?"

"I do feel a little better," Bellae said, closing her eyes to savor the aroma. "I can't believe how powerful the smell is."

"Bellae, you need to know how much you mean to me," Finn said.

"I know . . . I feel it!"

Figure 47: The Saatana *Division of the* Northern Dwarf *army wears red in honor of their namesake dragon. They have both infantry units and specialists who train and fight with the largest dragons in Verngaurd, the Saatana.*

"Life is too short not to value the important things, but not long enough to stress about those that aren't!"

"Thanks, Finn, for everything. When will we see the flowers?"

"It takes longer than you'd think. They're at the base of those volcanoes. The warm underground springs feeding the flowers keeps them blooming most of the year."

"How often do they erupt?" Lontas asked, more impressed with the sight of the volcanoes than the smell of unseen flowers.

"Constantly," Finn stated calmly as the color drained from Lontas' face.

"Con-constantly?"

"Don't worry. The Dwarves and dragons have irrigation ditches and reservoirs to make the lava flow where they want. They even have magma spas for the dragons, called kursteds."

"Magma spas!" Lontas repeated, shuddering at the thought of the Knights fighting something that enjoyed bathing in magma.

"That sounds cozy," Gimelli said, laughing.

"The Northern Dwarves also use magma for their foundries," Ritari said. "It's their secret to making rugged weapons like the fearsome draak swords carried by the Red or Saatana divisions."

"Red divisions?" Bellae asked, confused. "Like the Proliate?"

"No, they despise the Proliate. There are three branches to the Northern Dwarves' military: red, green, and blue. These correspond to the three different breeds of dragon. The red or Saatana divisions work with the largest dragons, the red Saatana. Some of those Dwarves help train them, and some are formal infantry. These are the dragons we will fight at the Tournament."

"The Green divisions work with the Vioma or green dragons. Some are infantry and some ride the green dragons ... Finn, what do they call them?"

"The green dragon riders are Aer Ridire. They serve as an air cavalry by riding wooden carriages loaded with crossbows."

"Do they ride blue dragons?" Jumeaux asked.

Finn laughed heartily. "No! They are too small. Plus, they can't fly and would be incredibly insulted, being uncommonly intelligent and crafty."

"They have full speech, right?" Lontas asked.

"Yes, the blue Kirvella dragons are quite loquacious and excellent leaders."

"I had a chance to study with them for six months. They are interested in philosophy, medicine, geology, and math," said Lovag.

"Dragon philosophers!" Lontas said, feeling exhilaration tinged with uncertainty.

"The Dwarves associated with the Kirvella dragons are few in number, but are the special forces of the Northern Dwarf army. It is a great honor to be elected to the blue Vasama division," Ritari stated.

Figure 48: Besides infantry units, some green Vioma Division fighters *called Aer Ridire train and fight on the large, green Vioma Dragons as air cavalry.*

Figure 49: The special forces of the Northern Dwarves, the Vasama, *are fierce fighters.*

"I miss working with them." Finn said.

"You worked with dragons?" Lontas asked excitedly.

Finn chuckled. "No, I worked with the Northern Dwarves. I did get to see them train the dragons."

"Are they really so different from Southern Dwarves?" Jumeaux asked.

Ritari laughed. "Don't ever ask a Dwarf that! The Northern Dwarves are taller, easier to get along with, and completely trustworthy."

"Around Southern Dwarves you keep one hand on your gold and the other on your sword. They are experts in deception, concerned only with profit. They invented prestidigitation, the art of illusion that Pumilus uses," Sorea commented.

"Why don't they ride the Red Saatana dragons?" Jumeaux wondered.

"I'm sure someone tried that . . . *once!*" Ritari chuckled.

"They are massive and barely controllable. I can't believe the Proliate and Magicians brought back the Dragon Battles," Sorea said.

"The Dwarves don't like it?" Gimelli guessed.

"No!" Finn said emphatically. "They hate the Dragon Battles, thinking it distorts their relationship. It's one thing to train them to fight an enemy, but fighting for sport is another matter. That's why it had been outlawed. I am stunned they agreed to bring it back one last time."

"How many of the Dwarves are Knights?" Gimelli asked.

"The Northern Dwarves have always been our staunch allies," Ritari said. "We used to have a ton of them become Knights, but currently we only have some Northern Dwarves at Toil Shaor, and none from the South."

"The Southern Dwarf Kingdom sent warriors to fight in the Dark War, but as many fought against us as with us," Finn said.

"At the massive Battle of Petturi, the Knights had thrown almost everything they had into the battle, and, for once, had the upper hand. We were starting to rout the Dark Warriors when the Southern Dwarves turned from their position on our right flank and attacked the center of our line. Our ranks were outflanked and quickly folded. The tide of battle turned, and we were obliterated," Ritari added.

"Half our Knights were killed and a quarter wounded. After that, the Proliators emerged and started beating down the Dark Warriors. The rest, as they say, is history."

"Why didn't we attack the Southern Dwarves?"

"They claimed to be under an enchantment from the White Wizard," Finn said, suddenly smiling. "The flowers!"

"Let's go, Crann!" he said, urging his horse to gallop.

Bellae screamed with surprise as Honey bolted forward.

"Slow down!" she implored, frantically pulling on the reins. Honey thrust her head forward, pulling Bellae up onto her well-muscled neck. The ground blurred below in a blend of green and brown. Bellae turned to see Crann and Finn falling behind.

"Stop!" Finn called as Crann dashed forward with all his might.

Suddenly Honey jumped into the air and they seemed to be flying above a cloud of color. Bellae relished feeling herself soaring above the ground. Shortly after, however, her stomach followed her body up, turning over as they plummeted down and Honey's legs were swallowed in a blanket of flowers. A surge of excitement ran through her, temporarily subduing her queasiness. After several more stomach-churning leaps, Honey abruptly stopped.

Bellae took several deep breaths before breaking her death grip on the reins and shaking out her sore hands as Crann charged towards them. Flowers of every shape imaginable spread out before them, creating an ocean of color.

"Imbecile! How dare you put Bellae at risk?" Crann neighed, storming up until the horses' muzzles were touching.

Without warning, Honey rose up briskly and brought her hoofs down, narrowly missing Crann's head but landing solidly on his right shoulder. Roaring in pain, Crann lurched to attack. Bellae leaned forward and he stopped, limping cautiously out of reach.

"Bellae, tell her to let you down and then back away," Finn said.

She translated his request, and Honey complied.

"Sorry, Bellae, I only wanted to run in the flowers," Honey stated.

"That was incredibly dangerous. Plus, you never strike any creature, especially Crann!"

"Take care of Crann. I'll lead Honey to Friar."

"There's something wrong with that horse!" Crann whinnied, wincing in pain as he gingerly put weight onto his right leg. *"It's not safe around that fool!"*

"Hey, I have you and Finn to watch out for me. I'm not worried. Let me see your shoulder," Bellae said, delicately rubbing it.

"That horse is evil," Crann huffed. *Sooner or later, you'll see I'm right."*

Scroll 8: Green Dragons

Bellae winced with sympathy as Crann gingerly limped, his crested mane, normally regal-looking, fell limply with each delicate hobble.

Finn began talking excitedly to Friar about something he was seeing, while at the same time, Crann abruptly stood at attention, his ears perking and rotating in search of a noise only he heard.

"Go, Finn!" Friar yelled.

The Elf climbed onto Honey, who instantly closed the distance to Bellae. Finn dismounted and jumped onto Crann who flinched with a painful neigh.

"Can he go?" Finn asked.

His heart answered yes, but his eyes announced no.

"Take Honey and be careful!"

Crann reared his head in protest, but Finn was already back on Honey and accelerating rapidly. He whooped with excitement at the speed of the horse. Crann reared his head incredulously, staring at Bellae with wide-eyed disappointment.

"Crann, you're in no shape to run."

"First you ride that leech of a horse, now Finn?" Crann turned away, quivering with anger.

Suddenly a bellowing howl startled the air to the north.

They searched the skies as Bellae moved closer and put her hand on Crann's shoulder.

"Vioma," Crann whispered.

"A dragon?"

"Actually, five green dragons. Bellae, you can't trust Honey," Crann said earnestly.

"She's been treated badly in the past. That's all. You'll see," Bellae said, nervous about the shapes enlarging on the horizon.

"Here they come!"

Numerous dark figures in the sky were rapidly approaching the Knights from the mountains. Bellae could sense their fierce anticipation.

As the dragons flew overhead Honey reared up, legs flailing, desperately reaching for them. Seeing they were moving towards the rest of the Knights, Finn wheeled Honey around and bolted back.

Figure 50: Vioma Dragon: *these midsize dragons can be up to thirty-feet long and, while fierce, have been domesticated enough to be ridden and used as the Northern Dwarf Cavalry.*

"Should we form up a defensive line?" Luchar asked as the rest of the Knights joined Bellae and Crann in the sea of flowers.

"It's the Vioma," Friar said confidently. After a moment of thought, his face furrowed, "However, after the trip we've had, I agree."

Ritari stepped forward. "Knights, form up! Squires, to the rear!

Pantteri and other competing Knights, in the center! Advance guard, to the flanks!"

Bellae gently led Crann towards the rear with the other squires.

"How is he?" Gimelli asked.

"He'll be okay with a little rest. I'm excited to see a Vioma dragon."

"Vioma-Shioma-who-cares-ioma. I can't wait to see the red Saatana, the *real* dragons!" Jumeaux bragged.

"Be very careful what you wish for," Friar advised.

By now the dragons were in plain sight and closing quickly. Honey peered competitively towards the dragons flying overhead, desperately trying to keep up.

The head of each dragon was fitted with a silver helmet, complete with holes for two large horns to arch up and out. Each of their armored necks held a Dwarf manning a crossbow. Three other Dwarf warriors wielded crossbows mounted on a wooden platform custom-built to allow maximum wing movement.

The Aer Ridire, or dragon rider cavalry, wore green tunics bearing a white outline of a dragon and carried two S-shaped swords. Their helmets had dragon wings sprouting from the sides.

The Dwarves yelled orders, and the dragons hurtled into a graceful aerial somersault before landing well ahead of the charging Honey.

Despite their size, over twenty-five feet long, the six Vioma Dragons had an intelligent look. The Dwarves gave several more orders. The green dragons said nothing, but seemed to understand as they crouched.

"Do they talk?" Gimelli asked.

"No, but they understand commands," Ritari answered.

"I am the commander of this division," one of the Dwarves said, quickly detaching himself from the carriage and sliding down a rope to get off his dragon. "We are the Aer Ridire sky riders. My name is—"

"Abhac?" Lovag interrupted.

"Lovag?" Abhac was tall for a Dwarf and, like most of his kind, incredibly stocky. His long, dark beard and scraggly hair billowed from under his helmet. He had a large, flat nose and spoke in a nasal tone. The two embraced and the shroud of apprehension vanished. The other Dwarves slid off their dragons to greet the Knights.

"It's been too long, old friend," Abhac said. "What brings you to our mountains?"

"We're on our way to the Tournament of Flags."

"You're a bit off course!" he laughed. "Perhaps you had your nose stuck in a book? Sometimes we had to force you to stop studying long enough to eat!"

"That sounds like our Lovag," Friar chuckled.

"My apologies," Lovag said. "Abhac and Aer Ridire, I present Friar Pallium from Castle Liberum. The Knights and squires are from the same."

"I have known Friar to visit our Dragon King, Abernan, and the Blue Dragon Counsel of Kirvella. You have long been our friend and are welcome," Abhac said.

Before Friar could answer, Honey burst into the group of the dragons, neighing and prancing with an arrogant swagger. Bristling and snorting, the green dragons surrounded the horse. Some bared their fearsome, dagger-like teeth as Finn struggled to move the horse away.

"What do we have here?" Abhac queried, angrily.

"This is Finn. He's with us!" Lovag replied quickly. "The horse, well . . . she's new and way too headstrong."

Honey bared her teeth and snorted at the increasingly annoyed dragons. Several reared up to their full height and roared. The Dwarves were yelling commands, trying to calm the dragons.

Bellae plunged into the scene, *"Honey, stop! These are friends. Move back!"* she commanded.

"I thought they were going to hurt you."

"Thank you, but they weren't," Bellae said as Honey nuzzled her face.

"You talk to animals?" the closest dragon uttered.

Bellae fearlessly approached as the curious dragon leaned in. *"Can I rub your scales?"* she asked when their faces were a few feet away.

The dragon arched his eyebrows. *"That would be nice."*

Friar introduced the Knights and squires, and the Dwarves returned the favor as Bellae continued to scratch and rub her smooth hands against the rough dragon scales.

"What's your name?"

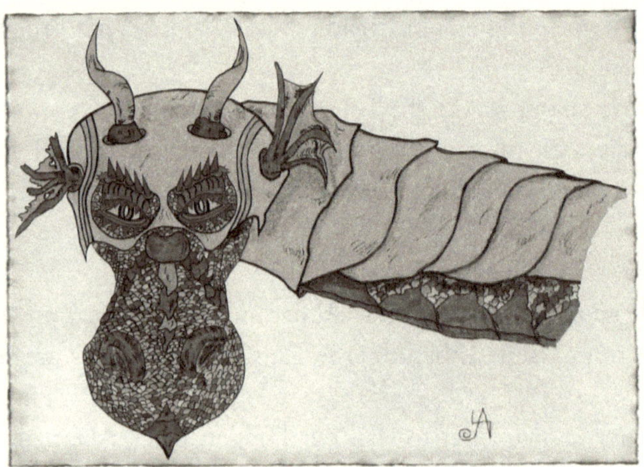

Figure 51: **Vioma Dragon Soma** *is known for a tattered right ear and befriending squire Bellae in the Storten Flower Fields.*

"The Dwarves call me Soma, but in my language, it's GGGGRRRHH-HEEEEUIIIIIOWTTTGGGG," the dragon howled.

"I think I'll stick with Soma," Bellae laughed. *"Oh! What happened to your right ear? It looks painfully tattered."*

"An old injury from when I was a fledgling."

"Does it still hurt?"

"Let's just say, some mistakes you never get over."

"You're still magnificent," Bellae said, in awe of the quilt of dark-green scales defending his body and his stark green and purple eyes.

Scroll 9: Fine Feathered Friends?

"Friar!" Lovag shouted. "Behind us!"

To the south of the Flower Fields, three Watchers hovered thirty yards above the ground. The one in the center, wearing a wicked smile, beckoned for them to come.

"What in the blazes are they?" Abhac asked.

"Foul creatures called Watchers!"

"Drivers to your dragons!" Abhac yelled. "Scout the area to make sure this isn't a diversion and that our mountains and the lady-Dwarf workers of the Flower Fields are safe. If the area is clear, return quickly. The rest of you Aer Ridire, advance on foot!"

"Knights form lines and advance with our brothers! Squires, march with us up to the wagons and then hold back with them."

As one they advanced with the Dwarves taking center, the advance guard to their right, and the competing Knights to the left flank.

"Welcome!" a Watcher said as the warriors emerged from the flower field.

"You are on our bequeathed lands sacred to, and protected by—" Abhac started.

"Don't care!"

"You are invading—"

"My patience only runs so deep, Dwarf!" the Watcher howled. "You are as naive as the hapless Knights! Innocence is always taken for granted until the season of change and your full immersion into the pain of reality!"

"What do you want, Watcher?" Friar asked.

"To help, of course. We will assist your adjustment to the life of pain descending upon you. I find it best to dip your toes gradually into the throbbing chaos of darkness that is Na Cearcaill!"

"Enough!" Abhac yelled. We have no patience for insolent intruders!"

The Watcher put his hand on his chin and raised his blood-red eyes with blue irises to the sky in contemplation, "Let's see, what can I conjure for *your* impertinence? I think . . . ah yes, that's it!"

The Watchers stretched out their arms and began to chant. The fissure-like lines coursing around their bodies radiated a bright-blue light as they intoned the loathsome language of Ifrean. After a few moments, a grey-white vapor began to rotate in an enormous oval, twenty feet off the ground.

"What's this?" Ritari asked.

"No idea," Friar stated. "But, we should halt!"

The Knights and Dwarves stopped moving forward and shored up their ranks.

The swirling mist began to firm up and enlarge as the center turned an undulating silver, almost like a mirror. One of the Watchers stopped chanting and took out krotala, two large clappers, and began to hit them together, creating a deafening racket.

"Thoughts?" Friar asked. He sighed as the others shook their heads.

"Where are the bloody dragons?" Abhac wondered. "They should have completed their sweep by now."

The Watcher stopped banging the clappers together and resumed chanting as the middle section of the oval turned from silver to dark billowing clouds looming over craggy mountains.

"The clouds within that thing are different, and I don't recognize those mountains," Abhac said.

Small black dots became visible in the distance within the mirror-like structure.

"It's a portal!" Friar said, turning around longingly, entreating the dragons to return.

"A gateway to where? More importantly, what's coming through?"

"That's enough!" the lead Watcher said, and they lowered their arms. The blue glow within their fissures faded as he spoke, "Isn't this exciting? Who knows what's coming through from the wonderful land of Ifrean?"

"Now we know how they are supplying their troops and moving them around so stealthily," Ritari seethed.

Friar nodded as Finn, Lovag, Arquero, and Sorea had their bows and crossbow ready. The dots began to grow larger, their shape becoming clearer.

"Are those birds? Seriously? You summon birds?" Luchar barked contemptuously.

Something in the way the Watcher smirked and raised his eyebrows, sending a dusting of flesh showering down, chilled Friar to his bones. Abruptly hundreds of the black figures burst through the magical gateway.

"Fire!" Friar yelled as their appearance took form.

Three arrows and bolt flew through the air, taking down four of the enormous bird-like creatures. Fearsome beaks held rows of razor-edged teeth. They had four large black eyes, two looking straight ahead and two on the sides of their head, and four smaller eyes arching menacingly just before the base of the beak. A tissue and feathered appendage spread across the top of their heads like a terrifying crown. Their two large wings had tube-like structures running down their length. Instead of a single tail feather, two large muscular cables ended in large fans of feathers for stability in flight. Their two claws were surprisingly small, appearing too minute to support their four-foot long bodies.

"Squires, arm yourselves and shields!" Friar screamed as the horde of creatures streamed towards the Knights and Dwarves. "There are too many for us to hold back!"

Luchar stepped out of line and swung his massive axe at the first bird. With a primal yell, he bisected the beak, cleaving its head completely in half, spraying blood several feet in all directions.

"Take that you bloody ugly … wait … these bloody beasts have giant spider eyes!" Luchar howled. "Friar they have other … really hairy legs!"

As his words faded the creatures slammed into the warrior's line, seeming to focus on the shield-less Dwarves. A large bird took down one of the Dwarves, its horrifying beak first knocked his sword away, then bit his hand clean off. Four hairy, spider-like legs emerged from its body and clamped onto the Dwarf as its small talons started to spin rapidly, ripping and digging through the flesh of the Dwarf's abdomen. They bore their way through his intestines, eventually clamping onto the hipbone for leverage.

A high-pitched screech stung the air as it flayed open its beak. In between the rows of sharp teeth, a fleshy pink tube emerged from the back of its throat. The tip of the tongue-like projection spread out five claws to reveal rows of honed spikes within.

The disgusting tube slammed in between the gaps of the Dwarf's helmet, the five claws easily plunged through his eye, following the optic nerve to the brain. The cylindrical tongue began undulating and a revolting sucking sound ensued as it slurped the Dwarf's brain from the cranium.

The nearby Dwarf warriors quickly hacked at the loathsome creature. One cut off the bird's head and another tried to pull the disgusting

Figure 52: With their dragons out scouting, the shield-less Northern Dwarf Warriors suffer badly as Watchers summon Stymphalian birds from Ifrean.

tongue from the eye socket, but the repulsive tube continued to undulate, dumping pureed brain from its severed neck onto the Dwarf's lifeless chest. As they pulled harder a surge of blood shot from the eye socket as they finally extracted the clawed tube. The tube-like tongue continued to spasm, desperately flailing and reaching out. With a cringe of disgust, the head was quickly discarded.

"Scelto!" Gimelli yelled, slashing fiercely at one of the giant birds hovering around her and Bellae.

Scelto jumped onto the wooden shaft of the carriage, vaulted over the horses and dove at the bird-like creature. Holding out his sword, he launched it forward. It shattered several of the bird's teeth before plunging through the back of the bird's head. His fierce momentum implanted the sword so deeply into its flesh, that the hilt rammed into the bird's beak. The bird's body flopped in violent spasms before the life drained from the eight inky eyes.

Another bird rushed at Scelto from behind and knocked him down. Scelto screamed as the bird's teeth bit into his upper back. Gimelli and Bellae shot forward and began slashing at the bird. Whipping around, the bird's head struck Bellae with such force she flew backwards. As she scrambled to find her dagger, Scelto exploded up, withdrew his sword from the carcass of the first bird and hacked the second bird's back. The cords leading to its tail feathers lashed around Scelto's ankles. Once securely wrapped around him, the creature flipped Scelto up into the air. He landed hard on his stomach, the air quickly departing his lungs.

Lontas joined Gimelli, both brandishing their swords. The bird let out a fearsome squawk before charging. Before it could get too close, an arrow from Finn sliced into its chest.

The bird faltered, giving Scelto time to recover and jump on its back with his sword raised above his head. Right as it started to twist around, Scelto drove the sword through the bird's neck. As it crumpled to the ground, he added several more blows for good measure.

"Bellae!" Crann cried out with a concerned neigh.

Despite his best effort, he could not fight to his beloved squire. Sensing an attack from behind, Crann turned and rose up on his back legs while lashing out with his front hooves. Two blows landed, one shattering the beak of the creature. Crann quickly spun around, thrashing the beast with his whip-like tail. The thick cords battered the flying beast to the ground.

Honey suddenly emerged to violently stomp the downed animal. The weight of the large horse combined with the ferocity of his blows quickly soaked the ground in viscera and blood.

"I like when they go squish! Honey bellowed. *"Let's kill them all . . . for Bellae!"*

Crann eyed the large horse suspiciously, but finally nodded, *"For Bellae."*

"Those 'birds' as you so eloquently put it . . ." the Watcher said. " . . . are actually the Stymphalian birds from the Stymphalia Swamp of Ifrean. While I can clearly see you are enjoying them, you haven't seen their most impressive trick!" The Watcher once again signaled the ghastly birds with a series of loud clapping noises using his krotala.

Ritari cleaved the head off one as the rest of the birds retreated and began flying in a large circle above the warriors. The Knights caught their breath, surrounded by the corpses of dead and dying birds and Dwarves.

"My favorite part!" the Watcher announced, lightly clapping.

"Friar?" Abhac mumbled.

"No idea what's coming, but shield wall!"

The Knights with shields locked them together. The Dwarves were shield-less and stood in anxious anticipation.

Bellae suddenly felt something familiar. Closing her eyes, she could feel panic and fear behind her. *My winged friend!*

She spun around to see the creature from the cemetery hurtling towards her, she could feel his deep concern and smiled. Her expression turned sour as she suddenly felt anger in the dragons that were now returning.

"Thank you, my friend, for watching over me, but you need to leave! The dragons are coming back, and they will attack you," Bellae said, waving him off. His excellent eyes easily read her lips and he reluctantly flew away.

"Quit being such a dunce and turn around!" Jumeaux hissed at his younger sister.

"Did I forget to mention the Stymphalian birds are man . . . and I guess now Dwarf-eaters who particularly love brains? Who said intelligence isn't an attractive feature?" The Watcher began laughing hysterically.

His humor turned to anger when the Knights and Dwarves did not join him, "Don't you get it? They love brains? Brains equal intelligence! It's a joke people!

"Anyway, for their next trick, see how the tube leading to the last three feathers on the tips of their wings is pulsating? They infuse those feathers with calcium, collagen, and phosphate! Anyone know what that means? No? It means they can turn their last three feathers to bone!"

The circling birds suddenly moved closer, the three most distal feathers on the wings closest to the warriors hurtled like arrows towards the earth. The ossified feathers splintered when colliding with armor or shield, but cut deeply into unprotected flesh.

"Get down!" Abhac yelled as he dove behind the Knight's shields.

The sharp and solidified feathers rained down on the line of warriors. Several Dwarves were instantly killed while others suffered numerous slices and wounds.

After releasing all the calcified feathers from one side, they reversed direction. Several hungry Stymphalians broke ranks and flew down towards the injured and recently killed Dwarves. As soon as they landed, their spider legs latched on, their talons dug through the abdomen to attach to the hipbone, and their spiked tongues pierced into the brains of the injured warriors. The Knights and remaining Dwarves hacked and beat on them mercilessly but for every one they killed, three more landed, eager to eat.

"Shields!" Friar yelled. "They're about to release the honed feathers from the wings on the other—"

Flames engulfed the air above as a dozen Vioma dragons flashed across the sky. The dragons did a looping somersault before unleashing another round of flames, immersing the Stymphalian birds in a storm of fire. As soon as the inferno ceased, the Vioma dragons flew into a vertical formation with three rows of four.

The Dwarf riders yelled, "Loose!" The suns overhead were almost completely blotted out as waves of crossbow bolts filled the air piercing into any remaining birds, some of which were already screeching within the devouring flames. The sickly smell of burning flesh and shrieks of pain filled the air.

The warriors below cheered as those above on the dragons let loose a stream of expletives. The portal vanished and the Watchers conjured red, semi-translucent shields around themselves. The dragons flew in circles around the Watcher's magic defenses, quickly discovering their flames and bolts would not penetrate the enchanted shields. The Dwarves and Knights on the ground dispatched the remaining Stymphalians with sincere animosity.

A blinding red light shot out of the three Watchers' shields, combining into a larger beam before incinerating the bodies of the dead Dwarves and Stymphalian birds creating a fiery pasture of burning flesh as the scorched carcasses of the last birds crashed to the ground.

"Move back!" Friar yelled. "We have seen this fire before, there is no putting out these magical flames and they will kill you! They stop only when everything is ash."

The Aer Ridire began shouting commands to their dragons, who responded by flying in a complex weave pattern. After other commands, the dragons took turns crashing their armored heads into the Watcher's magical shields. Back and forth they tossed the whirling and screaming Watchers.

"You cry like babies, you bloody jolts!" Luchar yelled. "Come out of those shields and I will smash your arid faces into oblivion!"

"I didn't think you knew what arid meant," Lovag joked.

After a few more commands several dragons hit the shielded Watchers straight up into the waiting tails of three other dragons that lashed their tails down like massive clubs, sending the Watchers within the red shields plummeting towards earth. Upon crashing down, the shields vaporized and their desiccated bodies thudded hard, sending a fine mist of dust showering up.

Laughing, the Watchers stood. "This is only the beginning of your end, fools!"

The three of them began chanting and vanished just as hordes of dragon flames engulfed the area. The dragons circled for several minutes to make sure the area was clear before landing.

The Dwarves dismounted, somberly standing over their fallen, and burning, comrades as the Knights and squires regrouped, cleaning off the blood and bird viscera.

"Thank you for fighting with us," Abhac said.

"It is we who owe you. Without your dragons, I fear we would all be dead."

"That was . . . unexpected . . . bizarre!" Abhac said, shaking his head.

Friar and Ritari recounted their previous run in with the Watchers and the minotaur.

"Bloody brain-sucking-spider-legged-birds, Watchers, and now minotaurs?" Abhac questioned. "The days keep getting stranger. I didn't think minotaurs existed."

"You don't have to believe in us for me to kill you!" a beast growled.

Off in the distance, an even larger portal than before swirled ominously as the thunderous stampede of hooves exploded.

"To your dragons!"

Figure 53: Saatana Dragon. *The largest of Verngaurd's dragons, the Saatana can be up to forty-five feet long. While unrideable, they can follow simple commands and be used in battle.*

Figure 54: A Saatana Dragon joins the fight. Twenty Red Dragon Warriors struggle to maneuver the giant dragon to join the battle.

The air cracked with a deep thunderous roar that shook the very ground.

Abhac laughed ominously as he turned towards his volcanic home, "Let them conjure whatever foul creatures from Ifrean they want. If they suffered under the Vioma, see how they like our red!"

"Is that the Saatana Dragon?" Lontas gasped.

The rattling of chains and a massive burst of flames rocked the sky as twenty Dwarf Dragon Warriors desperately struggled to maintain control over an immense red dragon. The monstrous beast seemed only mildly concerned with the orders being feverishly bellowed in his direction. Each movement of the dragon jerked the chains causing the Dwarves to surge forward, sometimes ripping them off the ground.

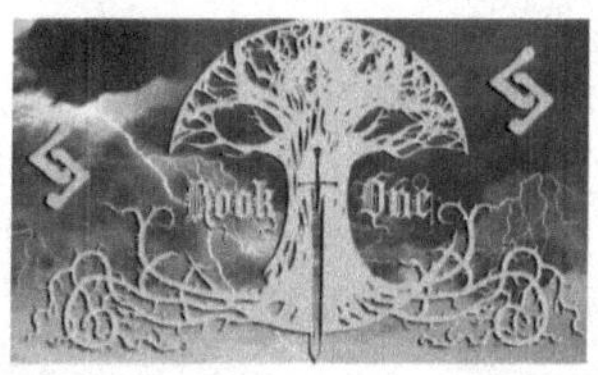

Book One's season of change came, as it is prone to do, without permission. Our journey slips from beneath rune Jera, ending as it began:
"The significance of each change of season is easily buried in the smallest of life's mundanities and trivialities. Yet, the true consequence of time's passage is there, blaring within the subtle disguise of a whisper for all who would listen."

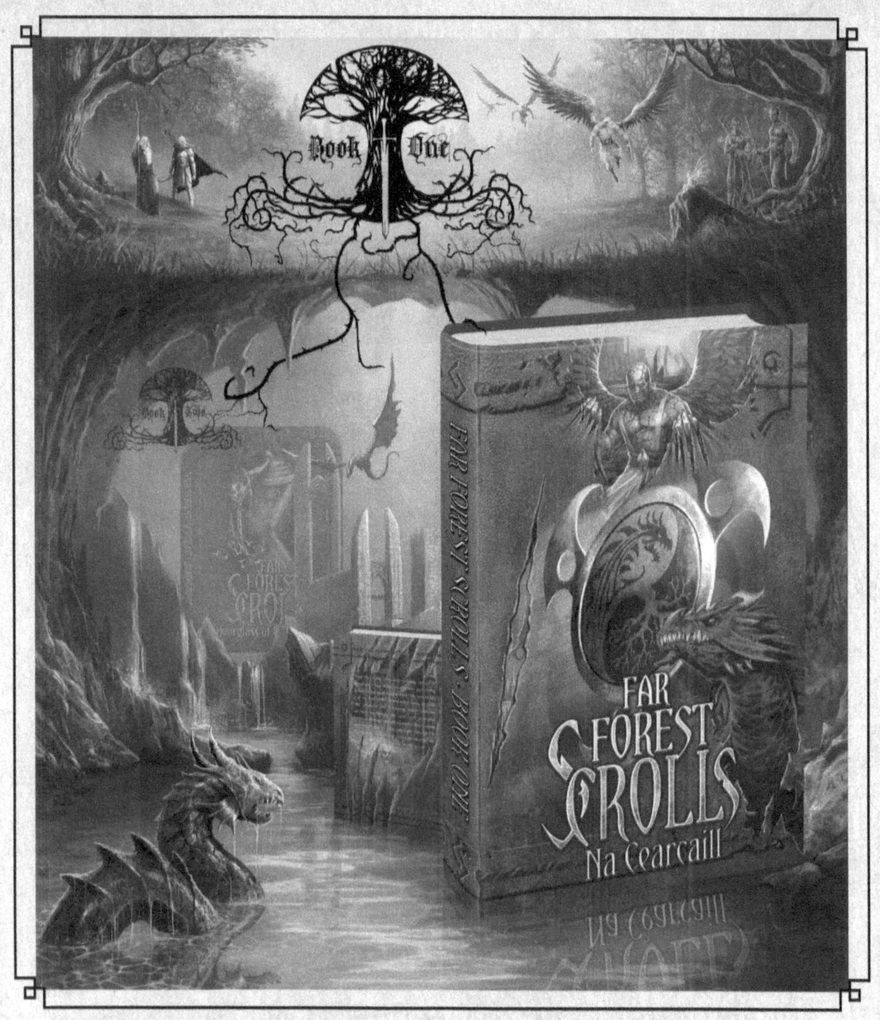

Figure 55: As water is appallingly absent in the desert of perpetuity make time to tread softly on your precious mundane days and enjoy each drop of life's liquid, each fellow on the journey, each experience as if it were a king's ransom, because each moment is, in reality, infinitely more valuable than some fictitious prize which, ultimately, is wryly fashioned of the same frangible dust as we are.

Each change deposited in our life delivers us
another uncomfortable notch closer to its
inevitable end. The darkness verily whispers
to all awake to hear the truth, giving birth to
that uneasy feeling endured with each change
of season, and, if we look up, squinting into the
heartlessly honest embrace of the cold,
starless night, we see the lonesome howl
of eternity mouthing its silent scream,
"There is no cure for your fragile mortality."

Figure 56: The journey through Book One fades as we cross into Book Two, represented by the rune of revolutionary change, Hagalaz. It denotes disruption, catastrophe, and unavoidable distress. For Verngaurd, and those you have met in Book One, it symbolizes a major shift in the reality of world order rumbling through every facet of life.

Figure 57: In Book Two the convoluted tale of friendship and betrayal reaches a boiling point at the Tournament of Flags. Will Verngaurd discover, and overcome, the forces trying to tear it apart? Or, will the world drown, sucked below the quickly falling sands within the Hourglass of Destruction they find themselves within?

For more information about Book Two visit:
www.FarForestScrolls.com

www.ingramcontent.com/pod-product-compliance
Lightning Source LLC
Chambersburg PA
CBHW050229110726
47898CB00007B/2076